Here's a sneak peek of
Winning the Rancher's Heart
by Pamela Britton

"You're a good man, Jaxton Stone."

Naomi sniffled.

No, he wasn't. He was having all kinds of inappropriate thoughts about her. Wondered what she would do if he bent and brushed her lips with his own. But he couldn't. Damn it all, he just couldn't.

"Sometimes," he said, "doing what's right for everyone takes a huge leap of faith, but I promise you, it will all work out all right in the end."

She turned to face him and he warned himself not to move. Not to stare at her lips. Not to lean in close to her. It was the hardest thing in the world to let her go.

"You're a good mom," he heard himself say, forcing himself to relax. "Have faith. Trust your heart. It'll never lead you astray."

She peered up at him, blue eyes wide, her hair spilling around her shoulders, and he felt himself falling...falling...

"Good night."

He ran.

Trusting the Rancher

Cathy Gillen Thacker & Pamela Britton

Previously published as *The Rancher Next Door*
and *Winning the Rancher's Heart*

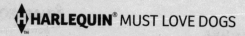

HARLEQUIN® MUST LOVE DOGS

ISBN-13: 978-1-335-69090-6

Trusting the Rancher

Copyright © 2019 by Harlequin Books S.A.

First published as The Rancher Next Door
by Harlequin Books in 2007 and
Winning the Rancher's Heart by Harlequin Books in 2017.

The publisher acknowledges the copyright holders
of the individual works as follows:

The Rancher Next Door
Copyright © 2007 by Cathy Gillen Thacker

Winning the Rancher's Heart
Copyright © 2017 by Pamela Britton

Recycling programs for this product may not exist in your area.

Printed in U.S.A.

www.Harlequin.com

CONTENTS

Cathy Gillen Thacker is married and a mother of three. She and her husband spent eighteen years in Texas and now reside in North Carolina. Her mysteries, romantic comedies and heartwarming family stories have made numerous appearances on bestseller lists, but her best reward, she says, is knowing one of her books made someone's day a little brighter. A popular Harlequin author for many years, she loves telling passionate stories with happy endings and thinks nothing beats a good romance and a hot cup of tea! You can visit Cathy's website, cathygillenthacker.com, for more information on her upcoming and previously published books, recipes and a list of her favorite things.

Books by Cathy Gillen Thacker

Harlequin Western Romance

Texas Legends: The McCabes

The Texas Cowboy's Baby Rescue

Texas Legacies: The Lockharts

A Texas Soldier's Family
A Texas Cowboy's Christmas
The Texas Valentine Twins
Wanted: Texas Daddy
A Texas Soldier's Christmas

Visit the Author Profile page
at Harlequin.com for more titles.

THE RANCHER NEXT DOOR

Cathy Gillen Thacker

This book is dedicated to
Lukas Frederick Gerhardt,
the "Third Musketeer," and the
proof that wishes do come true.
Welcome to the family, little guy.
The joy you've brought us
is indescribable.
And one more thing: if your two
older brothers try to give you the
business...you give it right back...

Chapter 1

"I take it you've heard the rumors," Luke Carrigan said as he ushered Trevor McCabe into the study of his Laramie, Texas home.

Who in the county hadn't?

Tired of his three daughters' well-known aversion to commitment, Luke Carrigan had vowed to take a hand in introducing them all to "suitable" men, in what Trevor figured was a vain hope they would soon settle down and have families.

What was it about their parents' generation, Trevor wondered, dropping down into the wing chair Luke indicated, that made them think marriage was essential to a person's happiness? He was content living the single life, and saw no reason to change his own circumstances.

"Don't worry, that's not why you're here," Luke continued.

Trevor held back a sigh of relief.

Luke sat down behind his desk. "I did want to talk to you about Rebecca, though."

Trevor tensed. Luke's second-to-oldest child had

been two years behind him in school. The two of them had nothing in common then—or now. He vaguely recalled Rebecca Carrigan as a rah-rah type who had always been busy organizing something.

"She has a tendency to go off on—well, let's just call them tangents."

Trevor didn't know what Luke was getting at, but he was willing to hear the noted family physician out and settled more comfortably in his seat. "Last I heard Rebecca was in Asia."

"Actually, she's been all over the world with the tour company she worked for."

Trevor shrugged his broad shoulders. "That's one way to travel the globe."

"Don't get me wrong. I'm very proud of how hard Rebecca has worked since she graduated college. Even more delighted with the staggering amount of money she has saved in the past six years." Luke paused and looked at Trevor, his eyes full of parental concern. "What worries me is what she plans to do with it."

Trevor grimaced. "Dr. Carrigan, I really don't think this is any of my business."

"You may change your mind when you hear what my second-to-oldest daughter has planned."

Trevor doubted it. Honorable men did not step in the middle of other families' contretemps.

"You know that small ranch you've had your eye on?"

Trevor tensed at the mention of his neighbor to the west. The fifty-acre tract was definitely in his sights, along with the much larger property on the other side of it, The Circle Y. "I gather you're talking about The Primrose?"

Luke dipped his head in acknowledgement. "Miss Mim is planning to sell it to Rebecca."

Trevor swallowed a curse. His jaw set. "That can't be right." *He and Miss Mim had an understanding.*

"I'm afraid it is," Luke replied. He didn't sound happy.

Trevor forced himself to put emotion aside and think about this rationally. "Your daughter doesn't have a background in ranching," he pointed out. Growing up, she'd never been a member of any of the agricultural groups such as 4-H. She'd selected SMU instead of Texas A&M, where all the agricultural students went, for college.

Luke shrugged. "That won't stop Rebecca. She wants The Primrose. She's leveraging everything to get it. And that's what has me so worried, the lengths to which she's willing to go." Luke paused before continuing. "I need someone who's been there to talk some sense into her, make her realize that buying and starting up a ranching operation is no game. It's grueling, twenty-four hours a day, seven days a week, work."

And probably harder than anything she had ever done before, Trevor thought. He wondered how long it would take her to give up and sell out, like every other dilettante who had a romantic instead of practical view of the ranching life. *Hell's afire.*

Trevor exhaled in slow deliberation. "What makes you think she would listen to me?"

"Nothing, except you're her age and well respected in the ranching community."

"Are you sure your daughter is planning to work the property? Or just reap the financial rewards? After all, Miss Mim has never actually managed it. She's leased it out to me, and other ranchers who needed extra land to run their herd." Trevor wouldn't have a problem with Rebecca living "next door" if she continued the lease.

Luke tapped his fingers on his desk. "If the risky financial dealings she's concocted with that San Angelo bank go through—and I have to tell you, right now it looks as if they will—Rebecca plans to breed alpacas."

"Alpacas!" Trevor echoed, gripping the arms of the chair. "She plans to raise alpacas in the middle of cattle country?"

"That's what she says unless someone can convince her otherwise. Which is why—" Luke leaned across his desk and looked Trevor straight in the eye "—since you're going to be living right next door to her, I've summoned you."

Rebecca Carrigan was just turning the corner onto the street where her parents lived when she saw Trevor McCabe driving away.

"I don't believe it," she muttered to herself as she squinted against the brilliant April sun. She had warned her father not to try and run her social life—or lack thereof—the previous evening, or interfere in her new career. Obviously, he hadn't listened.

Which left her two choices. Ignore what she had just witnessed, wait patiently for Trevor McCabe to make his move and then shut him down.

Or give chase and set him straight.

Always one to take charge when opportunity presented itself, she drove past the big turn-of-the-century Cape Cod she, her two sisters and brother had grown up in, and followed the dark green, extended cab pickup truck through the center of town to the feed store.

Trevor McCabe parked his vehicle in front of the

store, and before she could do the same, disappeared inside.

No matter, Rebecca decided, sliding her small yellow pickup truck into the last slot. She'd just follow him in and ask him to step out.

Keys in hand, leather carryall slung over her shoulder, she marched through the doors of the cavernous warehouse.

It was as busy as usual. Stacked sacks of feed took up the majority of space. The rest was occupied by shelves containing various home-veterinary supplies.

Half a dozen ranchers and hired hands stood at the cash register. Another five or six strolled the aisles, mulling over choices. In the middle of the action stood Trevor McCabe.

As always, Rebecca found the sight of the thirty-year-old rancher a little intimidating. It wasn't just that he was tall—he had to be six foot four—and buff in the way that men were who made their living through physical endeavor. It was the tough-but-smart aura he exuded, the cynical I-dare-you-to-try-and-put-something-over-on-me gleam in his hazel eyes. He'd had the same confidence back in high school, and it had only grown more daunting since. Not that she was going to let that stop her. Rebecca stepped right in front of him and tapped the toe of her boot on the cement floor. "Could I have a word with you?"

Trevor tipped the brim of his stone-colored hat away from his forehead and looked her up and down.

"Sure." He started to take her elbow.

Rebecca backed away. Suddenly, the thought of having a private conversation with this very grown-up version of Trevor McCabe seemed risky as all get out.

"Actually, I'd rather talk here," Rebecca said.

Trevor's lips compressed. "I don't discuss my private business in public."

No surprise there, given the fact that he probably didn't want everyone in town to know her father had just tried to convince him to make a play for her.

"Well, that's too bad because here and now is the only way we're ever going to converse." All Rebecca wanted to do was set the record straight. Let him know she was definitely not interested in him—romantically or any other way, no matter how ruggedly appealing he had grown up to be.

Their eyes met and held. Electricity sparked between them with all the unpredictability and danger of a downed power line. Rebecca caught her breath, deliberately held it. And prayed and hoped she would get what she wanted from him—a promise he would never meddle in her life, at her father's behest, or for any other reason. Independence mattered to Rebecca. She wanted Trevor—as well as everyone else in town—to respect and believe in her the way her family never had.

For a second, Trevor seemed tempted to hear her out but something—maybe it was the eyes of all the men in the feed store—had him doing otherwise.

"I don't think so." Trevor turned away.

Gosh darn it. What had her father said to him?

Unwilling to give up on this quest, Rebecca stepped closer. When he refused to acknowledge her, she tapped his arm. "I mean it, Trevor McCabe. You and I really need to talk."

His bicep flexing enough to get her to immediately drop her hand, he swung toward her once again. He spoke, carefully enunciating each and every word. "As I said, I don't think here and now is a good idea. I'd be glad to meet you later, however."

Rebecca just bet he would.

The sexual heat in his eyes said he wouldn't waste any time putting the moves on her.

She curled her fingers into a fist, to stop their tingling.

Noting he wasn't going to budge on this, and that everyone in the building was definitely staring at the two of them, she felt her temper getting the better of her, and snapped, "Fine, have it your way. I'll do all the talking." Rebecca pointed a trigger finger at the center of his chest. "And you, cowboy, can listen."

His brow arched. All conversation in the feed store had died.

Trevor had just dared her to go on.

Feeling the temperature between them rise, Rebecca propped both her hands on her hips. Perspiration gathered at her temples, on the back of her neck, in the hollow between her breasts. "I don't care what my father said to you." She paused to let the emphatic words hang in the air. "I am not—I repeat *not*—going to date you."

He stepped in closer. Amusement glimmered in his eyes. "Is that so?"

Feeling as if she had picked the wrong man to humiliate, even if it had been by his choice, not hers, Rebecca angled her chin higher. "You can bet your cattle ranch, it is."

Trevor rocked back on his heels, ran the flat of his palm beneath his jaw. "Well, that's interesting."

His rumbling drawl sent shivers over her skin. "Why?"

"Because I hadn't planned to ask."

Deep male chuckles surrounded them.

To her dismay, Rebecca felt her cheeks turn a self-conscious pink. "Then why did you even go and see my dad," she asked, "if you weren't willing to be part of his plan to get all of his daughters married off?"

A plan that Luke had told her started with her, since she was the daughter currently in so much "trouble." Why did her father have a problem with her running a ranch anyway?

"If you want to know why I was talking to your dad this morning, ask him," Trevor said.

"I'm asking you!"

Resentment sparked in Trevor's eyes. He hooked his thumbs through his belt loops and rocked forward on his toes. "Well that's too bad," he said, lowering his handsome face to hers, until they were nose to nose, "because what was said was strictly between me and your father."

Rebecca rocked forward on her toes, too. "But it was about me. Wasn't it?"

To her mounting aggravation, Trevor said nothing.

A discreet cough made them both turn their heads.

Rebecca caught sight of a well-dressed thirty-something cowboy she didn't recognize, lingering in the doorway of the warehouse, listening and watching all that was going on. Everyone else was looking at him, too, in the same way, which meant he was not known to people in these parts. The handsome blond-haired hunk lifted a hand in greeting to one and all and headed in their direction.

The stranger smiled pleasantly. "If it were me, I'd tell you everything you needed and wanted to know, and then some." He swept off his hat and waved it at the crowd. "Vince Owen," he introduced himself to one and all. "Trevor and I went to college together." Vince clapped a hand on Trevor's shoulder, grabbed his hand and shook it heartily. "Good to see you, buddy."

Trevor nodded, the expression in his eyes unreadable. "Vince."

Vince Owen turned to Rebecca. Charm radiated from him like light from the sun, as his gaze fastened on her face. "And you're...?"

Rebecca smiled, switched her keys to her left hand, and stuck out her right palm. "Rebecca Carrigan."

Vince clasped it warmly. "Good to meet you, darlin'. If you need anything, I'm at your service. I just closed on a ranch in the area—The Circle Y. You heard of it?"

Aware that Trevor had gone stone-still with something akin to shock, Rebecca paused. Ignoring the man who had given her so much grief in so little time—what did she care what Trevor McCabe's reaction to the news was anyway—she asked Vince, "It's right next to The Primrose, isn't it?"

He nodded. "And one ranch away from Trevor's Wind Creek Ranch, although I could be his next-door neighbor if I can snap up The Primrose, too."

"I doubt that will happen," Rebecca said politely, not sure she should say more until the papers were actually signed by her and Miss Mim.

"I agree with Rebecca." Trevor gave Vince Owen a long, steady look. "Last I heard, The Primrose wasn't for sale."

Which showed just how much Trevor knew, Rebecca thought, a tad guiltily. Miss Mim had told her Trevor'd had his eyes on her place, too, for quite some time now. But that was neither here nor there.

Deciding she had wasted enough time, she tightened her hand on the thick strap of her shoulder bag and took one last look at Trevor. "I meant what I said. I don't care what bill of goods my father tried to sell you about me needing a man in my life, Trevor McCabe." She ignored the chuckles of all the men gathered around them. "I'm fine as is," she continued stubbornly, holding Trevor's testy gaze with effort. "There won't be any connection—any private talks—between the two of us. And I'm *sorry* if my father misled you otherwise."

Trevor flashed her a grin that was more of a come-on than an expression of mirth.

"You don't look sorry," he remarked.

Knowing this wasn't a conversation that she would ever have the last word in, Rebecca merely rolled her eyes, turned and walked away.

As Trevor expected, Rebecca Carrigan had only to leave the warehouse before Vince Owen whistled. "That is one gal who needs a man to tame her."

Trevor had an idea what that would entail in Vince's opinion. Seething, he swung around on the man who had dogged his every step since the first day they'd met on the Texas A&M campus.

Trevor had vowed never to get tangled up in any of Vince Owen's cutthroat antics, no matter how much or how often he was baited. It had been a promise that had been easy to keep—until now. "Don't talk about her that way."

Vince offered the perverse smile Trevor had come to loathe. "If I didn't know better, I'd think you were sweet on her." Vince unclipped his BlackBerry from his belt and checked the screen, before hooking it back on his waist. "Not that it matters." Vince regarded Trevor steadily, his sick need to compete with Trevor as obvious and as powerful as ever. "Rebecca Carrigan is going to be mine before the month is out."

Trevor doubted Rebecca would fall for Vince's practiced lines, no matter how avidly Vince courted her.

Although Vince would never show the sleazy side of himself to Rebecca. To Rebecca, Vince would be all Texas charm and helpfulness. Like a chameleon, Vince had a talent for blending in—when he wanted to be inconspicuous. Right now, however, Vince's compulsive competitiveness had exposed his arrogance. Instead of making the friends he ought to be, Vince was making a statement about his own superiority to all the other ranchers in the feed store. A mistake in a place like Laramie, where folks didn't let anyone's head get too big for his or her hat.

"I think Rebecca just might have something to say about that," Trevor said casually, walking over to sign for the special bags of organically grown grain he had ordered for his calves.

Vince followed. He leaned against the sales counter. "Oh, I'll make her happy," Vince stated, loud enough for everyone to hear. He paused to let his words sink in. "And before I'm done, I'll bet you I get a ring on her finger, too." Vince turned to the other ranchers gathered around. He removed his wallet from his back pocket, withdrew two crisp one-hundred-dollar bills. "Any takers?"

It was all Trevor could do to hang on to his temper. "We don't make bets on the women around here," Trevor said.

Vince looked around, obviously disappointed no one else was reaching for their money.

With a slimy smile, Vince slid his wallet back in his pocket. "That's too bad for me—although it's probably smart on you all's part, because I'm going to win this wager." Vince tipped his hat, looked every man there in the eye and sauntered out.

"We don't need that element around here," Nevada

Fontaine, the feed store owner, grumbled in Vince's
wake.

No kidding, Trevor thought.

"How'd you get to be associated with him anyway?"
The farm equipment salesman, Parker Arnett, asked.

"We were both in the Aggie cattle management program at the same time." As much as Trevor had tried,
there had been no avoiding Vince Owen.

Vince had set his sights on Trevor early on, and com-
peted viciously with him ever since.

"You don't seem to be friends," fellow rancher, and
esteemed head of the local rancher's association, Dave
Sabado, remarked.

Nor would they ever be, Trevor thought, as everyone
looked at him. Trevor knew this was his opportunity to
tell everyone the whole sorry story. How ugly things
had gotten before he landed the top honors of his program at A&M, how he'd lost the affection and respect
of the only woman he had ever been serious about in
his life, how he had figured once he graduated he could
say good riddance to the fellow-ranching student who
had made him a target of the unhealthiest competition
Trevor had ever seen, only to find out the hard way
that Vince Owen's obsession with besting Trevor was
never going to end.

Unfortunately, that meant he'd be trashing another
man's reputation in public and Trevor made it a policy
never to do that. So he figured it best he keep his own
considerable resentment to himself. The men here were
smart enough not to fall prey to men of Vince Owen's
ilk, anyway. "Vince has a history of buying and selling increasingly bigger ranches. No doubt his purchase
of the Circle Y Ranch is just a temporary thing. He'll

make some improvements, stay just long enough to sell it for a profit, and move on."

"And meantime?" Nevada Fontaine asked, signaling some of his help over to begin loading the feed Trevor had just purchased into his pickup truck.

"I plan to do my best to steer clear of him," Trevor said, with a shrug.

"What about Rebecca Carrigan?" Nevada asked.

"I'll keep her away from him," Trevor said. No way was Vince Owen hurting Rebecca the way he had hurt Jasmine.

"If she hears about the bet Vince Owen just tried to make…" Parker Arnett didn't need to finish the thought.

"She won't, as long as none of us tell her about it." Trevor looked each and every one of the men who had witnessed the attempted wager, in the eye. "Agreed?"

Slowly, the others nodded.

"Good." Trevor breathed a sigh of relief. "'Cause there's no use hurting Rebecca's feelings." And no use in putting her in the middle of the continuing clash between him and Vince Owen. She'd have enough to deal with when she found out the ranch she wanted to buy was not for sale after all.

Chapter 2

"What do you mean you sold the ranch to Rebecca Carrigan?" Trevor McCabe said, an hour later. He stood in the living room of the Primrose Ranch house, watching Miss Mim pack up the last of her cherished travel guides and books. The community librarian and veteran traveler was like a second mother to all the kids in Laramie, maybe because she'd never married or had children of her own. Trevor had grown up knowing he could confide in her. "You and I had an understanding."

Miss Mim handed him the dispenser of packing tape. As always, she was dressed in an outrageously colorful outfit that clashed with her flame-red hair. Moving more like a twenty-year-old than the sixty-eight-year-old woman she was, she patted him on the arm, then pointed to the box. "I think the 'understanding' was more on your part, dear, than mine."

Trevor bent to line up the cardboard flaps. The tape made a ripping sound as it left the spool. "What do you mean?" he demanded, pressing the adhesive on the box with the flat of his palm.

Miss Mim unfolded the last cardboard moving carton and turned it over so Trevor could tape up the bottom of the box. She smiled at him fondly as he assisted her. "You have no problem making up your mind. And you always tell people what you want."

"You just don't listen," Rebecca Carrigan said, coming into the room.

Trevor hadn't known Rebecca was on the premises. It figured she would be. He turned to square off with her for the second time that day, felt his senses kick into high gear. It wasn't just that she was beautiful. It was the way she moved—with a kind of sexy, inherent grace. The way her lips curled softly and her chin tilted stubbornly. The slender curves hidden beneath the pink cotton shirt and faded jeans—along with her straight and silky honey blond hair, challenging golden brown eyes and delicate features—made it impossible for him to look away. Even though it was abundantly clear she wished he would disappear. "How would you know whether I pay attention or not?" he asked.

Rebecca shrugged in mute superiority and gestured at their surroundings. She took the deed out of her pocket and waved it in front of him like a matador waving a cape in front of a bull. "Case in point, cowboy, since this place is now mine, not yours."

Trevor felt like pawing the ground. Maybe because he had never been so ticked off, disappointed, and yes—humiliated. Figuring he would deal with Rebecca Carrigan later, he turned back to Miss Mim. "I told you I would buy The Primrose from you, at whatever price you deemed fair."

Miss Mim straightened and stated patiently, "And I said I would keep that in mind."

Trevor took over the job of fitting the last of her

books into the carton. "And then sold it to Rebecca without giving me a chance to even make a bid?"

Miss Mim stood back, to watch Rebecca load the filled boxes onto a moving dolly. "She needs the land, dear. You already have a ranch."

Frowning—it went against his grain to let a woman lift things when he was there and could do it for her—Trevor brushed Rebecca aside. "A ranch that you know I would like to expand."

Miss Mim led the way to the front door and held it while Trevor pushed the dolly through. "Perhaps you can make the same arrangement with her that you've had with me, regarding grazing rights."

Rebecca followed them to Miss Mim's aging Cadillac. She fit the suitcases into the backseat, while Trevor set the cartons in the already-crammed trunk. Rebecca closed the door. Trevor shut the trunk. The warm April air was scented with primroses and the earthier smells of new grass, sunshine and grazing cattle. Despite this being one of his busiest times of year on the ranch, it was also the most pleasurable. Well, not this year.

Rebecca flashed him another provoking smile.

"Not going to happen, Miss Mim," Rebecca said with a defiant toss of her head. "In fact," her eyes claimed and held his, "I need Trevor to move his herd off my land as soon as possible. Hopefully, today."

Trevor did a double take. He'd expected trouble from Rebecca Carrigan, but not this kind. "You can't be serious."

Rebecca's smile faded. "Oh, but I am."

Miss Mim chuckled and got her car keys out of her handbag. "You two are going to get along splendidly!"

Like hell they were, Trevor thought.

* * *

"How soon can I expect you to move your cattle?" Rebecca asked, the moment Miss Mim had driven off.

Trevor turned back to Rebecca, a stunned expression on his face. "Where is she going?"

Trying hard not to think what it was going to be like having this sexy know-it-all for a neighbor, Rebecca replied, "Laramie Gardens Home For Seniors. She's the new social director."

"She's supposed to be retired."

"Yes, I know." Rebecca turned her glance to the three pastures located at the rear of the property. The square plots were each ten acres, and surrounded by an aging brown split rail fence. A ten-acre hay field sat behind that. The house, barn and detached garage were situated at the front of the property, on the ten acres nearest the road. The Circle Y and Trevor's Wind Creek butted up on either side of her. She was now living smack-dab in the middle of two extremely ambitious men, both of whom coincidentally wanted her property for their own. Wasn't this going to be fun?

"So why is Miss Mim taking another job?"

Rebecca reluctantly directed her attention back to her "visitor." What was it about the McCabe men that made them think they had to know everything? "Apparently, Miss Mim has done all the traveling she wants now, and sitting around all day isn't agreeing with her. A lot of her friends already live at the seniors' home."

Trevor folded his arms in front of him. He reminded her of a general surveying his troops. "When is she going to move the rest of her stuff?"

"They've given her a furnished apartment, as part of the job. So all she's taking is her clothing and personal effects. The rest she sold to me as part of the deal."

"I want to buy the ranch from you."

Rebecca blinked. "What?"

"Add ten percent to whatever you paid her for it, and I'll pay it to you."

"Only ten percent?" she mocked. "Vince Owen has already been here and offered an additional fifteen."

"You're kidding."

Rebecca let her too-sweet smile fade. "Do I look like I'm kidding, cowboy?"

The corners of his mouth took on a downward slant. "What did you say?" he demanded.

"The same thing I'm telling you," Rebecca shot back. "No."

She wasn't surprised to see that Trevor looked relieved about that. Which led her to the next item on her agenda. "Back to the cattle. I need you to move 'em as soon as possible. And you'll need to make sure you clean up after them, or in other words, remove all the dung. I want those pastures clean as can be when I put my alpacas out there."

"You're planning to use all three?"

Rebecca nodded. "One for the females, one for the herd-sires and another for the nursing crias and their mothers."

"How big a herd are you starting with?"

"Ten. But I expect to expand rapidly." Rebecca gave him a moment to absorb all that. "So, can I expect this will be done today?"

Trevor begrudgingly relented. "I'll have to get some temporary help. I don't employ anyone else on a regular basis." He paused. "That may take a few days to arrange."

She glanced out at the far pasture, where he had some thirty steers grazing. "Or you could start right now," she suggested with a discreet lift of her brow, "doing it yourself." Seriously, how long could it take?

His hazel eyes darkened. "I can see living next door to you is going to be a challenge."

She slapped him on the back, rancher-style. Strode off, calling over her shoulder, "Cowboy, you don't know the half of it."

An hour and two phone calls later, Trevor met up with Tyler and Teddy at his horse barn. He'd known he could count on his triplet brothers to drop everything and help him out of this predicament, just as he had assisted them on numerous occasions, emergency and otherwise. The three of them were more than brothers and confidants; they were best friends. Their two much younger brothers, Kurt and Kyle, were growing up the same way.

"That totally sucks," Teddy said, after Trevor had finished filling them in on everything that happened that day.

The ever-practical Tyler shrugged. "Should have had a contract with Miss Mim."

Trevor brought out the lassos and handed one to each brother. "We've never had a contract on any of our arrangements. I just told Miss Mim what I wanted to do. She always said okay. When she needed something, she let me know, and I took care of it for her. I knew she'd want to sell the land eventually—she'd been thinking about moving into town for some time. I just figured when the time came she'd sell it to me."

Tyler carefully cinched his saddle. "When it comes to women, I've learned the hard way, never assume anything,"

Trevor squinted, grinned. "You talking about women in general or Susan Carrigan in particular?"

Teddy swung himself up into the saddle. "You ought to just go ahead and admit it, Ty. There's never going to be another woman for you but Susan."

Tyler guided his horse between Trevor's and Teddy's. "Susan and I don't get along."

"Sometimes you do." Trevor winked, thinking how smugly content his veterinarian-brother could be when his relationship with Rebecca's older sister, Susan happened to be humming along. And how miserable Ty was at times—like now—when it was "off."

"The two of you should just quit all the drama and get hitched," Teddy agreed, as they rode toward the pasture.

"You should talk," Tyler grumbled, with a sharp look at Teddy. "Since you've never had eyes for anyone but Amy Carrigan."

"Amy's my friend," Teddy muttered.

Trevor stopped at the pasture gate and dismounted to open it. "I don't see you dating anyone else—at least not for long."

Teddy turned his glance toward the cattle they were going to have to move. "That's because I've been busy getting my horse-breeding operation up and running."

Trevor knew how hard he'd worked. The Silverado was fast becoming known in Texas as the place to get quality, affordable quarter horses. "Now if you could only train a woman as well as you school a horse," Tyler teased Teddy.

Trevor frowned, his thoughts jumping back to the problem that had brought them all together on such short notice. "I could sure use a few tips on how to handle Rebecca Carrigan," he said, closing the pasture gate, before taking the reins once again.

"Burr under your saddle, huh?" Teddy replied.

Worse, Trevor felt responsible for protecting her, since it had been Trevor's lively public exchange with Rebecca at the feed store that had brought her feisty presence to Vince Owen's attention.

Rebecca didn't know about the bet the conniving jerk had tried—and failed—to make about her that morning. If Trevor had his way, she never would. What worried him was the thought that Vince was going to be living—at least part of the time—on The Circle Y Ranch, on the other side of Rebecca. If Vince were true to form, he'd soon be using his proximity to Rebecca every which way but Sunday in order to get to Trevor.

Vince's efforts to annoy, distract and otherwise make miserable were already working. Trevor's mind was on anything but the business he was supposed to be running on the Wind Creek cattle ranch.

Instead, he kept waiting for Vince to start up the ugly cutthroat competition again, via Rebecca, as a way of punishing Trevor for succeeding academically, professionally, romantically, where Vince had not. Knowing Vince, he'd probably go after the financial success of The Primrose Ranch and the Wind Creek cattle ranch before he was finished, too.

Unfortunately, the only way Trevor would be able to protect Rebecca and her newly acquired property was by befriending her first, a task not made easy by the fact that she thought, erroneously—her parents actually wanted the two of them to start dating. And was, of course, absolutely opposed to having anything at all to do with him. Now or in the future....

Aware his brothers were waiting on Trevor's response to his pretty new neighbor, he frowned and said, "You're right about that much. Ms. Rebecca Carrigan is going to be one royal pain."

As a kid she'd had a reputation for never listening to anyone in a position of authority. From what he could tell so far, that had not changed.

Tyler slowed his mount's pace as they reached the opposite side of the Wind Creek pasture and the gate that separated it from the Primrose Ranch pasture, where alpacas would soon be grazing. "Not to worry about it, bro."

Teddy winked and continued the ribbing, "If any man can handle her—"

And that was a mighty big if, Trevor thought grimly.

"—you can," Tyler said.

"Rebecca, dear, I've already thought of at least half-a-dozen things I forgot to get from the house," Miss Mim said.

"No problem, Miss Mim. I'll get them for you." Rebecca picked up the chalk from the tray on the message board in the kitchen. "Just tell me what they are and I'll make a list."

"My favorite vase, on the dining room table."

"Check."

Miss Mim rambled off four more items while Rebecca wrote. "And I was going to ask you for my binoculars on the hook by the back door, but I've changed my mind. I thought you might want to use those to keep an eye on your new neighbors."

Rebecca rolled her eyes, even as she took the binoculars and looped them around her neck. "Very funny, Miss Mim."

"I'm serious, Rebecca. Those two men are going to

be vying for your hand in marriage in no time. Just don't make my mistake and say no to romance, like I did. When you get to be my age, you'll find you regret it."

Rebecca knew that was true.

Although Miss Mim had been "family" to every parent and child who'd come through the Laramie Public Library, lately she'd been regretting the road not taken. Fortunately, Rebecca was saved having to respond by muffled voices on the other end of the connection.

"Dear?" Miss Mim was back. "The canasta game is about to start. I'll phone you later."

"When would you like me to bring the items by?"

"Two days from now—say around seven in the evening? I'm going to be busy prior to that."

"No problem."

Rebecca hung up the phone.

She walked around the house, gathering the requested items and slipping them into a cardboard box, all the while admiring her new home. It was hard to believe fifty acres of prime Texas acreage, never mind the pretty white stone ranch house with the rose-colored shutters and dark gray roof, was all hers now.

Miss Mim had inherited the seventy-five-year-old homestead from her parents and had taken loving care of it during the forty-two years she had resided there. Handsome dark pine floors shone beneath the delicate antique furniture. Upstairs, there were three bedrooms and a large old-fashioned bath with a claw-foot tub and pedestal sink. In the master bedroom there was an old-fashioned four-poster, matching wardrobe, chest of drawers and vanity. The second bedroom was a sewing room and the third, a study.

Downstairs, a formal parlor and dining room, suitable for entertaining, encompassed the front of the house. In the rear was a big kitchen, complete with trestle table and six Windsor chairs, fireplace and white stone hearth. Black marble countertops gleamed next to state-of-the-art stainless steel appliances and antique white cabinets. The combination laundry room and spacious food pantry were tucked behind panel doors.

Across the front of the house was a wide front porch. Instead of a patio or deck out back, there were steps down to the grass, and a flagstone path that led to a white stone gazebo, surrounded by primroses.

Beyond that was a big red barn and a good distance away from that, a white stone detached garage. Rebecca intended to park in the lane in front of the house and convert the garage into the official farm office, where ranch business would be done.

Figuring she should go down and take another look at the interior of the barn to see what if anything needed to be done before she brought animals onto the ranch, Rebecca headed out the back door.

She had just passed the gazebo when she saw three men on horseback cantering across Trevor McCabe's land, and onto hers.

Wondering whom he'd gotten to help him move cattle on such short notice, Rebecca picked up the binoculars from around her neck and stepped back into the gazebo.

It took a little focusing—and a minute for her to get a vantage point that avoided the stands of cedar and live oak trees between her and them—to get a good view of what was going on out on her land.

Rebecca smiled, identifying Trevor and his two oldest brothers.

When Trevor, Tyler and Teddy were younger, everyone had trouble telling the McCabe triplets apart. These days, it was no problem, despite the fact they all dressed in typical cowboy garb of hat, jeans, boots and cotton shirts. Although they all had broad shoulders, slim hips and fit, muscular physiques, their appearances differed. Trevor's thick reddish-brown hair was clipped so short it was barely visible beneath the brim of his hat. Tyler's hair was on the long side and brushed his collar. Teddy's hair was midway between the two and tended to kink up on the ends. Their differing personalities set them apart, as well. Trevor had a commanding air about him Rebecca found hard to ignore. Tyler was more aloof and had a gentle, assessing manner. Teddy exuded friendliness and a willingness to go the extra mile to help out a friend.

Hearing the phone ring, Rebecca went back inside. It turned out there was a problem with one of her alpacas. But at least she knew where help could be found. Assuming, of course, Rebecca thought as she picked up the binoculars and headed back to the gazebo, that Trevor and his two brothers hadn't left yet.

To Rebecca's relief she could easily make out Tyler and Teddy on horseback, moving the herd. Trevor McCabe, however, was nowhere in sight. Unless, Rebecca thought, getting down on one knee, he and his horse had disappeared behind that distant grove of trees....

Frustrated because she still couldn't locate Trevor, Rebecca adjusted the lens to the highest magnification.

A chuckle to her immediate right had her turning swiftly in alarm. Binoculars still resting on the bridge of her nose, she found herself close up and personal to a denim-clad zipper. Rebecca gasped and dropped the lens.

Smug amusement in his eyes, Trevor McCabe sauntered forward. "Find anything you like?" he drawled.

* * *

"You had no right to sneak up on me that way!" Rebecca scrambled to her feet, glad the two of them weren't as close as her initial view had seemed to indicate.

Trevor tipped the brim of his hat back. "Isn't that a little like the Peeping Tom calling the spy nosy?"

She told herself it was the heat of the spring day making her sweat. "I am not a Peeping Tom!"

"Well, you're not a spy, either." He abruptly changed from flirting cowboy to more sober rancher. "Which leads us to the question of why you're using binoculars on me and my brothers."

Rebecca ignored the heat of awareness rising up between them and forced herself to return his level gaze. "I need to talk to you about borrowing your livestock trailer tomorrow morning. I just got a call from the breeder. I have to pick up one of my alpacas tomorrow morning."

He lifted a brow. "Just one?"

"Blue Mist is pregnant. The vet in San Angelo doesn't want her traveling past tomorrow. He thinks moving her too close to her due date could jeopardize the cria—the baby."

"Why not pick up the rest of the herd while you're there, then?"

Rebecca inhaled the scent of man and sun and horse. "I'm not ready for them yet. But I can go ahead and pick up Blue Mist."

"Sure you want to do that?" he asked. "Alpacas are pack animals."

Now he was sounding just like the saleswoman she had just gotten off the phone with. Fortunately, Rebecca knew a hard sell when she heard one.

"That can wait until early next week." Rebecca knew she would have her hands full just managing one alpaca on her own. That went double for a pregnant alpaca. Besides, she wanted to make sure Blue Mist was completely comfortable and settled in before she brought in the other nine animals she'd bought. And then there was the matter of the balance due when she took possession of the animals. The temporary operating loan she had negotiated for start-up of the ranch was barely adequate. And she'd used most of her own savings on the down payment and mortgage fees for the ranch. She still had her credit card, but she didn't want to max out on that unless she absolutely had to. The remaining balance was her only safety net. And she still had so much to do before the Open House in less than two weeks.

"So can I borrow your livestock trailer?" Rebecca continued.

Trevor frowned. "I'd have to charge you for it."

Despite her tricky finances, Rebecca wouldn't have it any other way, since she absolutely did not want to be beholden to him. "I'd expect to pay a reasonable rent," she said hoping it wouldn't be too much.

"My price is one home-cooked meal."

Rebecca had been prepared to dicker over dollars. She opened her eyes wide, sure she couldn't possibly have heard right. "What?"

Trevor lifted his hands. "That's the arrangement I had with Miss Mim. Whenever I did a favor for her, helped her prune trees, or clean the shutters or whatever, she repaid me with a home-cooked meal and that is what I want from you, too."

Rebecca bit her lip as she tried to figure a clever way out of this that would not shut down all the help she was bound to need from him—in the short haul anyway. "Miss Mim is a fabulous cook." *So was she.* Trevor McCabe did not need to know that, however, lest he make a regular practice of demanding her culinary skills. She'd much rather exchange money or any other less personal commodity—like mucking out the pasture—with him.

"How well I know that," Trevor recollected. He ran the flat of his palm across his jaw. "That's what made working for her such a treat."

Rebecca could see he'd made up his mind about what he wanted from her. "I would prefer to pay cash."

"I don't take money from women. Or in other words—" he paused long enough to give his words an aggravating connotation "—my favors are not for sale."

Refusing to let him ruffle her, Rebecca tilted her head to one side. "And mine are?"

"I don't know," he replied. He leaned toward her and whispered conspiratorially, "Are they?"

Rebecca bit down on an oath. "Stop trying to get under my skin."

"Why," he countered, "when it's so much fun?"

For the second time in ten minutes, Rebecca found herself fighting a self-conscious blush. "Is there anything else you'd be willing to barter?" she asked.

He took a moment to consider.

Sexual chemistry arced between them, hotter than ever.

She held up her hand in halting fashion. "Never mind." Pulse racing, she shook her head in silent regret, mumbling just beneath her breath, "Forget I asked that." She forced herself to meet and hold his decidedly mischievous gaze. "When do you want to get your dinner?" she asked.

Her irritated tone brought a provoking smile to his

lips. "You make it sound like I'd be picking up a meal through a drive-through window."

"Pretty close, although to be generous, I will be delivering it to you." That way she could do at least that much of it on her terms.

He stepped closer, purposefully invading her space. "I don't think you get what I'm saying to you. When I say I want a home-cooked meal from you in return for borrowing my trailer, I'm talking about the two of us getting to know each other and sitting down to break bread together."

Just why he was suddenly so determined they be chums, she didn't know. But she didn't trust his newfound interest in her any more than she trusted whatever it was he had secretly been discussing with her father this morning.

Taking her time, she cocked her head and played with the ends of the braid falling over her shoulder.

Channeling Scarlett O'Hara—or maybe it was Calamity Jane—she batted her eyelashes at him coquettishly, asked sweetly, "I can't just put the food on the table and run?"

He stood, legs braced apart, muscular arms folded in front of him. "You only wish I were that easy to deal with."

No kidding.

He looked her up and down with lazy male confidence. "If you want my help, you have to sit down with me and regale me with your charming company every bit as graciously as Miss Mim always did. And in turn—" his gaze slid past the delicate hollow of her throat, past her lips, to her eyes "—I'll regale you with mine."

"Geez." Rebecca made a great show of blowing out an exasperated breath. "You drive a hard bargain."

He inclined his head in arrogant agreement. "Always."

It was time to get back to business. "I'll need the trailer at seven tomorrow morning," she said.

Trevor tipped the brim of his hat at her. "I'll be here, ready to go."

"I didn't mean you had to come with me!"

"That's the only way you can have use of the livestock hauler since I'm the only one insured to use it." Again, he appeared about as flexible as a thousand pound steer.

She took a deep steadying breath, tore her eyes from the masculine contours of his chest. "It's going to take half a day or more to do all the business with the breeder, talk to their vet, load up Blue Mist and get back here."

He shrugged his broad shoulders. "Then you better fortify me tonight with your culinary skills."

Once again, Rebecca found herself stunned by Trevor McCabe's temerity. "You expect dinner here tonight?" She'd been hoping to put it off at least a couple of days.

He declared victory with a sexy wink. "We'll just call it payment in advance."

Chapter 3

"Mom and Dad wanted to be here, too, but they both have to work evening hours at the hospital," Amy Carrigan told Rebecca an hour later.

Her three siblings had stopped in to congratulate her. They'd also brought housewarming gifts. Sunscreen and lip balm from Susie, who worked outdoors as a landscape architect and garden center owner and knew the importance of protecting skin. An indoor herb garden from Amy, who owned her own ranch and plant-growing business. And a deluxe first aid box from Jeremy, a family physician at Laramie Community Hospital.

"They said they'd be by later in the week," Jeremy continued.

"Right," Rebecca said.

Susie understood the hurt Rebecca felt—maybe because she had encountered resistance, too, when she had decided to eschew lucrative job offers and go into business for herself, right out of college. She and Amy had both been remarkably successful eventually, but there was no denying their first few years out of the gate had been so lean financially that their parents had worried constantly. Susie had taken the brunt of it, since she had been the first to take the leap.

"Just give them time. They'll come around, once they see you making a go of it," Susie encouraged, for once being more supportive than overly protective.

"And that Open House you're planning in two weeks to get your business off the ground will help," Amy added.

Rebecca hoped that was the case. Now that she was actually residing at the ranch, for all of…six hours…she was beginning to feel slightly overwhelmed by everything that had to be done, despite the steps Miss Mim had taken to make the transition easier for her by leaving the pantry, fridge and freezer stocked with fresh food and homemade entrees.

Lucky for her, Miss Mim had loved to cook for others.

"Just be glad you're not in my position," Jeremy lamented, "since everyone at Laramie Community Hospital still thinks of me as Luke and Meg's kid."

It had to be hard, Rebecca figured, taking a position at the same hospital where their physician father was Chief of Family Medicine and their mother an RN who supervised the entire nursing staff.

"You want to trade positions with me?" Rebecca teased. She stood on tiptoe to retrieve a glass casserole dish, then set it on the counter. "I'll be glad to let you cook dinner for Trevor McCabe."

"I still don't get why you agreed to that," Amy said.

"Yeah. Why didn't you just tell him to go jump in Lake Laramie?" Susie sipped the iced tea Rebecca had poured for everyone.

Rebecca shrugged and opened a foil-wrapped single serving packet marked Tex-Mex Chicken Casserole.

She dumped the rock-hard concoction into the dish. "I have to borrow a livestock hauler from somebody. He has one that isn't being used tomorrow. He lives right next door to me. He had no problem being neighborly."

Jeremy watched as Rebecca unwrapped another packet. "Maybe I should try his approach. It's certainly a novel way to get a date."

Rebecca regarded her siblings, her brows arched. "This isn't a date."

"Then what is it?" Susie persisted.

Rebecca popped the casserole into the microwave and punched Defrost. "It's an opportunity for me to start setting some boundaries with that handsome cowboy."

Amy tilted her head. "Interesting way to refer to your neighbor to the north."

"Come on," Rebecca huffed. "You all know what I mean."

"The question is, do you?" Jeremy asked.

Rebecca studied the dish in the microwave. "Trevor needs to understand I am no Miss Mim."

Her only brother chuckled. "I think he's got that part down already, giving how fast he's moving in on you."

The microwave dinged. Rebecca grabbed a pot holder and removed the dish. "For the last time, Jeremy, Trevor McCabe is not staking out any kind of claim on me tonight."

"If you say so." Jeremy looked over her shoulder. "And if I were you, I'd use about four of those if you don't want Trevor McCabe to leave hungry. Those are lady-sized portions." Jeremy patted his stomach. "I figure I could put away at least three of them, so he probably could, too."

"Good point." Rebecca went back to the freezer

and emerged with two more single-serve packets. "I wouldn't want him to leave hungry."

Susie studied her, ready to jump in, if necessary, and save Rebecca from herself. "That gleam in your eye means trouble," Susie said.

"Does it?" Rebecca asked innocently, wondering when Susie would finally realize that Rebecca could survive just fine without any sisterly—or parental—help?

Ever the peacemaker, Amy said kindly, "You could always ask us to stay for dinner, too."

Rebecca slid the extra portions on a plate, put them into the microwave and pushed Defrost once again. "If I did that," Rebecca replied, peeved Amy was now starting to meddle a bit, too, "Trevor McCabe would think I was hiding behind you."

"And what's wrong with that?" Susie demanded.

Rebecca reached for the herb garden and broke off sprigs of mint, cilantro, oregano, basil, rosemary, parsley and thyme. She got out a cutting board and began dicing up everything but the cilantro. "I am not afraid to spend time alone with him."

Amy frowned. "You realize you just mixed all those herbs together."

"Indeed, I do." Rebecca took the plate out of the oven, added the contents to the casserole dish, then picked up her spoon, and prepared to get to work. "And soon Trevor McCabe will, too."

The guilt started as soon Rebecca opened the door. She hadn't bothered to do more than wash her face and brush her teeth to get ready for her company. Her hair remained in the two loose braids she'd put it in that morning. She was still dressed in a T-shirt, jeans and boots.

Trevor had obviously showered before driving over. He was wearing a clean pair of jeans, a freshly ironed white Western shirt and dress boots. He smelled of soap and cologne. His reddish-brown hair was still damp, parted neatly on one side.

To make her feel even worse, he hadn't shown up empty-handed. He had a large wicker gift basket jammed with all manner of sauces and condiments, all bearing his mother's company's name—Annie's Homemade—and a plate of homemade ranger cookies.

Behind her, a less-than-appetizing smell filled the air. Rebecca tried not to think how the doctored casserole was going to taste.

To his credit, and her increased annoyance, he didn't react in the slightest to the rather unappetizing aroma scenting the ranch house. "My mom and dad sent you a housewarming gift, welcoming you to the neighborhood."

Rebecca studied the array of labels gratefully. She already knew Annie's barbecue sauce, ketchup, hot sauce, mustards and salad dressings were first-rate. "I didn't realize your mom had expanded into jams and jellies, too," she said. There was everything from boysenberry to apricot fruit spreads, as well as jalapeño jelly and chipolte pepper mayonnaise.

Trevor smiled. "Seems she's always perfecting some new recipe." He set the plate of cookies down on the kitchen table. "Better be careful or she'll have you acting as a taste-tester, too."

Rebecca nodded at the dessert plate. "Your mom make those, too?"

"No." Trevor took off his hat and hung it on a hook near the back door.

Rebecca studied the cookies. Golden-brown, perfect in size and texture. Her mouth watered, just looking at them. "Bakery in town?"

Trevor shook his head.

"Grocery?"

"Does it matter?" He was beginning to look a little annoyed. "I can vouch for 'em. They're good."

Rebecca slid one out from under the cover of plastic wrap. They smelled delicious, too. "I'm just curious." She bit into the confection, and found it rich and buttery and full of crispy rice cereal, oatmeal and coconut.

"I made 'em."

It took all her concentration to swallow. "You?" she sputtered, amazed.

Trevor shrugged. "My brothers and I all know how to cook. Even Kyle and Kurt."

"The younger two," Rebecca said, remembering.

"They're only seventeen and eighteen but they can grill a mean steak, scramble eggs. Throw together a salad. All the basics."

Maybe doctoring the food hadn't been such a good idea. She could have cooked normally and he likely would have been disappointed. Now, well, it was obvious what she had done....

"Anyway, I hope you like oatmeal and coconut...."

Like 'em? She was addicted to both. Even more annoying, it looked as though he was a better cook than she was, if the cookies were any indication.

"Can I help?"

Rebecca shook her head. Gestured for him to have a seat at the trestle table. She'd put herself at one end, him clear at the other. Four places and a vase of primroses stood between them. Aware the lettuce was beginning to wilt over the heavy application of buttermilk ranch dressing she'd layered it with a good half hour before, she set the wooden salad bowl on the table and went to the oven to get the casserole.

"I never knew you wanted to ranch," Trevor remarked.

Rebecca set two steaming plates on the table and sat down opposite him. "That's because I never confided my ambition to anyone but Miss Mim. She used to help me find books at the library."

"But you didn't study agriculture in college."

Deciding to start with her salad, Rebecca twirled a soggy piece of lettuce on her fork. "That's because I couldn't see myself breeding cattle or horses, or heaven forbid, pigs! I can't say chickens appealed to me much, either."

Trevor dug into his first course with an enthusiasm that made her wince. "So instead you took the job with that tour company and headed overseas."

That had been due more to a quarrel with her sister Susie and her father, over their outright betrayal of her in a romantic matter, than anything else. But Rebecca wasn't about to get into that. Especially since her relationship had never really been the same with her sister Susie, or her father, since.

Rebecca shrugged. "I'd always longed for adventure. The job provided that, and more." Plus, since she'd always been working and traveling and hadn't had to pay apartment rent, she'd been able to bank nearly her entire salary.

"I still don't see how you got from there to breeding

alpacas." Trevor finished his salad, and took a big bite of Tex-Mex chicken casserole.

It was all Rebecca could do not to gag herself as Trevor swallowed and followed his first bite of the main course with a gentlemanly sip of water.

She continued to play with her salad. "One of the European tours went to an alpaca ranch. I fell in love with the animals almost the moment I saw them, and when I found out how valuable their wool is—it's the finest in the world—I knew I'd found my calling."

"Sounds like you've given this some thought." Trevor got up and walked over to the gift basket. He came back with a bottle of Annie's Homemade Ketchup, with the familiar blue-and white-gingham label. He sat down and poured a liberal dose over the entrée.

"More than you could ever know," Rebecca replied.

He studied her while he ate. He didn't need sips of water now.

Rebecca on the other hand had all she could do not to gag on the mixture of incompatible herbs that she had added to the casserole.

Which served her right, she figured, for having done such an immature and bratty thing to begin with. She knew better than to treat a guest—even a self-invited one—this way.

"It's okay to be nervous about a new business venture," Trevor said eventually.

Finished with the meager portion she had put on his plate, he helped himself to some more, added ketchup, and—to her complete astonishment—dug right in.

"What makes you think I'm nervous?" Rebecca groused, not about to deal with one more naysayer in her life.

Her parents' worries, combined with her three siblings' unvoiced skepticism, had been more than enough.

Not that anyone had bothered to listen to the entirety of her plan. No, she usually lost them when they heard about the second loan she'd taken against the first, and the balloon payment due two weeks after closing.

Oblivious to the calculated financial risks she was taking, Trevor regarded her with a gentleness she didn't expect.

"You have the same look in your eyes that I had in mine when I closed on Wind Creek."

Rebecca couldn't figure out whether he was being straight with her or not. What he'd said did not sound like the Trevor McCabe she knew. "You. Mr. Big Shot Cattleman. Were nervous."

"Oh, yeah," Trevor replied. "As was my brother Teddy when he started up The Silverado." Trevor finished his second helping, and went for a third. "It's the same thing everybody feels when they buy their first car or home or pet, or accept a job. That what-have-I-gotten-myself-into-now panic. Buyer's remorse, some call it."

Rebecca added ketchup to her dinner, too, and found the condiment delicious and the casserole beneath just as unpalatable.

She toyed with the food on her plate, suddenly glad he'd brought this up. She needed some encouragement. "When does the panicky feeling pass?" she asked him.

"As soon as you get going." He flashed her a sexy smile. "Which is why it's probably good you're going to pick up the start of your herd tomorrow. Once you get busy caring for your alpacas, you won't have time to think."

Not thinking sounded good.

Rebecca started to relax.

Trevor smiled at her.

Too late, she saw the unexpected had happened... they were becoming more than neighbors...they were becoming friends.

"You didn't tell me you had a puppy," Trevor remarked a few minutes later as they cleaned up the dishes.

"I don't."

"Then you've got a visitor."

Rebecca followed his glance to the bank of kitchen windows overlooking the backyard. Sure enough, a chocolate-brown Labrador retriever was alternately nosing the ground and trotting briskly toward the house. When he reached the stoop, he let out a sound that was half bark, half whine. "Oh my goodness. He barely looks old enough to be away from his mama."

Trevor caught the puppy before he could dart past Rebecca, into the house. He lifted the squirming Labrador to chest level. "It's a she. And I'd guess, from the size of her, that she's about nine, ten weeks old, which means she probably just left her mama and the rest of her litter."

Interesting. "Does she have tags?"

"Nope." Trevor looked. "Just a collar."

She sure didn't look scared or lost. "Anyone around here have puppies recently?" Rebecca asked.

"Not that I'm aware. And this is a purebred, which makes her worth a pretty penny."

"You got that right," a male voice concurred.

Rebecca and Trevor turned.

Vince Owen strode toward them.

"This is Coco. I just got her today. I was bringing

her over to meet you and she got ahead of me. Trevor." Vince nodded.

Trevor nodded back, looking, Rebecca noted, no more pleased to see the Circle Y's new owner than he had earlier in the day.

"Rebecca." Vince leaned forward, and before Rebecca could stop him, kissed her cheek in Southern-style greeting.

Rebecca didn't know why she was annoyed. Having grown up in Texas, she had received many a casual peck on the cheek as hello over the years. None had ever bothered her. This one rankled. The way he subtly moved in between her and Trevor seemed meant to annoy his old college classmate. She didn't like being used as a pawn in anyone's game.

Trevor handed Coco to her new owner with a cynical look.

"I hope I'm not interrupting something," Vince said.

Rebecca sensed Vince wanted an explanation for Trevor's presence and perhaps an invitation to hang out for a while, too. She was just as inclined not to give it. Intuition told her that despite his smooth manner and cordial appearance, the handsome, blond Vince Owen was nothing but trouble.

Trevor looked at Rebecca, checking, she figured, to see if she needed him to stay. Knowing it would be easier to get rid of Vince and back to what she needed to be doing in preparation for the morning, Rebecca let Trevor know it wasn't necessary.

To her relief, Trevor took the hint, albeit with barely concealed reluctance.

Trevor slipped back inside the house to get his hat. "I've got an early day tomorrow. I better get going.

Vince." Trevor dipped his head in polite acknowledgment.

Vince nodded back. He waited until Trevor climbed into his pickup truck and drove away, then turned back to Rebecca.

"Like to hold her?" Without waiting for a reply, Vince thrust the puppy into her arms.

The chocolate-brown pup looked up at Rebecca with dark liquid eyes. As always, when confronted with puppies, Rebecca felt her heart melt a little. They were just so sweet, vulnerable, eager to please...

And given the packet of investment information she had yet to pull together for future customers of the Primrose alpaca operation, she really did not have time for this.

"My cattle won't be delivered for a few days. I've got two hired hands sitting idle. Should you need anything, be sure and let me know. I could send my cowboys over to help," Vince said.

"That's a very generous offer," Rebecca replied. But not, she figured, without strings. What kind, she wasn't sure she wanted to know.

"What are neighbors for?"

Rebecca petted Coco's head. She was a beautiful dog. Rebecca smiled as Coco licked her forearm with her velvety rough tongue. Too bad her new owner didn't seem half as smitten with the puppy as Rebecca was.

"You don't work the cattle yourself?" Rebecca asked.

Vince Owen shook his head. "I've got two other properties around the state. Have to ride herd on all of them." He withdrew a business card from his wallet, handed it to her. "Here are all my numbers. Should you need anything at all, just call. Meantime, as long as you and I are getting acquainted—" he paused to flash her a salesperson's winning smile "—I've got two tickets to the Laramie County Rancher's Association Spring Fling."

Rebecca already knew about the black-tie dinner-dance at the community center on Friday evening. "Thank you for the invitation, Vince, but I'm already planning to attend."

"With McCabe," Vince guessed, a hint of unpleasantness coming into his eyes.

Rebecca gave him the "attitude" she reserved for too-persistent men. "Alone," she corrected.

Relaxing, Vince gestured affably. "If we went together, you could introduce me around."

Reluctantly, Rebecca handed his puppy back to him. She didn't want anything or anyone interfering with her efforts to network and promote her new business. Vince could easily do just that, as could Trevor McCabe. "Laramie is a very friendly place. You won't have any trouble meeting people on your own."

Vince took her rejection with a graceful shrug. "Another time, then."

Not, Rebecca thought, if I can help it.

The tension between Vince and Trevor aside, there was something about Vince Owen she just didn't trust.

"So what's the story between you and Vince?" Rebecca asked Trevor the next afternoon, after they had returned. Her first stock purchase, the cornerstone of her alpaca breeding operation, Blue Mist, had weathered the trip back well, and was now grazing in the shade.

Trevor's hands tightened on the pasture gate. Up until now, he hadn't asked her anything about her other visitor from the night before, but she had felt his curiosity as surely as her own. "Why?" Trevor tipped the brim of his hat away from his face. "What did he say?"

"Nothing about you."

Trevor rested an elbow on the top rail. He looked out at the pregnant alpaca. "Then why are you asking?"

Rebecca finished filling the water trough and shut off the hose. "Because clearly the two of you are not mutual admirers."

Trevor tilted his head. "Happens sometimes."

She tilted her gaze in the same direction. "Usually, for a reason."

He raised one eyebrow. "Anyone ever tell you you're nosy?"

Her pulse picked up. "Anyone ever tell you you're maddeningly private?"

"All the time." He tapped her playfully on the nose. "And you didn't answer my question," he said.

She tried hard not to stare into his eyes as deeply as he was gazing into hers. "Inquisitive was the word Miss Mim used, I believe," she murmured, feeling her cheeks heat. "And yes, she said that all the time." She held up a finger as if lecturing to a student. "And you know what that means."

He waited.

"Once I have a question in my mind, I have to discover the answer." She paused for effect. "No matter what it takes."

"Threats don't work on me," he told her mildly.

She wrinkled her brow, the way she always did when working a puzzle. "Is that what Vince Owen did to you? Did he threaten you someway, somehow?"

Trevor scoffed. "You've been watching too many mystery shows on TV."

"But something despicable is going on here, nonetheless. Otherwise you and Vince wouldn't give each other those looks."

Trevor's expression remained impassive. "Looks," he echoed, as if he hadn't the slightest idea what she was talking about. Even though she knew he did.

"Like you can't stand each other but you're going to be polite because you've ended up living and working in the same place and to do otherwise would make everyone else even more uncomfortable and that would be ungentlemanly, and you were brought up, as a McCabe, to be a gentleman."

"Well, now that you've got it all figured out…"

"Okay. Don't tell me." Rebecca pivoted. "I guess I could always ask your mother."

He clamped a hand on her shoulder, brought her back around. "Why do you care?" he demanded.

She made her eyes go wide. "Because in case you haven't noticed, cowboy, I live between the Circle Y Ranch and the Wind Creek Ranch, and that puts me right smack-dab in the middle of you two guys. And although you might be willing to let that go, I assure you, Vince Owen will not."

Resentment warred with the curiosity on his handsome face. "Did you ask him?"

Why hadn't she? She could have. "I wanted to hear your side."

"And not his?"

Rebecca tried not to think why she automatically trusted Trevor in a way she couldn't seem to honor Vince. "Are you going to tell me or not?"

"Vince and I met at Texas A&M," he told her brusquely. "We were both studying cattle management. I was at the top of my class from the beginning—probably because I grew up on a cattle ranch and worked side by side with my dad, who happens to be one of the best cattlemen around."

It was more than that, Rebecca knew.

Trevor had a way with animals. An immense capacity for hard, physical, down and dirty work. And a need to achieve as deep as her own.

From what she'd seen thus far, Vince seemed driven by the outward trappings of success. Instead of being content with one ranch in one area of the state, he wanted three. He managed instead of ranched. And he already had his eye on the local social scene.

"Vince wanted to be the top student in our department. He was upset when he could not best me on exams and labs."

Okay. "And that's it?"

"Obviously, you've never had anyone continually competing with you. It grates on a person."

She studied him. "You think that's why Vince Owen bought a ranch so close to yours, don't you?"

Trevor clenched his fists in frustration. "It's not just this ranch. He dogs me all the time. I was asked to be a speaker on a ranching seminar last year. He found out and unbeknownst to me, got on the program, too. He found out what kinds of cattle I was breeding, started breeding that type, too. Bought a herd of heifers out from under me. Bought that land on the other side of you—the Circle Y—out from under me. I had offered the asking price to the previous owner, when he was ready to sell. Next thing I know he has accepted an offer from an intermediary for ten percent more. When I heard it, I had a sinking feeling who the new owner might be, but I didn't know for sure until Vince Owen walked into the feed store yesterday morning."

She glanced sideways at him. "Wow. No wonder you're annoyed."

Trevor dropped his hands to his sides and shrugged. "I just don't want to see you get hurt."

"I won't. I knew right off he wasn't the kind of guy I wanted to have as a friend."

"That doesn't mean he won't use you to get to me," Trevor warned.

"To use me, he'd have to get me to give him something. I have no intention of doing that. Now or ever," Rebecca said flatly. "I do want to thank you, though, for helping me go get Blue Mist this morning."

"No problem. I haven't been around alpacas since I was in college. I had forgotten how beautiful they are."

Interesting he would say that, Rebecca thought. It mirrored her feelings exactly.

As if realizing she was being talked about, Blue Mist ambled toward them.

The fawn-colored animal stood at almost five feet. With her gentle demeanor, long, sloping neck, sturdy giraffe-shaped body and dense, soft and fluffy wool coat, she lent a pastoral quality to The Primrose. Her cute oblong face and intelligent dark eyes only added to her appeal. Rebecca stroked her wool.

"How much do you know about shearing?" she asked Trevor.

He grinned. "I haven't tried it on my cattle."

"I'm going to have to do that once I get the entire herd on the property. It has to be done before it gets too hot."

He rubbed Blue Mist behind the ears. "You shear them once a year?"

Rebecca nodded. "In the spring."

Trevor dropped his hand as Blue Mist moved away

once again. "One question. How did an alpaca with light brown wool get the name Blue Mist?"

Rebecca had been wondering if and when Trevor would ask that. "She was born on a foggy morning, and when the owners first saw her, she was rising up out of a blue mist."

"Ah."

"It's a good name, I think. Prophetic."

"You mean romantic," he teased.

Rebecca couldn't afford to be thought of as anything less than business-minded. "I mean it spoke to me when I heard it. And when I met her, saw how gentle she was, and found out she was already with cria, I knew she was the start of my herd."

"Speaking of which…you and I need to talk about the fence around your pastures."

"Why?" Rebecca braced for news that would cost her more than she'd already spent. "What's wrong with it?" she asked in trepidation.

"The wood is breaking down in places."

She cocked her head. "You had your cattle in there."

His lips twitched. "Circumstances are different now. We're going to have my thousand-pound steers on my side of that fence, and your one-hundred-pound alpacas on the other."

"Are you saying your cattle are going to bother my alpacas?"

His hazel eyes glimmered seriously. "Not under normal circumstances, but we have to be prepared for the unusual."

She wished she could say he was joking. "Such as?"

"Predators getting in the pasture with your alpacas."

She would have laughed at the statistical absurdity

of the statement had it not been for his warning expression. "Are you trying to give me a hard time?"

"I'm trying to explain to you that even a stray cat or dog could spook your alpacas, and if they get spooked and start running and upset my cattle, we could have a stampede on our hands."

So it was back to the alpacas and cattle don't mix theory of ranching. An old wives' tale if she'd ever heard one. She planted her hands on her hips. "I think you're exaggerating."

He let his gaze drift slowly over her before returning to her face. He leaned down so they were practically nose to nose. "And I think you need mesh fence on the inside of the split rail borders, for safety's sake."

She dropped her hands and stepped back. "I can't afford to do that right now, Trevor."

He shrugged, as unconcerned with the financial details of the situation as she was obsessed. "Then I'll help you out."

His matter-of-fact offer sounded like a mixture of pity and charity. If she accepted either, word would get out, and she would never have the other ranchers' respect.

Rebecca shook her head, promising, "I'll get to it as soon as I can, but until then we're just going to have to make do."

Silence ticked out between them. "You sure that's a chance you want to take?" he asked eventually.

What choice did she have? She was on such a tight budget as it was, at least for the next month or so, the slightest catastrophe could catapult her into bankruptcy. Once she'd attracted outside investors, though, her situation would ease quickly.

Gulping around the anxiety rising up within her, she

tried to smooth things over while still stubbornly hold-ing her ground. "Look, Trevor, the rest of the herd won't be here for another ten days or so. As soon as I get past the Open House I'm having for potential investors, a week from Sunday," and get past the balloon payment that is due on my operating loan, "I'll take care of the fence. I promise."

Trevor looked like he wanted to continue debat-ing her, but when he finally spoke it was only to ask, "Where are you going to house your herd at night?"

"In the stalls in the barn. Which reminds me. I've really got to get cleaning if I want Blue Mist and that cria she's carrying to have somewhere to sleep tonight."

Trevor took the hint, and left to tend to his own herd.

Three hours later, Rebecca had scrubbed down the central cement corridor and two of the ten wooden-sided stalls. She was filthy from head to toe, and bone-tired to boot. Deciding to check on Blue Mist, she walked out to the pasture, and stopped in her tracks at what she saw.

Chapter 4

"Blue Mist doesn't appear to be in labor," Rebecca told veterinarian Tyler McCabe over the phone, minutes later. Struggling to recall everything she had read on the subject in preparation, and wishing her many books and articles—which were still on the moving truck due to be delivered any time now—were already in her possession, Rebecca continued describing the behavior of her prized alpaca. "She's pacing, but not rolling around in the pasture. What concerns me more than the humming sound she's making is the way she's drooling, how tense she is. The way she's stomping her feet and grinding her teeth."

"Her behavior is probably due to the fact she's been separated from the herd and placed in a new environment. But I'd like to take a look at her tonight anyway. I'll run by as soon as I finish up office hours here. Probably around seven or seven-thirty if that's okay."

"That'd be great. Thank you, Tyler."

"No problem. And let me know if anything changes."

"I will." Rebecca cut the connection on her cell phone and dialed again. She got the breeder, Helen Mc-

Namara, on the first try, and spoke with her, too. Helen suggested several ways to improve the situation, and offered her help. Forgetting her own timetable for getting her ranch up and running, Rebecca took Helen up on all of them this time.

Their plans set, the two women said goodbye.

Wishing she had listened to Helen's advice sooner, Rebecca pocketed her cell phone. She turned when she heard the sounds of wheels on gravel.

To her disappointment, it wasn't the moving truck she was expecting. It was the two people she least wanted to see at that moment.

She waited while her father's Suburban made its way up the drive to the house. "Mom. Dad." Rebecca nodded at Meg and Luke as they emerged from the vehicle.

Her mom was dressed in a light cotton dress and sweater, perfect for the warm spring weather, her dad a knit shirt, and slacks. They looked fit and trim. Regular visits to the salon kept the gray out of Meg's red hair, but Luke's sandy-blond hair was threaded with silver these days.

"We came by to see the ranch and see if you wanted to go to dinner with us," Meg said.

"Thanks for the invitation, but it's not a good time. I'm pretty busy."

"So we see." Luke looked past her disheveled appearance, toward the pasture. "That your first alpaca?" he asked, already heading toward the aging split rail fence.

As they neared, Blue Mist backed up and hummed and stomped even louder.

"Is something wrong with her?" Meg asked in concern.

"We think it's just homesickness, the fact she was separated from the herd. Tyler McCabe's coming out to check her this evening. The rest of the herd is going to be delivered tomorrow afternoon. She'll probably calm down when she sees the rest of her 'family.' In the meantime, it's been suggested that I go ahead and get her settled in a stall with food and water, so..."

"Is there anything we can do to help?" Meg asked.

Rebecca snatched the leather lead from the hook next to the gate, where she'd left it, and shook her head.

Talking softly, the way she'd been taught when she'd taken a seminar on the care and feeding of alpacas in Europe the previous year, Rebecca attached the lead to Blue Mist's halter and led her toward the barn. The animal relaxed almost immediately when she entered the six-by-ten confine with the high wooden walls. She settled onto the recently scrubbed cement floor with a sigh and "kushed" or lay down on her side. Rebecca removed the lead, then talked to her a little more. When she was satisfied Blue Mist was settled, Rebecca backed out of the stall and closed the gate.

Rebecca turned, to see her parents, watching. "Good job with that," her dad said, looking impressed.

Meg nodded in agreement. "I had no idea you were this good with farm animals."

"Even so, you think I'm crazy, undertaking this." Rebecca knew from the look on her father's face that his opinion hadn't changed in the least. Meg's probably hadn't, either.

Luke glanced at the interior of the barn. It hadn't been used to house animals for thirty years.

Meg walked out into the warm spring evening. The scent of flowers filled the air. Until now, she had kept silent on the subject, leaving the "heavy lifting" to Luke. Rebecca sensed that was about to change.

"We're so glad to have you back in Laramie again,

Rebecca, and we applaud your desire to be independent and run your own business, but we'd be lying if we said we weren't worried about what you're trying to do here."

Luke nodded. "I've done some research on alpacas."

"Then you know that compared to most types of livestock, they are very gentle and easy to raise."

"I also know what they cost. And I'm guessing you paid more for Blue Mist than for your brand-new pickup truck."

Rebecca didn't deny that was the case. "I'll make the money back and more. And I'll show you how I'm going to do that when I have my Open House the Sunday after next."

"All we're saying is that maybe you should slow down," Luke continued. "Take on a few animals, see how that goes before you invest every penny you have in this endeavor."

"You could start your own travel agency," Meg chimed in. "With your experience…you've been so many places. You would be great at it. You could still live on The Primrose. Have one or two alpacas for pets. You just wouldn't have to…"

"Labor like a farm hand?" Rebecca guessed where this conversation was going.

"Exactly," Luke said.

Rebecca was saved having to reply to that suggestion by another vehicle moving up the gravel lane that served as her driveway. "If you'll excuse me, I need to show the movers where to put my boxes."

Rebecca lifted the cross bar on the swinging wooden doors and opened up the detached barn-style garage that would soon be turned into the farm office. She greeted the driver and his assistant and indicated where she wanted the boxes stacked. The two men had just gotten started when a third vehicle drove up the lane.

"When it rains it pours," Rebecca mumbled, not all that sorry Trevor McCabe had taken this moment to drop by, too. She could use whatever distraction her neighbor provided, and then some.

Trevor drove past the movers and parked next to her parents' vehicle. Rebecca watched as he strode toward her and her parents. He said hello to everyone then grinned at her disheveled state. "Looks like you've been busy," Trevor drawled.

Rebecca noted he also looked a little worse for wear, as if he'd spent the day working, too. "Then that makes two of us."

"I stopped by to see if you wanted to borrow my pressure washer to clean out the barn," Trevor said. "I could show you how to use it, if you've never handled one."

Aware her parents were hanging on every word, Rebecca said, "I'd appreciate that. Thanks."

"Want me to go and get it for you now?" Trevor asked. "That way you'll have it when you need it."

"I'll ride over with you, if you don't mind," Luke said. "I've never seen your ranch."

Trevor's surprise faded as quickly as it had appeared on his face. "Sure."

Rebecca stepped between the two men. "Smooth, Dad. But you can stop trying to set up Trevor and I. He's already told me in no uncertain terms that he has absolutely no interest in dating me."

To Trevor's relief, Luke didn't even try to deny his supposed matchmaking before heading off to the Wind Creek with him. "Is that true?" Luke demanded as Trevor turned the vehicle around and headed toward the rural two-lane highway.

"Rebecca misunderstood why I was talking to you yesterday morning." Trevor eased back out onto the road.

"Did you tell her I asked you to talk her out of ranching?" Luke studied the feed corn growing in the field to their right.

"Nope," Trevor said as he turned into his own drive.

"Thanks. She wouldn't appreciate the behind-the-scenes interference."

He stopped to get the mail out of his box. "No kidding."

"I know you think I'm wrong for trying to change her mind about this."

Trevor shrugged and continued driving. "She's a grown woman."

"Who is still capable of making a mistake."

Trevor parked in front of the barn and cut the engine. "Maybe it should be hers to make. Look, Dr. Carrigan, I know you mean well. But Rebecca has a right to live her life any way she pleases."

Luke hit the release on his safety belt and pushed from the vehicle. "Even if it costs her six years of savings?"

Trevor led the way into the state-of-the-art facility. It smelled of disinfectant and spring air. "This venture of hers is not going to do that. Ranch land around here is only going up in value. Alpacas, while expensive, are a much sought after commodity, not just in Texas, but in the entire United States. There's a ban on importation. She's going to have to breed wisely to get the maximum value from her investment, but even if she doesn't, it's unlikely she will lose money, given the demand for the animals." He retrieved the pressure washer out of the tack room and carried it to his pickup.

Luke lounged against the pickup's gate. "That could all change if demand declines."

"True, but since it takes eleven months to produce a single alpaca, and alpaca wool is wanted world over, it won't happen any time soon."

Luke stuck his hands in the pockets of his slacks. "I heard what happened at the feed store with Vince Owen."

Trevor shut the gate. "Then you also know there were no takers for the bet he tried to make about Rebecca."

Luke exhaled. "Does she know?"

"No, and everybody there agreed she shouldn't. It would only hurt her feelings. Make interaction with him all that much harder. And since Vince owns the ranch on the other side of her now..."

Luke rubbed his neck. "Have the two of them met?"

"Yes." Trevor propped an arm on the side of his truck. "She doesn't like him."

Luke's posture relaxed in relief. "She's always had good instincts about people."

"About a lot of things, from what I see," Trevor concurred. He understood why Luke was protective of his second-oldest daughter, but protection wasn't what Rebecca needed.

Luke studied Trevor a long moment. "I never thought of you as a potential boyfriend for my daughter," he said. "But I want you to know, should you ever decide to pursue her, you have my blessing."

Trevor accepted the announcement with the respect it had been given. "I appreciate that, sir, but I would prefer you not mention this to Rebecca. It would probably blow whatever slim chance I have of getting her to go out with me."

A quizzical lift of the brow. "And do you want to go out with her?" Luke asked.

Trevor shrugged. "I don't think she wants to go out with anyone right now. She's got her hands full starting up her operation."

"Which is exactly why she needs someone like you in her life."

"Be that as it may, that's up to her to decide," Trevor said. "And with all due respect, sir, I suggest you back off and give her room to do it."

"So what's really going on between you and my dad?" Rebecca asked Trevor the moment the movers and her parents had left.

He turned and gave her a look that was pure innocence. "What are you talking about?"

So you're going to make me spell it out. "He obviously wanted to speak to you about something. Otherwise he wouldn't have ridden over to your ranch with you."

Trevor's hazel eyes took on a gentle expression. "He's concerned about you. I told him he didn't need to be. You're going to be a fine rancher. Yeah, there are bound to be difficulties, but there are people like me and my brothers and my mom and dad around to help you get acclimated to ranch living."

Trying not to notice how masculine and capable he looked in the dusky light, Rebecca propped her hands on her hips. "Why would you want to do that?"

He sauntered closer. "Same reason I'm loaning you my pressure washer." He playfully tugged at the end of one of her braids. "Because it's the neighborly thing to do." He paused, let his hand drop back to his side. "Ranchers help each other, Rebecca. That's the rule. You don't have to like your neighbor, or even know 'em, to lend a hand. And the expectation is that they'll help you back, when the opportunity arises. Otherwise, no one would be able to prosper. We'd all be taken down—financially and otherwise—by one emergency or another."

That made sense. Rebecca studied him. "I still feel like there's more going on here than I know."

The corners of his lips curved upward. "There probably could be." His glance sifted slowly over her face, lingering on the flush in her cheeks and bare lips before returning slowly to her eyes. "Did you know you've got cobwebs in your hair?"

Rebecca headed for the closest place to check her reflection—the side-view mirror on his pickup truck. She groaned at what she saw. "Not to mention dirt on my face! Why didn't someone tell me?"

He lifted one broad shoulder in an indolent shrug. "I'm guessing your parents didn't want to embarrass you."

Tingling all over for no reason she could figure, she demanded, "What was your purpose for keeping that info to yourself?"

The mirth in his eyes increased. A sexy rumble emanated from his chest. "I think you look kind of cute all dirtied up like that."

Loath to track any of the dirt into the house, Rebecca headed for the outdoor faucet. She turned on the water and washed her hands, then did the same to her face. "You make it sound like I was mud-wrestling."

Looking as if he wouldn't want to be anywhere else, he lounged against the side of the house, watching as she scrubbed her face with damp hands, rinsing and rubbing, until her fingertips came away clean. "Nah, just cleaning a barn. There are days when I've got muck on me an inch deep. That's why I put a shower outside my barn. You ought to think about it."

"You'd like that, wouldn't you? Me, naked as a jaybird, standing out in the open, under a steamy spray."

Trevor couldn't deny the notion had its appeal any more than he'd own up to his desire to watch over her and make sure she was safe. Ruthlessly, he pushed the steamy image her hot-tempered words had evoked away. He jabbed a thumb against his chest. "First of all, my outdoor shower has high wooden walls and a lock on the inside, insuring privacy. Second, I wasn't the one using binoculars on my neighbor last night. That was you, as I recall."

A fiery blush emphasized the sculpted curves of her cheeks. With a glare, she spun away, reminding, "I explained that!"

He had a fine view of her backside as she leaned over to shut off the faucet. And what a fine backside it was. "Mmm, hmm."

She marched right back to square off with him. "What do you mean, mmm, hmm?" She angled her chin at him.

Unable to resist, he tilted his head and ribbed her a little more. "I think you just like looking at me."

The humor left her eyes. "Don't flatter yourself."

If he hadn't struck a nerve, she wouldn't be half this upset. "Someone's got to."

She tossed her head. "You can leave anytime now."

"Not," Trevor countered, answering the challenge in her golden-brown eyes, "before I do this."

She had time to get away. They both knew it. Even

as they both realized she didn't really think he would do it. And it was the dare that had him stepping forward and wrapping an arm about her waist. He heard her soft gasp of surprise—and delight?—as he cupped his other hand beneath her chin and tipped her lips up to his.

The first contact was brief, like the flash of a Fourth of July sparkler.

"What was that for?" she asked, dazed.

"Heck if I know," he murmured, bending his head once again.

Their lips met, held. He felt heat, softness, but frustratingly, no surrender.

"I think there ought to be a reason," Rebecca gasped, coming up for air.

Desire roaring through him like a river after a heavy spring rain, Trevor brought her nearer still, until the length of her body was flush against the length of his.

Happy to be finally getting somewhere with her, he moved his hand around to the back of her neck, tilted her head up even more.

"And I think," she whispered as their lips brushed slowly, inevitably once again, "you ought to tell me."

Trevor'd never been one to dissect his desires. He wasn't about to start now. "Wanting you," he confessed, looking deep into her eyes, "is the only reason I'll ever need...."

The world narrowed to just the two of them, and that's when Trevor heard a low, irritating voice come out of the silence behind them.

"If I were you, Rebecca Carrigan, I'd ask for a heck of a lot more than that."

Embarrassed to be caught on the verge of totally making out with the man, Rebecca shoved at Trevor's chest then whirled to find herself looking at Tyler McCabe, vet bag in hand.

"Hate to interrupt, but maybe it's a good thing for you I did." Tyler winked at Rebecca and tilted his head at his brother. "Rumor has it Trevor's harder to catch than a rodeo bull."

Trevor shook his head at his sibling. "You're one to talk since you can't seem to stay with or away from Susan Carrigan."

Tyler's easygoing expression did not falter. "Susie and I are old friends."

And sometimes lovers, Rebecca knew. As long as Ty was in Susan's life, there wouldn't be room for any other guy. Problem was, Tyler seemed no more inclined to make any sort of lasting and/or romantic commitment to Susan than Susan was to Ty. So like dancers on a stage, they moved endlessly toward and away from each other, for reasons only the two of them knew.

"But enough about our love lives or lack thereof," Tyler continued. "I'm here to see Blue Mist."

"She's in the barn." Rebecca led the way.

Tyler and Trevor followed.

Blue Mist was still kushed on her side, humming softly.

Ty examined her. "She's not in labor."

Rebecca breathed a sigh of relief. Trevor looked pleased about that, too.

"But this kind of stress definitely isn't good for her cria," Tyler continued, listening to her heart and lungs.

Feeling almost as nervous as the mother alpaca herself, Rebecca shoved her hands in the back pockets of her jeans. "The rest of the herd is being delivered to me late tomorrow morning."

"That's good." Ty removed the stethoscope from his ears. "I imagine that will calm her immensely."

Rebecca hoped so.

"In the meantime, you might want to just keep her in here tonight." Trevor put the instruments back in his vet bag. "Check on her periodically through the evening. Then if she's calmer tomorrow, you can try and put her in the pasture once again."

Ty ran a hand down the alpaca's side one last time, then stood, and let himself out of the stall. He and Rebecca went over the regimen of vitamins and supplemental feed required for the mother-to-be, as well as the vaccination schedule for the rest of the herd.

"I'll get copies of all the records to you by the end of the week," he said. Tyler handed her a business card. "That's got my pager and home number on it. Don't hesitate to call if you need anything or have any questions."

"Thanks."

"And do yourself a favor. Watch out for this guy." Tyler kidded his brother and was rewarded with a playful punch to the bicep, reminiscent of their childhood when the three McCabe boys were the scrappiest, most mischievous guys around. "I heard he can be Trouble with a capital *T*."

Trouble was right, Rebecca found herself thinking, long after both men had departed, haunted by the sweet, hot kisses she and Trevor had shared. She hadn't been even half this physically attracted to Grayson Graham, and she knew how poorly that had ended. Plus, there were disturbing similarities to the two situations. Grayson had participated in private talks with her father, then refused to divulge what had really been said until the day he dumped her, and by then it had been too late. Her heart had been broken, her pride wounded so badly she'd had to leave Texas to begin to get over the betrayal.

Worst of all, her father still didn't think he had done anything wrong in keeping her in the dark. Luke thought—then and now—he had only been doing what a father should. Protecting her.

She would bet her ranch something similar was going on now between Trevor and Luke, Rebecca thought.

The question was what.

If Luke hadn't asked Trevor to pursue her socially, what had he asked him? she wondered as she showered and changed. Was Trevor looking out for her simply because Luke had asked him to do so? If that were the case, it somehow diminished everything Trevor had done thus far. And why would Trevor keep that a secret from her anyway?

Because she would have refused his help outright, on principle, that was why.

Rebecca sighed and went down to the kitchen to forage for some dinner. Too tired to cook, she made herself a sandwich and a cold drink, then finished off the meal with an apple and a handful of green grapes.

It had been an hour since she had checked on Blue Mist so she pulled her boots on and went out to the barn. Rebecca'd left a battery-powered light on a hook on the opposite wall, which cast just enough light to let the sweet-faced alpaca see where she was yet not interfere with her rest. It also gave Rebecca enough light to check on the expectant mother.

Blue Mist looked up at Rebecca as she entered the stall, her big dark eyes wide and serious. "How are you doing, sweetheart?" Rebecca asked gently.

Blue Mist responded by humming louder. But she

relaxed into Rebecca's touch. A good sign, Rebecca thought. It meant Blue Mist was beginning to understand that she would be the one caring for her from now on. "The rest of your buddies are going to be here tomorrow, so just hang on, you won't be alone much longer."

Rebecca talked to Blue Mist a few minutes more, made sure she had water, then let herself out of the stall. A glance at her watch showed it to be barely nine o'clock and already she was ready for bed.

Rebecca headed for the ranch house. She heard the phone ringing as she stepped inside.

"Rebecca, it's Vince Owen, I'm glad I caught you. Coco seems to have run off."

"What do you mean, run off?"

"I let her out into the backyard to take care of business about forty-five minutes ago. She disappeared into the darkness. I haven't been able to find her. I've been calling her, but I'm not getting any response. I thought—hoped—she might have shown up at your place, since she was there the other night. I hope she's not on the road, although I've got my two hired hands out there looking for her."

The thought of the sweet little puppy getting hit by an unsuspecting motorist was more than Rebecca could bear. "I haven't seen her, but I'll get my flashlight and go out and look around."

They agreed to take their cell phones—should one of them find her, they'd let the other know. Rebecca checked around the house, just to be sure, then headed out into the pastures, her powerful flashlight spreading a wide beam. She could see another flashlight, probably Vince's, coming across the property line onto her ranch from the Circle Y. Toward the two-lane road that fronted all three ranches, two more flashlights could be seen, probably those of Vince's hired hands.

Beginning to feel a little frantic, and worried about what would happen to the puppy if she got around the cattle on Wind Creek property, Rebecca flipped open her cell phone and dialed Trevor McCabe.

"What's going on over there?" he asked without pre-amble.

Figuring he'd seen the flashlights, Rebecca told him.

"I'll check around my property, too," Trevor promised.

Rebecca kept looking. Kept calling. Finally, she heard a small but distinct whimper, followed by a loud, pleading bark.

Chapter 5

Trevor turned his flashlight toward the sound. An arc of yellow light bathed the chocolate brown puppy as he scampered across the pasture toward Rebecca's kneeling figure. She welcomed the quivering animal into her arms while Trevor walked across the pasture to see what had attracted the puppy to the corner of the fenced-in area in the first place.

As Trevor suspected, Coco's presence on Rebecca's property was not coincidental. Trevor knelt to pick up three remaining nuggets of dry dog food hidden in the six-inch grass, and slid them into his pocket.

Scowling, Trevor headed back toward the action.

Vince came up to stand beside Rebecca. "You found the little scamp," he said.

"I think he scared himself, wandering so far away like that," Rebecca said, cuddling Coco closer, and laughing as the puppy licked her gratefully beneath the chin.

Trevor joined them.

"What are you doing here?" Vince asked Trevor.

"Trevor came over to help with the search." Reluctantly, Rebecca handed Coco back to her owner.

"I'll have to keep a better eye on this little one," Vince promised.

"You should," Trevor agreed, looking Vince in the eye. "Had Coco ended up in a cow pasture, instead of this one, she could have been trampled or kicked in the head by a steer."

Rebecca shuddered at the thought. Vince appeared unmoved and unconcerned. "Well, now that the calamity is over, I think I'll go back to the house," Rebecca said. She bade them both good-night, then headed for the ranch house, her long legs eating up the ground.

"Butting in where you don't belong, aren't you, fella?" Vince said, his flashlight still at his side, spreading an arc of illumination in the grass around them.

Trevor withdrew the dog food from his pocket and held it in his palm. "With good reason, apparently."

Vince shrugged, all clever innocence. "I don't know what that is supposed to mean."

Trevor put the kibble back in his pocket. "You planted that puppy in her pasture with a pile of kibble to keep it busy until Rebecca could find it. You're just lucky she didn't see the lengths to which you'd go to manipulate her."

Vince set the puppy down in the grass between them, where she nosed around, looking for more food. "So why didn't you tell her?"

Trevor's innate protectiveness heightened. Not sorry he had spared Rebecca the worry, Trevor glared at Vince. "She's got enough on her hands, getting her ranch up and running. She doesn't need you bothering her."

Vince smirked. "I don't know what you think is

going on here, McCabe, but no one, least of all Rebecca, has appointed you her protector."

Trevor took a step forward, even as Coco roamed an increasingly larger area around them. Trevor clenched his fists at his side. "I am not going to let you hurt her."

"The only thing I plan to do to her is pleasure her. The same way I pleasured Jasmine."

It was all Trevor could do to keep from punching Vince in the jaw. Knowing a free-for-all on Rebecca's property was exactly what his nemesis wanted, Trevor remained where he was, temper boiling, violence held in check. "You have a gripe against me then you come after me, but you leave Rebecca alone."

"Or?" Vince taunted.

Trevor scooped up Coco and handed her back to her owner, before the puppy could get lost again. "You'll have more trouble on your hands than you ever imagined."

"Don't tell me you slept out here."

The low sexy voice dragged Rebecca out of a heavy sleep. She opened her eyes to the sight of Trevor McCabe, leaning into the open window of her pickup truck.

Stifling a yawn, she said, "It was easier than trekking from the house to the barn to check on Blue Mist." Which she'd done every hour or so for the first half of the night, then gotten the idea to park her pickup next to the open barn door and sleep with the windows open, easily alert to any further trouble that might come up with her prize alpaca.

"Speaking of Blue Mist…how's she doing?"

"Better." Rebecca grabbed the steering wheel, moved her legs from the bench seat to the floor on the passenger side, and struggled to sit up. She felt as if she could have slept another ten hours or so.

Rebecca shoved the hair from her eyes and gave Trevor the latest news. "Blue Mist calmed as the night wore on although she was still making that humming noise about half the time. I'm sure she'll settle down when the rest of the herd gets here." Muscles aching, head still a little groggy, she got out of the pickup and tried not to notice how good Trevor looked in the early-morning light, even in worn jeans and an old concert T-shirt. "What are you doing here?"

Half his mouth crooked up in a tantalizing smile. "I came over to give you a hand with the power washing of the interior of the barn in exchange for a free meal."

Somehow, she'd never figured Trevor McCabe as a glutton for punishment. "Sure you want to do that after the dinner I cooked the other evening?" she teased.

"What was wrong with dinner?" he asked.

"It was awful."

He palmed his chest. "I ate all mine."

Yes, he had, with nary a complaint, a fact that made her like him all the more, since he had no way of knowing—yet—that was hardly an honest effort on her part. She headed back into the barn, feeling ridiculously happy when he fell into step beside her. She slanted him a sideways glance, wondering what it would be like to interact with Trevor like this every day. Even as friends slash mutual annoyances it was a tantalizing notion. "By the way, you didn't have to come over here last night," she remarked casually.

His expression grew resolute. "I thought we'd established neighbors take care of each other in the Lone Star State. And that goes double for ranching neighbors."

That was the problem. She could see herself getting used to him looking out for her, way too easily.

Wishing she'd had a chance to brush her hair and wash her face before meeting up with him, and change out of her rumpled T-shirt and jeans, Rebecca led the way to the first stall. Blue Mist was lying down on the cool and clean cement floor. The animal's soft humming picked up as Rebecca let herself inside. The feed she had left for her prized alpaca looked barely touched, but she needed more water.

"I hope she starts to eat soon." Rebecca stroked her soft woolly flank, then went to get more water from the spigot outside the door.

Trevor hung out next to the open stall door, patiently watching over the alpaca.

When Rebecca returned, Blue Mist was standing next to the feed bucket, eating. "How'd you get her to do that?" Rebecca asked in amazement, noting Blue Mist was no longer humming.

"Actually, I think it's something you did."

Rebecca set down the water bucket. "If that were the case, she would have been eating last night." She relaxed opposite Trevor, hands flattened on the wood behind her. "You sure you're not Dr. Doolittle or something?"

Amusement glimmered in his hazel eyes. Blue Mist stopped eating long enough to drink. "I can't talk to the animals…yet. My brother Tyler might be able to, however."

"Because he's a vet," Rebecca guessed, wondering how she ever could have had trouble telling the three guys apart. The triplets, though still identical, were so very different, Trevor so much more appealing than the other two, in so many ways….

"Because Ty's spent so much time around them,"

Trevor corrected, dragging her attention away from the masculine shape of his lips and back to the conversation. He gave her a hard look, as if wondering where her thoughts had drifted. "There are a lot of other ways to communicate with animals besides language," he continued.

As Blue Mist headed back to her food, Rebecca slipped from the stall. Trevor followed her. "A look, a touch..." She guessed.

"Right."

Trying not to think about the way Trevor looked at her—as if she were suddenly the most fascinating woman on the planet—and what the proprietary, light touch of his hand beneath her elbow meant, Rebecca led the way across the yard to the ranch house.

"I hope you don't think this is going to become a habit." She went to the sink and washed her hands. She had decided to take him up on his offer and cook for him because having help with such an arduous task like cleaning the barn interior was worth the aggravation of having him around.

Tall frame radiating barely leashed energy, Trevor waited until she was finished, then stepped to the sink. "Nah, of course not." He lathered up to his elbows with gusto. "Once you get it cleaned, that barn'll only need a power washing once or twice a year."

Pretty sure he wasn't that dense, Rebecca rolled her eyes. "I meant having breakfast here."

He rinsed his powerful arms one at a time. "I suppose we could always have it at my place."

Rebecca knelt to hunt for her favorite skillet. She pulled it out with a clatter. "Why would I be there?"

He watched her shut the cabinet door with her foot. "To help me with my chores?"

Rebecca released a long, slow breath. "I don't know anything about cattle."

Pleasure teased the corners of his lips. "I imagine you could learn if you wanted."

An answering satisfaction swept through her. She really shouldn't be enjoying these unexpected interactions with him quite so much. "How do you want your eggs?"

"Same way you're having yours."

"Migas it is, then."

"Want me to do anything?"

"Yeah, you can make the coffee and pour some juice for us."

"Toast?"

"If you wouldn't mind."

They worked in companionable silence. Rebecca whipped half a dozen eggs together in a bowl, added salt and pepper, and then cooked them in a skillet, waiting until they were almost scrambled before she added crushed tortilla chips and grated cheddar cheese. By the time she plated the eggs, and topped them with salsa and avocado slices, he had everything else on the table.

They sat down kitty-corner from each other this time. "For someone who has no interest in dating me you're sure hanging around a lot," Rebecca noted.

Trevor cleaned his plate, sat back in his chair. He studied her over the rim of his coffee cup. "That kiss yesterday has me thinking I might've been a little hasty."

A distracting shiver swept through her.

Tyler had been right.

Trouble with a capital *T.*

"That kiss, cowboy, is exactly why we shouldn't date."

* * *

Not exactly the response he had been hoping for, although it was pretty much the one Trevor had been expecting. He'd figured out in the last twenty-four hours that nothing about romancing Rebecca would ever be easy. But then, nothing worth having was ever easy, either.

"I don't follow," Trevor said, wondering if Rebecca had any idea how beautiful she looked, with her hair all mussed, her cheeks pink, eyes sparkling with a fiery light. Her jeans and the navy T-shirt she'd slept in might have been rumpled but they still clung in all the right places. And she still smelled of soap and shampoo....

"Then allow me to explain it to you," Rebecca began. "One embrace and you're suddenly all proprietary, coming over here last night, staying around even after we found the puppy and I headed inside, subtly but surely making sure Vince Owen felt your presence." She stood and began to clear the table.

Figuring cleanup should be a fifty-fifty proposition, too, he put the dishes in the dishwasher. Turned to see her wiping down the table and counters.

It was clear she had looked back at some point after going inside the house the previous evening, noticed he and Vince squaring off in the pasture and knew it hadn't been a social chat.

"It looked like you needed my help. Would you have rather I stayed away?"

"This isn't a competition." Finished wiping the counter, she headed for the door.

Tell that to Vince, Trevor thought.

He followed her outside. "I never said it was."

"Look, all three of us are neighbors. I'm smack-dab

in the middle of the properties. I don't care whether you two like each other or not. I plan on being friends with both of you."

He crossed the yard with her. "Good luck with that." Vince had never been good at being anyone's friend, which was part of what made him so jealous and envious of others who did have friends.

"Oh, I'll manage, I assure you," Rebecca said, shooting him another defiant look. "What was it you said to me yesterday? We ranchers don't have to like each other or even know each other all that well to help each other out?"

He snapped his fingers in regret. "Brought up short by my own words of wisdom."

"You've got to live by them, too."

She snapped the lead on Blue Mist and led her back out to the pasture.

Aware she was right—he couldn't afford to be the hypocrite among them—Trevor set up the pressure washer and vowed to do better at managing his reactions to Vince Owen.

The next few hours were spent cleaning out the interior of the barn. By the time they had finished, the musty odor was gone, replaced by the clean smell of the bleach and water solution. A gentle breeze blew through the doors. Rebecca was just as much a sight as she had been the previous day. Dirt smudged her face and hands and stained her clothes. But she looked happy and satisfied as she studied the stalls, as if her irritation with what she saw as his overprotectiveness were all but forgotten.

"What kind of cooling system do you have in your barn?" she asked.

Glad to have the conversation moved back to neutral territory, Trevor shifted closer. "Thinking about the summer heat?"

She nodded, looking around reflectively. "It's fine in here at night right now, but it's only April. By the time we reach July…"

Or even the end of May, Trevor thought, aware her ranch insurance agent would be bringing this up to her, too. "You're going to need a way to move the hot air out."

She nodded. "Alpacas carry the heat in the belly, so to cool them off you need to run fans at floor level. I'm thinking that it would be smarter to keep the temperature down overall and not have to worry about how to safely set up ten floor-level fans."

"For cattle we use a system of misters and fans mounted on the ceiling of the barn."

"The same has been recommended for alpacas. Did you install your system yourself?"

"Yes, but it wasn't easy. If you want my help on that—"

"Thanks, but I'm sure if you can do it I can manage to do it, too."

"Honestly, I wouldn't mind."

"And honestly, I think I've leaned on you, and your pressure washer, enough."

"You're kicking me out?"

She took his elbow and guided him toward the open barn door. "I'm sure your cattle miss you."

Trevor doubted that, since he'd tended to them before coming over here.

He lifted his hands in surrender. "Never let it be said that I can't take a hint."

* * *

"So how are things going out at The Primrose?" Miss Mim asked, hours later.

"Great, actually." Rebecca set down the box of forgotten belongings Miss Mim had asked her to bring to her on the public library information counter.

Although no longer the head librarian for Laramie branch of the Laramie County Public Library system, Miss Mim still volunteered on Thursday evenings. "The herd was delivered today." Already, Blue Mist had settled down, as had all the other alpacas. "I pastured the two males in the pasture furthest from the house, five of the females in the second, and Blue Mist and one other female in the one nearest to the house. I was a little worried about putting them in the barn for the night, but they all went right into their stalls, no problems, and settled right down."

"That's wonderful."

"Yeah." Rebecca grinned. She was exhausted, and her braided hair was still wet from her steamy shower and shampoo, but she had a deep sense of accomplishment, too. "I'm beginning to feel like a real rancher. But I need your help." No one could find information quicker than Miss Mim. "I have to put a mister and fan cooling system in the barn as soon as possible. I need to know which one I should purchase, what it costs and where I should go to get it."

"I'd be happy to help you look that up, dear." Miss Mim swiveled around to her computer, which was already logged on to the Internet. "But wouldn't it have been easier to just ask Trevor? I know he's put one in his barns. He told me all about it, at the time."

"I'd rather not."

Miss Mim raised a brow in silent inquiry.

"I feel I've leaned on him too much as it is. And while you're at it, can you price pressure washers for me? I need to purchase one of those, too."

Miss Mim found the Consumer Satisfaction Web site on ranch equipment, printed the appropriate pages and handed them over. "Networking is important, dear, no matter what profession you're in. There's a lot to be learned from your more experienced counterparts, and a lot you will someday be able to pass on to others, too. Which is why I hope you're planning to attend the Laramie County Ranchers Association Spring Fling at the community center tomorrow evening."

"I am." For advertising reasons only. She needed people to know about her upcoming Open House.

"Who is escorting you?"

Miss Mim might never have married but she had very definite ideas about what was proper, and what wasn't, when it came to social activities. Rebecca was pretty sure that young ladies driving themselves to black-tie dinner-dances was not an acceptable option in Miss Mim's view. "No one," Rebecca responded airily. "I'm taking myself."

Disappointment mingled with the hope in Miss Mim's blue eyes. "You could ask Trevor."

Enough already about Miss Mim's favorite ex-neighbor, Rebecca groused inwardly. Smile fixed on her face, Rebecca reported stubbornly, "He's already asked me, as did Vince Owen." She paused to look Miss Mim in the eye. "I'm not going with either of them."

"Any particular reason why not?"

Yes, and a very good one. "I don't need a man in my life."

Miss Mim smiled and wagged a teasing finger Rebecca's way. "Ah, but do you want one?"

Miss Mim's question haunted Rebecca all the way back to the ranch. Did she want a boyfriend? Up until Trevor McCabe had kissed her, she could honestly say she hadn't cared, either way. If a guy came along who interested her, she usually went out with him, until it became clear they weren't suited for each other after all. At times that realization took one date, some times half a dozen. But always there were difficulties that could not be overcome. She and "Mr. Wrong" realized they either had zero chemistry or wanted very different things out of life, and they parted ways.

Now, finally, she'd met a man whose kisses rocked her to her very core. He was a Texan who wanted to ranch and live in Laramie County, same as she. He had family in the area, to whom he was obviously close. He even lived next door.

He was also bossy, opinionated and way too protective of her. He seemed to have a problem letting her do things herself, her way. Yes, he had offered to help her out with ranching matters when needed, for a price, but deep down, she had the feeling he was just waiting for her to fail, so he could buy the ranch he'd already stated he wanted, and had planned to buy before she'd purchased it out from under him. And worst of all, he'd already had two private conversations with her father that she knew about. There might have been more.

That reminded her of Grayson Graham. No way did she want to be made a fool of again.

It had hurt too much the first time around.

And then there was the niggling unpleasantness between Vince Owen and Trevor, the undercurrent of competition that kept cropping up between them. Trevor had told her that Vince was the one competing with him, and given the fact that Vince had purchased a ranch in the vicinity of Trevor's home turf, that seemed to be true. But she also got the impression that Trevor didn't want Vince befriending and/or romancing her, and that Trevor—who'd initially announced he had no interest in dating her—would even put himself in the running for her boyfriend rather than see her hook up with Vince. And if that wasn't being competitive on Trevor's part, Rebecca didn't know what was.

The only safe route for her to take was to try and stay "neighborly" with both men, while keeping both at arm's length.

Maybe it was time for her to be thinking about having a boyfriend again. But for all their sakes, it wouldn't be either Vince Owen or Trevor McCabe.

"If I hadn't seen you getting out of your pickup truck, I don't think I would have recognized you," Trevor teased, falling into step beside Rebecca.

Rebecca picked up the skirt of her glittering turquoise evening gown as she made her way through the dozens of vehicles crowding the community center parking lot.

"I could say the same about you," she replied. She had never seen Trevor McCabe in formal attire and was unprepared for just how good he looked. The cut of the black tuxedo jacket and pants played up his fit masculine physique, while the snowy-white shirt contrasted nicely with the suntanned hue of his skin and the rusty brown of his short hair. He'd shaved closely and smelled of soap and sandalwood and leather cologne. His hazel eyes missed nothing as they took her in. Suddenly acutely aware of her exposed shoulders, the décolletage of her strapless gown, she turned her glance toward the door.

The dance had started nearly an hour ago.

Late getting home, even later taking care of her herd, she'd wondered at one point if she was going to make it at all.

"You had me wondering if you were even going to be here," Trevor remarked.

Rebecca stepped carefully up onto the sidewalk. She waved to someone else she knew. "I got caught in traffic en route home from San Angelo."

"What were you doing there?"

"I was purchasing a misting system for my barn." An action that had seriously depleted the remains of her operating loan. But with a searing heat wave now predicted for the middle of the following week, she didn't think she could wait.

He looked across his shoulder at her. "When's it going to be installed?"

"Whenever I get around to it."

He slid his arm beneath her elbow. "You're planning to do it yourself?"

Aware that anyone who saw them coming into the dance that way would think they were hanging out together this evening, she slipped away. "The salesperson said it isn't that hard."

He shrugged and held the door for her. "Maybe not if you're used to doing electrical and/or plumbing work yourself."

She turned sideways. Her dress brushed him as she passed. "The instructions are self-explanatory."

He smiled down at her and fell in step beside her. Once again his hand was on her, this time pressed to the middle of her spine. "Take it from someone who's done it, it's not as easy as it looks."

She flushed, heating at his light touch, aware they were already getting curious looks. "Thank you for the vote of confidence," she said sarcastically, giving him a narrow-eyed look.

He leaned down to whisper in her ear. "I'm not trying to undermine you."

She sucked in a breath. "Could have fooled me."

"Rebecca. Lovely as ever." Vince Owen joined them. He leaned over to kiss her cheek.

Something in her recoiled but aware others were watching, she forced herself to maintain a smile. "Hello, Vince."

"That gown new?"

Rebecca stepped back, away from both men. "I've had it for a while."

She had a closet full of evening wear left over from her career as tour director. She would have little excuse to wear any of the outfits again, yet she didn't have nearly enough blue jeans and denim work shirts.

"Well, you look lovely," Vince said.

"Thank you. Now if you'll excuse me…" Rebecca threaded her way through the crowd to Greg Savitz, her ranch insurance agent.

A few years older than she, the happily married father of four had taken over his father's business the previous year.

"How are things coming?" Greg asked. He led the way through the buffet line.

"Great." Rebecca picked up a plate, too.

"Good. As I told you on the phone, I can only give you a grace period of forty-eight hours. Now that you've got the herd out there, I'm going to need a check from you as soon as possible, as well as specifics on the herd, including health records, valuation and description of each alpaca you want covered."

"You're aware I want to go with monthly instead of bi-annual payments."

"Can't blame you for that."

Her insurance on the animals alone was going to run her several hundred dollars. That didn't include the land, the ranch house, barn and garage.

Greg gave her a sympathetic look. "I know it sounds like a lot, but with your herd alone valued at over one hundred thousand dollars, you can't afford not to insure them."

"I know."

"And speaking of the herd, I should have told you earlier that in order to go with the lowest possible rate, you're going to have a cooling system installed in your barn."

"I'm already ahead of you on that. I bought it today. I'm going to install it right away."

"Great."

As Rebecca headed for one of the tables, she ran into Elliott Allen, a banker with Laramie Savings and Loan. "Hey, I heard you went with a San Angelo bank for your financing on the property."

Rebecca nodded, aware Elliott Allen's bank had been the one most frequently recommended to her. Unfortunately, they were also very fiscally conservative lenders. "I needed to go an unconventional route, to get started."

"I understand." Elliott pressed a business card in her hand. "But if you ever want to refinance, give me a call." He winked and went on his way.

Well, that at least was positive, Rebecca thought as she found a seat at a crowded table. She chatted up her ranch while they all ate dinner. By the time she had finished, the dessert tables were being set up, and the dance band had started.

Rebecca passed out invitations to her Open House to everyone at her table, then rose to do more of the same.

No sooner had she started working the room, than Trevor and Vince were back. Vince approached her first. "I can see you're busy networking, but I need to talk to you about the fence on our property line."

Rebecca held up a hand, already knowing where this was going, thanks to her discussion with Trevor McCabe. "You don't need to worry about that. I'm planning to install mesh fencing inside the split rail as soon as I can."

Vince looked confused. "Why would you want to do that?"

"Because alpacas and cattle don't mix?"

"My cattle are not going to bother your alpacas. And I doubt your alpacas are going to want anything to do with my steers, when I get them in the pasture."

"Which will be?"

"The hired hands are going to start moving them in tomorrow." Vince took her elbow, and instead of guiding her to the side, as she expected, he escorted her onto the dance floor.

The next thing she knew, the two of them were dancing, and eliciting more than a few curious looks. "Who told you that you needed mesh fencing?" Vince tried to bring Rebecca close.

She used the pressure of her forearm on his chest, to push him away. "Trevor."

Vince shook his head. "Sounds like him. Take it from me, you don't need it. In fact, you don't need a lot of things people are going to try and sell you, like full insurance on your animals and a misting system for your barn."

"I wouldn't feel comfortable without either."

"Suit yourself, but it pays to surround yourself with like-minded business people, risk takers like ourselves, not naysayers. I admit I'm sometimes unconventional in my approach to things, and ridiculously old-fashioned in others, but bottom line, I now own three ranches instead of just one. My net worth is probably four or five times that of Trevor McCabe's and every other rancher in this county."

Rebecca didn't know about that. Trevor's uncles had been in the ranching business for years and owned some very prosperous ranches.

"If you want me to show you how to get maximum return on a ranching business with minimal cash outlay, I'd be happy to sit down with you and show you how, and it starts with alternative financing. But then, I gather you already know that, since you didn't go with the bank in Laramie."

"How do you know that?"

"I saw Elliott Allen trying to drum up business with you—he already did the same with me. Like you, I went elsewhere for funding where they had more competitive rates."

What had seemed like a good idea at the time, was now beginning to make Rebecca feel very nervous. "Speaking of ranching, I really need to continue to tell people about the Open House I'm having."

"I presume I'm invited, too?"

Why was her instinct to say no, when she needed every bit of outside financial investment she could get? "Certainly." Rebecca withdrew another small invitation from her purse and handed it to him.

No sooner had the dance ended, then Rebecca turned around, and found herself running full steam ahead into Trevor McCabe's chest. "My turn," he said, wrapping an arm around her waist as the music began once again.

"You really don't have to compete," Rebecca said.

"Who's competing?" Trevor replied, staying a respectful distance away, as they two-stepped to the beat of the popular country song the band was playing. "I want your attention. I've got it."

Rebecca tried not to think how right it felt to be held in Trevor's arms. "I don't want to be a pawn used in this rivalry between you and Vince."

He sobered abruptly. "I don't want that, either."

Looking into his eyes, she could almost believe him. Until Vince tapped on Trevor's shoulder and smoothly cut in, taking Rebecca back into his arms. Aware people were beginning to stare at them, Rebecca forced a smile, and firmly but surely extricated herself from Vince's arms. Only to find herself in Trevor's once again.

Then Vince's.

Trevor's.

Vince's.

"Hold it!" Rebecca wriggled free. Evaded Trevor's arms.

She lifted both her forearms, held them in front of her. "No more. Please. From either of you. Now if you'll excuse me…" She turned and headed for the dessert table.

"Wow, only back in town a week and already you've got two guys fighting over you," Amy remarked, joining her.

Rebecca made a face at her youngest sister, who was there with her pal since kindergarten, Teddy McCabe.

The two enjoyed a platonic relationship, but filled in for each other when one of them was currently unattached and needed a date for a function like this.

"Let's not talk about that," Rebecca said with a roll of her eyes. She looked at Teddy. As usual, he exuded friendliness and was always willing to go the extra mile for a friend. "How's your horse ranch doing?"

Teddy moved down the table, filling his plate with sumptuous treats as he went. "The Silverado is coming along nicely, thank you very much." He slanted her an affable glance. "How are things out at The Primrose?"

"Gearing up. In fact, I'm having an Open House from ten till four Sunday after next. I'd love it if you could come by, take a look around." Rebecca winked. "Maybe think about the financial advantages of owning—or leasing—an alpaca or two of your very own."

Teddy grinned, amused but not entirely opposed to the idea. "I'm not sure how well they'd do with horses," he said.

"No problem. I'm planning to board alpacas, too. That way you'd be able to breed your adult female to one my herd sires, sell the cria or offspring and reap the monetary rewards without doing any of the work. For a fee, of course."

Teddy studied her with the expertise of a person known for making sound investments, on and off his own ranch. "I assume you'll have a sales pitch ready?"

Rebecca nodded. "I'll be working on it all next week."

"In the meantime, how about giving Susie and/or Mom and Dad and Jeremy a call?" Amy suggested. "We haven't seen or heard much from you since you've been back in Laramie. We miss you."

Rebecca missed them, too. More so now that she

was close enough to visit whenever she wanted. Aware Trevor was still watching her, from a distance now, she looked away, admitting, "It's still awkward." As Rebecca looked in the other direction, she discovered Vince Owen watching her, too.

Her sister Amy, however, was not distracted.

Amy gently touched Rebecca's arm. "It's not going to get better unless you confront the problem head-on. Talk it out. Deal with it. Fight, scream if you have to, do whatever you have to do to move past what happened with that whole Grayson Graham mess once and for all."

Rebecca looked away, her emotions in turmoil. "I'm not sure I can, Amy." Her father and sister's betrayal of her still felt so acute. Made more so by whatever her father and Trevor McCabe were keeping from her now.

Chapter 6

"Talk about the perfect end to a less-than-perfect evening," Rebecca muttered as her pickup truck lurched to the side of the two-lane county road and skidded to a halt.

She slammed the door of her truck and made her way around to the right front tire. Just as she'd thought. It was flat. And here she was, out in the middle of nowhere, dressed in an evening gown, without an auto club membership to her name.

Her frustration erupted in a string of invectives. She kicked the tire with the heel of her evening sandal. Lost her balance. And would have fallen over had she not been able to grab hold of the passenger door handle.

Naturally, her temper tantrum did not go unnoticed.

Headlights bathed her in a yellow spotlight as another pickup truck slowed and pulled over, parking behind her vehicle.

Trevor McCabe got out and strode toward her. He'd left his motor running, hazard lights blinking, headlamps on. The light bathed his tall, muscled form. "Need some help?"

She didn't even have to think about it. "Nope."

He narrowed his eyes. "You can't fix a flat in an evening gown."

Want to bet? "If you can do it in a tuxedo, I can do it in a dress."

Trevor stood with his hands in his pocket. "Ever think your stubbornness is more trouble than it's worth?"

Rebecca marched back to get her jack, then realized she couldn't recall where it was stowed. Not about to admit that to him, or stand there reading her owner's manual while he watched, she lowered the tailgate and climbed up into the bed of the truck—a little less gracefully than she would have liked. Figuring the compartment that held the spare had to be there somewhere, she walked back and forth, looking for a latch.

"If you're looking for the spare, it's underneath the truck," Trevor said, retrieving something from his own pickup, and walking toward her once again. "Now, the only question is are you going to let me use this?" He held up a can of Fix-A-Flat. "Or are you going to force me to do it the hard way?"

Time is money, Rebecca reminded herself. "Fine. Use the can. What does it do anyway?"

He squatted down beside the air gage. "It inserts a complex liquid into the tire. The leaking air instantly polymerizes it to plug up the leak. And it also inflates your tire."

"Wow." Rebecca watched as her tire resumed its normal shape.

Finished, Trevor stood. "If there is a nail in there, this may not hold all that long. But it should be good enough to get you back to The Primrose."

"Thanks."

He smiled at her as if coming to her rescue yet again was all in a day's work and swaggered back to his truck.

Just to be on the safe side, Rebecca drove slowly.

Trevor was right behind her the entire way.

Instead of going on to his driveway, however, he followed her down the lane and parked just behind her, cutting the motor, but once again leaving his headlights on.

She met him in the lane, halfway between their two vehicles, wishing he didn't look so damn good. "You can go home now."

"Job's not done." He took off his coat and tie, and rolled up the sleeves on his pleated white shirt.

What would it take to make this man realize her difficulties were not his problem? "Yours is."

"How long do you think it will take you to change this tire?"

She tore her eyes from his brawny forearms. "Couple hours, I guess. I don't know."

He reached around beneath the truck. Half a minute later, both the jack and the tire were on the ground. "It'll take me fifteen minutes."

She had to admit it looked as if he knew what he was doing thus far. "It's not your responsibility," she repeated.

He patted her on the top of her head. "Anyone ever tell you graciousness is not your strong suit?"

Rebecca paced back and forth, the folds of her long silky skirt swirling around her legs. "I suppose you're going to want another meal for this."

He set up the jack and worked it like a pro. "Actually, what I'd really like is a cold beer when I finish."

A cold beer sounded amazingly good to her, too. "And that's all you want?"

He flashed her a crooked smile. "Well, if you're offering…"

Rebecca stilled him with an equally presumptuous look. "A chilled beverage is all I'm offering."

He slid his eyes to the hollow of her throat, to her lips and then her eyes. All innocence once again. "Then a chilled beverage is all I need."

She told herself the evening would definitely not end with her kissing him again. "Then you'll leave?"

He dipped his head in a gallant bow. "Then I'll leave."

Aware her pulse was racing as if he had made another pass at her, Rebecca left him to his work and went into the house. Five minutes later, she had changed out of her evening dress and back into her jeans, boots and a snap-front Western cowgirl shirt. By the time she had walked out the back door onto the lawn, he already had the damaged tire off and was fitting on the spare. She headed for the barn, checked on her herd. All were resting peacefully, even Blue Mist.

Rebecca made sure all of them had plenty of water to get them through the night, then she walked back out of the barn.

Trevor put the jack and the tire in the bed of her truck and turned off the headlights on his vehicle.

"In the house or out?" she asked.

"How about the gazebo? It looks like a nice place to have a drink."

"I'll meet you there."

Rebecca slipped back inside, got two beers, twisted off the caps and walked back outside.

To Rebecca's surprise, Trever stayed just long enough to have a drink with her. She told herself she was relieved when he left—and not disappointed.

* * *

The next day she rose early and headed for town. The first order of business was dropping by the insurance office to give Greg Savitz a check, the second, a stop at the vet's to pick up the prescription sedatives she was going to need for her alpacas when she undertook shearing later in the week, the third, Murphy's garage.

"So how did this happen?" Rebecca asked Mr. Murphy.

Mr. Murphy handed her the bill. "It looks as if the tire was punctured with a sharp object."

Rebecca reached for her checkbook. "You mean there was no nail in it."

Mr. Murphy nodded. "Just a small leak."

"How could that happen?" Rebecca asked.

"Sounds to me like it was deliberate," Vince Owen said, coming up to the counter. He had two cans of motor oil and a pair of windshield wiper blades in his hand.

"Could have been," Mr. Murphy agreed with a shrug. "Though why anyone would want to do that to you, Rebecca…"

Why indeed, Rebecca wondered.

Trying not to think how quickly her bank account was being depleted, she finished paying Mr. Murphy, then walked back out to her truck.

She was about to climb behind the wheel when Vince caught up with her. "I think I have an idea how that happened last night," he told her. "And it all has to do with me. And you."

"What do you mean?"

"Trevor probably told you the rivalry between us goes one way. Don't you believe it. He's just as competitive as I am. Otherwise, why would he have changed his mind about pursuing you?"

Vince's question was a good one.

A chill went down Rebecca's spine as she recalled that first morning in the feed store. What was it Trevor had said to her when she had accused him of being party to her father's matchmaking and let him know she wasn't going to accept a date? *"Well, that's good because I hadn't planned to ask...."*

There had been no doubt in her mind that Trevor had meant what he said.

And yet, mere hours later, he had started his sure but subtle conquest of her, inviting himself to dinner, turning on the charm...insisting they be friends as well as next-door neighbors. Vince had her attention now.

"According to the guys at the feed store, McCabe couldn't have been less interested in making you his woman—*until* I made it known that I wanted to date you," Vince continued. "And now here he is, doing everything and anything he can to publicly claim you. Including coming on strong at the dinner-dance last night, then coincidentally swooping in to your rescue right after."

Rebecca shook off the implication. "Look, it doesn't matter what Trevor does or says. The fact of the matter is I don't want to date anyone right now. And that includes you, too, Vince."

"That doesn't make me any less interested in you, but I can accept that. I tend to put business first, too. And I can see you have your hands full, making The Primrose operational. I'm not sure I can say the same thing about Trevor McCabe. Especially since..." Vince's voice trailed off. Frustration etched his features. He took off his hat and swept his hands through his sandy blond hair.

"You might as well spit it all out."

"Trevor wants to steal you the way he thinks I stole Jasmine from him, back in our college days. When the truth is Jasmine left Trevor after finding out what a cheating, lying, SOB he was. And then, she left me, too."

Rebecca spent the rest of Saturday alternately tending to her herd and painting the interior of the business office the light primrose-yellow she intended to use on all ranch correspondence. By nine that evening, the large cement-floored room looked less like the interior of a garage than it had, but it still had a long way to go.

During the day she would be able to open up the old-fashioned barn-style doors for light and ventilation, but at night, the single overhead bulb was not going to do it. So she went back to the house, got a couple lamps from the living room and got ready to give the walls another coat of paint.

She had just dipped her roller into the pan when the sound of a pickup rumbled in her driveway. Seconds later, Trevor strode in. He stepped around the towers of moving boxes in the center of the room. "Is there some reason you're not answering your phone?"

She straightened, and her grasp on the handle tightened. "I'm answering it."

"I've called ten times today. You didn't pick up once."

She studied the buttons on his starched tan work shirt. "I wonder why that would be."

For a long moment he didn't say anything, and she forced her gaze to his face. It wasn't just the aftershave clinging to his jaw—she could tell he had just shaved.

He also looked ready to go out. Not surprising, since he was single and it was Saturday night.

He continued to study her as if trying to figure something out. "Are you mad at me?"

Emotion bubbled up inside her. Relentless. Unmanageable. She tapped a finger to her chin, realizing too late it had paint on it. "Gee. Let me think. Yes. I believe I am."

He looked around, spotted a clean cotton rag on one of the boxes and handed it over. "Why?"

Embarrassed by her clumsiness, Rebecca dabbed at her chin. "Why do you think?"

He strode a little closer, still examining her like a specimen under a microscope. "I've no idea."

Rebecca scowled. Turning her back to him, she resumed painting. "Sure you do." She brushed the walls with harder than necessary strokes. "Just think a little harder."

A big hand captured hers. "If you're accusing me of something…"

Rebecca kept painting. "Now, you're getting the picture."

The pressure of his grip kept the roller from moving any farther. "I'd like to know what."

Rebecca swung around. "I found out what happened to my tire was no accident." Deciding that trying to paint and argue was a dangerous proposition, she set the roller carefully back into the pan, and paused to wipe her hands on the rag. "And I know all about Jasmine Whatever-Her-Last-Name-Was, too."

He didn't comment but the sudden way he let go of her and the lift of his brow said it all.

"Vince thought I should know how you make a woman think she needs help and then swoop in to rescue her. Apparently, it's your MO in the romance department."

The corners of his mouth turned down. "I don't know what you are trying to imply, but I did not damage your tire."

"Well, someone did."

He lowered his voice. "Did you ever stop to think that someone might be Vince?"

She'd never been the sort of person to accept gossip at face value. Yet something—maybe it was the strength of her attraction to Trevor—had her looking for any and every reason not to get further involved with him. Even if she knew said reason was flat-out wrong.

A guilty flush rose from her chest, to her face. Aware she was reacting presumptively, but unable to help it, she shrugged. Reminding herself that the only person who had come along to see her with that flat tire, the only person who had benefited from her "distress" had been Trevor McCabe, knowing the best way to get at the truth was to feign more knowledge than she actually had while simultaneously provoking emotion, she lobbed yet another outrageous remark his way. "Vince told me you'd blame it on him."

"Maybe," Trevor allowed slowly, bitterly, "because if your tire was indeed sabotaged Vince probably did it."

"And yet Vince didn't show up to rescue me and be my hero, did he?"

Trevor rocked back on his heels. "That would have been a little obvious, don't you think?"

A trickle of unease sifted through her.

Trevor had a point about that. Rebecca lifted a hand, then paused to level him with her gaze. "Truth to tell, at this point I don't think I care which one of you it was. Just know that I have no intention of becoming the next 'Jasmine.'" The two men could compete over someone—something—else.

His resentment filled the space between them. "Good to know you're interested in my side of the story."

She drew a conciliatory breath. "I'm listening."

He made a scoffing sound. "Too little, too late."

"Trevor." She moved to block his way. The hurt and outrage in his eyes flooded her with remorse. Too late, she realized if she wanted to put distance between them, she should have found another way to do it. "I want to hear your side."

Again, he was silent for a few moments. "So you can decide what's true and what's not."

"Yes."

"Thanks." His eyes narrowed. "I'll pass."

"What do you mean, you'll pass?" Who didn't want to have their side heard? Especially in one as messy as the one Vince had described?

"I thought you and I could be friends as well as neighbors," he drawled before turning and heading for the door without so much as a backward glance. "Looks like I was wrong."

Rebecca spent the rest of the evening alternately pushing away guilt and painting. Exhausted, she took a shower, and climbed into bed with the installation instructions for the misting system for the barn. It didn't take long for her to realize she was going to have to find a faster way to keep her alpacas cool before the mid-week heat wave. So once again she revised the work schedule she had devised to help her get ready for the Open House.

Fortunately, her brother and two sisters had meant

what they said about lending a hand, and gave up their Sundays off to come over. Rebecca handed out the construction masks. First up was Blue Mist. Because she was with cria, they had opted not to give her the sedative all the others had been given with their morning's breakfast. Susie cradled the quivering alpaca's neck and rubbed her behind her ears while they used an air hose to blow the dirt and grass out of her fleece. Jeremy held Blue Mist's hind legs, Amy her front. Rebecca manned the clippers, shearing the alpaca's tummy first, where the most valuable, softest fleece grew, then moving around to her back and sides, and finally her neck and legs.

With five inches of wool removed, she looked much skinnier. "She's got to be much cooler now," Amy noted, as they let the alpaca stand again.

"She'll feel even better once she delivers," Rebecca said as she put the valuable fiber into a plastic bag.

"When is she due?" Susie asked.

"Another two weeks."

Rebecca praised the alpaca for her cooperation and gave her a treat, then led her back to the pasture and got another female. As she led Midnight back to the barn, she couldn't help but notice Trevor, working the fence line closest to his ranch. He was too far away for her to tell what he was doing.

Unlike Blue Mist, who'd been relatively calm throughout the procedure, Midnight turned skittish the moment she saw the air blower.

"I'm surprised Trevor's not up here helping you," Susie remarked.

He would have been if I'd asked him, Rebecca thought.

"Did you ask if he wanted to lend a hand?"

"Yeah, with his experience with cattle, he'd probably be a lot better at this than we are," Jeremy said as he coaxed a recalcitrant Midnight onto the barn floor.

Aware her siblings were waiting for an answer, Rebecca shook her head. "I'm not really in a position to ask Trevor for any favors right now," she said.

"How come?" Susie asked.

Midnight flinched and moaned as Rebecca moved the clippers over her belly.

Briefly, Rebecca explained.

"Trevor McCabe would not sabotage your tire, just so he could come to your rescue later!" Amy said.

"I know that."

"Then why did you accuse him?" Jeremy asked.

"Easy," Susie cut in, as she sat, cradling Midnight's head in her lap. "Because he's getting too close, too fast. And Rebecca can't have that."

As much as Rebecca would have liked to tell her sister she was wrong, she couldn't. She had learned the hard way not to rush. Not to get too physical too soon. Not to confide, not to trust, not to open her heart up to lust and love, without putting on the brakes often and long, first.

Like it or not, Trevor McCabe made her want to do away with caution altogether.

He made her want to lean on him, go to him, include him in her life.

And she couldn't have that.

She had fought hard and long to be able to achieve financial independence and start up a ranch on her own. She was finally living her dream. Or trying to, if only the financial realities would stop getting in the way.

And yet she couldn't stop thinking she had been unfair to him. Really unfair. And that bothered her more than anything.

Trevor had nearly finished installing mesh fencing along the Primrose-Wind Creek property line when he looked up and saw Rebecca Carrigan marching his way. As usual, she was dressed in a T-shirt and jeans that attested to her willingness to get as down and dirty as the business of ranching required. A flat-brimmed hat shaded her face from the worst of the Texas sun. The pink in her cheeks deepened as she came to a halt just short of him.

Trevor kept right on working.

Rebecca propped her hands on her hips.

"I thought I told you I wasn't ready to put up a mesh fence," she said.

Wondering when he would stop wanting to haul her in his arms and kiss her once again, Trevor straightened slowly, tipped the brim of his hat back to better see her face. He rested an elbow on the top of the split rail wooden fence Miss Mim had installed, years before. "This mesh isn't on your property, it's on mine."

"I thought we were going to split the costs—and the decisions about this."

"Obviously—" Trevor pounded another five-foot metal stake into the ground, and attached another section of the rolled mesh fencing to the post "—after last night, that's not going to work."

She stomped closer. Her cheeks grew even more flushed. Her tongue snaked out to wet her lips. "About that—"

"I think you've said all you need to say." Trevor tried

but could not quite keep the exasperation from his low voice. "I got the point."

As the seconds drew out, her lips formed a delicious pout. "I was wrong. I know that."

Now, this was interesting. Trevor wiped the sweat off his brow with the sleeve of his shirt. In no hurry to let her off the hook, he studied her a good long time. "Wrong to what?" he demanded gruffly.

Abruptly she looked as frustrated with him as he still was with her. "To jump to conclusions." Her soft hands lifted in a conciliatory manner. "To even tell you what I'd heard in the first place."

Trevor dropped his sledgehammer onto the grass and reached for the cooler of water. He opened the spout and tipped the jug against his lips. None of this was as easy as she wanted to make it. With his free hand, he swept off his hat and let it rest against his thigh. "You think I want you keeping secrets from me, is that it?"

"No." She folded her arms in front of her contentiously and glared at him. "Of course not! Nor do I want you keeping vital information from me!"

"Vital information, huh?" he repeated in a tone meant to annoy her. He closed the spout with a snap and dropped the jug back into the grass. He dropped his hat and stepped forward, not stopping until he towered over her. "And just what vital information would that be?" he asked, ignoring the erratic intake of her breath and the clear definition of her breasts beneath the clinging light blue cotton T-shirt.

She tilted her chin at him and slapped her hands on her hips. Expressive brows lowered over her long-lashed eyes. "I still want to know about Jasmine."

He regarded her with silent derision.

Undeterred, she continued impatiently, "This is what

I know thus far. You had a girlfriend in college named Jasmine. You were serious about her. Your senior year, Jasmine caught you making out with another woman in the university lab, and she dumped you and turned to Vince. Vince and Jasmine started dating. And you've never forgiven Vince, even though Jasmine eventually dumped Vince, too. And that's what the rivalry between you two guys is really all about."

Leave it to Vince to twist things just enough....

Aware that she looked as miserable as he had been feeling since they'd had words, he told her tersely, "You've got your facts wrong."

She shrugged and kept her eyes on his. "So enlighten me."

He studied her brooding expression. "I wasn't with another woman."

She wanted to believe him. He could see that. She just wasn't sure she should.

Rebecca dug the toe of her dusty boot in the grass. "Vince said you were kissing someone named Valerie when Jasmine and he walked in that night."

Trevor had never been one to shift the blame for his mistakes, but in this instance, he knew he wasn't at fault. Stupidly naive, maybe, but not unfaithful.

He tugged off his leather work gloves, let them drop to the ground, knowing before he spoke how lame this was all going to sound, even years later....

With a weariness that went soul deep, he began. "Vince told Valerie I had a secret thing for her, that I was just waiting for some sort of sign from Valerie that she was interested, and as soon as I got it, I was going to break up with Jasmine and go after her."

Something in his words must have clicked, because

he saw a flicker of recognition or acceptance in Rebecca's eyes.

Trevor pushed on. "Vince arranged for Valerie to be in the lab the same time I was that night, then made sure that Jasmine was there, about the same time." He shook his head, recalling, "Vince and Valerie must have had it timed down to the second, because the moment Valerie grabbed me and planted one on me, Jasmine and Vince walked in. Vince had already told Jasmine I was fooling around on her, so when Jasmine saw Valerie making her move, she assumed everything Vince had told her was true. I tried to explain. She refused to listen to a word I had to say. So we broke up, and that was that." And Trevor had vowed to never again become entangled with a woman who did not trust him and believe him to be honorable.

"Just like I didn't want to hear your side of things last night," Rebecca murmured, looking distraught.

For a moment, Trevor's heart went out to her. Rebecca didn't deserve to be in the middle of any of this.

Had Vince not picked up on Trevor's attraction to her or wanted Rebecca's recently purchased property for himself, Vince wouldn't be pursuing her and causing mischief, now.

It was his fault, Trevor knew, that Rebecca had become a target for one of the most devious people Trevor had ever met.

"What else did Vince tell you?"

Rebecca took her hat off, too, and let it rest against her knee. She looked at it a moment before returning her glance to his face. "That you were only interested in me because you knew he was interested in me."

Rebecca took a deep breath and let it out. "Is it true?" she demanded.

Trevor knew he could sour Rebecca's view of Vince permanently simply by telling Rebecca about the bet Vince had tried to make about her.

But somehow that didn't set well with him, either.

If for no other reason than it would send Rebecca right back to Vince to discover the truth of that.

Figuring she couldn't be hurt by what she didn't know, hopefully would never know, Trevor shrugged. "I admit I don't want you involved with Vince Owen," he said. "I don't want to see any woman involved with Vince." His hands came up to cup her shoulders, and he pushed an errant strand away from her cheek. "But that sentiment has nothing to do with why I kissed you or helped you out."

Her palms flattened against the front of his shirt. "Then why did you do those things?"

Loving the warmth and softness of her as much as the spring sunshine overhead, he pried the hat from her fingers, tossed it in the grass and wrapped both arms around her. He pressed his lower half to hers. She surged against him. Everything that had been wrong righted. "Haven't you figured it out?" he teased, backing her up against the fence.

A shiver of desire swept through her, weakening her knees. Caution mingled with the yearning in her soft eyes. "Trevor..."

That was all the encouragement it took. He lowered his mouth to her and gave her a full-on kiss filled with passion and need. She gasped in surprise. He grazed her earlobe with his teeth, touched his mouth to her throat, the underside of her chin, her cheek, the tip of her nose, before moving once again to her lips. And this time, when he fit his mouth over hers, she was ready for him. Her mouth softened under his, opened to allow him deeper, wider access. She made a sexy little sound in the back of her throat, and then her hands were coming up, to cup his head. She was standing on tiptoe, pressing her body into his, tangling her tongue with his.

Rebecca hadn't figured she'd end up kissing Trevor when she'd come out here to talk to him, but now that she was in his arms, she couldn't think of anywhere else she would rather be. My heaven, the man was magic, his body hot and hard and she was the reason. He shifted again, flattening his hand down her spine, pressing her closer still, until there was no doubting how much he wanted her. Her body registered the intense pleasure, even as she generated more of her own, and she reveled in it, and wanted more.

Had he moved to take her then and there, she could hardly have said no.

Instead, he slowly, inevitably, let her go, and lifted his head.

"If we're going to do this," he said gruffly, looking down at her, "we're doing it right."

Chapter 7

Rebecca drew a jerky breath. Trevor was right. They couldn't continue this out in the middle of a field, where anyone who happened to be driving by could see.

"Your place or mine?"

He kissed her throat. "I don't reckon it matters. I'm sure we'll work our way to both eventually."

So he planned ahead.

So should she.

And paramount was keeping him from breaking her heart.

Wishing she had her hat on so she could shield her eyes from his probing gaze, she strengthened her emotional armor. "I'm just talking about a fling."

He ran his fingers through the sides of his hair. "One time," he repeated thoughtfully.

She nodded, aware her heart was still racing, her lips still tingling from the feel of his. "To get it out of our systems." Quench the desire building deep inside her.

His brows climbed.

"End the mystery of what it might be like and all that."

"I knew you were curious." His eyes alive and shining with suppressed devilry, he picked up her hat, settled it ever so slowly on her head. The corners of his mouth quirked upward. He focused with laser accuracy on her mouth, then teased, "I didn't think the need-to-know extended to this arena."

Not that he was protesting, mind you. It was clear from the evidence of his continuing arousal, pressing up against the front of his jeans, that at least part of him would be only too happy to discover what it would be like to be twisted up in the sheets with her.

Trying not to imagine how it would feel to have him buried deep inside her, she stated as casually as she could, "I don't make a habit of this." And that, in a nutshell, was the problem. She hadn't done this in forever.

Enter Trevor, with his sexy, oh so male presence, and what-I-could-do-to-you-if-I-only-had-the-chance hazel eyes.

She found herself at the melting point of butter on a hot stove. And damn it all, if the rancher next door wasn't hot as could be.

"I expect you don't, either," Rebecca continued stiffly, aware she was making a fool of herself by acting so uptight and methodical instead of loose and free as the spring breeze.

Worse, he saw right through her pragmatic act.

"You're right," he told her drily, calling her a liar with everything he didn't say. "One night—or maybe I should say one afternoon—stands aren't my thing."

"Then we agree, this—us—is an exception?" she plodded on determinedly. The kind of exception-to-the-rule that made life great.

He chuckled. "We're an exception all right. But this

chemistry between us is not going to end with a bang and a fizzle. When I make you mine—"

When, not if.

Rebecca focused on the words.

"—once isn't going to be enough." He lightly clasped her chin. "I can wait until the time is right." He leaned forward to brush her lips. "I trust you'll let me know when that is."

He paused to look deep into her eyes.

"But for now," he continued softly, knowing full well he'd just stolen her breath, again, "you and I both have work to do."

Rebecca didn't know whether to be impressed with his chivalry, relieved he'd had enough sense not to let them stray into territory they had no business exploring without some sort of commitment to each other, even if it was only for an ongoing love affair. Or frustrated she was going to go to bed once again with an ever-expanding To-Do List for company.

Maybe it was time she got a dog.

A puppy, like Coco, who'd be company for her, someone she could love and be loved by in return without having to worry about the complications a romance with a man brought.

As soon as she got her finances straightened out, Rebecca determined, and could afford the extra vet bills and food, she'd talk to Vince Owen, find out where he'd gotten his chocolate-brown Labrador retriever. And see about getting a "Coco" of her very own.

In the meantime, she had to take the fleece from the shearing to the local weaver recommended to her.

A quick call confirmed it would be okay to take it by for weighing and purchase that very evening.

So Rebecca showered, changed and drove off.

Unfortunately, the fleece didn't bring nearly as much as she had hoped. She'd only averaged eighty ounces per animal, instead of the maximum of one hundred and twelve. She'd gotten three and a half dollars per ounce, which was better than the low of two dollars per ounce, but less than the maximum of five.

"The more you pay for an alpaca," the weaver explained, "the better their fleece, and the more you'll get for it."

But the flip side of that was that a premium alpaca could fetch as much as four hundred thousand dollars per animal, and those animals were way out of her league, at least for now.

"You've done really well for a first shearing," the weaver said, as she handed over a check.

Unfortunately, "really good" wasn't going to cut it, Rebecca realized as she sat up late that night, going over her ranch books thus far.

Everything had cost more than she had anticipated when she had first drawn up her business plan two years before.

There were expenses—such as the mister and fan cooling system—she hadn't realized she would need, having done her preliminary training at alpaca farms in a much cooler environment over in Europe. Last summer's drought had pushed up the price of feed. Rising interest rates had ended up costing her more in closing costs on both her ranch mortgage and the financing package she had gotten on her herd of alpacas. And now she had a balloon payment due on her temporary operating loan that, although still payable, would leave her with exactly one hundred dollars in her bank account.

That wouldn't pay her mortgage for May or her utilities or gasoline for her truck or feed and supplements for her herd or the vet bills.

She was going to have to go back to the San Angelo bank where she had gotten the financial deal that had allowed her to start up her ranch and ask for an extension on the balloon payment on her operating loan.

So first thing the next morning, Rebecca took care of her herd and put them out to pasture. Then, armed with the facts and figures she had been up half the night preparing, got in her truck and drove to San Angelo.

Leigh Meeks, the loan officer, met with her right away.

But it wasn't to hear Rebecca's pitch, as it turned out.

"I'm sorry, Rebecca," the young woman in the pin-striped suit said. "We can't give you an extension. Our bank no longer holds your loan."

Rebecca blinked. "What are you talking about?"

"Your loan was sold to a venture capital group in Dallas last week. Edge Investments. They specialize in unconventional financial opportunities. They put out the word last week they were looking for alpaca ranches to purchase. Your whole loan package was transferred to them by close of business Friday."

"No one asked me!" Rebecca declared, upset.

"Read the fine print on your loan papers. We don't have to ask you. No one does. Edge Investments is free to sell your loan at any time, too." Leigh flashed a re-assuring smile. "This happens all the time, to regular mortgages, too. I'm sure it will be fine."

Rebecca felt as if she'd had the wind knocked out of her. It wouldn't be fine if Edge Investments refused to give her an extension on her balloon payment, and she was left with nothing in her bank account to pay her monthly expenses. She wouldn't be able to take care of her herd properly. Or pay her mortgage on the ranch. Without cooperation from her lender, she could be facing foreclosure and bankruptcy by summer! "How will I get in touch with them?"

"They're going to be contacting you."

"I can't just go ahead and call them?"

Leigh shook her head. "They need time to put your information into the system. I'm sure you'll get a letter in the next day or so, telling you who your new loan officer is. But I have to caution you, Rebecca, I very much doubt they will grant you an extension. They're in the business to make money, not give it back to customers. Your best bet, if you can't make that payment on schedule and have anything left to run your ranch is to try and refinance the whole package before the balloon payment is due, and just pay off the loan Edge Investments now holds in full."

Leigh's advice made sense, so Rebecca drove back to Laramie and stopped at the bank. She had gone to high school with the loan officer, Elliott Allen, and he was glad to see her there to do some business. He listened to her problem, and agreed to look at her situation, see what he could do.

Unfortunately, it wasn't much.

"You're aware you leveraged way too much with this first set of loans," he said, studying the figures. "Worse, the interest rate on the operating loan is variable and written so that every time the prime rate increases, or your credit rating takes a dive, your rate goes up."

Rebecca hadn't worried about the latter, because she was the kind of person who always paid her bills on time.

"I knew it was a risk. But I needed to get in and get

going, and I still think once I have my Open House on Sunday afternoon and get some outside investors to lease or buy some of my alpacas, and board them at The Primrose, that I'll be in good shape." Finances would still be tight for the first six months to a year, but after that…

"Tell you what," Elliott said. "You get some contracts signed over the weekend that will demonstrate you have a good income generated by your business and come back here first thing next Monday, we'll give your situation a second look. But you're still going to have to make that twenty-thousand-dollar balloon payment to Edge Investments, also due next Monday."

"Any chance I could get a loan for that folded into my new mortgage?" Rebecca asked.

Elliott Allen lifted a brow. "It might be possible to set up a line of credit against the ranch, once you can demonstrate you have some income coming in, not just money going out, but again that all depends on a revised business plan and a good showing at your Open House." Elliott stood to show her out. "If I may, I'd like to suggest you talk to Trevor McCabe. He's an ace at putting ranch projections together. He did one not too long ago that had us agreeing to lend him the money for two more ranches."

"The Primrose and…?"

"The Circle Y. Of course those sold to you and Vince Owen. But the bank still stands ready to lend him that amount should he find a comparable property."

No wonder Trevor was so irritated with Vince. On top of everything else, Vince had purchased the property Trevor had his eye on, to help him expand Wind Creek. "Is he still looking—do you know?"

"I don't know. I spoke to him at the dinner Friday

night, and he indicated he still hadn't gotten over losing out on the land adjacent to him."

Which meant what? Rebecca wondered as she said goodbye to Elliott Allen and walked out the bank doors, to the parking lot behind the building. That Trevor didn't just want her, he still wanted her ranch, too?

Could that be part of the reason he was pursuing her after telling her at the feed store he wasn't the least bit interested in dating her?

Rebecca scowled at the thought.

"That bad, hmm?" a low voice asked.

Rebecca glanced up to see her father standing in front of her. Obviously on his lunch break from seeing patients at the Laramie Community Hospital office complex, he had a stack of papers in his hand.

"I was afraid of this." Hand on her shoulder, he guided her to a shady place on the sidewalk, where they could talk, uninterrupted. He looked down at her compassionately. "It's not too late for you to take a more cautious approach to this whole ranching business."

Rebecca braced herself for the lecture sure to come. "Meaning?"

"It's clear you're in way over your head. But there is still time to back out or cut your losses."

Rebecca started to brush a hand through her hair, then recalled she'd put it in a sophisticated knot at the nape of her neck for her business meetings. "How do you suggest I do that, Dad?" she asked in exasperation.

"You could sell most of your herd, just keep one or two alpacas, to start. Get a job in town. Life would be a lot easier." Luke paused. "I happen to know they are looking for a new social director for the community center. Or you could train to be an occupational therapist at the hospital."

What was it Vince Owen had told her?

"Stay away from the naysayers.... Surround yourself with like-minded people."

Vince had certainly been right about that.

He had also said, *"Big risks lead to big rewards. Forget conventional when it comes to pursuing your goals. Take every shortcut you can. The important thing is getting what you want, when you want it."*

Well, Rebecca knew what she wanted.

"Or even go back to leading day tours around Texas," Luke continued helpfully.

Rebecca did her best to contain her hurt. "You have every right to your opinion, Dad. Just as I'm entitled to go after what I want, with no holds barred. While I'm fighting this battle, you have to back off."

Luke sighed, looking as if he wished he could give her a great big hug and instantly make everything better for her, the way he had when she was a kid. "That's exactly my point, Rebecca. It shouldn't be a battle. It shouldn't be this hard for you."

"Don't you look like you just lost your best friend," Trevor said.

Rebecca spread drop cloths over the garage floor. She had changed into an old souvenir T-shirt that had shrunk the first time she washed it, so it was much wider than it was long, ripped jeans and equally battered sneakers. "What are you doing here?" she asked, for the sake of her pride pretending she wasn't glad to see him at all.

If ever she'd had a day that left her feeling in need of rescue, it had been today. But she had the feeling if she let Trevor swoop in and help her with a revised business plan, among other things, that wouldn't be all he'd end up helping her with. And right now she had way too much on her agenda to even think about beginning a love affair with a man who had designs on her ranch, and the ranch next to her.

Trevor watched her move two sawhorses onto the center of the cloth, some five feet or so apart.

Like her, he was dressed for work, in a light blue chambray shirt and worn jeans that were frayed around the edges. He hadn't yet shaved, and the stubble gave him a rugged, sexy look.

Something hot and sensual shimmered in his eyes. "I came over to see if you wanted to go to a movie with me tonight."

Memories of the way he had kissed her the last time they'd faced off like this sent a burning flame throughout her entire body.

Mentally, Rebecca forced herself to douse the fire of desire.

She turned her attention away, and struggled with the unfinished wood door she had purchased at the home improvement center. "As in...a date?"

Trevor helped her situate the door across the sawhorses, his strong hands brushing hers. "If you want to call it that, sure."

She'd be a fool not to recognize all the pheromones flowing from his tall studly body. Rebecca was no fool. Mouth set in an uncompromising line, she nailed the door to the sawhorses. "I can't."

Laugh lines crinkled at the corners of his hazel eyes. "Because you're building furniture or because we didn't...?"

Pleased he had immediately figured out the use for the "desk" she had just made for her ranch office, Rebecca slanted him a glance meant to send him on his way. Better to get it all out in the open than stand around playing games. "Have sex?" she queried lightly, as if she hadn't been thinking about that possibility at all.

He moved lazily toward her. "Make love," he corrected, not stopping until he was close enough she could see the heat in his eyes.

It just figured he'd pursue her with romance.

Romance being the one thing she hadn't experienced in what seemed like forever, romance being the one thing that would leave her vulnerable, the one thing she couldn't afford to indulge in when her whole world was crashing in around her—financially, anyway.

"So back to why you can't?" he prodded, looking as if he wanted to do nothing more than take her in his arms and kiss her again.

"Because I have way too much to do."

And nothing he said or did was going to change that.

Finding the garage suddenly too intimate a setting for comfort, Rebecca went next door to the stable. She slapped a straw hat on her head, picked up a bucket of nutritional supplements disguised as treats and strode across the grass to check on the herd.

Trevor walked beside her. Blue Mist came over to the fence to investigate and Rebecca handed her a treat.

Trevor reached out to pat the alpaca's side. "She looks good."

Rebecca thought so, too. She took the hose from the pumping station next to the pasture and topped off Blue Mist's water trough.

"Nervous?"

Rebecca walked on out to the next field over, where the other females were pastured.

"How'd you know?" She tried to pretend she didn't appreciate the company.

Trevor tilted his hat back. "First time I birthed a calf, I was pretty edgy."

When they stopped at the fence, the other alpacas came over to get their supplements, too.

"How old were you?" Rebecca asked.

Trevor leaned against the four-foot-high mesh barrier he'd erected on the other side of the wood fence. As much as Rebecca was loath to admit it, adding the extra barrier of finely tempered steel did give her an air of serenity she hadn't expected. Doubling up on the fencing between his cattle and her alpacas had been a good idea. Mentally, she vowed to continue it on the other three sides of fencing for her pastures as soon as she could afford to do so.

Trevor smiled, recalling. "Fourteen. My mom and dad were off on Annie's Homemade business and Dad had left me in charge of the cattle. A thunderstorm blew up, and a tree was struck by lightning in the pasture where the cows that were ready to give birth were staying. The rain put out the fire in the tree, but the cows were completely spooked, next thing I knew one of 'em was in labor."

Rebecca imagined the harrowing chaos that had ensued. "Naturally, again, all did not go as planned."

"The calf was breech and the cord got twisted around its neck," he told her, his voice a little rough. "I had to reach in and pull it out."

"And it survived."

Trevor's gaze moved over the size of the pasture. "As well as the rest of the calves that were born that day." Trevor turned back to her with a smile. "Like I said, that lightning strike really scared 'em. Several of 'em went into labor that day."

The two of them ambled down to the last pasture, where the herd-sires were kept, the warm spring breeze ruffling her hair.

"Well, I guess I know who to call if I run into any trouble with Blue Mist," Rebecca teased.

Trevor watched as Rebecca dispensed the treats to the males. He returned her sidelong glance. "My brother Tyler?"

"He is my ranch vet."

Aware she'd slipped and started flirting with Trevor again Rebecca forced herself to adopt a more business-like attitude as she looked over at the Circle Y. Two large cattle haulers were backed up to the pasture, far-thest from the house, bawling cattle pouring out onto the field, their large muscular bodies crowding each other and kicking up clumps of dust and grass.

Rebecca'd grown up around a lot of ranches. She couldn't recall any looking that chaotic. "That been going on all day?" she asked Trevor.

"Since midmorning."

Rebecca frowned. "It looks like a lot of cattle to be putting in one pasture." It reminded her of rush hour in the city.

"Yep."

She studied his expression. "You're not surprised."

Trevor shrugged. "Vince likes to squeeze every penny out of everything he does."

"No matter the cost in other terms, I'm guessing."

Trevor said nothing. Just turned his glance back to his own ranch.

Rebecca pivoted to survey the Wind Creek. In con-trast, Trevor's place was downright pastoral, with the rolling green tree-lined pastures dotted sparingly with healthy-looking cattle, his white mission-style ranch house with red tile roof and white barns and outbuildings gleaming in the afternoon sun. "You don't run that many cattle in one pasture."

"And I won't. It's too hard on the grass, and bad for the cattle to be squeezed in that way."

"I'm guessing Vince Owen doesn't agree?"

"I push the envelope in one direction, he pushes it the other."

Admiring the restraint in Trevor's voice, Rebecca turned back to the Circle Y. From this distance, the cattle on the Circle Y versus the cattle on the Wind Creek didn't look all that different from one another, except for the obvious—they were different breeds. And different colors. Trevor's were white Charolais, Vince's Black Angus. "They don't look like they're suffering—yet anyway. I mean they're all pretty good sized."

He set his jaw. "He administers growth hormones and powerful antibiotics on a regular basis."

She studied him. "I'm guessing you don't."

"Mine are brought up on organic feed. No hormones. No antibiotics. Got fewer of them, but they sell for top dollar."

Which probably meant Trevor made as much as, if not more than Vince.

Trevor turned in the direction of the road. He inclined his head at Susie's green landscaping truck, turning into the drive. "Looks like you've got company."

Rebecca headed back toward the garage and Susie met her next to the barn.

Rebecca knew immediately that something was up.

"Dad told Mom about running into you at the bank today, and Mom told me."

"Great." Rebecca scowled. That was all she needed, her father spreading word of supposed impending failure as a rancher and a businesswoman.

"I came by to see what I could do," Susie continued, with her usual air of expertise.

Trevor started to edge away.

Knowing Susie would temper her remarks somewhat if someone else were there, Rebecca grabbed Trevor's shirtsleeve. Getting the message, he stopped trying to make a graceful exit.

Unable to hide her resentment, Rebecca told her sister, "There's nothing you need to do."

"It's not about need. There's plenty I *can* do for you if you'll let me," Susie said, with the too-helpful look that had irritated the heck out of Rebecca for as long as Rebecca could remember. It was the look that said Susie knew better, the exasperated but concerned look that conveyed Susie had to rescue her stubborn little sis yet again. And once again, in Susie's estimation, it was too late, the damage was already done.

With effort, Rebecca pushed back years of pique and tried to be as civil as she had promised herself she would be, in her dealings with her successful older sister.

Susie had been through a lot.

In some respects, Rebecca knew, Susie *was* wiser than her years.

But not, Rebecca told herself firmly, in this instance.

Rebecca plastered a pleasant smile on her face. "Assisting with the shearing yesterday was help enough, Susie."

"Your Open House is this Sunday, Rebecca. Today is Monday."

"Believe me, I know how much—or how little—time I have left."

Susie gestured at the garage that was supposed to be the ranch business office. "You're not going to get it all done alone."

Rebecca's spine stiffened. "You don't know that."

"I know this. If you were to scale back on what you were trying to do, between now and then, you'd have a much better chance of success on Sunday. Your operation has to inspire confidence, Rebecca, to attract investors. It has to state that the business is firmly under your control. At the time you have guests here, nothing can remain undone."

Trevor coughed and gave Susan a look that wordlessly instructed her to back off.

Rebecca glared at Trevor. "I can handle her."

Trevor lifted his hands in wordless surrender. Still facing them, he stepped away.

Predictably, Susie began to lose her temper, too. "You don't need to handle me, Rebecca. You need to listen to me. I know ways you can increase your cash flow immediately without having to get any more loans."

That sounded appealing but letting Susie get involved and tell her what to do would mean Rebecca was no longer in charge of her operation, Susie was. Rebecca couldn't have that. "Thanks, but no thanks," she told her sister flatly.

Susie blew out an exasperated breath. "You are so stubborn."

"And you," Rebecca volleyed right back, "are always barging in where you don't belong, telling me how to act and what to think. Except of course the one time that you should have told me everything…"

"You're talking about Grayson Graham."

"Who else?"

"Dad and I apologized for that!"

"And it was too little, too late, on both counts."

Susie blew out an exasperated breath. "We were try-ing to protect you."

Rebecca folded her arms in front of her. "Then, as now, I don't need your protection. I need you to treat me as a capable adult."

Susie glared at Rebecca, frustrated as always when a situation—or a person—was out of her control. "Add sensible to your list and you might actually get some-where," Susie muttered.

In her younger days, this would have been the per-fect point to throw an all-out temper tantrum. "You know what your problem is? You just never had any faith in me," Rebecca told her sister calmly. "You still don't."

Susie started to reply, then stopped, brushed a hand through her blond hair. She sighed, abruptly looking as hurt and disappointed as Rebecca felt that it had come to this—again. "Believe it or not, Rebecca, I did not come over here to fight with you," Susie informed her sadly.

Bitterness welled up inside Rebecca. Some things, it seemed, would never change. "Well, you failed on that count, didn't you?" Rebecca asked softly.

Trevor watched as Susie drove away. He turned back to Rebecca, like a principal chastising an errant stu-dent. "That was uncalled for."

"Who asked you?" Rebecca marched past him.

"She was trying to be *nice.*" He fell into step be-side her.

"She was *trying* to butt in." Rebecca slammed into the house, via the back door.

He strode in right after her. "Maybe you need her to butt in. She runs her own business. She started it from scratch. As a landscape architect who had to convince people to trust her from a young age, she knows a thing or two about presentation."

Rebecca stalked to the sink and pumped liquid soap into her palm. "More than you?"

"I don't have to sell people on trusting me with their money. Susie does." Trevor's voice gentled. He stepped in beside her to wash his hands, too. "What's going on with the two of you anyway? And who the hell is Grayson Graham?"

Rebecca blotted her hands on a towel, handed it over to him. "My college boyfriend."

Trevor took a moment to compute that. "Is he the guy everyone said you were about to get engaged to your senior year?"

Rebecca couldn't believe he remembered. "Yep."

"What happened?" Trevor lounged against the counter as she went to the refrigerator. "Did he have eyes for Susie?"

Rebecca set the pitcher of lemonade on the counter. "Not quite."

"She make a play for him?"

Rebecca aimed a lethal look his way. "No."

"Then…?"

"He was using me." Rebecca was so agitated she sloshed liquid over the rim of the glass. "Susie knew what he was up to, and she didn't tell me. She told *my dad* instead."

Trevor came to the rescue with a paper towel. "I don't follow."

Rebecca rummaged around underneath the sink for the spray cleaner. "Grayson Graham went out of his way to befriend Susie her senior year in college. Susie couldn't figure out why, since they didn't have much in common. Turned out Grayson knew my dad was on the admissions board for the UT–Dallas medical school, and Grayson wanted Susie to get him entrée to our dad. Susie refused. Apparently—" Rebecca calmed down as she began to clean "—Grayson had been told his MCAT scores were outstanding, but his grades from college were not. Without a certain grade point average, there was no way any med school in Texas was going to let him in. Grayson, who was brilliant but lazy, figured the only way to get around that was to get someone with influence—like my dad—to give him such a high recommendation the med school would have no choice but to admit him. When Susie refused to help him, Grayson asked me out."

"And Susie didn't tell you," Trevor guessed.

Rebecca added ice to both glasses. "Susie told me not to date him," Rebecca admitted reluctantly. "She *didn't* tell me why."

Trevor's hand brushed hers as she handed him the glass. "Would you have believed her, even if she had told you?"

His probing irked her. Rebecca lifted her brow. "That's not the issue."

He looked at her over the rim of his glass. "In other words, you would not have."

"The point is, I would have had the information." Rebecca gulped her drink and wiped her mouth with the back of her hand. "I could have decided for myself. At least, I would have been on my guard."

Thankfully, he did not argue that. "Where does your dad come into this?" Trevor asked.

Wishing she had on something other than the misshapen T-shirt and jeans, that would allow her look as pulled-together on the outside as she felt on the inside, Rebecca sighed. "Susie told him, too."

The look on Trevor's face said he knew what a mistake that was. "My dad agreed I needed to be protected, so the two of them concocted this plan to have Grayson come home to meet the family for a weekend." She flushed, recalling the stinging humiliation of that terrible time. "Fool that I was, I thought everyone was finally coming around to this wonderful college senior I was dating. And Grayson was so excited, so willing to become a member of the Carrigan clan, when he told me he wanted a private audience with my dad over the weekend, I thought he was planning to ask my dad for permission to marry me."

Trevor gave her a look that was so full of compassion she wanted to weep. "So you told everyone you knew...."

"Yes," Rebecca uttered miserably. She scraped the toe of her boot across the linoleum.

Trevor moved close to her side.

Rebecca continued looking at the pattern on the tile. "Grayson came home for the weekend, everything seemed to go great. My parents tried hard to get to know Grayson. Then, before we left, Grayson and my dad had their private meeting." Restless again, Rebecca began to pace. "I didn't know what was said, but I could tell—even though Grayson was all polite and everything—that Grayson was upset by whatever had transpired during their man-to-man talk. When we got back to school, I confronted him. I figured my dad had told him I was too young to be engaged. And I was all ready to comfort him, to tell him all we had to do was be patient."

"But that wasn't it."

"No. Grayson told me my whole family were jerks. I questioned how he could possibly have come to that conclusion when everyone had been so nice to him, and the whole story came tumbling out. By the time he had finished telling me his side of things, it was clear he had only pursued me to get entrée to my dad and he dumped me."

"And broke your heart in the process." Trevor's expression was grim.

Rebecca nodded, set her empty glass aside. "The worst part of it was that Susie and my dad both insisted they had only been doing what was right for me."

Trevor finished his lemonade in a single draft. "And you've been mad ever since."

Rebecca nodded. "For a long time, I was."

"Which was why you took that job after college with that tour company."

She gestured aimlessly. "That was part of it. The other part was I wanted to go off and see the world."

And she had.

Trevor came toward her, not stopping until they stood toe to toe.

Rebecca stood with her back to the counter, facing him, studying the strong column of his throat. "I thought things were going to be different now. I thought if I let them in on my dream, if I bought this ranch and started my own business they would stop treating me like a child."

Only it wasn't working out that way, she realized,

more discouraged than she could remember feeling in a very long time. Not nearly.

She looked up at Trevor.

Expecting sympathy, she was surprised to see none.

Chapter 8

"If you want to be treated like an adult, you have to act like an adult."

This wasn't the reaction Rebecca was hoping for from Trevor. "Criticize me while I'm down, why don't you?" She stormed from the kitchen and marched back to the office, ready to resume painting again.

"I'm not taking Susie's side against you."

She shot him a cold look. "Could have fooled me."

"Your sister may not have said what you wanted to hear just now, but her motivation in coming over here, and trying to help you out, was genuine."

"Don't you get it?" Rebecca pried open the lid on the paint can, gave the primrose yellow enamel a stir. "That's just the problem. Susie and my father didn't trust me to handle the situation with Grayson Graham without their behind-the-scenes protection, and they don't trust me to be able to pull off this business venture without their intervention. Nothing has changed and it probably never will."

He eased onto a low stack of book boxes. "It won't if

you keep up that attitude. There's nothing wrong with accepting a little help and advice."

Rebecca stirred with a vengeance. "You're telling me you let your dad and/or your brothers come over and tell you how to run the Wind Creek?"

Trevor stretched his long legs out in front of him. "I listen to their advice. Particularly when they have something to say that will help me. Then I decide what it is I want to do and do it."

Rebecca picked up a brush. "No hard feelings."

"None required. None meant, either."

She painted with long, even strokes. Gritted her teeth. "You make it sound so simple."

"It is simple."

She snorted.

"And there's something else, too."

Rebecca rolled her eyes. "Why is everyone so free with the advice where I'm concerned?"

"Just because Grayson Graham betrayed you, doesn't mean every other guy will."

She set her paintbrush down and wiped her hands with a rag. "Are we talking about every other guy or you?"

"Me." Trevor took her into his arms.

She splayed her hands across his chest. "I can't do this now."

His eyes glimmered with mischief. "What?"

She gasped as he sat back down on the box, taking her with him. One minute she'd been standing, the next draped across his lap. "Get involved with you."

He anchored one arm around her waist, tunneled his other hand through her hair. "Is that a choice to make?" His lids lowered to half-mast. "Or something that happens despite our intentions?"

Rebecca had told herself the next time he kissed her she would be prepared, she would have all her defenses up. That buffer fled the moment his lips made contact with hers. It wasn't so much the soft, sure feel of his mouth moving on hers, although that was tantalizing. Or the way his tongue dallied provocatively with hers, finding every sweet spot with ease. It was the way he took charge and dominated the moment, and her. The way he deepened the kiss and slid his tongue over the plump curve of her lower lip. The way he made her feel so ravished and cherished all at once.

As if she was meant to be with him, meant to do this. Meant to take this risk. Which was why of course she had to come up for air and say, "I've got so much on my plate right now…. Trevor… I can't risk…"

He nuzzled the side of her neck, finding the nerve endings just beneath her ear. He turned his attention to her lips again, kissing and caressing her with even less reserve. "Sure about that?" he murmured.

Rebecca was sure about one thing, as she allowed herself to melt into his touch, one last time before she forced herself to get back to work. No one had ever kissed her like this. No one had ever held her so close, and given so much or made her want to deepen the connection between them so very badly.

Which was why when the kiss finally halted, and the amazing intimacy ended, she felt stunned and bereft. Elated and confused.

"I've got to go back to my place, and finish up there," Trevor told her hoarsely, his expression reflecting her reluctance to get back to business as usual. "When I'm done, I'll be back to help you with all this."

"Oh, yeah?" Embarrassed to have revealed so much about her desire so readily, Rebecca vaulted off his lap.

Stalked away. "And what's that going to cost me?" She willed her knees to vanquish their trembling. "'Cause if you're looking for another home-cooked dinner…" She spun around to face him.

Or, heaven help them both, more of this…

His expression said, Game over.

"Don't you get it?" He caught her hand and pulled her against him, so there was no mistaking the desire dominating his lower half or the pounding of his heart beneath his shirt.

He paused to kiss her again, slowly, lingeringly, until she believed—as did he—they had something special, something neither could ignore.

He rubbed his thumb across her lips, looked deep into her eyes. "The pleasure of your company is gift enough."

Trevor returned about the time she had finished putting her herd in the barn for the night. He brought with him a picnic supper of cold fried chicken, potato salad, coleslaw, two bottles of ice-cold beer, a thermos of coffee and another plate of his homemade ranger cookies.

The fiercely independent side of Rebecca would have liked to say thanks but no thanks and send him on his way, but the more practical part of her was starved for food, and hungry for his company, even if he was an insufferable know-it-all from time to time.

So she made a big deal of sighing, and invited him to join her, as he must have known she would.

Grudgingly ignoring his satisfied smile, she dragged a couple of lawn chairs into the twilight.

In the distance, she could see Vince Owen and his cowboys unloading yet another two cattle haulers into the back pasture. Which made her wonder just how many cows Vince was planning to run on the Circle Y? Two hundred? Three hundred?

No one in Laramie ran as many cattle on such small pastures.

Of course, Vince could build more fence. He had plenty of land—fifty acres or more—that wasn't currently being used for grazing, in front of and to the sides of his ranch house, which was set back a ways from the road.

Not that it was any of her concern.

She had her own problems to deal with.

At the center of which was what she was going to do with her considerable physical attraction to Trevor McCabe, now that he had nixed the idea of a one-time-only no-strings affair.

Figuring she'd better get her mind on something other than the emotional argument and passionate kisses they had shared earlier, she turned her thoughts back to the business at hand.

In terms of ranching, she knew there was plenty she could learn from him. And as long as it was her idea, any "help" she received from him on her own terms, at her request...

"How long did it take your ranch to turn a profit?" Rebecca asked Trevor when they finished eating and went back to the garage to pick up where she had left off.

Trevor started painting the half a dozen bookshelves she had primed and Rebecca went to work on the battered wooden file cabinets she'd picked up at office surplus. "About a year," he said.

"What'd you do until then? How'd you make ends meet?"

Trevor moved the brush back and forth with steady,

rhythmic strokes. "I hired myself out as a cowboy to work other ranches, like my dad's, on a temporary basis."

Which was coincidentally exactly what her dad had suggested to her that very morning.

Rebecca tried not to wonder if he would make love with the same slow, steady expertise he did everything else. "That didn't make you feel like a failure?"

He shrugged, his frayed chambray shirt molding the contours of wide shoulders and broad chest. "Work is work. Besides," he teased her gently, his gaze roving her lips before returning to her eyes, "haven't you heard… pride goeth before a fall?"

She flushed, aware her lips were tingling the way they did when they kissed. "I thought the whole goal of being a rancher was to be self-sufficient."

"It is. But everybody's got to start somewhere. And unless you're having your success handed to you on a silver platter, it's usually at the bottom."

"I worried it might be too early to stop by," Meg Carrigan said at seven o'clock the next morning. She was wearing her nurse's uniform.

Rebecca shook her head. "I got up at five-thirty."

The two women hugged. "The question is, what time did you go to bed last night?"

Rebecca knew she had circles under her eyes. "One, maybe two."

"Oh, honey…" A wealth of love was in Meg's voice.

Rebecca lifted a hand. "I'm okay, Mom. I only need about four or five hours of sleep."

"You might be able to *get by* on that. You *need* seven or eight, minimum, to be truly rested."

"I'll work on that when I get my ranch up and running."

"So how are things coming?" Meg asked cheerfully.

"Let's look and see." Rebecca led Meg across to the garage. She opened up the doors. Meg gasped in delight at what she saw. Pale primrose-yellow walls, bookshelves, desk and files.

"You had built-ins put in already?" Meg asked.

Rebecca shook her head, pleased at the way the formerly rustic space was turning out. "All the furniture is used. I just cleaned it up and painted it a shade darker than the walls."

"Well, it looks marvelous. How'd you get so much done so fast?"

Rebecca thought about claiming superpowers but knew it would be pointless—Meg could read her like a book. "I, uh, had a little help." She saved them both the trouble of Meg prying the information out of her.

Unfortunately, Rebecca noted, as Meg lifted her brow, waited, that tidbit wasn't enough to satisfy Meg's need to mother her.

"Trevor McCabe was over here last night, painting, too," Rebecca said, doing her best to contain a self-conscious flush.

"Oh!" Meg looked thrilled.

Rebecca's brows climbed before any more conclusions could be leaped to. "He was just being neighborly."

"Oh?"

So her too-cool attitude wasn't working. Rebecca propped her hands on her hips. "Mom, please…"

"I gather this means the two of you are no longer quarreling."

Rebecca tensed at the assumption in Meg's eyes. "How'd you hear about that?"

"Amy said Sunday…"

"Amy needs to learn to be quiet."

Meg merely smiled and blessedly let it drop. "I brought you something. My laptop computer and color printer. And several reams of business stationery in the ranch's new signature color, Primrose yellow. I can use your father's, and/or my computer at the hospital, so I'm not in any hurry to get them back."

Rebecca's eyes misted. "Oh, Mom. Thank you."

"You're welcome."

"This is going to help me so much."

"I'm glad. In return, I want you to cut your father and Susie some slack."

Rebecca propped her hands on her hips. "Is there anything you don't know about?"

"Very little, as it happens. And I mean it, Rebecca. It's past time this feud between the three of you ended."

Rebecca began carrying the gifts to her office. "I'd be happy to call a halt if they'd quit trying to run my life."

"They mean well."

Rebecca set both on the desk. "Meaning well and doing well are two different things."

"So, they screwed up again by doing and saying the exact wrong thing. It doesn't mean they don't love you because they do—every bit as much as I love you, and yet you're never mad at me."

They went back to get the rest of the stuff from Meg's car. "That's because you know how to be supportive."

"Or because I leave the heavy lifting to them." Meg's voice gentled. "Listen to me, darling. It's true. I don't usually assume the role of bad cop because your father does it so well. And let's face it, it's more fun to be the good cop, but that doesn't mean I don't worry about you, too."

Rebecca refused to let her agitation show. "Your point?"

"Families are made up of people who are human, and that makes them inherently flawed institutions."

"Or in other words," Rebecca ruminated on a beleaguered sigh, "there is no such thing as a perfect family."

"Any more than there is a perfect person." Meg squeezed her hand. "You appreciate me because I don't expect you to be perfect, honey. I'm telling you, if you ever want to be happy, you have to stop expecting others to be faultless."

Rebecca was still thinking about what her mother had said to her when she saw the parcel post truck rumbling up the drive. Before she could do much more than step outside the office, he had dropped a big box onto her porch, lifted his hand in a wave and driven off.

Wondering what it was—she hadn't ordered anything—Rebecca went over to investigate.

The box bore her address all right—but Vince Owen's name. The package had been sent from a Dunnigan Dog Food care center in Dallas. Rebecca sighed. She could call Vince and ask him to come pick it up. Or she could run it next door herself, and leave it on his front porch.

Tossing the big cardboard box into the bed of her pickup truck, she climbed into the sweltering cab, put the windows all the way down and drove over, the unseasonably hot spring air wafting over her.

There were no pickups parked at the Circle Y.

Rebecca cut the engine, hopped out of the cab and ran the box up to the front porch. She had just dropped it when she heard a lot of loud, eager barking. Coming around the side of the house, she spotted a portable chain-link kennel, approximately six by ten feet, positioned beneath the shade of a tree.

Spying her, Coco got even more excited. She barked harder, running back and forth along the fence.

Unable to leave without at least saying hello to the puppy, Rebecca headed Coco's way. "Hey, girl, calm down now," Rebecca said, noting how hard the little dog was panting.

Rebecca knelt down beside the fence.

Whimpering hard, Coco stuck her tongue through the steel links, trying hard to lick Rebecca's hand, and nearly catching a baby tooth on the metal in the process. Rebecca looked around. Saw no one.

"I really shouldn't do this without at least asking permission," Rebecca told Coco, standing and walking over to the gate. "But what the heck…"

She slipped inside.

Coco took a flying leap, trying to jump into Rebecca's arms.

Coco whimpered harder, louder. Her rough eager tongue bathed the underside of Rebecca's chin. Her little body quivered as she settled in Rebecca's arms. Then she abruptly settled down, cuddling against Rebecca's chest and panted even harder.

Figuring she had time to comfort the lonely pup, Rebecca settled in the grass and stroked Coco's head, rubbing behind her chocolate-brown ears.

"Now, listen, little one, you've got to settle down," Rebecca soothed. "Running around like that in this heat can't be good for you, even if you have some shade. See that little doggy igloo over there in the corner? Yes, that one." Rebecca chuckled as Coco licked her hand. "It's nice and cool, and there's even a cushion in there for you to lie on. You've got two great big bowls of water and two more of food, so you're all set there. There's even a chew bone for you in the corner over there. And a corner of the grass that I can see you've been using for your own private potty. So you really are okay."

Coco turned her big dark eyes to Rebecca, whimpered more, then got up and walked on wobbly legs to her water bowl. She drank thirstily, emptying nearly half of it, before coming back to Rebecca's lap. She climbed back on and settled in, as if for a long nap.

"Oh, baby, I wish I could stay here and cuddle you all day long," Rebecca said, as Coco began nosing Rebecca's shirt and pants, in a way that told Rebecca Coco was picking up the scent of the alpacas on her clothing. "But I can't. I've got to get back and finish putting my office together, and see my herd has enough water in this heat—although like you they go right for the shade—and then get them inside the barn and settled for the night before the thunderstorms that are predicted for this evening appear."

Coco's expression turned alert and apprehensive.

Rebecca wondered if the pup had ever weathered a storm. Rebecca hoped she wouldn't have to do so alone and outside.

"I'm sure Vince or one of his two cowboys will be back by then," Rebecca said.

As if on cue, some of the cattle started mooing. Coco turned her gaze in the direction of the cows in the two big pastures that bumped up against Rebecca's pastures two and three.

"You agree with me, don't you, Coco?" Rebecca murmured, studying the wall of beef cattle. "There are way too many animals on those two patches of grass."

Oh, they had plenty of water all right. Feed and water troughs lined the entire perimeter of the aging split rail wooden fencing that fronted the Circle Y ranch house and barns. The problem was, some of the cattle seemed to be having trouble getting to it, as the biggest steers were blocking their way.

"Oh, well, it's not my problem," Rebecca said. "Nor, sadly, are you." Reluctantly, Rebecca stood and set Coco down.

Coco turned mournful eyes to Rebecca.

"Your owner will be home soon," Rebecca reassured gently. She leaned down to pat the pup on the head, and then quickly let herself out of the kennel.

Coco let out a bark in protest, then ran after Rebecca, jumping and leaping against the fence.

Knowing there was nothing she could say that would comfort the lonely little puppy, who like as not had many such days ahead of her, Rebecca grimaced and turned and headed for her pickup truck, empathetic tears running down her face.

Rebecca spent the rest of the afternoon unpacking her books and papers and trying not to think about Coco. She filled her bookshelves and file cabinets, set up several lamps and the floor fan that was going to have to do until she could install a window air conditioner, then unpacked the rest of the personal items in the moving boxes and carted those up to the house.

She had just finished with the last of the clothing, when she heard a weird trumpeting sound.

What the...

The noise got louder.

It was now accompanied by a fierce, barking that sounded all too familiar. *Coco.* Rebecca raced down the steps, through the kitchen, out the back door, just in time to see chaos erupt.

Trevor was deep in conversation with one of his business customers when he heard what sounded like a mini riot erupting. "I'm going to have to call you back," Trevor said, setting down the phone.

He raced for the door.

Midnight-blue clouds were gathering on the horizon with the typical speed of Texas weather. His herd was stamping and moving restlessly in response to the chaos on the next two ranches over.

A weird trumpeting sound pierced the air like a civil defense siren. On the Primrose, he could see the alpacas racing around the pastures like racehorses in training.

That couldn't be good.

On the Circle Y, dust clouds rose, and the Black Angus cattle moved toward the perimeter like a herd during roundup.

Trevor didn't have to think. He hopped in his truck and drove to Rebecca's as quick as he could, bumping along, avoiding fence and cutting through their front yards. By the time, he got there Rebecca was racing back and forth, shouting and calling at the cause of the commotion in vain.

"Coco! Stop it now! Do you hear me! Stop it!" she shouted, tears running down her face.

The puppy either didn't hear her—highly plausible given all the aggravated mooing and alpaca trumpeting going on—or was too worked up to mind. Didn't matter. Blue Mist was running around frantically, trying to get away from the dog, who was chasing her.

"You get Blue Mist!" Trevor shouted above the din. "I'll get Coco."

Trevor hopped the split rail fence and headed for the dog.

Thinking it was a game of chase, Coco tried to evade Trevor.

Trevor hunkered down, held his arms wide, waited.

The puppy ran back and forth, still barking, but clearly tempted. Trevor stared straight at him and waited some more.

With a joyful yelp, Coco raced straight for Trevor and leaped into his arms.

On the other side of the pasture, Rebecca was still trying to calm Blue Mist.

Figuring she knew the animal best, and would likely have better luck with that, Trevor took the puppy toward the Primrose ranch house.

He carried her inside, set her in the laundry room, shut the door and headed right back out.

Coco resumed barking. It hardly mattered.

Trevor had another emergency to attend.

Rebecca's alpacas were still stampeding. The storm was ever closer, lightning flashing in the distance, thunder rumbling.

Wincing against the piercing warning call of the alpacas and the deeper mooing of the fiercely upset cattle, he raced for his truck, got a lasso and returned.

"Head toward her and be ready to comfort her," Trevor shouted over the cacophony.

To his relief, this once Rebecca bowed to his expertise in such matters and obeyed. He threw the rope. It landed around the top of the alpaca's legs. He tightened the lasso just enough to cause Blue Mist to stumble. Rebecca was right there. She caught the stunned alpaca in her arms.

And that was when, unfortunately, all hell really broke loose.

Rebecca had just removed the lasso from Blue Mist's body and started leading her by the halter toward the safety of the barn when the earthshaking rumbling started.

Only it wasn't a quake.

And it wasn't a tornado.

Or even the fierce-looking thunderstorm drawing ever near that set her other nine alpacas into a frenzy. It was the sight of two hundred Black Angus cattle breaking through the barrier of the aging split rail fence between the properties.

The already-galloping alpacas were no dummies. They knew they were outweighed ten to one by the steers. Unable to get past the mesh Trevor had put up on the other side of the Primrose–Wind Creek property line, they headed for the only way out.

Spare minutes later, the two herd-sires barreled through the aging wooden fence line at the rear of Rebecca's property. The seven female alpacas broke through the fence separating pastures two and three and zoomed after the herd-sires, just ahead of the rampaging cattle.

Fortunately, the alpacas were lighter and faster than the Black Angus cows coming after them.

Unfortunately, all were running straight into the quick-approaching thunderstorm.

Blue Mist—perhaps exhausted from the ordeal—or perhaps just accepting the fact she now had a halter snapped to her lead, stayed with Rebecca.

"Take her to the barn and put her in a stall!" Trevor barked as the noise abated and animals scattered. He already had the cell phone out of his pocket. "I'll call for help!"

By the time Rebecca came back out of the barn, the skies had opened up, rain was pouring down. "My alpacas," Rebecca whispered, standing under the safety of the roof line, getting wet anyway.

Looking as if he didn't mind the drenching, Trevor gave her shoulder a reassuring squeeze. "We'll round 'em up. Don't worry. I've got half a dozen cowboys coming."

"How?" Rebecca trembled as the sky lit up with a jagged yellow flash, aware she could lose everything, including her precious alpacas. "How are you going to round them up?"

Trevor's jaw set. Determination radiated from him. "Any way we can. Most likely, horseback. But first we're going to have to wait for the thunderstorm to subside."

The thought of all that open countryside and the lightning flashing overhead terrified her. Glad Trevor was there, to see her through this, she bit her lip. "What if…?"

He shook his head, cutting off the thought. "They're animals, Rebecca. They'll know instinctively to seek shelter." He waited for a break in the lightning to push her toward the house, shielding her with his body as they ran.

He stopped just inside the door. "Meanwhile, I'm going to drive over and alert the ranches and country homes due south of us to the problem."

Glad he seemed to know just what to do, Rebecca nodded.

"I want you to stay here and work the phone. Call the sheriff's department, and the office of the Laramie

County Rancher's association and let them know what's happened, too. Have them help put out the word. Given all the cattle that are on the loose, we're going to need all the help we can get." Trevor stepped outside.

Rebecca caught his sleeve and pulled him back. "What about Vince?"

None of this would have happened if not for him.

Trevor grimaced. "I called him on his cell. He and his two hired hands are in Fort Worth—picking up more steers, if you can believe that. It'll be two hours or more before they can get back."

The next few hours were the tensest in Rebecca's life.

Help came from more people than she ever could have imagined.

Trevor's father, Travis McCabe, his two younger brothers, Kyle and Kurt, and his brother Teddy all showed up. They each brought half a dozen friends, and more vehicles, flashlights, lassos, cell phones and two-way radios than anyone had a right to expect. Neighbors and several members of the sheriff's department, helped out, too.

Before long, Rebecca started getting reports of alpaca sightings. With each alert, another alpaca was found or several more Circle Y cattle were rounded up.

Stacks of sandwiches and coolers of soft drinks were brought in. Rebecca made an endless supply of coffee.

By midnight, three quarters of the Circle Y cattle had been rounded up and pastured safely on other ranches. Rebecca had all but one of her herd back in the stable. And it was when the last one was being brought in that she first noticed something was wrong—really wrong— with Blue Mist.

Chapter 9

Knowing from the way Blue Mist was alternately pacing her stall and hopping restlessly up and down the birth of her baby cria was near, Rebecca raced back to the house through the pouring rain. Relieved the lightning and thunder had stopped, she got another stack of clean towels from the linen closet, the first aid kit Jeremy had given her the day she moved in and the book she had on birthing alpacas. She had read it cover to cover several times during the year she was planning the start-up of her ranch.

Heart racing, she carted the birthing manual back out to the barn. Blue Mist was still hopping up and down. Rebecca saw the cria's head had begun to crown.

She donned sterile gloves and stepped into the stall.

With a groan, Blue Mist lay down and rolled onto her side, panting and pushing hard.

Rebecca let her strain a few more minutes, until the head and the front hooves were all the way out.

Following the directions she had memorized, she broke the sack and cleared the airways.

The cria blinked, looked straight at Rebecca. But

did not seem to be any closer to coming the rest of the way out of its mama.

Rebecca touched the alpaca's shoulders gently. "Come on, Blue Mist, push a little more. You can do it."

Blue Mist strained, quivered.

The cria was making no progress.

Not sure how long the baby alpaca could stay that way, worried that the body of the cria was somehow wedged awkwardly in the opening, Rebecca reached in and began to gently work its front legs out.

One inch, two…

As soon as the front legs cleared, the rest of the cria's body came out. Rebecca made another check of the airways, was rewarded with a weak, mewling sound that was music to her ears.

Trembling with joy, she used a towel to wipe it clean and another to dry it off. She had just cut and tied the cord, dabbed the stub and area around it liberally with iodine, when she heard the rumble of a pickup truck, and the clanking of a cattle hauler, dragging behind.

Short minutes later, Trevor strode in, her herd-sire on a lead beside him. He was clad in a long yellow rain slicker. His hat looked drenched, as did his face and hair. "Got the last one here," he told her, looking over the top of the stall. A smile split his handsome face. "Hey, who is this?" Trevor said softly.

"Little Blue," Rebecca announced.

Positioning the cria close to Blue Mist, she stepped out of the stall, took the lead from Trevor. "Keep an eye on them for me a minute, will you?" she said.

"Sure." Trevor leaned against the outside of the door, while Rebecca grabbed a towel, and led Black Onyx down to his stall. She rubbed him down, checked for injury, and blessedly found none.

"You ever done this before?" Trevor asked.

Rebecca gave the herd-sire food and water, then walked back to where Trevor was standing.

"Birthed a cria? No. It was my first time."

"Looks like it's going pretty well so far," Trevor observed as Blue Mist got back on her feet.

Rebecca watched the alpaca sway back and forth, in much the same way she had earlier. "She's yet to finish her delivery and Little Blue has to stand on her own and nurse."

"That'll all happen, in due time," Trevor predicted.

Sure enough, Blue Mist began slowly but surely to deliver the placenta.

Seeing all was going exactly as it should, Rebecca turned back to Trevor, "Listen, about what you did for me tonight—"

He shushed her with a look. "It's nothing you wouldn't have done for me."

Rebecca checked on her alpaca, then turned back to him, "You were right about the fence."

Trevor's expression turned grim. He took off his hat and swept a hand through his damp hair. "I would have preferred not to be."

"How many cattle are still on the loose?"

Trevor undid the snaps on his coat. "Thirty or so is the rough estimate. Once steers get spooked like that, well, they can run pretty fast and far."

Glad the northern front moving through had forced the temperature down into the very comfortable low seventies once again, Rebecca asked, "What about Vince? Did he really bring more cattle back with him?

Trevor shook his head. "Nowhere to put 'em now. He sent them to another of his ranches, with the two hired hands he employs at the Circle Y."

"What about the rest of his cattle now?"

"The cattle ranchers with nonorganic herds are taking them in, five or ten here, five or ten there. It'll have to stay that way until he gets his fence fixed."

"Look," Rebecca whispered.

Little Blue was getting to her feet. Though wobbly, she was able to stand and find her way to her mama. Rebecca touched Trevor's arm. "I think she's going to nurse."

Little Blue rooted around, making that soft urgent sound, until she found what she was looking for. She fastened her lips over her mother's teat and began to suckle, awkwardly at first, then more and more confidently.

Rebecca and Trevor watched in silence, taking in the wonder of the moment.

Eventually, Trevor wrapped his arm around her shoulders. "You look tired," he said.

"I know. But I can't rest yet."

"Vince come by or send anyone to pick up Coco?" Trevor asked.

Rebecca shook her head. "I've been taking her out to go to the bathroom—on a leash—every couple of hours. I guess I should have tried to call Vince and let him know I have her, but I haven't really had the time."

"Morning is soon enough," Trevor said. "Meantime, can I get you anything?"

"Coffee would be great. But I gave the last of it away. There's none made."

"I'll go put on a fresh pot, and see to the pup," Trevor said.

He slipped from the barn.

Rebecca continued to watch the cria nurse until the

little alpaca had finished and both mother alpaca and cria lay down to rest.

Exhausted, Rebecca headed for the house.

Trevor was just pouring the coffee into two mugs when Rebecca stepped through the door. She looked gorgeous—tousled, exhausted and wet through and through. "Had I known you intended to make a run for the ranch house I would've left you my slicker."

She flashed a weary smile. "Then you would've been soaked to the skin."

Better than seeing her standing there, shirt and jeans clinging wetly to every delectable curve, Trevor thought.

She wiped her face on a dish towel.

Her hand trembled as she reached for the coffee.

His heart filled with a depth of feeling he didn't expect. "You've got to get some rest," he told her gruffly.

"I need to keep checking on Blue Mist and Little Blue for the next few hours, make sure they nurse again."

Trevor consulted his watch. "Tell you what. It's one-thirty now. I'll hang out in the stable, keeping watch over them while you catch a quick nap. I'll wake you at three-thirty. Or sooner, if need be. Tell you where things stand."

Her lips slid out in the stubborn pout he was beginning to know so well. And could never stop wanting to kiss.

She tilted her head at him, independent as ever. "It's not your job to watch over the animals on my ranch."

Just as it wasn't his job to want her so bad he ached. Trevor shrugged, adjusted his stance to ease the pressure building at the front of his jeans.

He turned away from her, and looked at the rain

still coming down in torrents. It drummed against the house and ground and filled the dark of night with a repetitive hush.

It was the kind of night a man and a woman should be huddled under the covers. Wrapped in each other's arms. After first...

Trevor swallowed so much coffee, he nearly burned his throat.

He really had to stop thinking like this.

Aware she was watching him over the rim of her cup, he told her the truth. "I'm too wound up to sleep for a while anyway. So I might as well be doing something productive." *Other than seducing you.*

Rebecca ran her hands through her hair, thinking. She sank into a kitchen chair, then started suddenly as the next thought hit. "Oh my... I forgot to ask. What about your herd, Trevor...?"

Finally, some good news. "All fine," Trevor was pleased to report. "Fence held. Didn't lose a one, although half a dozen of my white Charolais came nose to nose with some of Vince's Black Angus." At her surprised look, Trevor explained, "Generally, cattle herd together in a storm for protection. Especially when lightning and thunder are involved. Fortunately there was a double row of fence between them."

Rebecca propped her chin on her hand. "Why didn't yours stampede the way Vince's cattle did?"

Trevor grimaced, aware the whole calamity this evening could easily have been prevented with proper management. "I had far fewer animals housed in each of my pastures that adjoin your three. The cattle didn't feel they were trapped to begin with. Trapped cattle tend to be more nervous, kind of the way people are in crowds."

Rebecca worried her bottom lip with her teeth. "I

know what you mean about that. I hated some of the tours that had us packed in like sardines in a can."

Trevor pulled up a chair next to her. Their knees touched under the table. She didn't move away. "What was the worst?"

A rueful expression crossed her face. "I had a group of senior citizens who had always wanted to see the ball drop in Times Square on New Year's Eve, and they insisted on being right out in the middle of the melee." Rebecca made a comical face, recalling. "Of course they got too cold and had to use the facilities and some of them eventually needed to sit down and there was no place to sit down."

"I'm sure you handled it with aplomb." Just like the catastrophe tonight.

Rebecca flashed a weary smile. "I got everybody through it. And then swore never again. If a senior tour was crazy enough to try it, they'd have to get another guide."

"And did they?"

"Oh yeah." She sat back in her chair and stretched her long legs out in front of her. "There's no limit to people doing wild and crazy things."

If she stayed here much longer he was going to pull her into his arms, and he had no business putting the moves on any woman who had been through what Rebecca had this evening.

He stood and moved away. "I thought you were going to get some rest."

She exhaled slowly and stood, too. "You sure you don't mind?"

Although it took every ounce of willpower he had, he put his hands on her shoulders and pivoted her in the direction of her bed. "I don't mind."

* * *

Trevor should have known she wouldn't do as he ordered. Half an hour later, Rebecca stepped back into the barn. It had finally stopped raining and the air smelled as fresh and clean as she looked. He couldn't help it; he was glad to see her. "You showered."

She pirouetted so he could see her clean navy T-shirt and boot-cut jeans. "I'm glad you could tell."

"Well, I've got some good news for you." Trevor inclined his head at the stall that housed Blue Mist and Little Blue.

Blue Mist was standing patiently.

Little Blue was positioned beneath her, head tilted toward her mama's tummy, nursing contentedly.

Rebecca sauntered nearer. Hands in her pockets, she rocked back on her heels and observed. She had dried her hair, and left it long and loose, instead of putting it up. He appreciated the way she looked in braids but he liked her honey-blond hair this way, too, silky straight, swinging against her shoulders.

Reluctantly, Trevor turned his attention back to the activity in the stall. "That's a good healthy suckle," Trevor said.

Rebecca nodded, moving close. "Amazing how quickly they're up and running around, compared to human babies, isn't it?" she asked softly.

Sharing in her wonderment, Trevor wrapped his arm about her shoulders. "That's what comes from traveling on four feet instead of two." He appreciated the way she leaned into him. "Takes baby birds a mite longer, for instance."

She turned to face him, the warm abundance of her breast brushing his chest. "You're a regular font of information."

Trevor pushed away the urge to explore her soft womanly curves. "I did major in agriculture in college."

She released a beleaguered breath. "Bet you never figured you'd be helping a neighbor out by tracking down her alpacas."

"Actually," Trevor admitted reluctantly, "I was worried about that," which was why he had put up the double fence where he could, "but I never figured it'd happen the way it did."

Without warning, Rebecca's eyes filled with tears. Embarrassed by the show of emotion, she stepped away.

Guilt came, swift and hard. "I'm sorry."

"You didn't do anything to cause it." She wiped her lashes with the pad of her index finger.

He wrapped her in a comforting hug. "I didn't have to remind you of the enormity of what nearly happened right now, either."

"Damn, Trevor. I could have lost everything." Her voice was muffled against his chest. He felt the warmth of her breath through his shirt.

He sifted his fingers through the shimmering softness of her hair, lifted her face to his. "But you didn't," he said gruffly.

"Thanks to you." A hiccup caught in her throat, and then all the emotion she had been holding back this entire time came pouring out. She cried long and hard, the silent sobs shaking her chest. Her arms came up to wrap around his neck. He folded her closer still. Continued stroking one hand through her hair; the other gently massaged her back.

"Thanks to an awful lot of people," he added.

She sniffed. "But you're the one who rescued most of the alpacas."

"Only because I left the cattle finding to everyone

Cathy Gillen Thacker 163

else," he said, aware he had never felt like anyone's hero the way he did right now.

She looked up at him gratefully. "You saved my ranch, Trevor. You saved me."

She sounded so distraught he couldn't bear it. "You saved yourself with your cool head and ability to marshal all the help we needed to get the situation under control." He stroked her shoulder to quiet her.

"But the point is, I couldn't have done it without you, Trevor. If you hadn't been here to clue me in, taught me that ranchers help each other, told me whom to call tonight, I wouldn't have known where to start. I might have lost precious time. Might have…" Her voice broke.

She started to cry again.

And this time Trevor couldn't help it.

Couldn't not follow his heart and gut any more than he could have not helped her this afternoon when all hell broke loose.

"No more argument," he told her, gruffly glancing over his shoulder. "Little Blue and her mama are fine. We're getting you back to the house."

"Trevor."

Not about to let her argue her way out of what common sense dictated she needed—sleep, and plenty of it—he slid a hand beneath her knees and swung her, still crying, still protesting, up in his arms. He carried her out of the barn, across the yard. Clouds were dispersing. The hint of a crescent moon and a sprinkling of stars shone overhead. Everything smelled brisk and new.

He propped the door with his foot, then his back, and carried her on inside, not stopping to put her down in the kitchen as she probably expected, but moving deliberately through the house, on up the stairs, to the big four-poster bed she had bought along with the house.

He set her down beside it. "No argument. You're getting two hours of sleep. Right here. Right now."

Holding on to her with one hand clamped to her shoulder, he leaned across her to toss back the covers. "Now can you take it from here, or am I going to have to strip you down, too?"

She angled her chin at him, anger sweeping away her tears. "You are so hilarious, Trevor McCabe."

Trevor noted with pleasure his bold move had achieved something. "Well, at least you stopped crying," he noted in satisfaction.

Her golden-brown eyes sparked again—with an entirely different emotion.

"Only—" she went on tiptoe, surprising him as much as he had just stunned her "—so I could do this."

Okay, Rebecca thought, so this was not what she should be doing right now. Not nearly.

But she couldn't help herself.

She had been wanting to kiss Trevor ever since he had strode into the stable tonight, bringing the first two recovered alpacas with him. By the time he'd arrived with Black Onyx, some six more search and rescues later, she was so enamored of the strong courageous, generous-to-a-fault man Trevor McCabe had grown up to be she could barely stand it.

She had thought she didn't want or need any man to rescue her. She'd said she didn't want to be involved, physically, emotionally, or any other way with anyone right now. And she could hold to that decision easily, except when Trevor was around. And it was darn near impossible to force back the rush of emotion inside her when she was in his arms like this, feeling his mouth moving over hers.

He kissed her like there was no tomorrow. As if yesterday had always belonged to them, the future theirs for the taking. All she had to do was muster the courage to see where this blossoming friendship and fierce physical attraction between them led.

And that wasn't hard to do, either, not when his tongue was playing with hers, his hands were moving in her hair, the powerful muscles of his chest abrading her breasts. One arm slid down her back, flattening her against him, thigh to thigh. In the feminine heart of her, she could feel the tingly heat starting, her knees weakening, her whole body swaying as she threw herself into the kiss.

He stopped kissing her long enough to say, "This isn't…"

She caught his face in her hands, looked deep into his eyes, and whispered, "Yes, it is."

They were celebrating life. Victory. Over the elements. Over fear of intimacy. Over just about everything, because when she was in his arms like this, when he was sliding his hands beneath her T-shirt, over her ribs, to gently cup her breasts, she knew there was nothing finer, nothing more exciting or satisfying than the potential of making love with him.

"I want you." His lips left hers to take a thorough tour of her neck.

A shiver of want went through her. "I want you, too."

She parted the edges of his Western-style work shirt with a single jerk, sending the metal snaps flying.

He stopped kissing her long enough to grin as she smoothed her palms over the warm, satiny muscles of his chest. His pecs were tight, his nipples just as hard as hers.

Rebecca had never gotten why people in books and movies got so caught up in the touching, discovering.

Now, finally, she knew.

She couldn't get enough of him. The salty taste of his skin. The hardness of him, pressing through his jeans. The tenderness of his hands, as he divested her of her shirt, too.

Her bra went next.

His eyes darkened. She had never felt more beautiful than at that moment, seeing herself reflected in his gaze. "I knew it would be like this," he whispered, bending her backward from the waist. His lips touched where his hands had been.

Fire swept through her.

Aware this was every fantasy she had ever had come true, she gasped as his hands undid the snap and zipper on her jeans.

Holding her against him, one of her legs caught between both of his, he eased his palm beneath the elastic on her French-cut panties.

Quivering as he found her, Rebecca lifted her mouth to his. Kisses poured out of them, one after another. Feelings built. Desire exploded in liquid, melting heat. By the time he had her jeans and boots and panties off, she thought she was going to die if he didn't take her soon.

She helped him undress, too.

The first sight of him made her mouth go dry and her heart beat all the harder. "Oh. My."

"Why, Miz Rebecca, I think you're pretty sexy, too."

He searched his wallet, finally coming up with a rumpled condom packet that looked as though it had been there a while.

Grinning, he tumbled her onto the bed.

"Let me." Feeling sexier, more adventurous than she ever had in her life, she tore the wrapper with her teeth. Slowly, seductively helped roll it on. And then there was no more waiting. He was shifting her onto her back, parting her thighs with his knee, making sure she was as ready as he, and then one slow smooth motion later, they were one.

The first connection of body to body was magic. Their kisses only amplified it. And then there was no more waiting, no more patience, only white-hot heat, urgent need and passion and satisfaction unlike anything Rebecca had ever felt.

Trevor couldn't believe it was over so soon. He'd waited a lifetime to find a woman like this, a woman who could turn his world upside down, make him want, make him need, make him feel as if he could be everything to her, knowing damn sure she was all to him.

Fearing he was too heavy for her, he shifted off and away from her, taking her with him as he moved.

"I'm sorry," he murmured against the tousled silk of her hair.

Rebecca stiffened. She pushed herself up on her elbow so she could look at his face. "For...?"

Trevor let his hands sculpt the beautiful lines of her face, all the while holding her searching gaze.

"What else?" He flashed her a lopsided grin. "Rushing." He bent to kiss the curve of her shoulder, the U of her collarbone, the uppermost curve of her breasts. "When this happened, I had figured to really take my time. Make it last."

Rebecca sighed, stretched, glanced at the clock. "It is three-thirty in the morning," she reminded him.

Trevor wasn't using that excuse.

"The time doesn't have anything to do with it."

Trevor cupped the weight of her breasts in his hands, laved the tender pink tips with his tongue.

"I just couldn't wait to bury myself deep inside you. But now that we've taken the edge off, so to speak…"

Appreciating the way she quivered when he touched her, Trevor paid homage to her other breast. "We can do it all over again, and this time, sweetheart—" he paused to blaze a trail that went lower still "—I am really planning to take my time."

Trevor hadn't been kidding when he said he wanted to take his time making love to her, Rebecca thought half an hour later. If the first time they had made love had been all speed and heat, sheer male-female aggression and possession, the second time was all soft, hot languid kisses and tender-sweet caresses; it was finding a way to satisfy each other without bodies joining; it was finding humor in the lack of protection they needed to be really, truly together again.

Nevertheless, satisfaction came, for both of them, and they fell asleep wrapped in each other's arms.

Rebecca woke at four-thirty as Trevor was climbing back into bed. She lifted her head.

"I went to check on Blue Mist and her cria. Both are doing fine. When I left the barn, Little Blue was nursing again."

"Oh, good."

"I took care of Coco, too, so you've got another hour or two you can spend sleeping again. I suggest you use it."

And use it Rebecca did, snuggling right back into Trevor's arms.

She loved the way he felt pressed up against her, loved the warm safe way he made her feel.

Common sense told her she would be a fool to get too used to it; after all, they weren't even dating, but for the moment she intended to accept what joy came her way.

When the alarm rang at five-forty-five, she shut it off and eased out of bed.

To her relief, Trevor barely stirred.

Now that the tumultuous lovemaking was over, she needed time to sort out her feelings.

The sun rose in the east as she stepped outside and made her way across the yard, to the barn.

The herd was restless, but Rebecca didn't know what to do about pasturing them. The fence was broken down in all three sections. She had no rails to fix it. No mesh fence to put up. Meantime, thanks to Vince's neglect of his new puppy, she still had Coco to watch over, too.

Rebecca went back in the house, snapped a leash on the dog and took her out to the front yard, well away from the barn.

She was standing there, waiting for the chocolate lab to sniff out just the right spot, when Vince's Escalade turned in to her drive.

He parked, got out and came toward her. His eyes were bloodshot, his face rimmed with beard, his usual smug, superior attitude nowhere to be found.

"I heard you had my pup." He knelt down to pet Coco. Then stood. Shook his head. "I also heard she caused the stampede."

"It was a lot of factors," Rebecca said bluntly, not about to cut him any slack. "All combined, they led to disaster."

Trevor had been right, if she was going to pasture

alpacas next to their cattle, they needed better barriers between the three ranches.

She—a novice rancher—might not have known better, but someone with Vince's experience and background probably had.

Rebecca looked at Vince. "What are you going to do about the fence?"

Vince straightened. His glance touched on Trevor's pickup truck, still sitting next to her house. No expression readily apparent on his face, he turned back to Rebecca. "I'm going to put in barbed wire. It's the cheapest, most efficient way to keep 'em apart."

Rebecca stiffened in alarm. "I can't have barbed wire next to my alpacas."

Vince shrugged, unconcerned. "So double up on fence along the property line between the Primrose and the Circle Y. You can do whatever you want on your side, use mesh or more split rail. That's your business and your decision. But I've got to worry about my own. And right now I've got cattle penned up all over the place. I have to bring my herd back as quickly as possible. It's as simple as that." He took the leash from Rebecca.

The pup looked back at Rebecca, her expression sad as could be.

"What are you going to do about Coco?" Rebecca asked. If she'd dug her way out once, she could do it again. The Lab pup was lucky she hadn't been stomped to death in the resulting melee.

Vince shrugged. He patted the pup's head before putting her in his Escalade. "I'm going to do the only thing I can at this point—put her in the house, in a steel crate, and hire a dog walker to come by and care for her every day."

* * *

"It's a good plan, a reasonable one. Why are you upset?" Trevor asked over breakfast. "I'd think you'd have enough to do, just seeing to your own concerns."

Rebecca set a platter of fluffy golden-brown biscuits on the table. "He doesn't love that puppy."

"Vince isn't mistreating her, either."

"Coco's lonely." Rebecca sat down and took a stab at her eggs.

"She has a way of making friends. She'll find someone on his ranch—a cowboy, someone—to give her the affection she craves."

Rebecca tried to take comfort in Trevor's certainty—and worried anyway.

"And if she doesn't?" Rebecca found she had lost her appetite.

Trevor leaned over and fed her a bite of melon. "She will. Anyone who loves dogs is going to love that lab. They won't be able to help themselves."

Rebecca returned the favor, by hand-feeding Trevor a strip of bacon. She tilted her head. "So you think she's a cutie, too."

Trevor's brow lowered in gruff warning. "She's not our dog. Spend your time worrying about Blue Mist and Little Blue and the rest of your herd."

Another vehicle rumbled up the drive.

They looked out the window in tandem, saw Greg Savitz, the insurance agent stepping out of his car, a camera in his hand, a grim look on his face.

This, Rebecca thought, could not be good.

Chapter 10

Greg Savitz strode toward Rebecca and Trevor. The thirty-year-old married man was dressed for business in a shirt, tie and slacks. He had a camera in one hand, a clipboard in the other. "Heard you had a little trouble here yesterday."

Rebecca nodded.

Greg paused to shake hands. "I'm going to have to inspect the damage."

Rebecca had figured as much. "Will my policy pay for a new fence?"

Greg shook his head. "The coverage you selected only covers the outbuildings, the house and the herd."

Rebecca sighed. "That's what I thought." She led him into the barn. "Luckily, my alpacas are fine."

"You were able to recover them all?" Greg asked, pausing to make a few notes.

Rebecca looked at Trevor, unable to contain her gratitude for all he had done. "With other ranchers' help, yes."

"Well, that's good," Greg said, studying the rafters

overhead. "What about a mister and fan cooling system for this barn?"

"I purchased one. I'm going to install it as soon as possible."

"Yourself?" Greg gave her a surprised look.

"Yes," Rebecca said, trying not to think how difficult it was going to be to mount the turbofans on the ceiling, along with the low-pressure water nozzles, temperature gauge and PVC pipe.

Although it appeared to be costing him not to jump in and offer his help for that, Trevor let Rebecca conduct her business and remained silent.

Greg's brow retained a skeptical tilt. He took a few photos, then walked out of the barn to the latter two pastures, where the broken, splintered fence was evident. He examined the weak, weathered wood and took a few more pictures. Frowned.

"I can feel the bad news coming," Rebecca rocked forward on her heels. "You might as well spit it out."

"I screwed up by not getting out here to inspect the property at the time the policy was issued. I assumed everything was in order. I shouldn't have."

Dread pooled in the pit of her stomach. "What are you talking about?"

Greg rubbed at the back of his neck. "The incident yesterday indicates mismanagement on your part, Rebecca. As per the terms of the contract you signed, your insurance coverage has been suspended until a new fence is put in and a proper cooling and ventilation system installed in the barn."

"She's not going to need that temperature-wise for at least another month," Trevor put in, on her behalf.

"You and I know that," Greg agreed, "and had the fence been in satisfactory condition and the stampede yesterday not occurred, we would let that slide. But there was a big catastrophe here yesterday that could easily have been avoided. The insurance company can't overlook that."

Rebecca wanted to make sure she understood. "So you're leaving me without any coverage until those items are fixed?"

"I'm sorry, Rebecca. I've got no choice." Greg frowned. "And there's one more thing."

How could it possibly get any worse? Rebecca wondered.

"Because of the incident last night, the Primrose alpaca operation is now considered high risk, and your rates are going up another fifty percent, effective immediately."

"I don't know what I'm going to do." Rebecca paced back and forth. "I can't even take the alpacas out, except on a leash. I have nowhere to safely pasture them, now they know they can break through the existing split rail fence without much effort at all." Miraculously, the aging wood in the first pasture was still intact on all four sides. But she couldn't put all eleven alpacas in the same pasture at the same time, and she couldn't risk so much as a stray cat or dog getting into the pasture with them and causing another stampede.

She'd been lucky yesterday; she hadn't suffered any loss of life. Rebecca couldn't count on being that fortunate again.

Trevor regarded the waterlogged land with a pensive expression. "I've got to see to my own herd, but after that I can go into town and get some mesh fence. If we were to subdivide this first ten-acre pasture into three sections, you could put them all in here for now. There's plenty of room."

Rebecca had been thinking the same thing, but to hear it from him, rankled. He was speaking—and acting—as if he ran this property. And he didn't. She went toe-to-toe with him. "Don't you think that's my decision to make?"

Trevor gave her the same look Rebecca's father gave her whenever Luke thought she needed to acknowledge her inability to manage on her own and accept Luke's help. Trevor's lips formed an uncompromising line. "I don't want to play games with you, Rebecca."

One night of passion, and already he was trying to tell her what to do! She jerked her chin at him. "And I don't want you trying to take charge of my life."

His eyes narrowed. "You didn't seem to mind me helping you out with your problems last night."

"That's because it was an emergency situation and I had no choice!"

He stepped closer yet. "And this isn't?"

The heat from his body engulfed her. "I can manage my own affairs, thank you very much."

Unhappiness darkened his hazel eyes. "What are you trying to say to me?"

She swallowed, figuring he would not take this well. "I think last night was a bad idea."

Trevor's gaze raked her slowly and deliberately. "The me saving your ranch for you, or the part where we made love?"

The needling sarcasm in his low tone had her flushing self-consciously.

Determined not to back off from the boundaries she'd set, she said, "Both."

Ignoring the slight curl of resentment to his lips,

she continued resolutely, "It was great of you, Trevor. I appreciate it."

He braced his legs apart and folded his arms in front of him. "The taking charge of the alpaca rescue part."

"Yes. That part was wonderful. But—" Rebecca twisted her hair into a long rope and knotted it on the back of her head "—we shouldn't have started anything else no matter how grateful I was."

"Grateful," he echoed in disbelief.

She gestured listlessly. "You know how overly emotional I was after the birth of Little Blue."

His voice turned husky with the memory. "You were ecstatic. You had every right to be."

Rebecca turned her gaze to the sun climbing over the rain-drenched meadow.

The last twenty-four hours had been a roller coaster of emotion. "But my joy over that was no reason to tumble headlong into your arms." She was speaking as much to herself as to him.

"So you're saying that's all it was," he said as he searched her face. "A reaction to catastrophe and elation."

That was all it could be. "It was a lot to handle in one night."

He said nothing. He didn't have to—it was clear he didn't believe a word of what she was saying. She inhaled deeply and tried again, knowing even if she wasn't saying it right, their lovemaking had been too much too soon. "I've got enough on my plate already. I can't start a relationship." Especially with a man who could easily come in and take over every aspect of her life.

She didn't want to be told what to do.

Judged by what she did not do.

Abruptly, he looked as satisfied as he had when

they'd climaxed together that last time. "So you admit it wasn't just a fling on your part?"

She admitted she never had flings.

Working to keep him where she needed him—at arm's length—Rebecca swallowed and said, "I admit it was a mistake, one I have no intention of repeating."

The irked but undefeated look on Trevor's face as he walked away uppermost in her mind, Rebecca went back into the barn and set about giving all her alpacas food and water. Satisfied the herd was okay for the moment, Rebecca went back into the house. She put in a call to Tyler, telling him that Little Blue had entered the world, healthy as could be. The vet said he would be over later that day to check on the cria and again the following day to give Little Blue a CDT shot, Vitamin A and D, and a selenium shot.

Rebecca thanked him and telephoned her brother, Jeremy. "Are you working at the hospital today?" she asked.

"You know I have Wednesdays off, at least for now."

"Plans?"

"I'm going to look at ranch property for myself. See if I can't find something in my price range."

Rebecca knew his price range, fresh out of residency. If he wanted land with the house, whatever he could afford was probably going to be a fixer-upper, in the extreme. Although why Jeremy—who had zero interest in either crops or cows—was insisting on being a gentleman rancher, she did not know. "Can you put that off and come over and help me out? I've got to fix the fence. At least part of it, so I can put my alpacas outside."

"Yeah, I heard about that, but Susie is the one with the know-how in that department."

"She's mad at me."

"So apologize to her. You know you owe her."

"She'll think I'm only doing it to get her to help me."

"Well, if that's the case, I wouldn't blame her for not helping you." *Click.*

Rebecca stared at the phone. She couldn't believe Jeremy had hung up on her. Then again, that was typical for him, too. If he thought someone needed to do something, he would not help him or her avoid it.

Sighing, Rebecca stared at her phone. She dialed again. Grimaced.

Susie picked up on the second ring. "Carrigan Landscape Architecture."

"Hi, Susie."

"Rebecca."

At the sound of her older sister's stiff, cordial tone, Rebecca closed her eyes and rubbed at the bridge of her nose. She couldn't believe she was actually doing this, after making such a big to-do about being able to handle everything herself.

"Rebecca?" Susie said again, gently this time.

Rebecca drew a breath, tears of exhaustion pricking her eyes. "I need your help."

Susie was there an hour later with a roll of mesh fencing similar to what Trevor had strung along the property line, a sledge hammer and two bundles of metal fence stakes in the back of her pickup.

"There's no way we can do all three of your pastures," Susie said. "But we can at least get a half-acre run set up in the pasture closest to the house. You can rotate your herd in and out, until you have the time and resources to replace and repair all of the fencing."

"Thanks. I'm really going to owe you."

"No problem." Susie turned away without looking at her sister.

Rebecca caught Susie by the arm. "Susie. I really am sorry."

This time Susie looked Rebecca in the eye.

A mixture of guilt and embarrassment prodded Rebecca to continue. "It's not you, it's me. I'm the one who hasn't gotten over what happened before, with Grayson Graham."

Susie drew on her leather work gloves. As always, she did not suffer fools. "Don't you think it's about time you did?"

"Yeah, I do. Life is too short to dwell on what happened then."

"No kidding," Susie muttered in a way that reminded Rebecca that her older sister had been given her share of life-altering events to deal with, too, starting when Susie was sixteen. And yet somehow had come out all the stronger.

The two began to work, setting up stakes and rolling out fence. "This is really going to look bad at the Open House on Sunday, isn't it?" Rebecca said, after a while.

Susie wouldn't lie. "Yes. Having a temporary fence and pasture set up is only going to reinforce the word around town this morning."

"Which is…?" Rebecca asked, in dread.

"The Circle Y and The Primrose ranching operations are already out of control."

Rebecca knew she deserved at least some of the criticism. "What's the best way to repair the damage to my professional reputation?"

Susie pounded in a stake, then held it while Rebecca fastened the mesh fencing on the post. "Delay the Open House another month or so."

Together, Susie and Rebecca moved farther down the line. "I can't do that. I've got to be able to get some outside investors to put down money on Sunday if I want to pay off the balloon payment due next week on my operating loan."

Susie set up the next post with the casual expertise of someone who worked outdoors for a living. "You can't refinance?"

Rebecca made a face. "Not without insurance. Which was suspended until I get my mister and fan cooling system set up and all the fence repaired."

Susie sighed. "I wish I had the crew and the materials to help you, but I'm totally booked. Everyone wants new landscaping this time of year."

Rebecca told herself the sweat trickling down the back of her neck was due to the heat of the spring sunshine. "I'll figure something out."

"You sure?" Susie paused, all heart. "Because if it's just a question of money…"

Rebecca held up a hand. "I got myself into this mess. I'll get myself out."

Knowing time was of the essence—she now had less than four days to prepare for the Open House—Rebecca spent the afternoon rotating her herd-sires, females and nursing mother and cria, in and out of the single fenced pasture. It wasn't an ideal situation, but at least she was able to get the animals out of the barn for a few hours.

By the time evening came, she was exhausted.

And lonely as could be.

Part of her had expected Trevor McCabe to call or come by. He hadn't done either. It was what she wanted, for the two of them to maintain separate lives. So why was she so unhappy?

* * *

Thursday passed with no word from Trevor. Rebecca saw a lot of activity on his cattle ranch, though. For a good part of the day, his livestock had been loaded up and driven off for parts unknown. When Trevor wasn't doing that, he was out on his ranch, moving his remaining cows around.

Around dinnertime, she saw Tyler drive down to Trevor's place and walk out to the pasture with him, vet bag in hand.

Eventually, Tyler left the Wind Creek and drove over to The Primrose. "Everything okay over at Trevor's place?" Rebecca asked as she escorted him to the barn.

"No, unfortunately. Trev's got a real mess on his hands."

Alarm stiffened her spine. "Why? What's wrong?"

Tyler frowned. "He's got some sick cattle. We're hoping the whole herd hasn't been infected, but it's too soon to tell."

Maybe she shouldn't feel hurt Trevor hadn't called her to tell her what was going on over there—especially given how unhappily they had parted. But she did. "Is that why he's been taking cattle off the ranch today?" Rebecca asked.

"Using Miss Mim's binoculars again?" Tyler teased.

Rebecca blushed. Caught red-handed.

"Trevor told me about that," Ty said.

Rebecca shrugged. "They do come in handy. Seriously, what's going on?"

"Looks like some of Vince Owen's cattle infected Trevor's with an antibiotic-resistant bacterial disease."

Tyler's tone told her how serious the malady was.

"Can it be treated?"

"Yes. That's the good news. The bad news is the hit

Trevor is going to take financially because of the exposure." Briefly, Tyler explained, finishing, "This could severely impact his profits for the year. Worse, the other ranchers who rounded up and temporarily housed the Circle Y cattle are suffering the same fate with their own herds. This strain of bacteria wasn't present in Laramie County prior to this."

A fact which must make Vince Owen very unpopular, Rebecca thought.

"It could be an epidemic," Rebecca murmured.

Tyler nodded. "Starting to look that way."

Hating the one-sided turn their relationship had just taken—as if Trevor was good enough and smart enough to help her, but she wasn't viewed in the same way, Rebecca choked back her disappointment. "How's Trevor holding up?"

Tyler McCabe looked at her as if he knew there was a lot going on between her and Trevor. "You want to know that," Tyler said drily, "you need to ask him yourself."

The men in Laramie, Texas had a lot in common, Rebecca thought, after Tyler McCabe had given Little Blue and Blue Mist clean bills of health, and left.

They were always pushing a woman to do what they thought best.

Yet she couldn't just stand by and do nothing in Trevor's hour of need, especially given the way he had come through for her. So she did the neighborly thing. Whipped up some dinner and headed over to the Wind Creek, wicker basket in hand. After all, what was it he had told her, neighbors didn't have to like each other or even get along, to lend a helping hand?

Only after she arrived and heard the outdoor shower outside the barn going did she realize she should have called ahead, to let him know she was dropping by.

Too late. Trevor stepped out, dripping water, a large bath towel wrapped around his waist. The look on his face told her he had known it was her. He strode past her, through the grass, toward the ranch house. "I gather you heard the bad news."

Trying not to recall how that hard masculine body had felt pressed up against hers, Rebecca struggled to keep up. "That Tyler had to administer medicine to your sick cattle, which decreases their value substantially?"

His features were grim. He held the door to the mission-style ranch house. "Can't sell a cow as organic if it's had antibiotics."

Admiring the whitewashed walls and red tile roof, Rebecca stepped inside. The U-shaped home was built around a shaded outdoor patio. It had a beamed cathedral ceiling, a wall of windows overlooking the central courtyard. A masculine family room with oversize leather furniture and a big stone fireplace comprised the front of the home.

Rebecca handed over the picnic basket, watched as he set it down. "You're sure your cattle got it from the Circle Y cattle?"

"Oh, yeah." Trevor led the way down one wing, his bare feet moving soundlessly across the muddy-red ceramic tile floor, to the laundry room off the kitchen.

He plucked a pair of navy blue briefs and a clean pair of jeans off the top of the clothes dryer. "They were nose to nose with my herd the night of the storm. Vince puts antibiotics and growth hormones in his feed, which makes his Black Angus grow bigger, faster and increases their value, since beef is sold by weight. But it also leaves them vulnerable to infection from some pretty harsh strains of bacteria."

Rebecca turned away seconds before the towel hit the floor. "Which is what your cattle have."

She heard, rather than saw, Trevor clothe his lower half. "I hauled off all the sick ones—they're now getting treatment at Tyler's ranch."

Trevor strode past her, looking mighty fine without shirt or shoes.

Heartbeat accelerating, Rebecca ventured only as far as the entrance to the kitchen. "Tyler uses his ranch for treating sick animals?"

Trevor ventured into what appeared to be a bedroom. "Yep, Healing Meadow Ranch is primarily a large animal veterinary facility, or the closest thing we have to a large animal vet hospital in these parts." He returned, buttoning up a long-sleeved burgundy twill shirt.

Telling herself she most definitely did not want to kiss him again, Rebecca asked, "How long before the cows get better?"

Trevor shrugged. "Couple weeks, probably, before they get a clean bill of health and I can sell them."

"You have to do that?"

Trevor nodded, a mixture of fatigue and disappointment showing on his face. "They're no longer organic, and I can't risk infecting the rest of the herd. Unfortunately, they're not going to bring a market price like what they would have had they not gotten sick."

"That's awful."

His expression did not change. "It's life."

Rebecca edged closer, taking in the soap and fresh-air scent clinging to his skin. "Has this ever happened before?"

A flash of anger glimmered in his hazel eyes. "Not anywhere near this degree."

Wishing she could comfort him physically, the way

he had her, without it meaning anything, Rebecca asked softly, "How much of your herd are you losing?"

He shifted his gaze to her lips. "Roughly a third."

She felt herself flushing with heat. "No wonder you're upset." she said. "Is there anything else I can do for you?"

Any hint of Texas hospitality faded. He moved brusquely toward the door. "I thought you said we weren't going to do that anymore."

Rebecca had no choice but to follow. "Y-you know what I meant," she stuttered.

"No. I'm not sure I do."

She took a deep breath. "I'm trying to be a friend."

"I can see that." He opened the doorway. Hand to her elbow, he ushered her on through. "I'm not sure I'm ready to be 'just friends.'"

"So that's how you ended it, just walking away," Teddy McCabe said, an hour later.

"What choice did I have?" Trevor opened up a soft flour tortilla and layered it with strips of grilled fajita-style chicken and grated cheddar cheese. "I'm not going to pretend I don't want to be in her bed again. I do."

Teddy added salsa, lettuce, sour cream and guaca-mole to his. "You could try giving her a little room."

Trevor opened two longnecks of Shiner Bock, and handed one to Teddy. "The last thing a woman like Rebecca needs is 'room' to run away."

"You think that's what she's doing?"

How the heck should he know? "She doesn't want a man in her life." Not the way he wanted to be...

"Any man or just you?" Teddy grinned.

Trevor exhaled roughly. "Both."

"You could pursue her."

Trevor hadn't been brought up to take advantage of a woman. "I'm not going to twist her arm to get her in bed with me again."

"No. You'll just leave that to Vince Owen."

Trevor lifted his head. "What are you talking about?"

Teddy scooped salsa onto a chip. "He's still telling everyone in town that Rebecca is going to be his woman by the end of the week."

Trevor savored a bite of the delicious dinner and tried not to think how much better it would have tasted had Rebecca been here with him. "That'll never happen," Trevor said.

Teddy shot him a skeptical glance. "Are you sure?"

Trevor set his jaw. "Rebecca's not that much of a fool."

"Then why is Vince Owen running around bragging like it's already a done deal?" Teddy asked.

Why indeed...?

"And why did he tell everyone the romance is starting tomorrow night?"

"How bad is it?" Amy asked, the following morning.

Rebecca had called her as soon as she'd opened the morning's mail, and Amy had stopped by on the way back from delivering a flatbed of plants to several of Susie's landscape projects. Rebecca knew that Amy— who had started her own nursery business from scratch, would not only understand—she might be able to offer some concrete business advice.

"Pretty bad." Rebecca handed the letter to Amy. "The investment group that now owns my mortgage and operating loan says they are sending out a representative Monday morning at 10:00 a.m. My balloon payment of twenty thousand dollars is due before my temporary operating loan rolls over into a permanent one."

"It also says you must show proof of insurance before the loan can go to the next phase."

"Which is a problem, because my coverage was suspended until I can get the fence in, the mister and fan cooling system up in the barn."

"And you have the Open House on Sunday, too."

Rebecca nodded, feeling so overwhelmed she barely knew where to start.

"Everyone is busy with their regular jobs during the week, but I can round up a crew to help you with the fence and the misting system over the weekend," Amy said.

But would it be too little too late to try and do all that on Saturday? Rebecca wondered.

"Any chance Elliott Allen can help you out with a refinancing package?"

"I talked to him on Monday. He said he might be able to, if I were to come up with a better business plan."

"So what's stopping you?" Amy asked.

What indeed?

Rebecca spent the rest of the morning running the numbers. She was going to have to lease out all seven of her female alpacas for pregnancy, and convince investors to use her two herd-sires for studs... She could borrow money from Susie for her ongoing operating costs until she got her situation straightened out. But that would confirm her father's opinion that she was not capable of running a business on her own.

Rebecca could take Elliott Allen's advice and ask Trevor for help putting together a better prospective for the Laramie bank. But with Trevor still ticked off at her for deciding the two of them needed to go back to being just friends that didn't seem a palatable option, either.

Rebecca walked out to the pasture, where Blue Mist and Little Blue were taking a turn, grazing and basking in the warm April sunshine.

"So that's the new one," a low voice stated behind her.

Rebecca turned to see Vince Owen walking up to join her. He looked as though he'd had a little sleep, a shower and a shave. His clothes were expensive and neatly pressed.

Behind him, two more pickups with his ranch insignia rumbled up the drive. Eight dusty, sweaty cowboys got out. Two more trucks—an electrician's and a plumbing truck—parked behind them. Two additional technicians got out.

Rebecca noted the beds of the pickup were piled high with wooden split rail fencing, similar to what had crumbled under the weight of the stampeding cattle, and rolls of mesh, similar to what Trevor and Susie had already put up.

"I've been thinking and I feel awfully bad about what happened the other night. It was my fault for not keeping Coco inside the house. I know you've got this Open House coming up, and you can't expect to do much business if you've got pastures with big sections of broken-down fence. I was going to just go with barbed wire on my side, but after thinking about it, I can see your point. That won't look right on The Primrose, and it might be hazardous to your alpacas. So I'd like to make amends by having eight of my hired hands repair the existing wood fence, run mesh inside of that, and the electrician and the plumber put up the mister and fan cooling system in your barn. So what do you say?"

Rebecca would have liked to turn Vince down.

But he was right.

She did need help. Now.

Did it really matter where that aid came from?

What was it Trevor said to her? *"You don't have to like your neighbor or even know 'em to lend a hand. Ranchers help each other out. That's the rule."*

What Vince was doing would go a long way to repair the damage done. "I'll pay for all of the materials and go half with you on the fence labor. And I'll reimburse you for the installation of the mister and fan cooling system in the barn, but I'm going to have to do it over time."

"No problem. We can work out a payment plan later. Even barter for it, if you want."

No way was she cooking dinner for Vince. Rebecca regarded her next-door neighbor warily. "Like what?"

Vince shrugged. "You could take care of Coco for me—walk her and care for her—when I'm away from the Circle Y."

That, Rebecca wouldn't mind. She loved the little puppy. And if she could bring love and affection into the chocolate Lab's life…it would not only be a good deed, it would ease Rebecca's mind. "Sounds good," Rebecca said. "But even if I were to groom and board Coco, it would take years to pay off the labor charges that way."

Vince looked unconcerned. "Then we'll add other stuff, as well. The point is, we can sit down and figure all that out later."

Rebecca didn't want that hanging over her any more than she wanted to be endlessly in debt to anyone. "We'll negotiate suitable compensation as soon as the labor is done and we know what all the charges are," she said. "Tomorrow morning okay with you for that?" That would give her the night to think of ways to repay the debt that did not involve her coming up with a great deal of cash.

"Sounds great to me." Vince stuck out his hand, to conclude the business. As they clasped palms, he smiled. "Now, what else can I do to help you get The Primrose up and running?"

Chapter 11

"**I**'m over at The Wagon Wheel restaurant," Tyler told Trevor at seven-thirty that evening. "You'll never guess who's here."

"And I probably don't want to," Trevor grumbled.

"Rebecca is having dinner with Vince Owen."

Trevor tensed, aware this was his worst nightmare coming true. He shoved a hand through his hair. "And that's my business because?"

His brother's voice dropped a goading notch. "Don't pretend you don't care." Ty paused, then reported, "He's really turning on the charm."

Trevor's misery multiplied. He rubbed the back of his neck and struggled to keep his emotions under control. "Rebecca's a grown woman, Ty. She can have a meal with whomever she pleases." *Even if it twists my gut into knots.*

Tyler grunted. "You know as well as I do that she would not be having dinner with him if she knew about the wager Vince Owen tried to make about her."

That was true enough. Trevor still didn't want to hurt or embarrass Rebecca that way. He knew how sensitive she was, how vulnerable her pride, which had already taken a huge hit. He wasn't sure she could stand up and make her sales pitch at her upcoming Open House if she knew what had been said about her, behind her back, even if only one man had been doing all the boasting. Best, he figured, to continue to spare her that humiliation.

Trevor studied the collection of frozen dinners in his freezer, the meager contents of his fridge. "Rebecca's not foolish enough to fall for Vince's line." He took out the lone carton of milk and upended it, drinking the remaining tablespoon or two of milk.

"That's what you thought about Jasmine. And she sure fell for it, hook, line and sinker. Or am I remembering incorrectly?"

The memory stung. Nevertheless, Trevor refused to overreact. "It's probably just a business dinner."

Tyler scoffed, his disbelief evident. "You come over here and take a look for yourself. And then tell me that." *Click.*

Trevor told himself he wasn't going to go.

And he kept vowing that even as he grabbed his wallet and strode out to his pickup truck.

It wasn't as if Rebecca was his woman.

Or any of his concern.

She'd made it clear to him that despite the days of spending time together and helping each other out that culminated in a night of powerhouse lovemaking, nothing concrete had changed. The two of them weren't going to be more than friends.

He didn't owe her anything.

It wasn't his job to protect her.

Nevertheless, twenty minutes later, he found himself walking in to The Wagon Wheel restaurant.

Rebecca was still sitting with Vince.

It didn't look as if she had gone to much effort for the outing.

She was clad in a long-sleeved white T-shirt, denim skirt and boots. Her hair was in two loose braids. Her cheeks were pink. Her eyes were on Vince.

They appeared to be disagreeing about something, albeit very quietly.

Trevor watched as Vince leaned forward persuasively, took Rebecca's hand, in his. She offered a tight smile—the kind a woman gave when someone was hitting on her, in unwelcome fashion.

Trevor looked Rebecca in the eye. "Sorry I'm late," he fibbed. He turned to her companion. "Vince." Then back to Rebecca. "Ready to go?" he asked, pretending they'd had other plans that trumped whatever she was doing now.

Recognition flickered in Rebecca's eyes. "Oh. Yes." She eased her hand from beneath Vince's. She looked Vince Owen in the eye. "Thank you so much for the drink and appetizer."

"Your parents are expecting us," Trevor said.

"Right." Rebecca clasped her handbag, and stood. "I'll get back to you tomorrow with that list," Rebecca told Vince.

Vince smiled as if he hadn't had his date stolen out from under him. "You do that," he said.

Trevor slid his hand beneath her elbow. He escorted her from the restaurant.

She didn't speak until they reached the parking lot behind the building and climbed into his pickup. Her cheeks pink with embarrassment, she waited until he had eased behind the steering wheel before she inquired coolly, "I assume you were fibbing about the meeting with my parents?"

Trevor started his truck and backed out. "You assume right."

She shot him a withering glare as he paused to turn right. "Don't expect me to thank you for getting me out of there."

As it happened, Trevor thought as his foot hit the accelerator, that was exactly what he had expected. Along with a heartfelt hug of gratitude and a kiss or two. "Wouldn't dream of it." He pushed the words through his teeth.

An uneasy silence fell between them as they drove through town, and out onto the country road leading to their ranches.

She clamped her arms in front of her and stared straight ahead. "I can handle Vince Owen."

Trevor released a short, humorless laugh. "Sure about that?"

Rebecca turned her glance to the passing scenery. "At least he doesn't try to kiss me every time he sees me."

Trevor inhaled the juniper fragrance of the soap and shampoo she used. "Maybe not yet," he allowed.

Rebecca whipped her head around. As she turned to face him, her left knee came up on the bench seat between them. He didn't even know why he was trying to warn her off and/or talk sense into her. Or why the sight of her bare calf above the boot should be such an incredible turn-on. Except that he knew how soft and smooth and toned her body was.

"What's that supposed to mean?" she demanded.

French-cut cotton panties weren't that much of a

turn-on, Trevor told himself. *Unless, of course, Rebecca was wearing them.*

Aware Rebecca was still waiting for an answer, Trevor bit out, "Nothing."

Rebecca put her boot-clad left foot back on the floor with a resounding stomp. "Obviously, you charged into The Wagon Wheel, intent on rescuing me. From what? The evil clutches of that madman?"

A more apt description couldn't have been made. Well, maybe it was a little over-the-top.

"Just promise me you'll be careful," Trevor insisted.

Rebecca threw up her hands, clearly not believing a word he said. "Of what exactly?" she snapped in mounting frustration.

Trevor knew the words sounded ridiculously paranoid even as they came out of his mouth. "Vince Owen is not a man you can trust. In fact, the more generous and helpful he seems, guaranteed—the less trustworthy he is."

"You sound jealous."

Trevor feigned cool. "You think so?"

"I know so!"

"Well, then." Trevor steered over to the side of the road, into the grass and put the truck into Park. "If I've been tried and convicted in your eyes," he drawled, releasing the catch on his safety belt, "I might as well do this."

Trevor hit the emergency blinkers and moved across the bench seat. Ignoring the astonished look on her pretty face, he took her into his arms, and covered her mouth with his.

He expected her to put up a fuss. But the deeper he kissed her, the more passionately she kissed him back.

His tongue touched hers. She met him stroke for

stroke, parry for parry. He groaned, crushing her closer against his chest, and heard her soft telltale whimper of acquiescence. And that was when the Escalade slowed, passed by, moved on. But not before they both got a look at the driver.

Vince Owen's face, turned straight at them was all the reminder Rebecca needed. Letting loose with a most unladylike word that perfectly summed up the situation, she extricated herself from the warm, hard cradle of Trevor's arms. "I hope you're satisfied!" she fumed.

Looking as if he wanted nothing more than to haul her back in his arms and resume kissing her with even more passion, Trevor stayed where he was. He lifted a querying brow.

"Obviously what happened just now was all for your rival's benefit," Rebecca stormed, her emotions vaulting completely out of control.

"Like I knew Vince was going to drive by here and catch us!" Trevor scoffed.

Rebecca tapped a lecturing finger against the hardness of his chest. "First of all, *you* were kissing *me,*" she pointed out.

"And you were kissing me right back!"

Her temper skyrocketing, she ignored that obvious truth. "And second of all, if he were going back to his ranch, he would have had to take this road to get there." A fact Trevor obviously knew.

"If I had wanted Vince to see me kissing you, I would have laid a big one on you in the restaurant."

Working to slow her thundering heart, Rebecca shrank against the window. "And sacrificed your reputation as a Texas gentleman? I don't think so."

Trevor shook his head, his expression unerringly

grim. Without another word, he fastened his seat belt, put the pickup truck in gear and steered back out onto the road.

Rebecca would have liked nothing more than to continue arguing with him.

Afraid they'd end up kissing again if she did so, she kept quiet until they arrived at The Primrose.

"Thank you for the ride home," she said politely.

"You're welcome." Trevor got out, too.

She dropped her purse inside the back door, then headed across the yard. "I'm not inviting you in."

Trevor looked as though he was settling in for the long haul. "So we'll talk out here."

Deciding the best thing to do was ignore him, Rebecca went in to the barn.

To her amazement, the fan and mister cooling system was up. A flick of the switch next to the door and a raft of cool air went flowing through the barn.

Aware they wouldn't need the system this evening, she turned it back off. Walking up and down the stalls, she checked on her herd. All had eaten their evening meal and still had plenty of water. Little Blue was nursing contentedly while Blue Mist stood by patiently, every bit the gentle, protective mama alpaca.

Satisfied all was well for the moment, Rebecca strolled back out of the barn. Flashlight in hand, she walked through all three pastures. The broken-down fence in pastures two and three had been completely repaired, sturdy mesh placed inside the perimeter.

Best of all, the Black Angus that had been moved back onto the Circle Y had been pastured on the other side of the ranch, well away from Rebecca's property line. That could only help her when she held her Open House on Sunday afternoon.

"I'm sorry I didn't get around to helping you with all this," Trevor said eventually, as they cut through the landscaped backyard, toward the ranch house.

Was that what he thought this was all about? Shocked, Rebecca turned her glance to Trevor. "I know you've had your hands full with sick cattle, and all that."

They stopped at the gazebo.

He sat down on one of the stone benches, gestured for her to do the same. "Sorry I messed up your date with Vince."

It was her turn to scoff. "No, you're not."

He flashed the sexy grin that turned her inside out. He rubbed his jaw, lifted his shoulder in a hapless manner. "Okay, I'm not." He watched as she settled a safe distance away from him. "Are you dating him?"

"No." Rebecca told herself she was glad they had the width of the gazebo between them. "Course not."

"Then why were you having dinner with him?"

She flattened her hands on either side of her and stretched her legs out in front of the bench. "He wanted to talk ranching."

Trevor watched her tug her skirt as low as it would go and cross her legs at the ankle. "And you wanted to listen."

Rebecca ran her fingers across her denim-clad thigh. "I felt I owed him that courtesy after he provided the labor for the work that had to be done around here."

"And?" Trevor's gaze seemed fixed on her hand.

Rebecca swallowed and looked Trevor in the eye. "It was a mistake. The way Vince does business will not work for me—it's too close to the financial edge. He's all about taking whatever shortcut he can find to get whatever goal he's set, regardless of whoever else he might mow down in the process. He seems to think that's just the cost of doing business, ranching or otherwise."

Trevor did not look surprised. "That sounds like Vince."

"And there's something else," Rebecca found herself admitting. She studied Trevor's expression. "The whole time Vince and I were in the restaurant, we were getting funny looks from the other diners. Or at least the men that were there."

Trevor shifted his gaze toward the house.

She knew a man avoiding answering when she saw one.

"Why? Did you have spinach and artichoke dip on your chin?"

Rebecca stood and walked over to stand next to him. "I'm serious, Trevor. Even before you showed up to publicly spirit me away, people were looking at me like I was…really stupid…for being there with Vince."

Trevor shrugged and turned his attention to the stars and the full moon shining overhead. Slowly, deliberately, he got to his feet. "Maybe they think you can do better, too," he said eventually.

Rebecca had to tip her head back to see into his face. "By dating you?"

He tilted his head down, slanted her a look. "There are worse things."

He had a point there. Rebecca sighed. "Like sleeping with you and telling myself it'll be okay."

"It would be all right," he countered softly, "if you'd let it continue."

A shudder of awareness swept through her, weakening her knees. "Friends and neighbors shouldn't make love on a whim," Rebecca insisted stubbornly.

"You're right about that," Trevor said.

Rebecca looked at him, unable to hide her surprise.

"But what if it's more than a whim?" Tenderness emanating from him, he sifted both hands through her hair. "What then?"

Rebecca knew, even before Trevor shifted her close and flattened a hand against her spine, that he was going to kiss her again. Gently, this time. Inquisitively. And that sensual exploration turned out to be even more devastating than the caress he'd laid on her when their passions were stoked, and their tempers were raging.

Sheer physical desire she might have been able to resist.

She definitely could have turned away any attempt to dominate her through sexual expertise.

But gentleness—wanting—were something else, especially when his emotions so closely mirrored hers. She hadn't been able to stop thinking about the way he'd made her feel, so cherished, so desired. Beautiful. Womanly. She hadn't been able to stop thinking about the expert caresses of his fingertips searching out all the pleasure points of her body, or the way he seemed to know intuitively what she needed.

She moaned as he cupped her face in both hands and held her head under his. She trembled as he caught her bottom lip between his teeth, and worried it gently with the edge of his tongue. And then he was kissing her full-out again, pushing her back against one of the white stone pillars, the warmth of his body blanketing hers.

Dampness pooled low, mingled with tingling heat. When he urged her up on tiptoe, inserted his knee between her thighs, she complied. His lips slid down her neck, even as his hands slipped beneath her T-shirt, to find the clasp of her bra. "I've missed you so much."

His confession thrilled and comforted her, and prodded her to honesty.

"Me, too." She stretched sinuously, as his palms kneaded her swollen flesh. "Too much."

Which made her wonder why she was fighting him, fighting this, anyway....

She felt his smile against her ear. Softly, he declared, "No such thing."

She gasped and he took her mouth again, hotly, decisively.

His thumbs traced the tender crests, rubbing back and forth, creating a hot, aching need.

"Oh, yes," she said, between slow, sipping kisses that had her arching wantonly against him. "There is."

She caught her breath as his hands found their way to the hem of her denim skirt, lifted it slightly, eased beneath.

"Not where we're concerned," he told her gruffly, in a way that almost had her believing it.

And then he was kissing her, again and again. His hands slid up her thighs, found their way between.

The next thing she knew, her panties were easing down. He was touching her there. Creating ripples of fire, of need.

She caught her breath as the sensations mounted, spread.

Trembling against his hand, she felt herself begin to slide inexorably toward the edge.

"Not...without...you," she said.

She struggled to find his zipper, pushed it down, even as the heat of his kisses spread outward, through her chest, across her shoulders.

The scent of his soap and cologne filled her senses as

he brought her to the brink, and she tortured him, too, first with delicate touches, then full-out exploration.

Wild with sensation, caught up in the recklessness of the moment, they drove each other into waves of passion, until neither could stand it anymore.

Catching her by the hips, he lifted her against the stone. The chill at her back contrasted with the heat in front of her, the rumpled clothing crushed between them.

And then he was part of her again, searching, taking.

Bringing her closer yet.

Both hands cupping her bottom, he held her right where he wanted, right where she needed to be, and then there was no more thinking, no more holding back, only hot, wet kisses and hotter pleasure.

She trembled and cried out.

He caught the sound with his mouth, and then, he, too was moaning, shuddering, thrusting ever deeper.

Together, they surrendered to the inevitable, to each other, to whatever this was, and would always be.

Rebecca came back to reality slowly.

She couldn't believe she had done this again.

Couldn't imagine *not* doing it again.

He set her down gently, brought up her panties, lowered her skirt. A kiss to the side of her neck, her ear, her temple. Then he was zipping up, fastening his belt. "Let's go upstairs to your bed."

Trembling, Rebecca armed herself with her only defense against him—humor.

She flashed him a crooked smile that belied the vulnerable way she felt inside. "You always want more."

Emotion trembled in his voice. "I want you."

"Trevor…"

He clasped her shoulders. "I want you, Rebecca. And I know you want me."

Rebecca tried to deny it. But when he put his lips to hers, when he kissed her like that, and swung her up into his arms, and carried her across the yard, all her excuses, all her defenses, began to fade.

"We're going to have to talk about this," she warned.

He swept through the door. "In the morning."

"Trevor—"

He strode up the stairs. "Talking about this always gets us into trouble, Rebecca."

He had a point there, she conceded reluctantly.

He made his way down the upstairs hall, to her four-poster bed. He deposited her next to it. "Feeling on the other hand, acting on those feelings, always leads to something good."

Rebecca trembled with a mixture of anticipation and need. "Lovemaking, you mean."

"And feeling close to you. And being close to you. And having you close to me."

Close felt good, Rebecca noticed as he divested her of her clothing, and helped her remove all of his. Close felt very good.

Giving in, Rebecca let him lead her where he wanted her to go, and in return, she led him, too.

By the time they fell asleep, she felt sated, secure and, much to her surprise, very much as if she was falling head over heels, deeply, irrevocably in love.

"You probably don't want to talk about this," Trevor said, the next morning. Nixing the idea of having breakfast together—and not so coincidentally, conversations just like this—Rebecca had dressed and headed straight to the barn at the crack of dawn. Figuring, hoping, he'd take the hint and go on back to Wind Creek.

He hadn't.

"Then I'm guessing we shouldn't," Rebecca replied, pasturing the last of her herd.

She didn't want anything ruining the wonderfully wild and passionate night they'd shared.

She was afraid if they talked too much, something would.

"I have to know."

Obviously not finished lending a hand, Trevor walked back to the barn with her.

"What kind of deal did you make with Vince Owen for all that labor on the fence, and the cooling system in the barn?"

Still doing her best to chase him away, Rebecca donned her leather work gloves. "Are you worried I might be offering him home-cooked dinners?"

Briefly, sheer male possessiveness flashed in Trevor's eyes.

Ignoring her hint, he pushed the wheelbarrow to the last stall. "Did you?"

Rebecca shoveled waste from the stall floor. "No. Of course not."

Trevor moved from stall to stall, right along with her. "Then what did you offer him?"

Rebecca welcomed the fresh morning air, moving through the barn, dispersing the fecund smell of animals quartered overnight.

She set her jaw. "And this is your business because…?"

Trevor's steady gaze never wavered. "I care about you."

Care. Not love.

He helped her empty the contents into the compost pile Susie would later pick up, to turn into fertilizer.

"I don't want to see you in a bad situation," Trevor continued.

Now he was sounding like her dad, and Susie, way back when. They'd tried to protect her, too. "You really don't trust me, do you?"

"In what sense?"

Hooooo boy. Not a question the rancher should have asked.

"I'm not worried about you being unfaithful to me," he said.

His confidence both thrilled and annoyed her. She wanted him to be possessive in a sexual and romantic sense. Yet she wanted her freedom to do as she pleased, without worrying over his reaction, too. "That's good." She paused to wet her lips. "Although..."

He lifted a brow.

Throwing caution to the wind, she finished her thought. "I don't recall anyone saying anything about being exclusive."

"We're exclusive, all right," he told her gruffly, the same kind of passion in his hazel eyes that was there every time he took her into his arms.

Rebecca knew, as a fiercely independent woman, she should have resented the assumption on his part.

She didn't.

Maybe because...although he hadn't told her he loved her, the way she now knew she loved him...his attitude was still a step in the right direction. The direction she wanted them to go.

"Then what are we arguing about?" she asked, perplexed.

He brought his arms up to hold her close. "You. Being in over your head."

Resentment rankled in her heart once again. "And not having the sense to know it?" She elbowed her way out of his embrace.

He caught her to him once again. "I didn't say that."

She planted her hands on her hips anyway. "But you think it."

"Look." Trevor sifted his hands through her hair, tilted her face up to his. "I know Vince. He's never been the kind of guy that gives something for nothing. There isn't a philanthropic bone in his body. Yet he lends you eight of his hired hands, brought in from all three of his ranches, to make the necessary repairs."

Rebecca sighed. About that much at least she had a very plausible explanation. "Vince said they were in the area anyway, to move cattle to his other two ranches. He also said he felt bad about Coco digging out and causing the stampede that caused the damage, and he wanted to make reparations."

Trevor stepped back and away from her. "That sounds good on the surface."

Rebecca studied him. Suddenly, she had the same strange feeling she'd had at the restaurant last night, as if she was the only one not in on the joke. "Is there something you're not telling me?" she asked quietly.

Now it was Trevor's turn to look and act uncomfortable with the direction the conversation was taking. He walked over to the first pasture, now divided into thirds, and looked out to Blue Mist and Little Blue. "I just know how devious he can be when he wants something."

Rebecca watched the nursing cria and patient mother with the same wonder she felt when she'd delivered Little Blue. "You're thinking about what Vince did to you and Jasmine, to break the two of you up."

Trevor acknowledged this was so with a slight dip of his head.

"He's made no secret he's interested in me. I've made it clear I'm not interested in him that way."

Trevor rested his palms on the top of the rail. "That's what has me worried."

Rebecca studied the large capable hands that had made sweet, wonderful love to her throughout the night.

Sighed.

"The sick competition thing again," she guessed.

Trevor shrugged. "Vince's going all out for you that way doesn't make sense on a rational level. When it comes to me, Vince isn't reasonable."

Rebecca rubbed the toe of her boot on the soft green grass. "I still don't get what that has to do with the work his men did on my property."

Trevor directed his gaze from the rest of her sedately grazing herd, back to Rebecca. His attitude was as blunt as his voice. "Did you or did you not make a deal with him to reimburse him for his help?"

A little taken aback by how strong Trevor was coming on, Rebecca found herself admitting, "Vince and I agreed to work it out later, by cash or barter or whatever combination seems to work."

Trevor's frown increased. "Barter?" he repeated.

Rebecca's exasperation grew exponentially. "It's no big deal, Trevor. We talked about me taking care of Coco when Vince is unavailable. I'm *not* going to be cooking any meals for him. In any case, he's going to send me a detailed write-up for the labor charges."

Not appeased in the least, Trevor ordered, "When

you get it, I want you to let me know what the amount is. I'll loan you the money. You can pay him off."

Rebecca harrumphed in contempt. "That would be like robbing Peter to pay Paul." *I think I've done enough of that already.* She started to turn away.

Trevor clasped her elbow lightly, pulled her back. "Listen to me, Rebecca. You don't want to put yourself in a position of being indebted to Vince Owen, in any way."

She wrested free of him, threw up her arms and stomped backward. "What I don't want is you telling me how to run my ranch or deal with my neighbors!" She gave her words a moment to sink in, then stared him right in the eye and continued, "I'm a grown woman, Trevor, perfectly capable of figuring out the right and wrong thing to do."

He stopped grimacing long enough to open his mouth.

She held up a hand before he could interrupt.

"I know I'm going to make errors, Trevor. Every rancher does in the start-up process. But it's up to me to overcome whatever mistakes I render. All I want from you—all I *insist* that I have from you—is respect! And if you can't give that to me—" she paused to draw a last, enervating breath "—then you shouldn't give me anything at all!"

Chapter 12

No sooner had Trevor left to care for his own animals than Vince knocked on Rebecca's door.

Fresh from the shower, her hair still wet, she had on no makeup. She felt oddly vulnerable as she opened her front door.

Vince's glance took in the fine fabric of her stone-colored slacks and notch-collared blouse. "Business meeting today?" he asked her.

For reasons she didn't want to examine too closely, Rebecca did not want to tell him her plans.

"Something like that."

She nodded at the file folder of papers in his hand. "Is that the labor charges for the work yesterday?'

"Yes." Vince handed her the manila folder. "I wrote it up, just like you asked."

Rebecca leaned against the banister.

Her eyes widened as she perused the figures.

"Five thousand dollars?" she asked.

"I employ the best in the business," he said. "Their contract states they get paid double time for anything not in their specific duties. And, of course, the plumber and electrician who put in the mister and fan cooling system each charge two hundred dollars for emergency calls plus last minute rates, which are substantial. And then there were the materials."

Trevor had been right to mistrust Vince Owen.

Rebecca stared him down. "This is awfully steep."

Vince flashed an unsavory smile. "Are you backing out on the deal we made?" he asked.

"No." Unfortunately, it was too late for that. It was her own fault, Rebecca knew, for not having talked money and got a firm estimate before one minute of work was done by anyone. Had she done that, she wouldn't be in this mess now. "But I'm going to need a day or two to figure out what kind of repayment schedule I can handle."

"I'm a patient man," Vince said. He looked past her. "Is that coffee I smell?"

Her deeply ingrained Texas manners forced her to smile and ask, "Would you like a cup for the road?" *Before I do what Trevor said I should have done in the first place, and boot you out of here on your tail.*

Once again, Vince Owen was all genial charm. "That would be very nice, thank you. Unless you could join me for one now?"

"I'm afraid not. I've got an appointment. But I'll be glad to get you a cup to go." Rebecca led the way into the kitchen.

"I have to tell you," Vince continued, "I was very sorry our dinner ended so abruptly last night."

Rebecca had only agreed to have a drink with Vince, and then only because that was the only way he would discuss ways she could improve her business plan.

It did not appear that it would be helpful to point that out to him.

"I should have told you about my previous engagement."

"You should have told Trevor that you and I weren't finished, and advised him to go on without you. Where was it you said you were going? To your parents?"

Caught in an obvious fabrication—albeit a social, romantically motivated one—Rebecca flushed. "Turns out we had the wrong night for that."

Vince flattened a hand on her kitchen counter. "You don't have to lie to me, Rebecca."

That was about all she and Vince agreed upon.

"All right. I won't." Rebecca paused. "You might as well know anyway. Trevor and I are…seeing each other."

Vince's expression turned droll. "I gathered that when I saw his truck pulled over on the side of the road, the two of you going at it like a couple of love-starved teens."

Rebecca handed Vince his coffee. "I think you should go."

Vince accepted the travel mug full of coffee that had been on the warmer far too long. Looking in no hurry to go anywhere, he folded his arms in front of him. "Aren't you the least bit curious about the group that holds the mortgage on this place now?"

Rebecca tensed at the clever cruelty she saw in his eyes. "I know who they are, that they specialize in buying up high-yield, unusual investments."

"Do you know who owns Edge Investments?"

Rebecca gestured inanely.

"Perhaps," Vince advised her in a low, silken tone that sent a chill down Rebecca's spine, "you should find out."

* * *

Rebecca would have liked to go straight to the library to research Edge Investments but she had a handful of invitations to deliver, including one to Trevor's uncle Wade McCabe, a multimillionaire who had made his wealth by investing in growing businesses, in addition to the oil wells his wife, Josie, a wildcatter, had founded.

Figuring if anyone in Laramie would know just what kind of outfit Edge Investments was, Wade might, Rebecca stopped by their ranch first.

After inviting the handsome older couple to the Open House the following day, Rebecca filled Wade McCabe in on the recent turn of events regarding her property loan. "The new mortgage holder is sending a representative out to collect the balloon payment, Monday morning. I'd like to know what to expect."

"Trouble, is my guess. I'm sorry, Rebecca. That outfit is known for snapping up high-risk, high-value investments and forcing the property owners into bankruptcy and foreclosure."

Rebecca let out the breath she had been holding.

This was getting worse with every moment that passed.

She should have listened to her father, and gone a more conventional route for her financing and started her alpaca operation much more slowly.

She should have listened to Trevor and stayed the hell away from Vince Owen.

But she hadn't done either, and now she was in a mess from which she wasn't sure she was going to be able to extricate herself.

"Are you feeling okay?" Josie Wyatt-McCabe asked.

Rebecca nodded. "Do you know who owns the company?" she asked.

Wade shook his head.

"Edge Investments has such a bad reputation within the Texas investment banking community, I don't think the real owners want their names associated with it. They have a CEO, of course, sitting in the Dallas office, but he's only twenty-four, and nothing more than a figurehead."

"Maybe Miss Mim can help me find out more," Rebecca said.

Wade paused. "I hate to see anyone taken advantage of, Rebecca. If you find yourself in need of rescuing…"

The magic words she did not want to hear.

Rebecca forced herself to appear a great deal more confident than she felt. She declined their generous offer, smiled and shook hands with both. And headed for the next person on her list.

By noon, she had personally dropped off a dozen more invitations.

At Laramie Gardens Home For Seniors, Miss Mim and the other residents were eagerly awaiting her arrival.

"Thanks for letting me practice my sales pitch in front of you," Rebecca told the group assembled in the meeting area.

She set up a projector and passed out copies of the information packets she had prepared. Then she began her prepared spiel.

The senior citizens were generous in their comments and suggestions on where she needed to improve. Rebecca accepted them in the helpful spirit in which they were given. Consequently, her second run-through was much better. Clearer, more concise. Energetic. "I just wish you all could see the alpacas in person, particularly Little Blue and her mama, Blue Mist," Rebecca said, as she packed up her stuff for transport back to the ranch. "They are so sweet. You'll never see a more adorable ranch animal."

"Maybe we could do a field trip," Miss Mim suggested.

"That would be wonderful." Rebecca smiled.

"Tomorrow afternoon okay with you?" Miss Mim asked.

"You'd be willing to sit through this a third time?" Rebecca asked in amazement, as everyone nodded.

"It'd give us a chance to see the darling alpacas. And enjoy the flowers and the beautiful April sunshine and refreshments."

Refreshments! Oh heavens, Rebecca hadn't even thought about that.

"You do have food and drink planned, don't you, dear?" Miss Mim asked.

I will have, Rebecca thought.

"Because if not, I could…"

Rebecca lifted a staying hand. "There's just one favor I need you to do, Miss Mim," she asked the former librarian. "And it's a big one."

Trevor had just finished his morning chores when the phone rang. "I'm glad I caught you. We need to talk," Luke Carrigan said.

Trevor knew if Luke was summoning him, he wanted to talk about Rebecca. "When and where?"

"My office in the hospital annex. How soon can you get here?"

Trevor consulted his watch. "An hour."

Saturday afternoon, the waiting room was deserted.

Luke ushered Trevor into his private domain. He motioned for Trevor to take a chair and settled behind his desk. As Trevor had expected, Luke wasted no time in getting to the point. "I want to know your honest assessment of how Rebecca is doing."

"Fine." Better since they'd made love again and spent the night wrapped in each other's arms.

Not so good since they had disagreed that morning, over his efforts to protect her from whatever Vince Owen was going to pull next. And Trevor knew Vince was up to something.

"Meg and I were out of town at a medical conference, but we heard about the stampede and the trouble that followed the moment we got back."

"It was a harrowing experience, but she got through it with flying colors in the end. Even delivered her very first alpaca, Little Blue, on the ranch, all by herself."

"That's great."

"I know you've had your doubts about Rebecca being a rancher. I had mine, too, but I have to tell you, your daughter is amazing."

"She's got what it takes to make a go of it?"

"In spades, sir."

Luke rubbed the corner of his mouth with his thumb. "I know the Open House is tomorrow afternoon."

"Yes, it is."

"And Rebecca's invited everyone she knows who might possibly be interested in investing."

"That's right," Trevor said, proud of the audacity Rebecca was exhibiting.

Luke drummed his fingers on his desktop. "She hasn't come right out and said so exactly, but her siblings think she's got everything she owns on the line this weekend. Is that correct?"

Trevor looked Luke in the eye. "These are questions you should be asking Rebecca."

"I would if I thought I'd get a straight answer."

Trevor knew what Luke meant. Rebecca was pretty prickly when it came to doing this by herself, for herself. "She hasn't discussed the financial particulars with me, either. But I know she would appreciate your moral support. And anyone else you can wrangle up to be there."

"Meg and I talked last night." Luke rocked back in his swivel chair. "We're prepared to write a check that would cover her expenses and immediate debt. We have no idea how much that is."

Trevor understood Luke's intentions were good. They were still dead wrong. "I think that would be a mistake. Rebecca would resent it and completely take it the wrong way."

Luke rocked forward once again. "We want to take some of the heat off so she can relax and enjoy her Open House and not feel pressured to sell, sell, sell."

Beginning to see why Rebecca got so aggravated with her successful physician father, Trevor exhaled slowly. "First of all, she's in business to market her alpacas. Tomorrow's event will be good experience for her. She may or may not meet her goals—although given how hard she's been working, not to mention how much she loves caring for her animals, I think she just might. In fact, I think she's going to surprise a lot of folks with her expertise. I know she did me."

Luke scowled. "I don't want her to be embarrassed."

Trevor shrugged amiably. "Then don't do anything to embarrass her."

Silence fell as Luke thought about that.

"Speaking of embarrassment," Luke continued eventually, "what was the deal between you and her and Vince Owen at The Wagon Wheel restaurant last night?"

Trevor swore silently to himself. He had hoped Luke wouldn't hear about that.

"A patient who saw it said Vince looked furious when you waltzed in there and stole his date."

"It wasn't a date, it was a business meeting," Trevor corrected irritably. "They were just having a drink."

"Apparently, Vince Owen didn't see it that way. He was madder than a hornet when he paid his bill and stormed out after the two of you left. Probably because he thinks you're interfering with that boast he made, about making her his woman before the month was up."

Trevor winced at the memory. "I'm sorry to hear Vince Owen's ire made other diners uncomfortable."

"But you're not sorry Rebecca's taken a shine to you, are you?"

No, couldn't say he was.

Deciding discretion was the better part of valor, Trevor met the older man's searing gaze. "What precisely are you asking here, sir?"

Luke sobered. "What every good father wants to know. What exactly are your intentions toward my daughter?"

"Given the way we parted company this morning, I wasn't sure how glad you would be to see me," Trevor drawled.

Very glad as it happened, Rebecca thought, her pulse jumping at the sight of him.

Her intellect, however, was a lot more cautious.

Rebecca knew they needed more than passion and friendship to take their relationship to the next level. They needed to trust each other deeply.

And trust was the one thing she struggled most with. She wasn't used to getting what she wanted in the romance department, and she had never dreamed she could want a man as much as she wanted Trevor McCabe, or be cared for so intensely in return.

The deep satisfaction and joy she felt whenever she and Trevor were together had her waiting—wrongly or rightly—for the next catastrophe in her life to occur.

Trying not to notice how good he looked in the casual shirt and jeans, she replied, "That all depends whether or not you're ready to give me the respect I deserve."

The look in his eyes gentled. "I've never disrespected you, Rebecca."

Hurt trembled deep inside her. Stubbornly, she reminded, "You haven't believed I could handle everything I need to handle on this ranch, either."

To her relief, he held up both hands, looking genuinely contrite. "My mistake. One I promise not to make again."

Wanting to be perfectly clear, in hopes they'd never have a similar argument again, Rebecca said, "I can handle all the challenges in my life. Including the ones you'd rather I not have to deal with." *Like Vince Owen.*

"Fine. Although I should remind you that you're back in Texas now, and Texans do *whatever is necessary* to take care of their women."

"Even giving them free rein?" Rebecca teased.

Trevor stepped across the portal and took her in his arms. "In your case, I guess I'm going to have to." He lowered his head for a steamy kiss.

Rebecca kissed him back with all the affection building up inside her.

"So how's the work going?" he asked, when they finally broke apart.

Rebecca took him by the hand and led him into the

living room. "You know how I was worried last night because I hadn't received that many RSVPs?"

"I believe you mentioned it twenty or thirty times." He settled on the sofa beside her.

"They started coming in today, by phone and e-mail." She showed him the list. "Trevor, I've got seventy-five acceptances!"

"That's great."

"And fifty more maybe's!"

"Even better," he said cheerfully.

If only it were that simple, Rebecca thought, with an inward groan. "And not nearly enough food or drink to give them."

"No problem. I can make a grocery store run."

She made a face. "This isn't a poker party, Trevor. I can't just give them potato chips and soda."

Trevor looked at the cookbooks spread across the coffee table. "Obviously, you had more in mind for the reception part of the afternoon."

"Hot hors d'oeuvres. Fancy little desserts. Finger sandwiches. Texas beer. Wine. Plus, someone to organize the spread while I concentrate on talking business with my guests. If I could afford to call a caterer, it'd be no problem. But…"

He put a silencing finger to her lips. "Phone your siblings. Ask them all to bring something. Same with your mom and dad. I'll call everyone in my family who can cook. It can be their ranch-warming gift to you. And don't give me that I Want To Do Everything Myself look, Rebecca. Yes, you're begging for favors, but these are acts of kindness we will return in spades, because that's what family and friends do for each other. There's no shame in asking for help when you need it."

"How come you're always on the giving end and never on the receiving end of things, then?"

"Because I've already been through the start-up phase of my ranching career. As you soon will be, too."

Rebecca made another face at him.

He pulled out his cell phone. She picked up hers. They started dialing.

Fifteen minutes later, Meg Carrigan and Annie Pierce McCabe had both volunteered to set up and oversee the buffet tables, and they had the beginnings of a spread that would make Martha Stewart proud.

"Everything will be here an hour before the guests arrive. Guaranteed." Trevor handed over the list of items being donated to the event.

Rebecca added it to hers and perused them with a satisfied sigh. "I still need beverages and ice," she stated with a frown.

"Make me a list. I'll go get it and while I'm in town, I'll pick us up some dinner."

Rebecca couldn't help it. She felt that she was imposing far too much. "You really don't have to do all this," she told Trevor softly.

To her surprise, he agreed with her. "You're right. I don't."

Her heartbeat sped up. "Then why are you?"

He smiled, shifted her onto his lap and kissed her again. Deeply, irrevocably.

She was trembling when he let her go.

"That's why," he told her softly.

Because he wanted to make love to her again? she thought. Or for a deeper, more emotional reason?

She knew what she was hoping for, but no more confessions were forthcoming as Trevor smoothed the hair from her cheek, looked deep into her eyes. "Besides, there's something I forgot to do in town, too. And I better hurry before it's too late."

He touched his lips lightly to hers, and slipped out of the ranch house.

Her lips still warm and tingly from his kiss, Rebecca watched him go. It was hard to believe how much she had come to care for Trevor McCabe in so little time. Harder still to imagine her life without him, ever again.

The telephone rang.

Seeing from the caller ID it was Miss Mim, Rebecca picked up the phone. "Tell me you found out who owns Edge Investments," she said.

"I did," Miss Mim replied. "But you're not going to like it."

That, Rebecca noted, an earthshaking five minutes later, was the understatement of the century.

Figuring there was no time like the present to confront the most underhanded person she had ever come across, she got in her pickup and drove to the Circle Y.

Vince opened the door.

Coco shot past him and went straight for Rebecca. Rebecca bent to pet the chocolate Labrador retriever. Coco responded by licking Rebecca's arm, and wagging her tail so hard she nearly fell over.

"I figured you'd be stopping by this evening," Vince said casually, motioning her inside.

Rebecca remained on the porch of the Circle Y ranch house.

Reluctantly, Rebecca turned her attention from the love-starved pup, straightened slowly. "I'd prefer we talk out here."

"Suit yourself." Vince shut the door. Waited, an expectant look on his deceptively handsome face, while

Coco sat on Rebecca's foot, her weight braced against Rebecca's leg.

Wishing she could just take the puppy home with her once and for all, Rebecca forced her thoughts to remain on the disturbing problem at hand, and the neighbor who might just be trying to ruin her. "You own Edge Investments."

Vince smirked at the way the eager puppy turned, and tried to climb up Rebecca's leg. "That's right."

Feeling a little canine protection might not be a bad idea, Rebecca picked the twelve-pound puppy up and cuddled her against her chest. "You purchased the loans on my property deliberately."

Vince noted the way Coco settled down immediately, before returning his impassive gaze to Rebecca's face.

"I had the feeling you might need my help."

Rebecca recalled the letter she had gotten in the mail.

"Is that what you call it?" She worked to keep the emotion from her voice.

"Threatening to foreclose on me if I don't have my insurance in place and the balloon payment on Monday morning?"

"I helped you get the property back to an insurable state."

Vince was acting as if she should be *grateful* to him.

"The question is why if you intend to try and foreclose on me?" Just how sick was this man?

"I don't want to force you from your property, Rebecca," Vince told her calmly. He stepped toward her, took the puppy, opened the door and pushed Coco inside. "I'd like nothing more than to have you living next door to me and Trevor McCabe."

"Providing?" Rebecca ignored the heart-rending barking on the other side of the closed door.

"You let the world know—starting tomorrow, at your Open House—that you're my woman." Vince turned and frowned as the ruckus continued.

"But I'm not your woman," Rebecca pointed out, a great deal more tranquilly than she felt. Inside the house, the barking turned to pitiable whimpers.

Vince folded his arms in front of him and continued. "I'm a much better companion for you. You'd know that, if you gave me half a chance. Plus, I can afford to give you anything you need, including money. If you're with me, Rebecca, you and your ranch will want for nothing."

Rebecca stepped back, away from him. She propped her hands on her hips. "I can't believe this," she muttered, not bothering to hide her revulsion.

His persuasive smile faded. Coco raced to the window and began barking there. "Then you better start," Vince warned, his low tone as chilling as it was matter-of-fact. "I'm through playing around, Rebecca. Finished losing you to an idealistic loser like Trevor McCabe. I want you in my life and in my bed."

Trevor had been right—Vince Owen took "unhealthy competition" to a whole new level.

Rebecca forced herself to ignore Coco's pitiful whimpering. Not easy when the sound alone was enough to break her heart. "Why?" she asked Vince. "So you can parade me around Trevor like a red flag in front of a bull and stick it to him that way?"

Vince's expression hardened. "Trevor McCabe needs to understand once and for all that I'm superior to him in every way." He paused, continued smoothly, "You can help me accomplish that."

How could she not have realized how vicious Vince Owen was? "You understand that not only am I not physically or intellectually attracted to you, that I also find you extremely loathsome?"

Excitement gleamed in Vince's eyes. "The fact you find me personally despicable will only make it that much more thrilling in the bedroom."

Feeling as if she was going to be sick, she stepped completely off the porch. "Information garnered from personal experience, no doubt."

He shrugged and made no apology.

Rebecca clenched her fist, her keys digging into her palm, as the puppy began barking hysterically once again. "I'm not going to let you blackmail me."

Smugness creased his features. "You've got a night to think about it. I trust by morning you'll have figured out your ranch means more to you than whatever it is you think you have going with Trevor McCabe."

Rebecca told herself the tears of anger and frustration welling behind her eyes were for the puppy, not herself and the unholy mess she had just gotten herself into, all by not listening to Trevor's cautions. "And if I don't?"

Vince lifted his hands in the most casual of gestures. "Then you better have a twenty-thousand-dollar check for Edge Investments on Monday morning, to make that balloon payment, as well as some sort of repayment schedule set up for the five thousand dollars labor charges you owe me," he told her with a cool, satisfied smile. "Or your days on The Primrose Ranch are going to be over, sooner than you think."

Chapter 13

"I know it's early, but you all need your beauty sleep tonight," Rebecca told the female members of her herd as she snapped leashes on all their halters and prepared to lead them, en masse, from the pasture to the barn for their nightly feeding and bedding down.

Refusing to let Vince Owen's threats throw her off course or depress her, she went right back to the work schedule she had set for herself.

"We've got a big day tomorrow, and I'm counting on every one of you to look and act especially adorable to dispel the rumors of your waywardness earlier in the week."

Pewter Percy, one of the herd-sires snorted in reply, as Rebecca passed his stall. "Yes, I know it wasn't your fault. You didn't start that stampede, and given the size of the Black Angus cattle running toward you, you had no choice but to run for your lives, as far and fast as you could. The way I see it, that just proves how smart alpacas are, what survivors you are. And I'm a survivor, too," Rebecca continued, stabling one female alpaca after another. Enough of one to overcome even the toughest opponents, without running to anyone else for help.

She was an adult—perfectly capable of handling this all on her own.

Black Onyx tilted his head, skeptical as always. The fact he happened to be male doubled her irritation. "Now, don't look at me like that, big fella. I know it looks bad on the surface." Like Vince Owen might actually take everything from her if she didn't capitulate to his demands and sleep with him, just to tick Trevor off. "But I know what I'm doing. And the fact of the matter is, we're almost there." Rebecca finished stabling the animals and took all the leather leads and hung them on a hook near the door. "We just have to hold on a little longer."

"Of course I know Trevor would help me. If Trevor knew what happened tonight, he'd probably go over and punch Vince Owen in the nose and help me get the money to pay off the sleazy jerk, to boot. But that wouldn't be right." Rebecca moved on to the stall closest to the door that contained the newest member of her herd.

Little Blue edged closer, drawn to the emotion in Rebecca's low tone. Blue Mist looked equally concerned.

She knelt down to check mother and cria. "That would be letting him solve my problems for me, and although it's tempting to let him do that—you don't know how tempting—I got myself into this mess. It's up to me to get myself out. And I can do it, too." Satisfied all was well, Rebecca stood.

Blue Mist nosed her cria into the corner of the stall. Getting the message, Little Blue began to nurse.

"All I have to do is let people know what a good investment alpacas are, and get them to sign up for leases tomorrow. Then I'll have the money to make the balloon payment on Monday morning and time to refinance the balance with a reputable banker like Elliott Allen, which is who I should have gone to in the first place. And I'll be able to concentrate on building this place up to be the best alpaca ranch in Texas...."

"Telling bedtime stories to the herd?" Trevor asked, strolling in.

Rebecca smiled, her heart quickening, as always, at the sight of him. She hated keeping things from him, but this was her problem. "Something like that," she drawled.

He looked around in admiration. "It's amazing, how far you've brought this place in just two weeks."

Rebecca made no attempt to contain her pride and contentment. "Thank you."

"I'm serious. You're turning out to be one heck of a rancher, Rebecca Carrigan."

Now if she could just figure out how to get Vince Owen out of her and Trevor's life, once and for all.

Pushing aside the guilt she felt for not confiding her latest challenge to Trevor, she adopted a deceptively light tone. "I'm glad you finally figured that out."

"After tomorrow everyone else in Laramie County will know it, too."

Rebecca drew a breath. "I hope so."

"I know so." The corners of his eyes crinkled. "Ready for a surprise?"

She loved it when he looked at her like that, as if she was the best thing that had ever happened to him. Determined to stay in the moment, she edged closer. "That all depends. What is it?"

"Come and see." Trevor took her by the hand.

Propped up against his pickup truck was a large, rectangular-shaped present.

He stood back to watch. "Open it."

Rebecca pulled at the ribbon and tore off a corner. It didn't take her long to discover what it was. A big wooden sign in the signature ranch color of Primrose yellow. Bold black letters proclaimed, The Primrose Ranch. Huacaya Alpacas for Lease, Sale and Boarding.

Emotion clogged her throat. She determined not to cry.

He edged closer. "I noticed you didn't have a business sign next to the road. I figured we could put this one up for now. Then if you wanted to change it out for something else later—"

Rebecca let go of the sign, wreathed her arms around his neck and silenced him with a kiss. "That's the best present I've ever received! Thank you so much!"

Twenty minutes later, Trevor pounded a stake into the ground next to the mailbox. The elegant-looking sign was attached.

Trevor and Rebecca stood back to admire it in the fading daylight. "I should get a camera," Rebecca said.

"We'll do that tomorrow," Trevor promised, lacing an arm about her waist, shifting her close. "Meantime, we've got dinner to eat. And knowing you, probably a hundred last-minute details to tend to," he said.

He wasn't far off.

Rebecca still had investment brochures and information packets to print and put together. Individual pictures of the alpacas to arrange in the slide projector she had borrowed from the public library. White folding chairs to arrange in the office, where the presentation was to take place.

Finally, near midnight, there was nothing more that could be done.

Trevor came up behind her, wrapped his arms around her and buried his face in her hair. "You've got to get some rest," he murmured against her ear.

Happiness unfurled inside her. "I know."

He turned her to face him, tenderness etched in his expression. "Do you want me to go or stay?" he asked her gently.

How had she ever lived without him in her life? Without this? She smiled, rose on tiptoe, wreathed her arms about his neck. "What do you think?" she whispered.

He rubbed his lips on hers. She opened her mouth to the pressure of his, encouraged his tongue to dally, even while hers did the same. "That kiss feels like a yes."

She drew back, already working free the first button on his shirt. "It's also an invitation to shower." Her fingers touched warm, muscled skin.

He playfully touched his nose to the bridge of hers. He leaned forward, his forehead touching hers, and held her face between his hands. "With or without you?"

Lusty images filled her head. The knowledge he wanted her as much as she wanted him was almost as powerful an aphrodisiac as her growing feelings. "Your choice."

He grinned unabashedly and looked deep into her eyes. "Then you know what I choose." Hand in hand, they started for the ranch house.

No sooner had the door closed behind them than he found the corner of her mouth, and the center, exploring until the need pooled deep inside her. Her nipples ached for his touch. Her lower half strained against him. "We're never going to get upstairs if you keep kissing me like this," she warned, as his hand closed over her breast, claiming the soft flesh and teasing the nipple through the smooth cotton T-shirt.

"Oh, we'll get there," he promised in a low, husky voice that heightened her anticipation all the more, the hard length of him pressing into her. His eyes were slightly glazed. "One article of clothing at a time."

She had time to draw a breath, and then his mouth was on hers again, and they were kissing as if the world was going to end. She lost her boots in the kitchen, along with his. Her T-shirt next to the stove. Her bra in the hall. Not to be outdone, she got his jeans off in the foyer. His shirt at the bottom of the stairs. By the time they had reached the bedroom, they were breathing erratically, and skin to skin. Her inhibitions fled, dwarfed by the need to make hot, soul-searing love with Trevor McCabe. And judging from the way he was looking at her, kissing her, touching her, he wanted to take his sweet, lovely time with her, too.

Legs trembling, body aching, Rebecca bypassed the bed in favor of the shower. She'd had far too few moments like this in her life....

And nothing...nothing...even close to Trevor McCabe.

He grinned as she turned on the spray and pulled him in along with her. As always, it took a moment for the water to get warm. They laughed and shuddered as the cold spray hit their bodies. Shivering, she came toward him. The unique male scent of him filled her senses. He clasped her to him, his palms spreading heat across her skin. By the time the kiss ended the moisture pelting them was warm and enticing.

"Allow me." Rebecca grabbed the bar of juniper-scented bath soap, and rubbed it across his chest, back, down his thighs, between. He groaned as she rinsed with the handheld attachment.

"My turn." Eyes darkening, he backed her against the wall. Took his time lathering her body, even longer rinsing. Her nipples budded. The skin between her thighs grew slick.

She arched against him, impatient now, longing for the ultimate closeness. She'd never felt more alive, never felt so safe, warm and protected. Loved, even though he had never said the words out loud.

The thing was, she realized, as she kissed him back, her hands caressing every inch of him, she loved him, too.

He gripped her bottom and stroked her where their bodies met. Drawing her leg up, she settled against him. "Uh-huh," he said. "In the bed."

It took forever to towel dry, even longer to get situated between the sheets. Wild with yearning, she rolled onto her side.

He lay beside her, stroking, caressing, taking his time. Kissing her slowly, completely. Demanding the same. Until he was on top and her legs were wrapped around his waist. Holding her arms pinned above her head, he pushed inside her, timing his movements, building their pleasure, taking her with him to the very depths. Focused on one seductive plateau after another, she clenched around him, gasping his name, and then there was no more time, no more playing, no more holding back. They were pushing toward the edge, falling, racing, feeling. Climaxing together in mind-blowing passion. Floating freely, slowly... coming back down... shuddering together...holding each other... loving... kissing...and starting all over again.

* * *

"I have to tell you, Rebecca, what you've done here is downright amazing," Elliott Allen said.

Rebecca had asked the Laramie banker and her ranch insurance agent, Greg Savitz, to arrive early for a private tour. They had viewed the barn, visited all eleven of her alpacas grazing sedately in the pastures, taken in the new ranch office in the old garage and ended up in the gazebo, where a small refreshment table had already been set up.

Rebecca poured iced tea for Elliott, lemonade for Greg.

"Does this mean my insurance is now reinstated?" she said.

Greg nodded. "In fact, everything now looks so good, I'm going to talk to the home office about bringing your rate back down to where it was."

"Thank you." Things were so tight financially, every little bit was going to help.

Greg went off to join Trevor, who was standing in the yard, talking to his father and hers, who had shown up early, along with Annie and Meg. Banished from the kitchen, the men set up folding tables and chairs in the shade.

Now for the real test. Rebecca turned to Elliott. "Have you had a chance to look at the new business plan I faxed you last night?"

Elliott nodded. "I reviewed it before I came over here. It looks good, Rebecca. If you can meet your financial objectives today, I'll have no problem getting the loan committee to approve a new financing package for The Primrose."

Rebecca smiled.

Finally, it seemed everything was going her way.

She had the ranch she had always dreamed of owning, an alpaca operation and a man who made her happier than she ever imagined she could be.

All she had to do was stand up to Vince Owen and show everyone she could handle anything that came her way—even a deliberate attempt to ruin her newfound romance and drive her into ruin—all on her own.

Trevor knew something had been bothering Rebecca the previous evening. She had been too quiet one minute, chattering like a magpie the next. It could have been just nerves over the official opening of her business, all the guests she was expecting, the fact, with all eyes on her, she really wanted to succeed.

That was a lot to handle for someone who had only been in the ranching business for two weeks.

His gut told him it was more than that.

There'd been a reckless-to-the-point-of-desperation quality to their lovemaking. As if one of them had been going off to fight a war.... And then there was the way she had been holding on to him last night, in her sleep. Not just snuggling close, the way she had before. Holding on for dear life.

Something had happened to change her mood during the time he'd gone into town to get her ranch sign, and the other items she needed. What, he didn't know.

He'd find out.

But it would have to wait until after the Open House, when she had accomplished the goals she had set out for herself.

Fortunately, he had a lot to keep him busy.

Trevor's brothers arrived just ahead of feed store owner, Nevada Fontaine, Dave Sabado and tractor salesman Parker Arnett.

Trevor had just said hello to the group when Vince Owen sauntered over.

Not surprisingly, given the havoc his substandard ranching practices had caused earlier in the week, Vince got a polite but cool reception from the group of men. A fact, Trevor noted, that seemed to push him to further ruthlessness.

His expression smug, Vince tipped his hat back, and abandoned even the pretext of politeness. "You all ready to see me win my bet?"

Trevor tensed.

This was the lowlife he knew, the one who had dogged him all through his university days.

Glances darkened as the men closed rank around Vince. "You can't have a bet if no one agrees to wager," Nevada Fontaine reprimanded, mocking Owen's tone.

A distance away, Trevor saw Rebecca glance over. Tense.

Because she knew the history between the two men and intuitively anticipated Vince might try and make trouble with Trevor today? Or had something else happened…something he knew nothing about?

"And the way I recall it," Dave Sabado continued, oblivious to the dark nature of Trevor's thoughts, "you got no takers."

Parker Arnett put in, "Besides, seems Rebecca Carrigan is already spoken for."

It was time to stake his claim. "They're right. Rebecca is with me now," Trevor announced flatly.

"Really?" Vince taunted, rocking back on his heels. He regarded Trevor with arrogant derision. "Is that why she rushed over to my place last night, the moment you left for town?"

Trevor knew Vince well enough to ascertain when

he was telling the truth. Or at least the part of it that Vince wanted Trevor to know.

And there was fact in this.

Which was probably why Rebecca had been so single-minded and hyperactive last night. Because Vince had said or done something to try and upset her. And knowing Rebecca, she had determined to handle whatever it was on her own.

Tyler and Teddy McCabe stepped forward in a way that reminded Trevor of their "Triplet Threat" days. In true "One for all, and all for one" fashion, Teddy glared at Vince. "We don't want any trouble here today, Owen."

Tyler flanked Vince's other side. "We'd hate to have to bodily throw you off the property, but if you don't behave yourself, starting now, we'll do just that."

Trevor nodded, glad he had his brothers for backup. "No one is ruining this day for Rebecca." *Not even you. Snake belly.*

Vince held up both hands, backed off. "Fine." His complacency remained unaltered. "We'll just see what happens."

Vince strolled off.

It was all Trevor could do not to throw him off The Primrose, anyway.

Rebecca walked briskly up, what Trevor imagined was her tour-guide smile fixed firmly on her face. "What's going on?" she murmured, taking Trevor by the elbow, and leading him over to the side of the house, by the back door, well out of earshot of the guests roaming the property.

"The usual." He clamped down on his temper. "Vince was just trying to get under my skin."

Worry darkened her eyes. "What did he say?"

Trevor figured he could ask Rebecca about Vince's

comment and find out what had really happened between Vince and Rebecca later. "Nothing that bears repeating," Trevor said, more concerned about her than himself. And at the moment, she was looking mighty pale. "You about ready to start?"

Rebecca nodded, took a deep, relieved breath and folded her arms in front of her in a defensive pose. "I just hope I can pull this off."

Trevor had the feeling her sudden anxiety had something to do with Vince Owen, which made him want to throttle the man all the more.

"Are you kidding? You're going to be fantastic," he said, giving her elbow a squeeze.

As it turned out, there were so many people there, Rebecca had to do her presentation three times, and each time, it was a standing-room-only crowd.

By the time the afternoon had ended, she had leased out all eight of her female alpacas for the next three years, she had eight orders for stud service, and Miss Mim and a group of other seniors had arranged to buy Little Blue outright and board her on the ranch. A dozen others were interested in leasing and/or buying arrangements, as soon as Rebecca was able to expand her herd. She collected ten percent of all monies owed when the contracts were signed, as per her business policy. Rebecca couldn't stop smiling as she said goodbye to everyone who had come by.

Finally, it was just Rebecca and Trevor.

And that was when Vince Owen chose to appear once again.

Rebecca had hoped that when Vince realized she wasn't going to capitulate to his demands, that he would slink away to the hellhole from which he had risen. Apparently not.

He walked toward Rebecca, his expression ugly. "You made a mistake here today," Vince told her.

Rebecca put down the serving platter in her hand. "You're the fool, for ever trying to blackmail me in the first place," she muttered furiously.

Trevor looked at Rebecca.

Relieved to finally be able to tell Trevor everything without fear he would try and solve her problem for her, she explained, "A company Vince owns, Edge Investments, now holds the mortgage on this place, as well as my operating loan. Vince told me yesterday that if I didn't tell everyone I was his girlfriend today that he would foreclose on me tomorrow morning if I couldn't make the balloon payment." Rebecca turned to Vince. "But thanks to my success this afternoon, I'm going to be able to pay that off. Then I'm going to refinance and never have to worry about being blackmailed by you again."

To her dismay, Vince smirked as though he still held the high card. "It's not that simple."

Trevor moved closer to Rebecca. "Sure it is," Rebecca said.

Vince's seedy grin faded. "There's the matter of the five thousand dollars labor and material charges you owe me. I expect immediate repayment on that, too. Or I'll be forced to take you to collections and sue you for nonpayment of debt."

Rebecca's spirits sank like a stone in the bottom of a pond. She'd thought she was finally in the clear financially!

"That wasn't our agreement and you know it," she stormed.

Vince stared her down victoriously. "I've got eight cowboys, a plumber and an electrician, who saw us shake hands on it, before work ever commenced."

Shock reverberated through her. "You said I could have as much time as I needed for that. That all you wanted from me today was some sort of repayment schedule, which I have!"

"Funny—" Vince rubbed his jaw "—I don't remember it that way. In fact, the way I remember it, *the entire payment is past due.* You were supposed to give me a check at the time I presented you with the bill yesterday morning. You didn't. Being the generous man and neighbor that I am, I gave you another opportunity to pay me again last night, and again you refused."

The lie was so outrageous it took her a moment to recover. Trevor looked as if he was about to take Vince's head off.

"I'm not going to let you get away with this," Rebecca said through her teeth.

Vince smiled at both of them and slowly dropped his hand to his side. "You're not going to have any choice. You can't refinance with a lien on your property, and I plan to put a lien on this place first thing tomorrow morning. After that, I'll use your nonpayment of your debt to trash your credit rating, which will make it impossible for you to refinance with anyone else. And your drastically lowered credit rating will force me to up the interest rate on your mortgage, as per terms of your original loan agreement. By the time I'm done with you, you'll be begging me to foreclose on this ranch and put you out of your misery. Of course, all that could change if you agree to go on a few dates with me."

Rebecca threw her hands up in frustration, paced a distance away. "What is it with you? Why are you fixated on this dating thing? When you know I'm not the least bit attracted to you?"

"Because," Trevor told her grimly, "he can't stand the thought of not winning the wager he tried to make about you the first day he came to town."

Rebecca blinked, sure she hadn't heard right. But apparently from the looks on both men's faces, she had. "What bet?" Rebecca asked warily.

"He said he would make you his before the month is out," Trevor replied in a low, bored tone. "And get a ring on your finger, too. The dates he wants are a precursor to that."

"Well, it's not going to happen." Rebecca whirled back to Vince. "I don't care what you threaten me with."

"We'll see about that." Vince flashed an evil smile and walked off.

"Unbelievable," Trevor muttered under his breath, watching him go.

When they were alone again, Trevor looked at Rebecca with calm self-assurance. "Don't worry about the five thousand dollars. I'll transfer funds to your bank account first thing tomorrow morning."

Rebecca struggled to take it all in. The demands, the betrayal, the fact that her finances, which looked so rock solid for the next six months a few minutes ago, were now tilting precariously again.

"You can pay me back whenever," Trevor continued.

Rebecca blinked. "That's your solution?" she said softly. *"To give me money?"*

Trevor shrugged. "If there's no lien, you can refinance."

She moved one hand slightly. "That's not the point."

His eyes narrowed. "Then what is?"

Feeling more of a fool than ever, Rebecca studied

him. "When did you find out about the bet Vince Owen made about me?"

"Tried to make," Trevor corrected, irritation on his face. "No one at the feed store would wager with him. And I knew about it at the time. I witnessed it."

"And didn't see fit to tell me?" Rebecca asked, enraged.

Trevor regarded her calmly. "I didn't want to hurt your feelings."

Rebecca's anger mounted. "So instead you let me go on interacting with that sleazy lowlife without any knowledge of what Vince was doing and saying behind my back."

Trevor spread his hands. "I was protecting you."

She moved forward until they were only inches apart. "I don't want your protection! Who else knows about this?"

"All the men in town."

Rebecca noted there wasn't an ounce of apology in his hazel eyes. "My father?"

"Yes," Trevor replied curtly.

Shame warred with humiliation. "When did *he* find out?"

"He knew about it the first day he came to see The Primrose Ranch."

As she recollected, it all made sense. "Which is what you two were talking about when he went over to your ranch to get the pressure washer," she said through her teeth.

"He wanted to discuss it with me, yes."

"And *he* didn't tell me, either!"

Trevor folded his arms across his chest. He did not try to conceal his irritation. "We agreed to spare you the embarrassment."

"How very kind of you." Rebecca flashed a saccharine smile. "Did it ever occur to you that I wouldn't be in the mess I am right now if you had only told me what was going on from the get-go? Had you told me that Vince tried to make a bet about me, had you warned me in advance about his substandard ranching practices in regard to his cattle, I wouldn't have given him the time of day, neighbor or no, I would have known to install fencing right away."

"If you recall, I tried to talk to you about that. You wouldn't listen."

Rebecca went on as if Trevor hadn't spoken, "And I certainly wouldn't have accepted his offer of help with the new fencing and the installation of the cooling system in the barn!"

"So you made a mistake—"

Tears burned behind her eyes. "That could cause me to lose my ranch!"

"I told you," Trevor corrected with exaggerated patience. "You're not going to lose The Primrose. I'm not going to let you lose your ranch. And neither is your father. Although a lot of what just happened could have been avoided if you had waited for me to help you with the labor on the fence and the cooling system in the barn."

Rebecca reached out to steady herself on the back gate of his pickup truck. "You had all you could handle with your sick cattle. And time was running out."

"I would have organized a group of guys to help me get it all done before the Open House and you wouldn't have been charged anything. And—" his voice dropped an accusatory notch "—I could have prevented what happened just now if you had told me that Vince was blackmailing you!"

Rebecca spun away from him. She shoved her hands through her hair. "It wasn't your problem!"

Hand on her shoulder, he whirled her back around. "Don't you get it?" His hold on her tightened possessively. "Everything that happens to you is my concern."

Blinded by equal parts hurt and fury, she shoved away from him. "Next thing I know you're going to be challenging my competence and telling me how to run every aspect of my life."

He gave her an if-the-shoe-fits look, and said, his voice soft as silk, "Just admit you were wrong not to come to me for help and tell me what was going on with Vince at the time it was going on, promise me you won't shut me out like that again, and we'll let it go."

The hell of it was, he didn't even realize he was being condescending. But she sure as heck did. She stepped forward, not sure whether to deck him or kick him in the shin; she only knew she wanted to wound him the way he had her. "We'll let it go?" she repeated on a soft, bitter laugh.

He nodded, still ready to forgive and forget.

She wasn't. And might never be. Rebecca balled her fists at her sides. "You're unbelievable, you know that?" When he didn't react, not in the slightest, she let her voice drop to a feral growl. "Get off my property."

His brow arched as if her words did not—could not—compute. "You're throwing me out?"

She scoffed, too devastated to continue. "What else would you expect me to do after the way you've undermined and disrespected me—not just today, but from the very moment we met up again in the feed store?"

His contriteness faded. "I'm not going to apologize for protecting you."

That was the problem. He just didn't get it. Pretending she'd seen this coming all along, Rebecca replied sadly, even as the happily-ever-after she'd wanted for them slipped through their fingers, "I didn't think you would."

Chapter 14

"What in the world is going on over there?" Susan asked.

Amy moved to the kitchen window overlooking the Circle Y Ranch. Rebecca's two sisters had spent the night with her, alternately consoling her and brainstorming ways to immediately come up with the five-thousand-dollar labor charges she needed to pay off Vince Owen, and keep a lien that would damage her credit rating from being attached to her property.

Rebecca didn't know how she would have lived through the last twelve hours without them.

Her sisters were not just stellar independent businesswomen, with a lot to teach her, as it turned out, they were also very sympathetic when it came to the sheer stupidity of men in general, and Trevor McCabe in particular.

Rebecca only wished she had called on them sooner, instead of insisting on sorting out all her financial problems herself, her own way, without any family help.

Maybe if she had let Susan and Amy closer, she

would have been so busy hanging out with them, she wouldn't have gotten so involved with Trevor McCabe.

And maybe not. Rebecca sighed.

Even now, as furious as she still was with Trevor, there was just something about him that made her heart go pitter-patter and turn her world upside down. And honestly, how foolish and naive was that?

How ridiculously romantic?

"It looks like a parade of pickup trucks." Amy sipped her coffee.

"I see a few SUV's and sedans in the mix," Susan noted.

"As well as a coupe or two." Amy's nose wrinkled in perplexity. "What do you think it means?"

Susan and Amy turned to Rebecca.

As if she should know.

"I have no clue. And when it comes to Vince Owen, I really don't care. Let's just get these papers signed, the checks written, so I can run them to the bank before ten o'clock."

The three women sat down.

One last time, they went over the business contract their cousin, Claire McCabe Taylor, a Laramie attorney, had helped them draft via phone and email, the previous evening.

They had just finished signing when they heard a parade rumbling up Rebecca's drive.

Admittedly curious, the three women stepped out onto the front porch of The Primrose ranch house. Cowboys and prominent business people of all ages poured out of vehicles and congregated on Rebecca's front lawn. Neighboring ranchers; all three of the Mc-Cabe triplets; their two younger brothers, Kyle and Kurt; their father, Travis McCabe; as well as ranchers Brad McCabe, Shane McCabe; and the husbands of all four Lockhart sisters were among those standing together. Rebecca recognized a dozen other members, including the president of the Laramie County Rancher's Association.

But it was Trevor McCabe, stepping forward as leader of the group, who had her heart pounding.

"First off, every man here owes you an apology," Trevor began bluntly.

"Including me." Rebecca's father moved to the front of the group, to stand beside Trevor.

Traitors both, Rebecca thought.

"We should have told you from the get-go about the wager Vince Owen tried to make about you two weeks ago," Nevada Fontaine said.

Dave Sabado agreed, "You're one of us, Rebecca, same as any other rancher."

Parker Arnett added, "The fact you're a woman is neither here nor there. We should have leveled with you like we would have talked straight to any man."

Luke Carrigan nodded, his expression contrite. "We're all guilty here, and we apologize."

Teddy McCabe stepped forward, too, pausing only long enough to shoot an apologetic look at Rebecca's sister Amy, before continuing frankly to Rebecca. "We also want you to know that you don't have to worry about Vince Owen any longer."

That sounded good to Rebecca even as she determined not to show her relief, lest it be perceived as a sign of weakness.

"He's decided to leave the county, effective immediately," Tyler McCabe said, with the same practical gentleness he used on his veterinary patients and their owners.

Although she was more than capable of keeping Vince off her property, even if she had to get a shot-gun to do it, Rebecca knew getting him to leave the county was more than she could have wrangled on her own. "How'd you manage that?" Rebecca asked warily.

Travis McCabe looked at the group around him with paternal authority, "I'm thinking maybe we all should let Trevor explain that to Rebecca."

Amy and Susan got the hint.

"Good idea." Her sisters were off the porch in no time flat.

Before Rebecca could voice "Wait!" everyone had scattered. Truck doors were slamming. Engines start-ing. Vehicles were rumbling off in the same orderly fashion they had driven up the driveway.

Once again, she and Trevor were very much alone. Pretending her life was just fine without him, she faced him. "You want to tell me what's going on?" She made no effort to hide her cantankerous mood.

He stopped a few feet from her and looked into her eyes, his tone as flat and pragmatic as hers was curt and emotional. "I called everyone for an emergency meeting last evening, explained what Vince Owen was trying to do to you. This morning, we let him know as a group that we didn't need his kind around here."

Rebecca knew when she was getting the cleaned-up version of events. "Vince Owen wouldn't just leave be-cause he found himself unpopular."

"You're right. He wouldn't. But he *would* depart to avoid multiple lawsuits lodged against him, due to the spread of livestock illness and property damage the gross mismanagement of his cattle caused."

Trevor withdrew a sheaf of legal papers from his

back pocket. He handed them over, managing not to touch her in the process.

Trying not to feel bereft at the loss of personal contact, Rebecca scanned them quickly. "This affidavit states that Vince—not I—is the person responsible for the five-thousand-dollar labor charges on my property, and that he incurred them as fiscal reparation for the damage to my property, caused by his stampeding Black Angus cattle."

"Right. So the threat of any lien being placed on your property is now gone. Should he so much as think about trying anything else, we all have our lawsuits ready to go. And they'll stay that way, until the statute of limitations runs out."

Which meant they'd have years.

Realizing this would also mean she would no longer see Coco, Rebecca sighed, and forced herself back to the business of the day. "I still have to make the balloon payment."

"Yes, but now you'll be making it to my uncle, Wade McCabe."

Rebecca lifted a brow.

"He and his lawyers are over at the Circle Y right now, completing the sale of the mortgage on the Primrose to one of Wade's investment groups. They're paying cash. So as soon as the papers are signed that threat will be gone, too."

Rebecca wanted to berate Trevor for doing that, too, but figured it would be hypocritical when the reality was, she felt nothing but relief she would not have her fate in the hands of Vince Owen in any way, and none of this was anything she could have managed on her own.

Still, the idea of being beholden to a McCabe, when she had just broken up with a McCabe…

She swallowed. "I had planned to refinance with Elliott Allen, at the Laramie Bank."

Trevor nodded respectfully. "And you can still do that, no problem, hopefully under much better terms than your old mortgage. In the meantime you won't have to worry about Vince. He no longer has any hold on you, financial or otherwise."

Finished, Trevor started to walk away.

Once again, too much was happening, too soon.

Rebecca strode after him before she could stop herself. "Trevor!"

He turned.

"Why did you do all this?" Rebecca asked, her heart in her throat. "Especially after the way we parted yesterday."

Was it because he loved her, after all? Because—like her—he was beginning to realize he couldn't bear the thought of a life without the passion they'd shared and the intimacy they'd found?

Trevor rocked back on his heels. He rubbed a hand across his mouth and chin. "Because I owed you," he said, lowering his voice to the soft, seductive lilt she knew so well. "You were only in this mess in the first place because Vince wanted to use you to get to me," he told her sorrowfully. "And because what he tried to do to you just wasn't right."

"Well, his explanation makes sense," Jeremy said to Rebecca several hours later when he stopped by to see how she was doing.

Rebecca stared at her only brother. She had been hoping he would shed some light on the situation, him being a guy and all. "It was so matter-of-fact."

Jeremy paced back and forth, checking out the alpacas grazing sedately in the grass. He looked at her over his shoulder. "Would you have preferred to have him crying in his hankie?"

The depth of her exasperation made her tense. "You know what I mean."

"Yeah, I do." Jeremy smiled the way he had when they were kids. "You're still sweet on him."

That, Rebecca didn't want to hear, think or feel. She gave her brother a quelling look. "Trevor and I are over." She slid her hands in the pockets of her jeans. "The truth is, we never should have started anything up."

"Yeah, I can see how you'd think that." Jeremy leaned on the pasture fence. "He just moved heaven and earth to get you out of trouble you never should have gotten yourself into, because he doesn't care a lick for you."

Rebecca rolled her eyes and corrected Jeremy's way-too-romantic version of events. "He rounded everyone up to chase Vince Owen out of Laramie because Vince Owen is nothing but trouble and it was the right thing to do for everyone, not just me!"

Jeremy chuckled. "You keep telling yourself that."

"Now he has nothing to feel guilty about," Rebecca continued stonily, studying the beautiful blue of the Texas horizon. *Except breaking her heart into a hundred million pieces.*

"Probably not." Jeremy strolled amiably closer. He tugged one of her braids. "You, on the other hand, are a different story."

Rebecca arched her brow at Jeremy.

He scolded her with a shake of his head. "Here you go again, letting your stubborn pride get in the way of your happiness."

She folded her arms over her chest, over her heart. "That's what *you* think I'm doing."

"Not just me, Rebecca. Everyone in the family knows what a mistake you're making, refusing to forgive Trevor for trying his hardest to keep you from being hurt."

Put that way, her actions did sound stupid.

Had Trevor given her the slightest sign that he still cared for her, she would have been back in his arms in two seconds.

The problem was, he didn't call her. Not that day. Or the next, or the next.

Didn't email.

Didn't come by to check on Little Blue and Blue Mist and the rest of her herd.

Didn't bring her dinner or invite himself to dinner, in return.

He worked his ranch.

She worked hers.

Days passed. One after another.

Vince Owen packed up and left, just as he said he would.

Rebecca refinanced her property with the Laramie bank.

And she missed Trevor McCabe more and more every hour, every minute, that passed.

Finally, the following Saturday evening, she mustered up her courage, baked a batch of ranger cookies, got herself gussied up and drove over to his place.

Lively country-and-western music filled the air as he answered the door. While she had been pining away, Trevor McCabe looked as if he'd never felt better.

Obviously just out of the shower himself, he was

clean shaven and nicely dressed, in a white Western shirt, dress boots and jeans.

"Here to congratulate me?" he said with a sexy smile.

Actually, to make a peace offering. But now that he'd mentioned it… "For what?" Rebecca asked.

"Purchasing the Circle Y."

Which was, coincidentally, a property he had wanted all along, Rebecca realized with a start. The only thing missing from his equation of perfect happiness was the Primrose, which she still owned.

"So your ranch is now twice the size," she affirmed.

"That's right." Pride and contentment radiated in his low tone.

"And you've got two houses."

"I'm planning to turn the one at the Circle Y into a business office."

"Congratulations," she said stiffly. *Now she was buffeted on both sides by Trevor McCabe land, which was going to be nothing but a constant reminder of all she'd had, and then lost.*

Trevor tilted his head, studying her aggravated scowl. "I thought you'd be happier for me."

I would be if I thought you still cared.

"Happier to know you've got a neighbor on both sides you can rely on," he continued, a questioning look in his hazel eyes.

She caught a whiff of the slow roasting beef brisket, the yeasty smell of fresh-baked bread. Unable to totally keep the jealousy from her voice, she thrust the peace offering at him and backed slowly toward the door. "I feel like I'm interrupting."

The sparkle was back in his eyes. "You're right," he agreed cheerfully. "I'm not alone."

Rebecca bit down on an oath. "You've got a date."

Why was she surprised? Just because the thought of *her* going out with anyone else was incomprehensible did not mean *he* was as foolishly single-minded.

He made a seesawing motion with his hand. "More like a lifetime commitment."

The notion rocked her back on her heels. She'd thought they would have time to make amends, to see if they couldn't get past this and pick up where they'd left off. "You're engaged?"

His smile was as soft and enticing as his kisses had once been. He took her hand and tugged her close. "Why don't you come and see?"

Rebecca liked to think of herself as a mature adult, but this was too much. She put up a palm to keep him from coming any nearer. "Thanks, but no."

He came closer, anyway, wrapping an arm about her waist. When she would have pushed away, he held fast. "The thought of me with another woman really bothers you, doesn't it?"

Rebecca regarded him with haughty cool. "I just think it's a little soon."

"Mmm." His voice was a sexy rumble in his chest.

She tried not to notice how warm and solid and enticingly masculine he felt. Or how good he smelled, like soap and cologne. "You don't seem surprised."

"Why would I be?" he asked compassionately and calmly. "I feel exactly the same way about seeing you with anyone else."

Feeling a chink in her emotional armor, she wrinkled her nose at him. "And yet you haven't called, haven't emailed, haven't dropped by."

His gaze remained on hers, as steady and strong as his presence. He cupped her face in his free hand. "I was waiting for you to come to me."

Her heart began to pound. Hope rose deep within her. "You were so sure that would happen?"

"I know what you feel for me," he told her in a low voice, husky with emotion. "I know how rare it is." He paused to give her a long, hot kiss. "I know a love like ours doesn't come along every day." He paused to kiss her again, deeper, more soulfully. "And I know there is no way on this earth that I am ever going to be anything but more in love with you each passing day."

She blinked, wanting to be sure she hadn't imagined this. "You—?"

"Love you," he said, the depth of his contentment sweeping over them both. "Yes, Rebecca, I do. Just as you love me."

She couldn't help it—she began to smile, even as her stubborn independent nature reasserted itself. "I never said that," she reminded.

He grinned, triumphant. "You didn't have to." He held her tight and buried his face in her hair. "It was in your eyes every time you looked at me." He leaned back slightly. "It was in every kiss, every caress, and it was certainly there in spades every time we made love."

She bit her lip, savoring the way his arms felt around her. "Then why didn't you come after me?"

His expression gentled once again. "I knew you needed time to sort out your business affairs, process everything that's happened and discover what was in your heart and mine."

Also correct. "And now that I know?" she asked cautiously, wondering where they went from here.

"I'm hoping you'll marry me." He held her face in his hands and kissed her tenderly. "Maybe not today, or tomorrow, but one day, when you're ready, I want you to be my wife."

Rebecca resumed breathing.

"But it's got to be on one condition."

She blinked back the mist of emotion. "Somehow, I knew there would be a catch."

He sobered, every inch of him resolute male. "You're going to have to let me do the man thing and protect you, just as I expect you to do the woman thing and watch over me. Because that's what people who love each other, who care for each other, do."

She flashed her untamable grin at him. "Spoken like a true Texan."

"Through and through. So is it a deal?" He waited.

But not for long. "Yes," Rebecca said firmly, looking him right in the eye. "I'll marry you."

"When?"

The man did not waste any time. But then he never had. "Six months from today."

That quickly, it was decided. Which gave them plenty of time to start kissing again. And kissing and kissing.

She was ready to head for his bed when he murmured against her lips, "There's just one more thing."

Of course.

"You're going to have to accept part-ownership of one of your wedding presents now."

He certainly planned ahead.

"Because it's very important we share in the responsibility." Trevor said soberly as he took her by the hand.

She went along willingly. "Now, you're confusing me."

He winked. "We've got room in our life for one more, don't we?"

Oh yes, back to the mysterious "guest" in his kitchen.

"That all depends on who it is," she cautioned wryly.

"Trust me. You're going to love her as much as she already loves you."

Rebecca certainly hoped so.

They rounded the corner.

Coco was curled up in a wicker basket in a corner of the kitchen, fast asleep.

"She was sold with the Circle Y ranch," Trevor said.

Rebecca wasn't surprised the puppy had been so readily given over. Vince Owen did not have the temperament or the time to successfully care for a puppy. Trevor, on the other hand, had love and patience in spades, as well as an amazing rapport with all animals.

Trevor knelt down beside the Labrador retriever. Gently touched the back of her soft chocolate-colored head. "Hey, sleepyhead, wake up."

Coco opened her eyes. Stretched. Saw Rebecca. And shot up like a stone coming off a slingshot. The next thing Rebecca knew she had her arms full of wiggling, happy puppy.

"I think she's as glad to see you as I was," Trevor drawled.

Rebecca could not stop laughing as Coco licked her beneath the chin. A fiancé and a puppy all in one night. "This is the best present I've ever received. My only question is how did you get her to sleep?" Rebecca rubbed behind the Lab's ears.

"Lots and lots of exercise. Or as Tyler told me, 'a tired puppy is a happy puppy.'"

The theory seemed to work. "Good to know."

Trevor bent and snapped on a leash. "What do you say the three of us go for a walk? Then we'll come back, have dinner, put her down for the night, and see if we can't find a way to amuse ourselves…."

* * *

"This has got to be one of the proudest days of my life," Luke Carrigan told Rebecca six months later.

"And to think," Meg Carrigan teased her husband with spousal affection, "she managed to find a man to marry without your assistance."

"Now," Luke stated, with a playful glance at his son and other two daughters, "if only her siblings could settle down, too."

"My medical practice and my ranch is all I've got time for these days," Jeremy said.

"No kidding," Susan teased. "That place of yours is in such bad shape it'll take light-years to fix up."

"You won't find any woman willing to share it with you, until it's at least somewhat habitable," Amy agreed.

"That's the plan," the energetic bachelor, Jeremy, grinned.

Luke turned to Susan. "Don't look at me," she said. "I'm not about to head down the aisle any time soon, except as Rebecca's maid of honor."

"I'd happily get married," the incredibly romantic Amy begged to disagree, "if I could only find someone to fall madly in love with, too."

"It'll happen when it's meant to happen," Meg stated with maternal confidence. She looked at her husband. "And not a moment before, no matter how much *meddling* anyone does. Meanwhile—" Meg stepped behind Rebecca to adjust her tiara and veil. The two women's eyes met in the mirror "—I want Rebecca to know how very happy I am for her, too," Meg said in a low voice so choked with sentiment it brought tears to everyone's eyes. "She's accomplished so much in such a short period of time."

Rebecca turned to face her family. "I couldn't have done it without all your support, though, the way you all lent a hand with the shearing and the Open House. Not to mention helping me figure out how to get more out of the land."

"It was your idea to reduce the size of the pastures to more manageable levels, and lease out the rest for planting," Amy pointed out.

"But you contracted for the property to expand your nursery business, and Susan brokered the deal and directed her landscaping crews to help refence the fields." Rebecca paused. "I couldn't have accomplished near as much without all of you."

"That's what family's for," Meg said.

The wedding planner knocked and stuck her head in the door. "Time to get the show on the road, folks," she said.

Wedding music sounded in the chapel beyond.

Jeremy escorted Meg to her mother-of-the-bride seat in the front of the church. Susan paired up with groomsman Tyler McCabe. Amy stepped off with Teddy McCabe. Luke offered Rebecca his arm. Together, they walked through the pews of well-wishers, to the altar, where Trevor waited.

Rebecca had only to look into his eyes to know how beautiful she looked. And heavens, he was gorgeous, too.

Her heart brimmed as her father kissed her and gave her away and then she and Trevor stood before the minister, hand in hand, ready to pledge their future together.

"…I take thee, Trevor…"

"….as my lawfully wedded wife…"

"…joined together, let no man put asunder. Trevor,"

the minister finished, beaming, "you may kiss your bride."

And with Coco watching contentedly in the wings, on the end of a primrose-yellow lead, Trevor did.

* * * * *

With more than a million books in print, **Pamela Britton** likes to call herself the best-known author nobody's ever heard of. Of course, that changed thanks to a certain licensing agreement with that little racing organization known as NASCAR.

But before the glitz and glamour of NASCAR, Pamela wrote books that were frequently voted the best of the best by the *Detroit Free Press*, Barnes & Noble (two years in a row) and *RT Book Reviews*. She's won numerous awards, including a National Readers' Choice Award and a nomination for the Romance Writers of America Golden Heart® Award.

Books by Pamela Britton

Harlequin Western Romance

Cowboys in Uniform

Her Rodeo Hero
His Rodeo Sweetheart
The Ranger's Rodeo Rebel
Her Cowboy Lawman

Harlequin American Romance

Rancher and Protector
The Rancher's Bride
A Cowboy's Pride
A Cowboy's Christmas Wedding
A Cowboy's Angel

Visit the Author Profile page
at Harlequin.com for more titles.

WINNING THE
RANCHER'S HEART

Pamela Britton

Dedicated to my darling Lysy Loo,
the daughter of my heart.
We love you, Alysa Panks.

Chapter 1

"Is this it?" T.J. asked, his left elbow brushing her own as her son wiggled on the old Ford's front bench seat.

Naomi Jones stared at the sign hanging above the dirt road, clenching her palms against the sweat that formed.

Dark Horse Ranch.

"Yes." She sighed. "This is it."

"It doesn't look like much of a ranch," said her other child from her shotgun position. Samantha sounded about as enthusiastic as a dental patient about to undergo a root canal, but these days her teenage daughter didn't sound enthusiastic about anything.

She had a point, though, Naomi admitted, but she knew from experience you couldn't see much of the place from the road. Just a bunch of valley oaks dotting the acreage and the needle-straight line of a road, one that headed toward some low-lying foothills not too far in the distance. It was dusk and the sun had just started to set behind the hills. The dew point had risen and it released the scent of herbs in the air.

New life, new beginnings, she reminded herself.

Goodness knows she'd made a mess of the old one.

Not at first. At first it had been heaven on earth. But then Trevor had died and everything had changed, and not for the better. These days Samantha was either a perfect princess or perfectly horrible. It was clear she needed to rein her in. And T.J. Poor T.J. had been bullied since his first day of elementary school. She hoped like heck the move would help.

Here we go.

Her old truck rattled forward. Someone had hit her pickup in the back and taken off without leaving a note. She didn't have the money to fix it, so duct tape held parts of the bumper together. She should probably have it fixed before it flew off on the freeway or something, but that was what this move to California was all about, too. A good-paying job. A place to live—for free. And, once she sold her home in Georgia, money in the bank.

"Wow," T.J. said.

She'd been so deep in thought she hardly noticed their surroundings. She looked up at her son's gasp of amazement and spotted it. Beyond the oak trees, nestled into a craggy hillside, stood a house. A very big house.

"I know, right?" she said, guiding the old truck toward the redwood-and-glass monstrosity. It should look out of place in the middle of the country and yet the home seemed to have sprouted from the very rocks it sat upon. She'd watched enough shows about architecture on television to know it'd been designed by a naturalist, someone who wanted it to look indigenous to the landscape, and had probably cost a small fortune.

"Is that where we're going to live?" T.J. asked with a tone of reverence.

She glanced at Samantha to gauge her reaction, but as usual, her thirteen-year-old had her head buried in her phone. Then again, in her present frame of mind, they could probably pull up to Buckingham Palace and Sam would pretend indifference.

"We're actually living around the left side. In the maid's quarters."

Sam snorted. Her daughter hated her new job title: housekeeper. One of many things Sam had given her grief about when she'd learned they were moving.

"Can we go inside?" T.J. asked. He pushed his thick-framed glasses up on his nose.

"Not the big house," Naomi said, smiling when she spotted the way his red hair stuck up on one side. They'd had the window down at one point. "We need to settle Janus into his new digs."

She glanced in the rearview mirror. The Belgian Malinois must be lying down because Naomi couldn't see his head between the bars of the plastic crate.

"He's going to love it here," T.J. said, wiggling on his seat.

At least one of them was happy with the move, although they weren't completely free of Georgia just yet. She still needed to go back and arrange for all their furniture and belongings to be stored and/or sold. And she'd have to move some of it out west, which meant another long drive.

"I thought you said there would be horses," Sam grumbled as they pulled up in front of their new home.

"They're here." *Somewhere.* According to the owner's sister, Lauren Danners, they'd built the horse facility out back. Lauren had been the one to hire her because her brother, Jaxton Stone, was always out of town. Hooves for Heroes was a therapy center for soldiers with PTSD, although she'd never seen it. A state-of-the-art facility. New, she'd been told. Very expensive.

She pulled up to housekeeper's entrance on the left

side of the main house. Slipping out of the truck, she tucked her cell phone in her back pocket and took a deep breath of the chamomile-scented air. It had rained recently; that was the reason for the moisture in the air. She could smell the earth and the wild oats that grew between the trees. The moisture had settled on the granite stones that ringed the base of the house, turning them a dark rose color. A door had been placed in the middle of the wall—an ornate maple door with a fan-shaped paned window set into the top of it. Narrow windows sat on either side of that door, a small deck with redwood steps leading to the entrance. She wanted to buy some plants for the railings when she had some extra money.

"It doesn't look like much," Sam said.

"Wait until you see the inside."

Lauren had shown her around the fully furnished apartment when she'd flown out for the interview. Three bedrooms. A kitchen. Even a family room that overlooked a back patio with a pool right outside. Not her own pool, of course, but the owner's. She'd been told her kids could use it, though, as long as she checked with Mr. Stone first.

"Why don't you let Janus out?" she asked T.J. "He can check out our new place, too."

Her son dashed to the back of the truck, dodging suitcases and boxes to get to the beige-colored kennel. Poor dog had been cooped up for at least three hours.

"Use the leash," she warned. The last thing she needed was her husband's ex-military dog running off and getting lost. That would be a disaster.

"Can't we, you know, find a place of our own to live?" Her daughter's face was a mask of distaste as she stared around her. "I don't want to share a house with someone I don't know."

Naomi resisted the urge to make her own face. "We're not sharing a house, kiddo. We have one right here." And it's free. And furnished. And requires no commute.

Sam flicked her long brown hair over a shoulder. "Yeah. The servants' quarters."

Was it illegal to spank kids in California? She doubted anyone would blame her if she did. "Sam, please. Give this a try."

"Whatever." She flounced off, heading for the front door.

T.J. came up beside her, Janus by his side, the dog's dark eyes catching on something near the front of the house, although what she couldn't tell. He was forever looking for trouble, compliments of his military training.

"Don't worry, Mom. She'll get over it."

The fact that her ten-year-old son tried to console her shouldn't surprise her. He'd been doing that for the past two years, ever since Trevor had died.

"I hope so, bud," she murmured.

She'd been told the front door would be open, and it was. The apartment, which took up a whole corner of the owner's mansion, was just as spacious as she remembered.

"Wow," T.J. said again.

Definitely bigger than their place in Georgia, not that Sam would admit it. She just slumped down on the couch to their right, eyes glued to her phone.

"I'm going to go meet my new boss." Naomi tried to inject perky self-confidence into her voice. "Sam, can you and T.J. try to unload some of our stuff?"

Sam didn't answer, just kept clicking buttons.

"Sam."

Her daughter eyed her from above the top of her phone. "Fine."

She winced inwardly. The whole journey out to California, she'd tried to convince her daughter that the move was for the best. They'd be near the kids' grandparents once they made the move out west, too. They'd be living on a ranch. They could even have their own horses down the road once she sold the house. Sam had always loved horses. But Sam hated to leave her friends. She didn't like California, although she'd never been there before. She hated that her mom would be a housekeeper. Why couldn't she do something different? Why couldn't they stay in Georgia? And on and on it'd gone.

"I'll be right back," she said, trying to hide her disappointment. At least T.J. was happy. Her son was going from room to room, sounds of "wow" and "cool" being emitted periodically.

As if she didn't have enough to worry about, a sullen teenager only added to the mix. Jaxton Stone's sister had said he was a nice man: the perfect brother, she'd said. He worked super hard, which was why he needed a live-in housekeeper. Apparently, her new boss was always off somewhere in the world. He ran a military contracting company. She'd had to Google what that was, a sort of army-for-hire type of thing. They provided protection for corporate executives, too, something she'd never heard of before, but was apparently necessary if the company was big enough that it could afford to pay a ransom. She'd been shocked to read just how dangerous foreign travel could be for the head of a big company, and her new boss made a living keeping those corporate head honchos safe. A very good living, by the looks of it.

Off you go.

She stepped outside and skirted the house to the main entrance. At least her surroundings were pretty spectacular. The home sat on property that looked like something out of an old Western movie, or maybe *Bonanza*. Rolling hills were covered by dried grass, trees casting inkblot shadows on the ground, taller mountains in the distance. She'd had to cross through those mountains to get to Via Del Caballo, so she knew the ocean lay on the other side. It might have rained this morning, but it was clear now, a few patchy clouds off in the distance. She took a deep breath of the freshly scented air and then squared her shoulders. Lauren had constantly mentioned how great her brother was. She hoped her boss's sister hadn't fudged the truth.

The front door sat atop a row of steps like the opening to a Mayan temple. She was just about to make the sacrificial ascent when a sound caught her attention. A dog sat on the massive porch that framed the front of the house. It stared at her curiously from its position by a redwood chair with maroon cushions.

"Hey there, boy," she said, climbing the stairs quickly. Some kind over overlarge terrier, she thought, smiling at the way tendrils of hair came together at the crown of its head and made it look like it had a Mohawk.

"Bad hair day?" she asked.

The dog just thumped its tail. Skinny little thing. She wondered if it were ill or something.

She smiled down at it and eyed the place. Should she just walk in? Ring a bell?

She pressed the doorbell, stepped back, the dog watching her as she stood there, then moved forward and rang the bell again.

Was he home?

She'd been assured someone would be there to greet her this morning. And the apartment had been unlocked. Maybe he'd stepped out?

She wondered what to do. Wide beams stood above her, the wooden rails reminiscent of pictures she'd seen of Camp David. It smelled new. Like varnish and wood and fresh paint.

He must not have heard me. She peeked through one of the massive windows that lined the front. She didn't see anybody, so she went back to the door, turning the handle just to see if it was open, not to go inside or anything.

The alarm nearly deafened her. She had to cover her ears it was so loud. The dog that'd been on the porch ran away so fast she wished she could do the same.

Whoo-a-whoo-a-whoo.

What had she done? She hadn't even opened the dang thing.

Dear Lord.

She stepped back from the door, staring at it, as if she could somehow will the alarm to shut off.

It swung open.

Blue eyes stared down at her. That's all she caught a glimpse of before he went back inside. Through the open door she watched as he turned toward an electronic console on the wall, pressed some buttons and silenced the alarm.

Her ears rang. Her face blazed. Her smile nearly slipped from her face.

"Good morning." She tried to brazen it out.

He slowly placed his hands on his hips, and as Naomi looked into his gorgeous eyes, she knew nothing would ever be the same again.

* * *

"Do you always just walk into people's homes?"

The redhead's smile grew even more strained, and he recognized the grin for what it was—a show of bravado that fooled no one.

"I didn't walk in, I promise." She lifted her hands. "I just tried the door."

"Soooo you could walk in?"

"No, no." She shook her head, a mass of red hair falling over her shoulders. "I was just seeing if someone was here. I wasn't going to walk in."

"Mom!" Behind her, a dark-haired girl came to a stop on his gravel driveway. "Are you okay?"

She turned to greet the teen. "I'm okay." She waved her away. "Just a little misunderstanding."

A little boy, younger than the girl and with hair as red as his mom's, skidded to a stop next. "Man, that was *loud.*"

"I take it those are the kids?" he asked.

She glanced back at him. "Yup."

Which confirmed that she was Naomi Jones, although her Southern accent gave it away. The friend of a friend that his sister had interviewed and loved, and whom he'd been forced to hire because Lauren felt sorry for the single mom of two. That wasn't surprising given that his sister had been raising a child all on her own, but that would soon change since she'd met Brennan Connelly.

"Can I see the inside of your house?" the boy asked, lifting up on his toes as if he might be able to peer over his mom's shoulder.

The girl smacked him on the head.

"Ow!" the boy cried.

"Come on." The teen gave them what could only be

called a glare of derision. "Let's let Mom do her *house-keeping* thing."

His gaze caught on the woman in front of him, just in time to see her wince. "I'm so sorry."

He'd have to have been a real jerk not to accept her apology. His men might call him a hard-ass, but it really wasn't true. Well, most of the time.

"It's okay." He stepped back from the door. "Come on in."

"Thanks."

She glanced around, her gaze coming to rest on a granite water sculpture at the center of the main foyer. The sound of running water soothed troubled souls, his included.

"I love your house." She stopped in the middle of the foyer, her eyes—the prettiest shade of blue he'd seen in a long, long time—traveling around the interior. "It reminds me of a guest lodge or something."

"Thanks."

Those eyes landed back on him. "I'm Naomi Jones, by the way."

He could tell she wasn't sure if she should hold out a hand or simply stand there and keep smiling.

He took the guesswork away from her and stuffed his hands in his pockets. "Nice to meet you."

He saw something flit across her eyes, something that told him he might have just offended her, or maybe disappointed her. "You, too." She stuffed her own hands in her pockets.

Interesting. Usually mimicking someone's gestures was a sign of submission, but he doubted that was the case here. He'd seen her tip her chin up a tad. Those bright blue eyes of hers had grown a little less friendly, too.

"So, those were your kids?"

"Yes. T.J. and Samantha."

"And you've settled into the apartment?"

"Well, no. We only just got here. I was told to come straight to you when we arrived. So you could meet me."

Check her out, his sister had said, although he hated the way saying the words made him feel. His sister had said she was perfect for the job, but that didn't mean he would think so, too. He'd agreed to hire her as a favor. He'd been telling himself for the past two weeks that he should trust his sister's judgment, but as Naomi stood in front of him he wondered what the hell he'd gotten himself into.

"Why don't we go talk in my office?" He motioned that she should follow him past the sunken living room that overlooked the front of the property and up some stairs to his left. He'd had very few people to his private retreat. He could probably count the number on one hand, but he wasn't surprised by her reaction to the vaulted ceilings and the wrought-iron balustrade as she followed him up the wooden steps. It'd taken a year to build the place, and another three months to build the massive covered arena and apartments out back. He'd spent those last several months flying back and forth between his corporate offices in San Francisco, interviewing hippotherapists and psychotherapists, and securing the purchase of the livestock for his ranch. It'd been a hell of an endeavor, but he'd gotten it done.

"My sister tells me you've done this before?"

"Well, not quite," she said, taking a seat opposite his desk. He watched as she immediately shifted first left and then right, solidifying his own thoughts about his new furniture. Not comfortable. He'd hired a decorator, and he'd begun to suspect that she valued form over function. He liked things the opposite way, something he'd clearly neglected to convey. In his line of work, things needed to be efficient. Someone's life might depend on it.

"I used to work as an event planner, and before that, I worked for a hotel doing the same thing. But I started out in housekeeping. Worked my way up while I attended college, that sort of thing."

He'd known that. He'd read her résumé a time or two. "Why do you want to move all the way out to California?"

She stared into her lap for a moment, resting her hands on her jean-clad legs, sunlight from the tall windows in front of her emphasizing the red of her hair. "The kids' grandparents are moving out here." She looked up and met his gaze. "My kids love them. I didn't want Sam and T.J. to be that far away."

"So you chucked it all?"

He didn't mean to sound critical, but he could tell by the way she furrowed her brow that she took it that way. "We don't have anybody else. No other family, no aunts or uncles, and life in Georgia is…challenging."

"More challenging than moving all the way to California?"

There went that chin again. "We needed a change."

A big change. At least from the sound of things.

He leaned back. He sat opposite her since he didn't need to see the view. "This job won't just be about housekeeping. I know that's what my sister told you, but it's going to be way more than that."

She tipped her head, leaned forward a bit. Her body language told him she didn't mind this change of plans.

"You'll still be keeping house to some degree," he explained, "and managing my household—buying groceries and whatnot—but whoever works here needs to be flexible, too. They need to understand that one day they might be asked to cook for me when I'm in town, or clean a guest apartment, or help one of our guests in some way. It won't be easy, but it'll be interesting. You do know how to cook, don't you?"

"You wouldn't ask me that if you'd tasted my Southern pecan pie." She beamed, and he had to admit she didn't look a thing like he'd expected. He'd expected older. More…harried-looking. She had two kids and he knew that couldn't be easy.

Drop-dead gorgeous, that's what she was.

Even in an off-white long-sleeved T-shirt as plain as day. He didn't normally notice such things, not when all he cared about was if someone could do a job properly, but the visual image in his head was so far from the reality that it startled him.

"What about you?" he said. "Do you have any questions?"

"Yes." She pinned him down with a stare like an entomologist would a cricket. "You won't be bothered by two kids and a dog, will you?" She looked around her as if envisioning two terrors inside his home.

"I would expect them to stay out of the way."

And suddenly she appeared amused, her blue eyes lighting up from within, her whole face transforming, and if he'd thought her beautiful before, that was nothing like the way she looked with a smile on her face.

"I can't keep my kids in a kennel."

"No, of course not, but kids are always off doing things, at least in my experience. As far as your dog, I would appreciate you keeping him on a leash, at least until we know how he'll react around horses."

"You don't think *your* dog will mind having a new dog on the property."

"What dog?"

Her brows drew together. "The one on your porch. Or it *was*. It ran off when the alarm sounded."

"What?"

"By the front door. But like I said, it ran off."

"I don't have a dog."

"No?"

He shook his head. "If you see it, please let me know. I'll have to call someone to catch it."

"No. Don't do that. It's better to try to re-home a stray."

"We don't know it's a stray."

She frowned. "I think it is. It looked skinny."

And she cared. With concern clouding her eyes, she looked younger. She couldn't be much older than thirty.

Younger than you.

Much younger.

"Let me know if you catch it and we'll go from there."

She nodded. "Anything else?"

"One last question."

She waited quietly. He admired the way the sunlight set strands of her hair afire before he admitted he shouldn't be noticing that type of thing.

"What if you change your mind?"

"About what?"

"The move. Working as a housekeeper. Living on the ranch."

She lifted her chin a tiny fraction, but enough for him to realize she was sensitive about the issue. "I won't. We even drove my old Ford truck all the way out here. And

I've started the school enrollment process for my kids. They'll be all set to start at their new school in the fall."

He studied the woman in front of him. Lauren had told him Naomi worried that her husband's death had affected her kids far more deeply than she'd surmised. That they were having problems in school and that a move all the way across country would be good for them. He couldn't say he agreed. Then again, he didn't have kids, so who was he to judge?

"All right then. I guess we'll see what happens."

"Terrific."

"And your first task will be helping to organize a party I'm having here in a couple of weeks. Local military brass. Short notice, but I'm sure I can easily pull strings and get people here. You'll have an unlimited budget to make it an affair people will remember. I want to make a big splash."

Her mouth dropped open. "I—"

"You've planned events before, or so you said."

He saw her take a deep breath. "Of course I have. I just didn't think I'd be starting so soon."

"Is that a problem?"

"No. Not at all."

"Good, then I'll take you on a tour of the ranch next." She seemed surprised again.

"Unless you'd like to settle in first."

"No, no. That's okay."

"Good." He glanced at his watch. "And before I forget, here's some information I put together for you. My cell phone. Email. Etcetera." He slid a manila envelope forward. "Meet me in front of your apartment in ten minutes."

She lifted a hand, saluted. He lifted a brow. She

smiled and stood up, envelope held in front of her like a shield.

"It was nice to finally meet you."

"Same," he said with a dip of his head.

He watched her slip away, but when she left he spun his chair so that it faced the windows. Maybe he shouldn't have left the hiring of a housekeeper to his sister. He had a feeling Naomi Jones might prove to be a handful, although he had no idea why he felt that way.

Her eyes sparkled.

As if she saw the world from the big end of a telescope and what she spotted amused her. Usually, he hired people who were far more serious, but he supposed that was to be expected given the nature of his work. Naomi seemed...complicated.

He hated complications.

Chapter 2

"Can I tour the ranch with you?"

T.J.'s face was imploring and it killed Naomi to shake her head. "Honey, there'll be time to show you around later today. Let me spend some time with my new boss first."

"But I thought you weren't going to start work until next week," he said.

She'd thought so, too, but she should have known her new boss was a workaholic. His sister had told her how often he was out of town. That he was driven and impatient and yet the kindest man she'd ever get to know. She'd have to take his sister's word for it. So far she felt...nervous. He had the ability to escalate her pulse, and not because he was good-looking, although he was that, with his dark hair and blue eyes. Handsome and intimidating as hell.

"Plans changed." She brushed her hand through T.J.'s hair. "But I promise to explore with you later on today."

When she got off work she would make sure to show T.J. the ranch, although she'd forgotten to ask Jax Stone about her hours. And what days she'd have off. And a whole host of other questions because when she'd looked into his eyes she'd just sort of gone *ooohh*.

Someone beeped a horn. Janus stood up from his position at Sam's feet and began to growl.

"Nein," she softly told him. That was all she needed to say for the dog to rest his head again. That was the last thing she needed—for Janus to start attacking the door. "Stay inside," she told her kids, although she doubted Sam heard her. Earphones didn't quash the sound of music that emanated from the tiny white buds. Her daughter would be deaf by the time she was fourteen.

"Can I go see the pool?" T.J. asked, eyes filled with hope.

"No."

His lower lip stuck out. "But Mom…"

"Just stay here. Sam." He daughter continued to tap something out on her phone. "Sam!"

That got her attention, but she seemed completely put out that she had to remove one of the buds from her ear. She did everything but roll her eyes.

"Keep an eye on T.J."

T.J. wiggled. "I don't need a babysitter."

The horn beeped again. Janus barked. Naomi turned to the room and said, "Stay."

"Mom. I'm not a dog."

"I know that. I meant all of you. Don't leave."

She slipped outside before T.J. could start complaining again. "Sorry," she told her new boss, drawing up short at the sight of the all-terrain vehicle he'd arrived in. It looked like something the military would use—all camo paint and big black bumpers and a cab framed by a roll cage.

"Was that your dog I heard?"

She nodded, her face coloring a bit because it was only then that she realized she hadn't told his sister exactly what kind of dog she'd be bringing with her.

"That did not sound like a small animal."

Once again she found herself tipping her chin. "He's a Belgian Malinois."

He knew what that was, she could tell by the way his blue eyes narrowed. "You have a Malinois?"

She nodded, decided that she should just spit the rest of it out. "He's an ex-military war dog."

His lips pressed together before he said, "What are you doing with an MWD?"

"He was my husband's."

Trevor.

Her high school sweetheart. The man she'd known instantly that she would marry, even as young as she was. She tried not to let her emotions show, but she saw Jax's gaze hone in on her own. It still hurt, although she'd hoped, goodness how she'd hoped, that it would have faded by now. At least a little bit. She prayed the move would help. Less of a reminder of what her life had been like before.

"You took possession of him after he died?"

She nodded. "Smartest thing I've ever done."

He stared at her a long time. "Come on," he said. "I'm sure you want to spend time unpacking when we're done here."

"It's fine," she said, forcing a smile as she slipped into the passenger seat. "How far away are the horses?"

"Not far," he said. "I wanted the guest quarters to be within walking distance of my home."

Jaxton Stone was rich. Not that she hadn't already known that. Not that she cared, but she could tell he was more than just well-off.

She'd found out about Dark Horse Ranch through Trevor's best friend, Ethan, who'd taken on the role of surrogate brother over the past year. Ethan's brother-in-law Colt had told her Jaxton owned the company Colt's brother, Chance, used to work for, and that they'd been in combat together once upon a time. And that Jaxton was the type of man who'd give his left kidney to someone. It was Ethan, Colt and Chance who'd convinced the reclusive Jaxton Stone to move to Via Del Caballo and build his therapeutic horse ranch for combat veterans. Naomi loved the idea so much she'd asked if he was hiring, and voilà, here she was. Except given their description of the man, and then after meeting his sister, she'd expected someone completely different. Guarded. Not this...stern taskmaster who didn't seem to have the muscles to smile.

"I love your home."

He put the vehicle in gear, the clutch lurching them forward so that she grabbed the roll cage to steady herself, the metal cold beneath her fingers. It was far cooler than she'd expected. She'd be chilled within a matter of minutes in her long-sleeved T-shirt and jeans.

"Thank you," he said, shooting her a glance, looking like any rancher on any given day, on any other average ranch, in his black cowboy hat and jeans. The road followed the curve of the hillside, and she gasped at what stood on the other side. A massive equestrian complex, one made out of thick beams and with a steeped roof and tall windows across the front. It was all off in the distance, but close enough that she and the kids could walk, and all tucked away in a little valley behind his house.

"Wow."

She hadn't meant to say the word aloud, but it escaped before she could stop it.

"It turned out nicely, I think."

He *thought*? The ranch was a showplace. Long, rectangular buildings were usually plain and ugly, but whoever had designed his house had also designed his barn. It had thick beams jutting out, not just across the front, but along the sides. Massive double doors—two stories high—were set into the front so they could be opened or closed, but they were cleverly designed so that it looked like the short end was all one big wall of windows. It wasn't just a barn, she realized then. It was an arena.

Amazing.

It wasn't that she hadn't seen stables before. Ethan's sister-in-law, Natalie, owned an equestrian facility twice the size. It was the sheer newness of it all that blew her mind, that and the knowledge that before his arrival, none of it had been in the center of the valley, one with a small lake in the distance and hills that had been browned by the June sun.

He drove forward again. "I'd like to have the party down here, in the arena, so people can mill around and see what we've built. I'll invite some of the country's leading experts on post-traumatic stress disorder. Anyone who needs a room can stay in the guest quarters."

And he wanted to do this how soon? She gulped at the thought, but something told her Jaxton Stone didn't know the meaning of the word *failure*.

"We'll need to ensure we have plenty of food on hand, and maybe hire a caterer if you think it'll be too much. You should probably get me a list of local media. I'm hoping they'll take one look at Dark Horse Ranch and spread the word about what we hope to accomplish here. I want this facility to be the best therapeutic ranch on the West Coast. I want to change lives here. Help people. Make things better."

She turned to look at him, stunned to realize this wasn't just a passing fancy or some kind of tax write-off. She could hear the sincerity in his voice, earnestness mixed with hope and maybe even longing.

He cared.

"Let me show you the arena and the corrals and the horses we've purchased for the program first. That's something Colt and Ethan are helping me out with. I don't know a whole heck of a lot about horses, but I'm learning."

For the first time he had become animated, showing her the state-of-the-art, climate-controlled arena—actually driving through the center so she could see the iron stall fronts to her right and the polished wooden beams—every inch the masterpiece that his home was. The kids would go nuts when they saw it.

"The horses have been carefully selected for the program." He motioned toward a dark bay horse that peered at them curiously from the other side of a stall front. "And they're turned out to graze in the evening, something that's good for them."

He showed her the turn-out pens next, driving behind the barn.

"The pastures are so green compared to the hills."

"We're on an aquifer. That's where the water for my lake comes from. That's what keeps everything green. Natural springs." He pointed toward the horse pens. "The Reynolds family could have charged me a small fortune for this property, but they sold it to me cheap. Actually, their home's just a few miles away from here as the crow flies. They still ride their horses out by the lake."

She smiled at the mention of the Reynolds family. She adored Colt and Chance and their sister, Claire. Particularly Claire, who'd taken such good care of Janus when he'd been in her care. Claire owned a military dog rescue and she was married to Ethan, who was a veterinarian.

"This is my favorite animal." He pulled to a stop in front of one of the horse corrals, getting out and heading toward the brown horse that walked toward them. "His name is Zipping Down the Road. Zippy for short. He used to be some kind of famous show horse, an actual world champion or something, but his owners retired him a few years back and he's been a therapy horse ever since."

She watched from her seat in the ATV as he walked up to the animal in question, holding out a hand, letting the horse sniff it before moving up next to his head and patting his neck.

"Looking for a treat?" he softly asked. "You know I have them somewhere, don't you?"

Who was this man? she found herself wondering, watching as he fished a baby carrot out of his back pocket and then gently fed it to the horse. His whole face had changed. Gone was the stern taskmaster. In his place stood a man with soft hands and warm eyes.

"Come here and pet him."

Okay, so there was the taskmaster again, but that was okay. She smiled because she'd been worried the kids would hate him. That her new boss seemed cold and distant and that he wouldn't like her children. But for the first time she saw the man who'd spent millions of dollars on a state-of-the-art facility for wounded warriors. A nice man. A caring man. A man with a gentle spirit.

Their gazes connected as she slowly moved up next to the horse.

"He's gorgeous," she said, and she couldn't hide her smile because it felt so good to pet one again. It'd been years, but she'd always been a horse-crazy girl. "I bet you were really something in your younger years," she told the animal, leaning in next to his nose and inhaling the sweet animal scent that only horse lovers understood. The horse did the same thing right back, smelling her loose hair and tickling her ear and making her giggle.

When she drew back she felt his gaze on her, her smile fading at the look on his face.

"What?" she asked.

He stepped away. "Nothing."

For some reason she felt the need to explain her reaction. "It's been awhile since I've gotten to pet a horse."

"So you've been around them before?"

"Oh my goodness, yes." She patted the animal on the softest part of its body, its muzzle, a place that felt like velvet. "When I was younger I used to ride all the time. My mom showed horses and I did, too, up until her death when I was sixteen. My dad died at the same time. Car accident."

And even after all these years, it still ached like the dickens. She wasn't all that close to her in-laws. They hadn't approved of her being a blue blood. That's what Trevor had called her. He must have seen the twinge of pain in her eyes because he crossed his arms and drew himself up, the softness in him fading.

"We should get back." Had her words upset him? "You have a lot of work to do," he added.

He'd gone back to the uptight, aloof business owner, and for the life of her she didn't know why. She was the one with a sad past. First her parents and then her husband had died. Some days, it just didn't seem fair.

"Sure."

She reluctantly returned to the vehicle, gazing at the sorrel horse that watched them drive away. They headed back in silence, and Naomi wondered if she should ask him about her kids, if it'd be okay to show them around, but something made her hold back.

"Thank you for the opportunity to work with you," she said when he dropped her off.

"Don't thank me, thank my sister." He glanced at her quickly. "I'll expect you to start work at eight tomorrow morning. Feel free to show your kids around. You might not have time over the next few weeks."

He left her standing there, the tires even kicking up a little bit of gravel as he headed back to the garage on the far side of the house. Naomi watched him drive away with dread in her heart.

What have I done? she wondered.

And was it too late to change her mind?

Chapter 3

She would be here any moment now. He listened for her footfalls on the steps leading to the second floor. She had her own entrance to the house, through the kitchen, and he suspected she'd make use of it today.

He'd given her the pass code and instructions for his alarm yesterday, although he probably should have given her some kind of schedule, too. An oversight he would soon rectify. He stared out the row of windows that stretched across the second story of his home office, not really focusing on the view.

She still wore her ring.

And yesterday, when they'd talked about her husband's dog, she'd seemed lost. It had hit him hard for some reason. Maybe because she reminded him of his sister, who'd been through the same thing. There was just something…sad about her that had touched him when she'd told him about the Malinois, and then later, when she'd been petting Zippy.

His gaze slid over the front of his property, watching for movement in the brush. *Old habits die hard.*

Something stared up at him. Jax froze.

A dog. Big dark eyes held his gaze. If not for the contrast of the dark hair against the muted gray trunk of an oak tree, he wouldn't have seen him at all.

"Well, I'll be—"

She really *had* seen a dog. There'd been a part of him that had wondered if she'd imagined it. Maybe confused a fawn for a canine. Or a coyote for a domestic dog.

"Am I late?"

He didn't turn around. "That dog is back." It was crazy the way the animal stared up at him, almost as if he saw him through the glass. Maybe he did.

"Is he brown?"

He nodded.

"Mohawk?"

"What?"

"Never mind." She came forward. "Where?"

He pointed. "Out by that tree."

The smell of her body lotion or perfume or whatever wafted toward him. Vanilla and lemons.

"We should try to catch him."

She sounded as Southern as Georgia peach pie. He finally looked away from the dog to peer over at her. Even in profile she was deeply and extraordinarily beautiful. She'd worn her hair loose around her shoulders, the bulk of it resting against an off-white sweater. An ambient morning glow filtered in through his windows and highlighted the paleness of her skin and the gorgeous blue of her eyes.

"Stay here."

He didn't give her time to respond; frankly, he was almost glad to leave her side. He didn't like noticing how stunning she was. She worked for him. Her looks were something he didn't want to dwell too deeply upon, so he stepped away from her, ducking through the entrance of his office and turning left, toward the massive stairwell that bisected the house. He'd always thought stained wood and wrought iron balustrade just a tad over the top, but it served its purpose well. He headed straight for the front door.

"Do you have a leash?"

She had clearly ignored his order to stay put. Why didn't that surprise him? "No."

"Maybe I should go get one of mine."

He burst out onto his porch. The dog didn't move. He headed toward the tree that it cowered behind, noting the matted fur and the skin that hung off its bones like a coat that was too big. It seemed to be some kind of terrier breed, an overgrown Toto that'd gotten too big for the basket. And it looked like it had a Mohawk. That was what she'd meant earlier.

"That's him. That's the one I was telling you about."

"Go call animal control."

"No."

He glanced over at her sharply. She didn't seem to notice, just moved past him. "Let's see if we can catch him first." Her feet crunched on the rocks of his gravel driveway.

"Leave it alone. It might have rabies."

She stopped, turned to face him, the look on her face the same one she no doubt gave to her kids when they said something ridiculous, like maybe a candy bar would be good for breakfast. It raised his hackles. He'd been up for hours and he was pretty sure the scruff on his chin and the ends of his hair stood up on end, and he was tired, which might explain his cranky mood.

"I sincerely doubt it has rabies. Like I said, we need to catch it." She turned back to the animal. "Poor thing. It's been weeks since he's had a good meal."

"All the more reason to call animal control."

He turned to go back to the house to do exactly that, but she half turned and caught him with a "No," and it was hard to say who was more startled, because she stared down at their joined hands for a moment, then jerked her gaze up at the same time she released his fingers.

"I mean, please don't do that. Not right now. Let's see if we can catch him first."

"I don't think he wants to be caught."

"Come here, Fido," she crooned softly, once again ignoring him.

"Fido?" he heard himself say.

"Shush," she told him.

Shush?

She hunched over a little, and God help him, his eyes dropped to her backside and the way her jeans clung to her curves and he forgot his disgruntlement and cursed inwardly instead.

"There you go," she crooned softly as she moved toward the oak tree near the edge of his driveway. "Don't be shy. Remember? We met yesterday."

The dog didn't move and Jax found himself eating his words because the mutt didn't run away at all. He reached out with his nose, sniffing her.

"Do you have a rope?"

"Uh, I have no idea." And if he did have one, who knew where it was. He'd paid someone to move him in. The past couple months had been a constant game of hide-and-seek.

"A belt then?" She glanced up at him, still standing next to the dog, gently stroking his head, her wedding ring catching his eye. "Or a tie?"

"I'll go see what I can find."

This wasn't how he'd envisioned his morning going at all. He'd imagined her sitting across the desk from him. Had planned to give her a to-do list a mile long. That would have kept her out of his hair. Instead he found himself standing in front of her and contemplating the odds of her obeying an order from him to let animal control deal with the situation.

"You know what? You stay here. I'll go inside. I have a leash we can use." A smile stretched across her already wide mouth.

"Here. You take him," she added.

But the moment she moved, the dog bolted. "Hey," she cried, making a lunge for him. She landed on air, her breath rushing out of her with an *oomph*.

She immediately rolled onto her back, Jax torn between revulsion and dismay because she'd managed to cover the front of her pretty off-white sweater with streaks of dirt.

"That little jerk," she said, using her hands to sit up. The dog ran away like he'd been struck by a bolt of lightning. "Now we'll never catch him."

"Told you we should have called animal control."

"I can't believe he did that."

He moved forward, holding a hand out to help her up. She took it willingly, and the way she smiled at him, her eyes bright and twinkling, her whole face lit up, it socked him in the solar plexus. Man. She could sell rain to Noah with that grin.

"Perhaps you'll listen to me next time."

He hadn't meant the words to come out sounding so stern, but he saw her smile falter.

"Perhaps I will."

She flicked her chin up and Jax couldn't decide what

her best feature was, her stunning eyes or the power of her grin.

She pulled her hand out of his grip and brushed herself off. "Looks like I'm going to have to change." Her hands dropped back to her sides. "Maybe I can get my kids to catch him when he comes back."

"Maybe."

What the hell was wrong with him that he watched her hands on her breasts, that a part of his mind went on its own little safari wondering if they were as firm as they...

"Meet back in my office when you've changed."

He turned away before she could spot the bright shade of red that ran up the side of his neck, at least judging by the heat that scorched his skin. And the way he clenched his hands. Or the way his whole body had tensed.

Mother of two, remember. Widow. Still wears the wedding ring.

Did he need a better reason to steer clear?

"What a mess."

Naomi stared at her reflection in the mirror and spotted a leaf in her hair. Could she have made a bigger fool of herself?

"Are you sure he ran toward the road?" T.J. asked.

He was excited beyond belief at the prospect of a hunting expedition. He'd even changed into a camouflage outfit.

"I'm sure. But you're to stay within sight of the house, you hear me?" He ran out of her bedroom. "And take Sam with you."

"Really, Mom?" her daughter drawled.

"Really, Sam," she called back. She didn't know what

had happened to her sweet daughter, but she'd disappeared into a cloud of puberty.

She dashed into the bathroom as big as a hotel room to fix her hair, the sound of the front door closing behind her kids echoing through the house. She couldn't believe the size of her new digs. It was nearly a hike from the front door to the back to her massive bedroom and the walk-in closet that housed her pathetic wardrobe.

It took her a quick second to brush her hair. She stepped back to examine her long-sleeved white shirt— her standard uniform for life, that and jeans. It might be June in California, but the lack of humidity made it feel like winter in Georgia.

Off you go for round two.

Her own entrance to his home was at the very back of her apartment, beyond a door that might look like a linen closet but wasn't. There was a hallway with a washer and dryer to her right, and beyond that another door that led to his house. The security buttons beeped as she punched numbers. A long beep sounded when she'd finished, followed by a *snick* as the door unlocked. She half expected him to be on the other side. Maybe pop out from around the hallway that led to his kitchen.

And what a kitchen it was—like something that belonged to a reality cooking show, one where celebrity chefs and top models cooked. Large rectangular terracotta bricks made up the floor. The entrance at the end of her hallway was an arch, one made entirely of bricks. As were the walls. In the far wall sat a giant stainless steel hood with a double stove beneath.

She reached out a hand and glided a finger across the island in the middle. The off-white marble was cold to the touch. Not even the fixture that hung above it—

three lights made into one—could warm its surface. The whole house felt that way, she thought, entering the main foyer. It was stunning. A true work of art, but unlived in, which was strange because she knew Jax's sister had lived in the apartment she'd taken over, and she must have cooked in the kitchen a time or two. She paused for a moment at the entrance to the living room, trying to put her finger on what it was.

No plants. Not even a fake one.

To her right sat a sweeping staircase, and just beyond that, a cobblestoned fireplace. But if she owned this gorgeous place she'd have stuffed a massive ficus in the corner. Maybe even some pointed palms at the corners of the couch in the sunken living room. Something that would catch the light from the double row of windows and set off the granite floor. Whatever. Not her place, and it never would be. What *was* her problem was the granite floor. She could see her reflection in it and she didn't want to think about how much work it would be to maintain it. No wonder he needed a housekeeper.

She turned toward the stairs, but she paused as she stared out the cathedral windows along the front. T.J. ran through the grove of trees across the road, clearly on the trail of something. Sam followed reluctantly behind, her brown hair long and down her back, head bowed.

She had her phone.

Dear Lord in heaven. She might have to have the thing surgically removed. For a moment she contemplated telling her to put the thing away and keep an eye on her brother, but the property was fully fenced. How much trouble could they get into searching for a dog? Besides, she needed to get to work.

Work.

She had a list of chores he wanted done daily. And

now he wanted help planning an event. She placed her hand on the smooth burl railing. And he wanted her to act as a maid. And a hostess. Lord, it sounded like she'd be busy in the coming weeks. But busy was good. Busy kept her mind off thinking of Trev and how much she missed him still.

"Knock, knock," she said, rounding the corner of his office. There was a double row of windows downstairs and the same in his office, although she could see the A-line of the roof from where she stood because the second-floor windows were snug up against it. Jax sat behind a massive desk made out of a slab of burl that matched the stairwell railing.

"Take a seat." He waved toward the same chair she'd sat in yesterday.

"Okay, I meant to ask you, but what is it made out of?"

He motioned with his hand as if the answer should be clear. "It's a tree root."

She felt her brows lift. "Of course. What else would it be?"

He seemed puzzled by her lame attempt at humor. It made her wonder yet again what she'd gotten herself into.

"Are your kids looking for the dog?"

"Out there right now." She took a seat, the wooden surface uneven and uncomfortable.

He leaned back in his chair and he seemed such a contradiction. He lived on a ranch, yet he looked more like the CEO of a big corporation with his short-cropped hair, the ends dipped in gray. He wore a white button-down shirt, and from what she could tell, jeans and boots. No cowboy hat today. Probably no big buckle. No wide smile of greeting, either. His sister was so sweet and open, yet his face was as closed as the garage door on the other side of his home, his entire demeanor unapproachable. Even his office was a contradiction. It was meant for show. All wide-open space, expensive furniture and sparse furnishings, and yet he had a Lego cowboy sitting in between two massive computer screens, one of them with a COWBOY TOUGH sticker stuck to the back.

She caught him staring at her. Something in his eyes made her smile fade.

"So I thought it would be a good idea to give you a to-do list this morning." He glanced at the screen on his right.

She shifted in her seat. A to-do list? In addition to her housekeeping list? The man knew how to keep a woman busy.

"Great."

He slid a sheet of paper in her direction. "You'll see the first item on the list is to call animal control."

She almost shoved the thing back at him. "No." And she even surprised herself with the sharpness of her tone.

"Excuse me?"

It was the third time that day she'd said no to him, but she didn't care. "I told you we should catch him."

"He's a stray."

"He's lost and alone and scared. I see it in his eyes. I refuse to send him to a place where he'll feel even more alone and afraid."

He shook his head. "You presume he's lost. It's more likely that he was dumped."

Her stomach lurched at the thought. Who would do such a thing? "I still don't want him to go to a shelter. They'll kill him."

"Not necessarily. Someone might adopt him."

"A dog like that? One that doesn't want human company? No."

She could tell he wasn't pleased by her argument. Great. Five minutes into her meeting with the man and already she'd managed to antagonize him.

"Just let the kids try to catch him. I'm sure once Tramp realizes we want to help him, he'll come around."

"Tramp?"

She nodded. "From the movie. Doesn't he look just like him?"

"I don't know. Never seen it."

She sat back in her seat, winced when her spine made contact with the back. "Never?"

He shrugged. "What can I say? I don't watch a lot of TV."

The poor, sad little man. "Well, trust me. He looks just like him."

"I'll have to take your word for it."

She glanced down at the list he handed her again. "Research caterers?" She tipped her head up. "I don't have a computer."

Another blank stare. "Not even a tablet?"

She shook her head. "I had one, a laptop I mean, but my daughter dropped it on the way here. It fell out of the back seat of my truck and shattered the screen. I have a smart phone, but that's it."

His look was akin to someone being told ten plus ten was two. For some reason, it made her want to smile. Nerves, she told herself. Smiles and silly giggles had always been her go-to reaction when she was tense.

"Will that be a problem?" she asked.

He slowly shook his head. "I'll have a laptop delivered to you by the end of the day."

Of course he would. She glanced down at the list again. "I guess that means I can't do items three, four and five, either. I'd need access to email for that."

"You don't have email?"

"Of course I do, I just think it'd be easier to research and solicit bids from caterers using a laptop instead of a phone, don't you?"

He pressed his lips together. "Okay then. Maybe now would be a good time to go over the housekeeping list I gave you yesterday."

"Sure."

His brows drew together. "Is there something wrong with your chair?"

She realized then that she'd been shifting around in it a lot. "This thing is like some kind of medieval torture device. Clearly, whoever you asked to decorate this place didn't actually expect anyone to live here."

He kept doing that—kept looking at her like she had Christmas lights hanging from her nose. Just then the phone on his desk rang. He glanced at the number and answered. He listened intently for a moment and then replied in perfect French, something she didn't understand, and he spoke it so fluently and so well that it was her turn to have her mouth drop open.

Who *was* this man?

She'd been expecting a sun-bronzed, boot-wearing cowboy. Maybe someone quite a bit older than her. But someone who was kind and approachable, like his sister. Instead she sat across from Clint Eastwood in his younger years. Maybe when he'd played the role of Dirty Harry.

He hung up and said, "All right, let's go over the list I gave you yesterday."

"I don't have it with me."

"That's okay." He clearly had a copy because he read from it. "Floors. As noted, use your best judgment when those need to be done. I'm not around a lot of the time, so you might not need to do them very frequently." He met her gaze for a moment, but quickly looked away. "Windows, as needed. You'll find all the cleaning supplies in a pantry in the kitchen. I've tried to think of everything you'll need. Let me know if you'll need anything else."

She nodded, not that he was looking at her.

"Dusting, empty the trash, cleaning the light fixtures—that's all self-explanatory, and like the floors, I'll leave that up to you."

He set the paper down. "One thing I wanted to mention was laundry. It's not on the list, but I was going to ask if you'd mind doing mine in addition to your own."

"No. I don't mind at all." Could he see how flushed her face had turned at the thought of folding his underwear? She hoped not.

"I don't expect you to iron. And if something needs to be dry-cleaned, I'll take care of that myself." He picked up the list again. "Let me know if you think anything needs to be professionally cleaned. Carpets. Drapery. And keep your eye on fixtures and whatnot. This is a new home, but things can still break."

"Got it."

He set the list down again. "Did my sister tell you what I do for a living?"

She sat up straighter. "Yes."

"Good. You should know I have accounts all over the world, which means I travel a lot."

"She mentioned that, too."

"Although I've slowed down lately. I've made a commitment to my sister and nephew. I try to spend as much time as I can with them, although sometimes it's just not possible—my work takes me away from home. That's where you come in. I'll need you to keep an eye on the place. I've hired someone to manage the ranch and all its livestock affairs, but he's coming all the way from Texas and he won't be here for a couple of weeks. Until then, the Reynoldses are a big help."

"That's who we should call about Tramp. Claire Reynolds has her dog rescue." She couldn't believe she hadn't thought of that before. "She'll know what to do."

He nodded. "Good idea. You can add that to your to-do list."

The phone on his desk rang again. She expected him to pick it up. Maybe start speaking in Russian or something. Nothing would surprise her with this man. Instead he ignored the call.

"Back to the security of the ranch." He leaned toward her. "No houseguests."

She lifted her brows. "None?"

"Not unless they're authorized by me."

"Not even the tooth fairy?" She couldn't resist. He just seemed so stern.

He'd gone back to staring at her again. "Tooth fairies are the exception."

"What about Santa?"

"Approved."

"And the Easter Bunny?"

"Roger that."

"My kids will be relieved."

Lord love a duck, was there an actual living, breathing smile on his face? She'd made him smile. She had no idea why that filled her with such a sense of accomplishment, but it did.

But then the smile faded. He stared at her. She stared

back, and she realized she liked him. She had no idea why. He hadn't exactly been all warm and fuzzy. She'd spent most of their time together arguing with him and he didn't seem to mind. Actually, he seemed to enjoy their tooth fairy conversation.

"Anyone else?" he asked, lifting a brow.

"I'll let you know."

"Good." He glanced at his open laptop again. "Once you receive your laptop you'll receive a pass code for my wireless network. Under no circumstances is it to be shared."

"Not even with my kids?"

"They can have it, too. Just not anyone outside the ranch."

"Got it."

"You should also be aware that there are security cameras. They're discreet, but they cover a wide variety of angles, so be mindful."

"Good to know in case one of my kids gets lost."

"Also, from time to time I'll have guests. When that happens I'll expect you to remain out of sight."

Guests, hmm? Of the female variety, she supposed. That, too, made her blush because she couldn't imagine what she'd do if she stumbled upon a naked guest.

"And I don't think I need to remind you to keep…" He looked up at her. "What are their names?"

"Samantha and T.J. We call her Sam for short."

"Please keep Sam and T.J. out of my house. Unless there's an emergency."

"They were already told, but I'll remind them."

"And I should probably meet them. Bring them by tomorrow."

Without thinking, she saluted. His brows lifted. She

smiled. He stared at her again, a long, drawn-out stare that made her uncomfortable.

"So that's it for yesterday's list. Do what you can with today's to-do list. It should be self-explanatory. You can add calling Claire and asking her if she'll help you with that dog." He stood. "Let me know what she says."

"What about cooking for you?" She tried not to fidget as she stood in front of him. "I have to confess, I'm dying to use that oven."

He appeared to consider her words. "You won't have to cook for me much. I like to graze more than eat big meals."

"Not ever?" She couldn't contain her disappointment.

"And when I do cook, I actually enjoy cooking myself."

Once again, her mouth went slack. "Really?"

And there it was again: the soft chuff. Definitely laughter.

"Yes, really."

"So I guess it's back to my hidey-hole then."

"Let me know how it goes."

She nodded, resisted the urge to smile one last time, then turned and walked away, but as she traveled across the cavernous width of his office, her tennis shoes making nary a sound on the hardwood floors, she had the strangest sensation. He watched her. She was so sure of it that she paused at the doorway, glanced back.

Their gazes connected.

She froze. She wasn't sure why. It was the look on his face. It wasn't one that made her think he was attracted to her in any way shape or form. To be honest, she'd been on the receiving end of those looks more than once since Trev had died. No, it was more like she was a weed he'd spotted in the fancy hedges outside.

Her lips lifted in an automatic smile. He didn't smile back. She turned her smile up to its full wattage. Still no response. Good heavens. The man had the personality of a wooden stick.

"See you later."

And then he did something she didn't expect. He saluted to her. It made her laugh. She didn't know why, but it did, and she didn't mind letting him hear it as she walked toward the stairs.

Chapter 4

She'd laughed at him.

It bothered him. Actually, a lot of things about her bothered him. Her looks affected him in a way he didn't want to admit. The thought of her washing his undergarments had filled him with mild horror, and yet before he'd met her he'd planned for his new housekeeper to do exactly that. Now...?

He was so deep in thought about her that he jumped when his phone chimed. Incoming call from a number he didn't recognize.

"My kids didn't have any luck finding the dog," said a deeply Southern voice. "So I called Claire and she's on her way over with a trap. She thinks we'll have no problem, but we both agree he's not going to a shelter."

He just shook his head, not that Naomi could see it. "Fine. You catch him. You deal with him."

"Sounds good. I told her to meet us out front."

"Us?"

"I presumed you'd want a say in where we place the trap."

She had a point.

But it wasn't until he was outside, watching her round the corner of his house, that he admitted he'd been kidding himself. He could have left the matter to Claire. She was the professional dog handler. But he'd wanted to see Naomi. Had wanted to look for that mischievous grin of hers again.

Why?

It alarmed him, the realization that he was attracted to her.

Claire wasn't there yet, but Naomi spotted him sitting on the porch, the maroon cushions beneath him not the least bit comfortable. He really would need to do something about his furniture. He couldn't have guests over and have them sit on... What was it she'd called it? Medieval torture devices.

"My kids are bummed they won't get to catch Tramp."

She smiled in amusement and it brightened her face in a way that made him want to... He frowned. He didn't know what it made him want to do.

She crossed in front of him, a hint of vanilla trailing in her wake, and sat on the matching redwood seat.

"Ugh." Her smile faltered, but only a little. "Did they use rocks for stuffing?"

"It's the buttons," he said, shifting in his own seat.

She leaned over, her long red hair swinging forward. It was later in the day now and the sun loved the color. It set the strands afire in such a way that he knew it was natural. All of her was natural, from the dark brows to the thick lashes to the bee-stung lips.

"You mind me asking who decorated? I might hire them to make furniture for my kids to sit in when they're bad."

Almost, *almost*, he laughed. He caught it just in time.

He didn't want her to know how easily she charmed him, not since they'd be working so closely together. "You might be onto something."

She straightened suddenly, and he realized a white van was coming down his long drive. They had an uninterrupted view of the land. He'd planned it that way. In his line of business, you always used the terrain to your advantage. Nestled up against a hill, it wouldn't be easy to breach his home from the back, just the front, and he'd helped mitigate the weakness by clearing his property so that only oak trees remained. No shrubs for people to hide behind. Not that he expected enemies. Still, it was always good to be prepared.

"Claire," Naomi said, standing and already on the move.

He'd somehow forgotten that they knew each other. Although Ethan had recommended her for the job, it was clear she'd formed a bond with the man's wife based on the way she ran to Claire's vehicle, her image reflected back to him on its surface.

"That was quick," he heard Naomi say as Claire exited the van.

"I only live half a mile away," Claire said.

The two women hugged and drew back, and Jax realized he'd never seen Claire smile before. Not truly smile. The grin she gave Naomi could have beamed signals up to the moon. They both turned and started walking toward him.

"Are you and the kids settling in okay?"

Naomi nodded. "The kids were all over the place this morning looking for the dog. T.J. said he had a blast. Even Sam seemed to have enjoyed herself. The fresh air is probably good for them."

"I can't wait to meet them. And to see Janus."

"You will. We can all have lunch together."

"Perfect."

Naomi's face was an entire movie cast of emotions, Jax realized, and he couldn't look away. Everything she felt showed. Perhaps that was what fascinated him. In his line of work you never let anyone see what you were thinking. Naomi let it all hang out.

"So you found a dog," Claire said when she made it to the porch, her own ink-black hair loose around her shoulders. Up until he'd met Naomi, he'd thought Claire had the brightest blue eyes he'd ever seen. Now he realized they hadn't even touched the surface.

"He was on the front porch when I got here yesterday."

"And you tried to catch him."

"Actually, no. I thought he belonged to Jax." She glanced at him, smiling. "It was only later that I realized my mistake, and when we tried to catch him earlier, he ran away."

Jax stood, and he didn't hesitate to open his arms. Ethan's wife was petite as a butterfly, but she had the strength of an armored truck. Her son, Adam, had been diagnosed with cancer at a young age. But throughout his many treatments, she'd been there for him, nursing him and caring for him, and you would never have known how sick Adam had been watching him ride around the ranch these days. She'd truly been through hell and come out on the other side and he admired her for it.

"What?" she asked, drawing back. "Tired of chasing bad guys? You have to run off a poor, defenseless dog?"

"It wasn't my fault the dog got away."

"Sure it wasn't."

He just shook his head. "We need to catch it."

"Catch him and feed him and get him cleaned up," Naomi interjected. "Then we'll decide what to do with him."

Jax crossed his arms in front of him. She stared right back, not backing down. It made him want to kiss the defiance right off her—

Whoa.

What?

"Okay, you two. Whatever you decide to do, we have to get the dog first. I'll go get the trap, show you how to work it."

Naomi was still staring at him. He shifted his gaze to Claire.

"I should fire you," he heard himself say, and it shocked the hell out of him because he'd never, not *ever*, said such a thing to an employee.

"Even if you do, I'm still going to leave here with that dog."

And she would, too. They stared at each other, Naomi's jaw thrust forward in what he'd come to realize was stubborn defiance. Yet far from making him mad, it made him want to smile.

His gaze moved to Claire. She stared at the two of them in avid fascination. For some reason he went from amused to uncomfortable.

"Let's go get your trap," he told her.

They set the trap away from the main house, not that it would work.

"We're not going to catch him this way," Naomi said.

Claire glanced at the house where Jax had disappeared to a few moments ago. "Don't tell *him* that."

They both stood back, staring at the wire cage with

a can of cat food on the trigger. "He's the bossiest man I've ever met."

"He has to be in his line of work."

She felt her lips purse. "I guess. But I have to confess, I'm worried about how he'll react to my kids."

"They haven't met?"

"Not really. When we arrived I hid them in the apartment."

Claire smiled. "Trust me. You have nothing to worry about. He has a nephew he adores. I've seen them out together. He's a different man around kids."

"I hope so."

Claire tipped her head. "You still having trouble with Sam?"

Naomi looked away for a moment. "I don't know if it's hormones or if there's something else that has her upset. All I know is the move hasn't helped matters."

"I bet it hasn't. But take heart. There's so much to do here. Once you get her involved in 4-H and the ranch animals, she'll perk up."

"I hope so."

"Maybe I can talk to her. You know, sometimes it's easier to open up to a stranger."

"Not Sam. She's like a clam." Naomi shook her head. "As opposed to T.J. He's an open book."

"It'll be nice to finally meet them."

"I'm sure they'll be grateful for the company. I think they're kind of bored."

"They'll settle in. And when school starts, they'll make friends."

"I hope so. I don't think I could take another year of T.J. being bullied. And his glasses being broken. And being called a nerd and taunted because he's not athletic. Poor kid has been through enough."

Claire's eyes saddened. "You've all been through enough."

And now she was in a new place with a new boss and a new life. Some people might call her crazy. It wasn't that. More like…desperate.

"Come on. I'll introduce you."

But Claire didn't move. "It's going to be okay, you know. The kids will be fine. And Jax might come off as tough, but on the inside he's complete mush."

"I'll take your word for it."

Claire touched her arm in reassurance. "You're going to impress the socks off him."

Impress? Doubtful.

Her friends loved him so he must be a good guy, but she had a feeling he was a workaholic. He would expect a lot and give back all he had in return. But there was something else about him, too. He had a young face, but his eyes…they were old. She'd seen the same kind of eyes on men who'd returned from the Middle East. Trevor had come home looking like that, but she'd always been able to tease a smile back onto his face. Maybe that was why she'd stood her ground with Jax. He reminded her of Trevor, and she'd automatically reverted to form. Goading him into laughter. Saying whatever thing came to mind. Making him smile until the kindhearted Jax made an appearance.

She couldn't decide if that was good or bad.

Chapter 5

"Do you think I'll get to ride a horse soon?"

Naomi pulled the covers up to T.J.'s chin. Her big ten-year-old. Never too old to have her tuck him in at night.

"I think it's possible. I'll talk to him about it in the morning."

T.J.'s warm hand fell on her own. His eyes earnest. "You like him, don't you, Mom?"

She leaned toward him. "Of course I do."

She'd spent the day working her tail off for the man, but she supposed that was a good thing because it kept her mind off the move and worrying about her kids. After she'd finished, she spent the rest of the evening unpacking their clothes and tidying the apartment.

"Is he nice?"

"He is."

She'd stood up to him about Tramp, and rather than get angry, he'd let her have her way. In hindsight, she probably should have kept her mouth shut. Too much was riding on this to blow it with her new boss.

"Do you think I'll ever get to see the inside of his house?"

"Of course you will."

Please keep Sam and T.J. out of my house.

His words made her bite back a frown. She didn't blame the man. She really didn't. But that was the problem. One minute he let her tease him. The next he was so stern. Such a contradiction.

"I wish I didn't have to go to school."

The words drew her instantly back to the present. "You have months before you have to worry about that."

Her son fiddled with her fingers. "You think they'll be nicer here?"

She leaned down, touching her nose to his before drawing back. "I know they will."

"Sam won't have any problems." He frowned. "She gets along with everyone. Especially the boys."

And that *was* the problem. She'd noticed Sam was just a little too into some of those boys, especially given her young age. It had scared her. She worried that her daughter was so in need of male attention, she looked for it in the wrong place.

Oh, Trevor. Why'd you have to go and leave us?

As if sensing her thoughts, Janus sat up from his position alongside T.J.'s bed. The dog rarely left the boy's side.

"Sam will need to make new friends, too. And you'll both have all summer to do so. You'll feel better about school once you get to know people."

She squeezed his fingers then leaned down and kissed his forehead. "Sleep tight."

Janus's tail thumped when she rose to leave the room. "Keep the bad dreams away," she told the dog, who lay back down.

She would swear the dog's mouth lifted in a smile. Her husband's dog was the smartest animal she'd ever met. He'd helped T.J. through some rough nights. For whatever reason, her son had nightmares about Trevor's death and Janus seemed to sense them. They'd gotten better with time, probably in part because of Janus, but every once in a while they would strike. And it broke her heart.

The sheen of her son's tablet screen caught her eye. It sat on his night table, a piece of furniture that had probably cost as much as her truck. The whole place was decorated with finely crafted pieces that she worried incessantly about her kids scratching.

"Good night," she told her son, and then, before she could think better of it, grabbed the tablet. It was part of the mom code that your kids got all the fancy electronics before you did. T.J. used it to read books and play games and watch videos. But it had internet.

You shouldn't.

She wanted to. She couldn't deny it. She wanted to know more about Jaxton Stone.

She passed Sam's room. Another perk of the job. Her daughter had her own space now, too, instead of sharing a room with T.J., not that she seemed to care. She didn't even look up as Naomi passed by. Too busy reading a book, and to be honest, Naomi was glad. Better that than texting her friends or being online and maybe meeting some boy that was really a perverted old man. She hated the internet and the trouble her kids could get into. Too much surfing could lead to trouble.

Like you're about to surf?

Yeah? So what, she told herself, settling down on a plush couch. She tried entering his name first, surprised when his picture and bio came right up. It was just a snip from his website. Darkhorse Tactical Solutions, or DTS. She clicked on the full link.

Founded nearly two decades ago, Darkhorse Tactical Solutions (DTS) owes its success to Jaxton Stone. A former MI (Military Intelligence) specialist for the Army, he holds a PhD in strategic management and a BA in political science. One of the youngest owners of a military contracting firm, Mr. Stone brings a unique blend of experience to DTS, one gained while serving three tours in the Middle East. He speaks three languages, is highly decorated, and prides himself on putting the safety and security of his clients on the same level as those he employs.

She leaned back. Three tours. That was a lot of time spent overseas. Now that she thought about it, that explained the stony appearance. He'd learned it from the military, where you were taught to keep your thoughts from showing on your face.

She clicked on the DTS homepage. There was a picture of men in camo with the desert as a backdrop. It took her a moment to realize that the man in the middle, the one with dark protective glasses and at least three days' growth of beard, was Jax. He was younger, and he held some type of assault rifle, but she recognized the stern expression on his face. The caption read, "Jaxton Stone, Founder (middle)."

She studied him. It made her wonder what he'd been through. What he'd seen. Based on what she'd learned from Trevor, none of it had probably been good. But he was single. How much harder would it be to bear the burdens of your terrors when there was nobody to lean on once you came back home? Maybe that was why he'd started his security firm. Maybe he'd needed to surround himself with men who understood.

She set the tablet down. She had no doubt Jax was

a nice man. He clearly had a code of ethics, too. You didn't get medals from the Army unless you did something pretty spectacular. But rather than reassure her, the realization that she worked for a man a lot like Trevor unnerved her. Most of the men she'd met since Trevor's death were ordinary and uninteresting. Jaxton Stone definitely wasn't that.

War hero.

A man who didn't brag about his accomplishments or display them in any way. A man who gave one-hundred percent of his time and effort to the company he ran and the men who worked for him. He would be a fantastic boss. She should consider herself lucky to have gotten a job with him, especially one that included lodging and a fancy ranch for her kids to enjoy.

She nibbled on a nail. She needed to put aside her concerns. From here on out she would focus on the positives, not the negatives. She would be the best damn employee Jaxton Stone had ever seen. When she was done planning this party, he'd wonder what he ever did without her.

Jax wondered if he should have hired her.

The next morning he found himself staring out the windows of his office again, thinking he could probably hire an outside housekeeper, one who didn't come with kids and a dog and a pair of stunning blue eyes. He could outsource the event planning to his main office. It might make things a little difficult, but it could be managed.

And then she'd be without a job. And homeless. And in a strange state.

The thought had him spinning to face his computer. He should focus on work, so he shot off a quick email to his IT guy, asking if her laptop had been delivered yesterday. Brady's response was nearly instantaneous. It would arrive today, and there was an apology for the delay. That was how Jax operated. Quickly. Efficiently. Fluidly. He was so involved in shuffling through emails and fielding phone calls that he hardly spared a thought for the delivery truck that came and went. Jax knew she was on his network when a chat box suddenly appeared.

Hey there, boss.

He hesitated a moment. If he replied it might open up a conversation, and he really didn't need that right now. He was in the middle of a sensitive negotiation between an Israeli business mogul who needed security for his wife when she came stateside for a few weeks. The man might be richer than Croesus, but he always drove a hard bargain, which was probably how he got to be so rich. Drove him nuts.

I see you received your laptop.

He'd typed without thinking, his fingers flying across the keyboard before he could stop himself, and damned if he knew why.

The software told him she was typing, and he found himself holding his breath as he waited for her reply.

I did, but it's like driving a new car. I don't know where anything is and I keep waiting to crash it.

He smiled, glanced at his email inbox, thinking Yosef might have responded. He hadn't and so he typed:

You found the chat icon quickly enough.

That's because I love to talk.

He sensed that to be true. He'd watched her standing outside with Claire earlier, talking animatedly.

Hello? she typed.

At least you can admit your faults.

Ouch.

He'd been teasing a bit, unusual for him. But, of course, she didn't know that. Don't worry. I'm used to it. My sister could talk the ears off a marble bust.

Your sister is adorable.

On that they could agree. Still, he couldn't help but type: You wouldn't say that if you were helping to plan her wedding.

I would LOVE to help her plan her wedding.

You're hired then.

He'd been half joking, but once he typed the words he realized Naomi might not want to add to her already huge to-do list.

Do you mean it?

Twenty-four hours ago he would have added to her workload without a second thought. He gave a lot to his employees, but he expected a lot, too. Suddenly he wondered if sometimes he asked too much.

Only if you want to.

Her response was immediate. I do!

He nodded even though she couldn't see it. I'll check with Lauren then and see if she minds.

Got it, boss.

She didn't say anything further, and anyway, his email binged and he saw at once it was Yosef, but it surprised him how much he wanted to go on chatting with her. Instead, he busied himself with more work, checking in with his men in the field. There were new contracts to assign. Jobs to be billed. He had a host of staff in the Bay Area, but he kept an eagle eye on things because that was just his way. Control freak, his sister said. Obsessive, some of his employees claimed. He called it detail-oriented, and in his line of work that could save your life.

He just hoped he didn't scare Naomi away.

His fingers froze on the keyboard. What an odd thing to think. His management style was to set the tone of employment right from the get-go. Employees either lasted or they didn't. He wanted Naomi to last.

It's because she reminds you of your sister.

Was that it? he asked himself. Or was it really the intense attraction he felt every time she walked into a room?

Whatever he felt, he would keep it under wraps. They both had too much to do to have it any other way.

* * *

"Knock, knock."

He'd been waiting for those words since he'd first sat down to work this morning. Crazy. And she waltzed in like she owned the place, red hair flying, lips lifted in a smile, a sheaf of papers in her hand.

"My liege," she said with a small bow, but then she straightened a bit and he spotted the hint of color that spread from her neck and up to her cheeks, almost as if she didn't mean to tease him.

"I'm sorry," she said.

Just as he suspected. The words had slipped.

"No. It's okay." He tossed his own sheaf of papers across his desk, the documents sliding for a bit before coming to a stop near the edge. "What do you have for me?"

"A list of potential caterers." She sat down in front of him, and her smile could warm even the hardest of hearts. "Thank you Google and Yelp."

"Are they local?"

She nodded, pushed a lock of her hair behind her ear, revealing the plumpness of her lobe. Why was he staring at that lobe? Why did he have to force his gaze away? "I figured you'd want to patronize local businesses."

"I do."

"So here's my list. Of them all, I'd recommend Bill's Barbecue. He does a lot of local events. Crowd favorite. Voted Best of Via Del Caballo for five years in a row. For an outdoor event, I think he'd be great. And since you want the event in the arena, I was thinking we could drape a canvas top from the center, sort of like a circus tent, and lay down a portable floor. We could set up an open bar in the grooming stall, let your guests actually interact with the horses. Later we could take them on a tour of the guest apartments above the arena. I think it would be perfect."

It would be perfect. Clearly she understood what he was trying to accomplish. He wanted to show off the facility, yes, but he also wanted to make a statement. Local brass needed to understand that he was utterly committed to making Dark Horse Ranch one of the premier therapeutic ranches in the nation. Holding the event down at the arena was a masterstroke. People could see firsthand what he had to offer.

"Book the caterer," he said. "Reserve the tent or whatever you plan to put in the center of the arena. And the tables and chairs. Everything you need—you have some excellent ideas."

She beamed. "Far out. I'll get on it right away."

Far out?

He shook his head, and that's when he saw it. On the screen to his left was the image of a dog, one that stood on his front porch, eating out of a can of...cat food.

"Son of a—" He stood abruptly.

"What?"

"He's back." He pointed to his computer screen.

"Who?"

"That damn dog."

She stood up, leaning toward him, the scent of her catching his attention. He actually had to close his eyes.

"He's got the cat food." She drew back. Thank goodness she moved away. "The little sucker outsmarted the cage."

"Clearly." He stood, started to head for the door.

She beat him to it, blocking his way. "No," she said, holding out her free hand and pressing it against his chest.

He froze.

She did, too.

Her hand. He stared at it for a moment, shocked. None of his other employees had ever dared to touch him in the past. Okay, they'd shaken his hand, but it wasn't just that she actually touched his person. No. Her fingers were soft and petite and so warm.

"I'm sorry," she said for the second time that morning.

I'm not.

The words were on the tip of his tongue, hovering there, about to jump off, but he talked them back from the edge, reminded himself that she worked for him.

"I wasn't going to try to run him off," and even to his ears the words sounded strained.

"I know that, but we have to do this carefully so we don't startle him."

She looked up at him so imploringly, her blue eyes the color of butterflies. She reminded him of the beautiful creatures. Someone who might fly away at the slightest touch.

Whoa, whoa, whoa. Where had that thought come from?

"What do you suggest?"

"I'll go out first, from my apartment, walk up to him slowly. He's met me before, so he won't be scared. I'll catch him somehow and we'll bring him inside."

"Good plan."

She smiled, and it was like dropping off the edge of a building. His head swam for a moment and he had to resist the urge to take a step back.

"I'll grab one of Janus's leads on my way through the apartment," she said.

Why did he react so strongly to her smiles? What was wrong with him?

She left in a hurry. He followed, and much to his chagrin, caught himself glancing down at her backside. She wore a white long-sleeved shirt, and her jeans sparkled with rhinestones. That was what caught his eye.

At least, that was what he told himself.

"You stay here," she ordered, and then the smile notched up a degree. "Be ve-wee, ve-wee qwiet," she whispered in an Elmer Fudd voice. "Whee'rhuntin'wabbits."

Her lips twitched, laughter hovering just at the edge of her mouth and, damn, she did it for him.

He wanted to kiss her.

She turned just in time, because had she been staring at his face, she might have caught the way he swiped a hand over it. Might have seen the way he turned away from her, reeling.

He desired her.

There was just one problem. She still wore a ring on her finger. Clearly, she still had a thing for her husband. He doubted she was the type to have an affair with her boss, too. And the fact that he was even thinking that scared the crap out of him.

Get a grip, Stone.

She was just a woman. A very pretty woman. He'd faced far more serious threats to his peace of mind. Hadn't he?

There was something fundamentally wrong with having to sneak up on a dog. It didn't help that her kids had begged and pleaded to help out on her way through the apartment. Naomi slowly rounded the edge of the house, glancing back just in case her kids decided to ignore her order to stay inside. Only as she turned the corner did she realize she needn't have bothered sneaking up on Tramp. He'd known she was there. The moment she peeked around the edge of the porch, he tilted his head, eyes shooting right to her.

Well, alrighty then.

"Hey there, boy," she crooned.

Through one of the tall windows she spotted Jax. He stared down at her in a way that made her skin tingle, although why that was, she had no idea. He was just watching her. At least he'd done as she'd asked and stayed put. Tramp seemed to be responding well to her presence. He hadn't fled, not even when she took a step toward him.

"Don't run away," she said softly.

He bolted—right for her.

What?

One minute she was standing, the next she was on her butt and being licked to death. "Tramp. No." Which came out sounding like, "Trampth. Noth."

"Naomi," someone yelled. Jax, concern evident in his voice.

"It's okay." She grabbed Tramp by the collar, clipped the leash to it. "I'm all right."

She looked up, froze. He stared down at her, and there was such a look on his face, one she didn't immediately recognize.

Possessiveness.

She leaned back in surprise. "I'm fine," she gasped out.

He was probably just protective by nature. There was no reason for him to stare down at her possessively. He was her boss, not a boyfriend.

She blushed at the thought of *that* ever happening.

Tramp realized there was another human there and

decided to check him out in the same way he'd checked her out—by jumping up on him.

"Down," he ordered as she scrambled to her feet. Her butt throbbed. The cheeks on her face had warmed, too. She decided to avoid eye contact. Clearly she was reading things on his face that weren't there.

"Let's get him inside before he slips his collar," he said.

"Good idea."

But they had to half drag, half lead him there. When they made it to the porch, his claws skittered across the surface, as if digging into the wood could stop his progression forward. In the end Jax had to push on his rear end to get him through the door—just in the nick of time, too, because he slipped his collar the moment the door closed behind him.

"Tramp, stay." But the dog bolted. "No!" Naomi cried as Tramp jumped up on Jax's fifty-thousand-dollar couch.

"Down," Jax ordered next.

The command worked, but the way the dog came at them was all wrong. He used a side table as a springboard. A glass lamp ended up a casualty.

"Hey," she cried again, charging toward the wayward dog. Jax did the same thing. They nearly bumped heads before they both drew apart in surprise. Another crash. A statue had fallen over, one she hadn't even seen before. Another moment where they both ran toward the dog. Tramp didn't notice and didn't care. He had the biggest canine grin on his face she'd ever seen. Considering he hadn't wanted to enter the house, it surprised her. It was as if he'd spied that sofa from outside the house and determined that one day he'd use it for a doggy trampoline.

"Grab him," Jax ordered.

She was trying, but he slipped her grasp. She straightened up and yelled at the top of her voice, "Tramp!"

To her absolute and utter shock, the dog slid to a stop, turned and headed right for her. She could read the intent in his eyes.

"No." She held her hand out.

Jax took the blow in her stead. One moment he stood behind her, the next he was in front of her and Tramp was rearing back, and they were like two objects colliding at the speed of light, their impact a big bang of canine tomfoolery.

"Jax!" she heard herself cry, for some insane reason trying to catch him. It didn't work. The weight of them all was too much. Jax took the brunt of it. She fell hard, too. Tramp seemed to think it all good fun because he bounced up and down on them both, pink tongue hanging out, muddy paws leaving prints on her shirt.

"Sit!" Jax yelled.

Tramp sat.

It was like the moment after a bomb blast. The instant where all was quiet and you tried to take stock of what'd just happened.

"He knows sit," she said in awe.

"Clearly he does."

"And you thought he'd been dumped."

"Clearly he was, and probably because he doesn't listen."

Tramp just looked at them both, happiness shining from his eyes, and Naomi started to laugh. She couldn't help it. Here she was in one of the most prestigious and most gorgeous homes she'd ever seen, and one four-legged canine had managed to ruin it all. Well, just the living room.

She expected Jax to sit up, to scowl, to frown at her in a "see, I told you so" sort of way. Instead he tipped his head so they were eye to eye, and her whole world tumbled end over end because of the look on his face. She could have sworn she saw his gaze dart to her lips, but he pulled it back again and her own humor faded as her heart began to *thu-dump, thu-dump, thu-dump* in her ears.

"You okay?" he asked gently.

No. She wasn't okay. Not at all. Her heart pounded. Her skin tingled. Her chest rose and fell.

"Yeah, I'm good."

His gaze dropped to her lips again. She looked at his lips, too, and then he rolled toward her and she could feel his breath on her face and she thought he might… That he could possibly… That she wanted him to…

He got up.

If she'd been a candle she would have melted at his feet. He waved a warning hand at Tramp. She forced herself to breathe.

He held out a hand. "Now that we've got him, what are we going to do with him?"

"A bath." Her lips trembled. "I'll have the kids give him a bath."

He stared down at her, hand outstretched, and she stared at his masculine fingers and wondered if she had the courage to clasp them.

Tramp took the decision out of her hands, shooting toward her and sliding his tongue across her face.

"Hey," she cried, sitting up. Somewhere, almost out of the range of her hearing, she thought she heard him say, "Lucky dog."

Chapter 6

He'd damn near kissed her.

Jax tried not to think about that as they headed toward the door to her apartment. Okay, more like forcibly pushed the almost-kiss from his mind.

"Did you catch him?"

The words were said by an exuberant little boy who'd clearly been waiting for them. T.J.'s eyes fell on the dog behind them. "Cool!"

"Where's Janus?" Naomi asked.

"In the front, staring out the window," T.J. said, half turning. "Janus, *bliff*." He brought his hand to his chest to emphasize the German command because clearly Janus wasn't at the window anymore. The dog stopped in his tracks, but Tramp had caught sight of him and in a matter of seconds he was at the end of the leash, whining, crying, barking. Janus didn't move, a testament to his military training.

"This isn't going to work." Naomi's daughter had to yell to be heard. "You can't just bring a strange dog in here, Mom."

She was right.

"You can give him a bath in my tub," Jax offered.

"Really?" the little boy said.

"Tramp, come," he ordered, pulling the dog back. The crazy canine didn't want to listen again, furthering his suspicion that lack of self-control was clearly why he'd been dumped in the country.

"Come on, Tramp," Naomi said.

Somehow they managed to drag and pull Tramp back into Jax's home. When they closed the door, he settled down a bit, but only a bit.

"I'm T.J., by the way," said the little boy, his glasses reflecting the light of the kitchen window.

"Nice to meet you, T.J."

"This place is amazing," he said, staring around him in awe.

"Should we give him a bath in here?" Naomi asked.

"I doubt we'll be able to get him near a sink. Probably best to use the tub in my bedroom."

"Cool!" T.J. cried. "I get to see your house."

The boy reminded him of his nephew, especially when he raced toward the entrance to the kitchen. Tramp clearly wanted to join him, because it took everything Jax had to stop the leash from sliding through his fingers.

"Wow," the boy said, staring around him, mouth slightly open.

"Nice, isn't it?" his mom asked.

Did he need a better reason to keep his eyes and hands to himself? Jax wondered. She was a mom. His employee. He shouldn't be staring at her lips and wondering what they might taste like.

"Head up the stairs," he told T.J. Actually, it was good to have the boy out in front of him. Tramp clearly wanted to meet him, because he eagerly followed in his wake. "Head left at the top."

But T.J. had stopped on the landing, peering down below him and into his living room. "This is like the Stark mansion."

Naomi laughed, glanced up at him. "If you knew how much he was into comic books, you'd know that's the biggest compliment he can give."

Tramp was finally able to sniff the boy. T.J. pulled his gaze away from the interior of his house and squatted down. "Hey there, boy."

Yup. Just like his nephew. The same soft touch with animals. The same enthusiastic smile. The same zest for life.

"I'll take him," T.J. said, looking up at Jax.

"No, that's okay," Naomi said. "Let Jax do it, Teej. He can be a lot to handle."

"Awww," the boy said, but then he straightened up and clapped his thigh. "Come on, boy."

And that's how Jax found himself directing everyone into his bedroom, although why he suddenly felt self-conscious about a room Naomi would one day clean, if she hadn't already, he had no idea. He walked past them and opened the bathroom door. Tramp didn't follow; he realized why when he turned back. Both Naomi and T.J. stared around his bedroom in awe, and Tramp refused to budge.

"This is unbelievable." T.J.'s gaze caught on his massive bed. Jax's gaze caught on it, too, but for a whole other reason. And that made him feel like some sort of disgusting creep because he really shouldn't be wondering what T.J.'s mom thought about the bed. He really shouldn't.

"It's gorgeous." Her Southern accent was seasoned with pleasure.

She liked it. He shouldn't care, but he did.

"I spent a lot of time designing it," he admitted.

His bedroom took up the entire southern side of the house—second floor because he couldn't sleep in a room that was ground level. Too easy to break into. Like the front of his home, each end of the house had peaked roofs, and beneath that, walls of glass. From his vantage point he could see the lake, and way off in the distance, the Reynolds property and the glint of a metal roof that was Natalie's covered arena. In the winter, when the grass was green and the lake was full, it would be stunning. He wouldn't know, having just moved in at the beginning of spring, but it was something he looked forward to.

"You could see all the way to the beach from here," T.J. said.

He smiled. "Not quite."

Tramp's nails dug into the Berber carpet, making a popping sound as they all three moved toward his bathroom. "All the way at the end, to the left."

He made the mistake of looking at Naomi, and he saw that she stared at his king-size bed. She must have sensed his gaze, because she half turned and then her body twitched as if it was a physical shock to catch him watching her.

"It's big," she said, and there it was again. The hint of color at her neck. It once again spread up into her cheeks. "You could fit a football team in it," he thought he heard her murmur. But there was admiration on her face and in her voice, and it pleased him.

His bedroom, of all rooms, was the most "him." He might not have been born on a ranch, but he was a cowboy at heart. He'd always been drawn to horses. As a kid he'd watched every old Western movie he could get his hands on, usually starring John Wayne. In hindsight that was probably why he'd joined the military. He was a good guy chasing down bad guys. This ranch was a way of letting the cowboy side of him show through, and so the walls were the same redwood as outside. In front of the tall windows opposite his bed were comfy beige chairs with separate footrests in front. He'd positioned them near enough to the cobblestoned fireplace in the left corner of the room that in the winter he'd be able to feel the warmth of the flames. He saw her gaze catch on the wrought iron light fixture that he'd bought from an old saloon. Some nights he'd stare up at the thing and wonder about all the people who'd stood beneath it over the years.

"It's like a hotel," T.J. said, once again coming to a stop.

"You like it?" he found himself asking.

"I do," T.J. answered, but it was Naomi that Jax watched.

"It's beautiful," she said. "But are you sure about this?" She motioned toward his bathroom.

"It'll be fine." He led the way. Here the granite floors were rough, not polished smooth, and rust and brown in color. A square piece of off-white carpet sat in front of the double vanity, and it was the rug she stared at.

"Holy guacamole," T.J. said. "That's not a bathtub. That's a swimming pool."

Naomi seemed equally shell-shocked. "What if he tries to jump out the window?"

Around the tub they'd used stained glass for privacy—horses against a blue backdrop in a field of gold—and it was, quite frankly, his favorite feature of the house. "He won't jump out of that."

The look she shot him said, "Famous last words," and then she glanced back at the tub again. "All right, T.J. You're going in there with him."

"Cool."

"Although you might need a lifejacket," he heard her mumble.

"Should I get naked?"

"T.J. No." Naomi shot him a look of horrified amusement. "Just roll your pants up."

Tramp, by now, sensed his impending doom. The dog had put on the brakes, despite the sight of his favorite new human climbing into his tub, sans shoes, jeans rolled up. He tried to skitter back toward the door.

"How do you turn the water on?" T.J. asked.

He didn't blame him for asking. He'd had the same reaction when he'd seen the stainless steel fixture shaped like a Santa sleigh. There were no knobs.

"It's all done with a remote control." He pointed toward the edge of the triangular-shaped tub. "The buttons at the top are hot and cold."

"I'll do it," Naomi said. "You try to get Tramp in the tub."

That ought to be interesting.

"He's shaking." T.J. had to raise his voice over the sound of the running water. "I think he knows what's coming."

"I think so, too," Naomi said.

That made three of them. Sure enough, the moment he tried to wrap his arms around the dog's midsection, he bolted for the door.

"Tramp!" Naomi cried.

Jax reached for him as he tried to shoot by. Somehow, he didn't know how, he caught him midstride.

"Come on, boy. This is for your own good." Dog paws waved in the air as if he still tried to run.

"He doesn't think so," she said.

Tramp wanted none of it, and the look on that dog's face… Jax didn't know whether to laugh or pet him. There was such a pathetic expression of "don't kill me" on his face that he found himself leaning down. "It's okay. No one's going to hurt you."

The dog stared up at him, his big brown eyes shielded by bushy brows that reminded Jax of a walrus.

When he looked up he realized Naomi and T.J. stared at him, the craziest expression on Naomi's face, a smile on T.J.'s.

"I think he likes you," the boy said.

"Come on," he told the dog, heading toward the tub. The dog didn't move. Tramp went slack as Jax lifted him over the edge.

"What about shampoo?" Naomi turned back to the bathroom.

"It's in the dispenser there. It's for human hair, but it'll have to do. You have to pump it."

It wasn't easy to slide the dog into the tub without falling in himself, but it helped that T.J. was inside, waiting.

"Do you have any cups or something we could use to scoop water?" she asked.

"Downstairs," he said. "I'll go get them."

"No. I can do that. I'll see if I can't get Sam up here to help, too."

"Good luck with that," T.J. said, squatting down next to the dog. "Hey, boy," he said gently. "I'm not going to hurt you."

But Tramp eyeballed the liquid that steadily rose. Jax knew it would be a matter of time before he tried to jump out again. "All right. Make room."

"What?" T.J. asked.

"I'm coming in."

He sat on the edge of the tub, pulled off his boots and socks, and rolled up his jeans. For a moment he contemplated changing into a T-shirt, but he didn't want to be right in the middle of changing when Naomi, and maybe even her daughter, came in.

"I hope Tramp appreciates this." He gingerly stepped into the tub. Honestly, he'd never used it before and Naomi was right. He damn near did need a lifejacket. He understood why Tramp stared up at him in terror. From Tramp's point of view, it probably seemed like a giant crater, one quickly filling up with water.

"Sam will be up in a minute." Naomi drew up short at the sight of him, the arm that held blue plastic cups dropping to her side. Then she smiled again. "Good idea."

"I need a cup, Mom." T.J. held out a hand. Naomi gave the boy one, setting the other one down on the rim.

"I think the water's going to soak my jeans." Jax looked up at Naomi.

She'd begun to roll up the sleeves of her shirt.

"You coming in, too?"

"I think the more we all pitch in, the faster this will get done."

"Good thinking, Mom."

So that's how he ended up holding Tramp's collar while the two of them scooped water over the dog's back. Good thing, too. The first time they poured water over Tramp's back, the dog lunged, but between them all they managed to keep him inside the tub.

"Okay, what do you need me to do?"

They all three looked toward the bathroom door. Sam stood there, her dark hair pulled into a ponytail, an expression of extreme boredom on her face. She always looked that way, Jax was starting to realize.

"Perfect timing," he heard T.J. say. "Right when we're almost done."

"Shut up, brat," Sam said.

"Towels," Naomi interjected, making him think their verbal warfare was a common occurrence. Distraction was a good technique to head off a fight.

"Where are they?" Sam asked.

"In the cabinet behind you," Jax said.

"I bet this is what the White House looks like," she muttered, turning toward the cabinet.

"Poor guy," Naomi said, ignoring her daughter. "He's been lost a long time. He's so skinny."

And scared. And Jax wouldn't be human if it didn't tug at his heart.

"We'll get him fixed up."

He met her gaze. Their heads were only inches apart, and she smelled like vanilla and lemons again. Moisture clung to her skin, highlighting the striking perfection of it, her lashes so long they nearly touched her eyebrows. Her lips were red and he realized it was because she kept biting them in concentration. He had a hell of a time pulling his gaze away.

"What are you going to do with him once you're done?" Sam asked, having come back with the towel, and there was a look on the girl's face, one that made him feel suddenly self-conscious. He hoped like hell she didn't think he liked her mom or anything, because he didn't. Not like that. "You can't keep him in our place, not with Janus."

"First things first." Naomi blinked at Jax a few times before looking up at her daughter. "We're going to dry him off. Then we're going to take him for a walk, and after that we'll put him in the laundry room until we're sure he'll get along with Janus."

"Really?" Sam said, and it wasn't a supportive *really*. More like a "good luck with that" really.

"Don't be such a doubting Thomas."

Naomi turned back to him with a smile on her face, her red hair falling over a shoulder, and the look she gave him was full of cheerful optimism. He drew back. God, what was it like to be her? To say it would all work out and to actually believe it? To go into something with such confidence? In his experience things rarely worked out as planned.

"And what about after all that?" her daughter asked.

"We're going to take him to the vet to see if he has a microchip, and then we're going to find his home, either his old one or a new one." She leaned down, lifting the dog's face and asking him, "Okay?"

Tramp bolted.

"No!" she cried, reaching for the leash. It slipped from her grasp.

Jax tried to grab it, too, but the dog scrambled out despite their best efforts. Tramp didn't count on slick paws and a wet floor when he landed. The moment he tried to gain purchase, he slid sideways. Sam reached for him, but Tramp saw her coming and clambered toward the bedroom.

"Get him!" T.J. cried.

All three of them dashed out of the tub, but it was too late. The dog headed for the door like a linebacker on Sunday morning. They should have closed the bathroom door, Jax realized, an oversight on their part because the dog didn't want to stop.

"Darn dog!" Sam yelled, trying to grasp his tail.

They disappeared around the corner and Jax figured they were doomed. Once the dog spied the open bedroom door he'd make a break for it.

Only...the door wasn't open.

Sam must have closed it on her way through. Tramp ran toward it, stopped, then ducked left. He knew what would come next. Sure enough the dog headed for his bed.

"No!" they all cried.

Too late. Up he went, Sam reaching him first, the girl trying desperately to grab the leash, but his bed was big and the dog was quick. He jumped off the other side and headed back the direction he'd come, spotted the three of them and turned toward his fireplace, hitting the rack that held the tools and scattering them everywhere.

"Get him," Sam ordered.

How one dog evaded them all was anyone's guess, but evade them he did, Tramp dashing around and between and over the bed until they'd covered every square inch of his bedroom more than once. A picture was knocked from the wall. Some books from a shelf. A carpet runner flipped sideways. It wasn't until T.J. dived headfirst onto the bed, Tramp captured beneath him, that they were able to get close. To give the dog credit, he didn't try to snap at the boy, just attempted to wiggle out beneath him.

"I got him," T.J. cried.

Naomi grabbed the end of the leash. Sam grabbed the collar and Tramp looked up at them all, mouth open, eyes wide, his expression clearly asking, "What now?"

Jax almost laughed. Naomi let out a snort and

clapped a hand to her mouth, eyes wide. Sam smiled. T.J. started to giggle, too.

He felt an emotion build inside him then, something he hadn't felt since his sister and her son moved out of the house. A kind of satisfaction. He tried to analyze it, couldn't come up with a reason why he felt that way, and so instead he said, "I guess he's dry now."

Which made all three of them laugh, which made the satisfaction turn into something else, something he couldn't identify, and that scared the hell out of him.

Chapter 7

"He doesn't smile very much."

Naomi kept her gaze on Tramp as they walked toward the horse barns, Samantha's observation having the ring of truth. T.J. had insisted on going for a walk once she was done with work, and she didn't blame him after being cooped up in the apartment all day. She'd made a ton of progress on her to-do list. She'd worked far more than eight hours, popping in to see her kids and check on Tramp throughout the rest of the afternoon. She figured it was the least she could do after completely wrecking Jax's morning with the Tramp Fiasco, as she now called it.

"He's just a very busy man," she said, watching as T.J. rounded the corner with Janus leading the way. The two dogs had met face-to-face, and much to her surprise, Janus seemed unfazed. She would still lock Tramp in the laundry room for now, but at least their first meeting hadn't been a complete disaster. Tomorrow she'd take Tramp to get scanned. Later tonight she'd work on flyers. All in all, a productive day.

"I don't get why you'd want to work with him," Sam

said, hands in the pockets of her denim jacket, brown hair in a ponytail. She looked about five years old, but Naomi knew it was just an illusion. Her daughter had slipped right into puberty without her realizing it.

"It's a great job." She'd told Sam that at least a hundred times on the way out. "Not many jobs give you a place to stay for free. Plus a great salary. And it's close enough to Nona and Papa that you can visit them. And I'll have flexible hours. I get to see you guys all the time. It's a win-win."

"Not if your boss is a jerk."

"He's not a jerk." And it surprised her how quickly she came to Jax's defense. Claire had been right. He seemed tough on the outside, but inside was a different story. Look at how he'd jumped in to help with Tramp. For whatever reason, he just liked to keep his emotions to himself.

"He likes you."

That made Naomi stop. "What makes you say that?"

Sam stopped, too. Her blue eyes had the strangest expression in them. "You should have seen the way he was looking at you."

She dismissed her daughter's observation with a swipe of her hand. "He was probably just thinking about what a crazy woman I am for bringing a dog into his house."

"No, Mom." And if Sam had had glasses, she would have been looking over the rim of them. "He was staring at you like you were some kind of giant ice cream cone."

Her cheeks flamed, even though she knew her daughter had to be wrong. Still, just the thought of Jax, maybe, possibly, sort of liking her filled her with an odd sort of glee, an excitement that instantly changed into a massive dose of guilt, or maybe horror. She didn't have feelings about her boss. She almost told Sam that she didn't know what she was talking about, that she was too young to recognize attraction. But these days that type of comment would be the opening salvo to a verbal war, so she kept quiet and decided to change the subject.

"Are you excited about your trip with Nona and Papa?"

"You don't like him back, do you?"

So much for changing the subject. Why did it feel like she was about to tell her daughter a lie? "Of course not. Not like that," she quickly amended. "He's a nice man, but he's my boss. I'm just excited about working for him. It will open so many doors, especially once we sell the house."

Her daughter narrowed her eyes and Naomi wondered what she would do if she ever decided to date someone. She had a feeling Sam would consider it a betrayal of her dad's memory if she took the plunge. Thankfully she had no plans to bring a man into her life anytime soon.

"Will we be able to pet the horses?" T.J. called from up ahead.

They'd rounded the corner of the hill, the arena and pastures spread out in front of them. The fact that neither T.J. nor Sam reacted to the site of the massive structure told her they'd seen it before, not that she was surprised. They'd canvassed a wide area looking for Tramp the other day. She just hoped they'd obeyed her instructions to stay away from the horses.

"Head for the sorrel horse in the pasture."

Her son turned back to her, a puzzled look on his face, and she knew immediately what the problem was. "The brown horse," she said, pointing and holding back a laugh, one that changed to a sigh of near sadness. She loved horses, had missed being around them. A part of her wondered how different life would have been for her kids if her own parents hadn't been taken from her all those years ago. It would have been great if they'd been able to afford one.

T.J. ran off, and Janus instantly matched his steps to her son's. Tramp whined, but she settled him with a pat on the head. She expected Sam to run off, too. Sam was her horse-crazy kid, and yet she stuck by her mother's side. That was part of the reason why she'd decided to move, too, so Sam could get closer to the animals she loved.

"Don't you want to join your brother?"

"In a minute."

Uh-oh.

"We're leaving next week," her daughter said.

"Yeah. Disney World. Are you excited?"

It had been one of the bummers about starting to work in California so soon. She would miss the kids' first trip to the world-renowned amusement park. It was one their grandparents had been planning for nearly a year, but she hadn't wanted to ask for the time off, especially once she'd heard about Jax's party. Though if she were honest, it didn't upset her too much. She and her mother-in-law didn't exactly see eye to eye. It been one of the toughest decisions of her life to follow them to retirement on the West Coast. In the end the fact that the kids only had Trevor's parents left—no aunts or uncles or another set of grandparents, just Rose and Walt—had decided the matter. And then she'd heard about the job less than two hours away from where Rose and Walt had bought a home and it'd seemed like fate.

"I wish you could come, Mom. I just don't like you here all by yourself."

All by herself. As in alone with Jax. That was what this was about.

"I'll be fine."

Sam just stared. Naomi felt heat stain her cheeks once again. "Sam. It's not like that."

She lifted a brow. Behind the bravado, something like worry flitted through her daughter's eyes. "Really?"

"Really," Naomi said emphatically.

"Can I pet him, Mom?"

T.J. stood by Zippy's head, bouncing from foot to foot. Janus stared up at the horse, ears pricked, slightly crouched, as if daring the animal to try to nip his human.

"Go ahead, hon. He won't bite."

They'd passed by the massive riding complex without Naomi noticing. That startled her, but she supposed she'd been pretty deep in thought, still must have been because Sam had hung back, and it took Naomi a second or two to realize it. She stopped and turned back to her daughter, her blue eyes full of some emotion Naomi didn't recognize.

"Do you still love Dad?"

The question took her by such surprise it literally robbed her of breath. "Of course I do, honey."

Sam's gaze scanned her face as thoroughly as an FBI agent. "Do you miss him?"

"More than you know."

At last the fear in her daughter's eyes started to fade away. Satisfied, Sam turned to the horse, and Naomi was pleased to note the interest in her eyes. She watched as she tentatively approached the animal, but it was Naomi's turn to hang back.

Her daughter's question hadn't been random. She'd

asked because she was afraid she might be ready to move on with her life. It was the first time Sam had ever done something like that and it made Naomi realize when the time came, if it ever came, she would have to give her kids a heads-up.

But it wouldn't come to that. Not for a long time.

It was the smell that caught his attention.

It'd been a restless night, and as always happened when he couldn't sleep, he buried himself in his work. He'd spent the entire night getting caught up, although that was nearly impossible to do given how many clients he had overseas, but he knew the day would come when he'd have to leave the peace and sanctity of his ranch. Some things, like hiring new employees and soliciting new clients, simply couldn't be done from home.

But that smell…it was like something from his past. He couldn't put his finger on it until he followed his nose out of his office and down the staircase. He heard music, a frisky beat that he recognized as a current hit. His nose led him into his kitchen, and Jax stopped in his tracks at the sight and smells that greeted him.

"There you are," Naomi said in her Deep South drawl. "I was wondering if I'd manage to lure you down."

"You're cooking."

Her smile could have charmed birds from a tree. "I sure am." She pointed with a pair of tongs toward the center island that he rarely—come to think of it, that he'd never—used. She'd put down placemats and kitchen crockery that his designer had picked out for him months ago.

She smiled. "Already cooked my little ones their

own breakfast. No big deal to come over here and do the same."

"I told you it wasn't necessary to cook me meals."

Her smile slipped just a little bit. "You did, but you've been working so hard up there, I doubt you even thought about eating. Go on." She clacked her tongs together, pointing toward a bar stool.

He didn't want to. He really didn't. But he also didn't want to see that smile fade, because she looked adorable standing there in a denim button-down shirt that'd been rolled up at the sleeves and a white apron tied behind her. She'd piled her thick red hair atop her head in such a way that it seemed ready to tip off the side, yet it somehow stayed in place as she opened the oven and grabbed…

Waffles. He loved waffles.

"Where's Tramp?"

"I'm still keeping him in the laundry room for now. He met Janus last night, but you never know. The kids already walked and watered him. I called Claire. I'm going to take him into the Via Del Caballo Animal Clinic later today."

He sat down. She placed the tray of waffles down in front of him and he realized that was what he'd smelled. Sugar and flour and eggs.

"I figured we could make this a working breakfast seein' as how I know how hard it is for you to pull yourself away from your desk." She grabbed a spatula.

And God help him, the smell of those waffles made his stomach growl. She had bacon, too. He saw that when she put another plate down. And a bowl of freshly cut fruit, although where she'd gotten it he had no idea. And what appeared to be warmed-up maple syrup.

"Want some OJ?" she asked, grabbing a pitcher. She

poured him a glass without waiting for an answer, then leaned her elbows on the counter and waited for him to take a bite, her brows lifted in anticipation, the look on her face one that told him how much she enjoyed cooking and how much she looked forward to seeing his reaction to her food.

He took a bite. Soft, fluffy waffle melted in his mouth and he very nearly groaned.

"Good?" she asked.

He nodded because, honestly, he didn't want to waste time talking. Only then did he admit how famished he was and how much he needed to eat, and so he did. Naomi stood across the counter from him, resting her chin on her palms, her smile getting bigger and bigger as he wolfed down the first waffle. She served him another one without asking. This time, however, she grabbed a sheet of paper from the counter behind her after she'd served him.

"Okay." She grabbed a pen from a cup he didn't remember having, but that she'd clearly found somewhere and placed on the center island. "So I've booked the barbecue guy." He watched her tick off an item while he kept on eating. "He's not cheap, but what are you going to do? I've also taken the liberty of hiring a band. I know, I know, I probably should have consulted you, but in the interest of saving time, I just did it." She peeked up at him. "I hope you don't mind heavy metal."

He nearly choked. She laughed and he stopped chewing because, damn, she was beautiful. Even with her hair hanging haphazardly off her head and wearing a baggy shirt and that white apron, her beauty couldn't be denied.

"I spent yesterday afternoon calling every local politician I could get a hold of. Well, their secretaries and whatnot. And then I called the town mayor. And the local sheriff, who I understand you know, and who said he'd be happy to attend. So far I have forty people attending—"

Forty?

"—and probably more by the time it's all said and done. Your new hippotherapist, for one. And the ranch manager, who are both arriving the same week." She checked off another item.

She set the paper down. "I was thinking maybe we should offer horse rides to your guests? I mean, the goal is to get people talking about Hooves for Heroes, yes? It'd make for some good press to take pictures of people on horseback, especially the non-horsey type. Heck, we might even score some national coverage. And I think the politicians would be more apt to remember your program the next time they're considering a VA bill if we showed them a good time, so an open bar for sure. Might need to get them liquored up to get them on a horse."

He set his fork down, leaned back, and he had to admit it. She'd impressed the hell out of him. Not only with her cooking, but with her smarts.

"The big top will arrive at 0700 next Saturday. It'll be a circus theme. I'm going to hire extras, too. You know, clowns with top hats and superlong ties, maybe some acrobats. I think it'll be fun and different from the usual rodeo-themed events Claire tells me are popular around here." She met his gaze. "So I ordered invitations, put a rush on them because we're so short on time. I mean, in reality, we should take a few months to plan this event, but it is what it is so I'm taking the plunge and moving ahead at light speed. Hope that's okay."

He took a sip of his orange juice. She'd really taken

the ball and run with it. "Talk to our new ranch manager about the guest rides. It's a brilliant idea."

Her eyes lit up.

"It's all great. Better than I could've managed in such a short amount of time."

"Thank you."

Something about her smile filled him with an emotion he couldn't identify, not at first. But then he had it. Pleasure. He liked seeing that grin.

He grabbed his plate. "I'm done."

"I'll take that."

"You don't have to." He headed toward the sink.

"Actually, it's my job."

Yes, it was, but it made him feel somehow rude not to pick up his own plate. Frankly, it made him feel odd to think of her cleaning his house, too. He didn't have time to analyze that, though. Just as he didn't want to analyze why pleasing her pleased him.

"Listen, I wanted to ask you something."

The tone of her voice caught his attention. He turned back from the sink, leaned against it. She did the same thing against the center island, and he could tell from her crossed arms that she was uncomfortable with what she had next.

"I was wondering if my kids could use your pool. I know that's a lot to ask, but T.J.'s been dying to jump in."

"I don't mind them swimming. In fact, my nephew is coming over in a bit to ride horses. Why don't we let them all swim together?"

Her whole face lit up. "That would be great."

And there was the strangest look on her face. It was as if she'd stepped back and looked at him through a looking glass, and now she saw him differently, and maybe she did see him differently, but then she looked down and the spell was broken.

"I'll go tell them."

"Go on ahead."

She turned and headed back to her apartment and he stared after her. Letting her kids swim was no big deal. It was no more than he would do for any other employee.

That was what he told himself, and man, he almost believed it. The thing was he didn't mind sharing his pool with family. Naomi was an employee, though, and usually he kept a strict line between the people who worked for him and himself. But it wasn't just the thought of breaking his personal employer code that bothered him. It was just the thought of seeing Naomi in a bathing suit that made him wonder if he'd lost his mind.

"Uncle Jax!"

Kyle scrambled out of his future stepdad's truck faster than a colt coming out of a bucking chute. "I got in. I got in."

There was no sense in asking what he'd gotten into. Since he'd first heard about the junior rodeo state championships, Kyle had one goal in mind—performing there. He'd been carefully tracking his points for two months.

"Way to go, buddy." He gave him a high five. "Go on in and get saddled up while I talk to Bren."

Behind him, Bren Connelly, newly reelected sheriff of Via Del Caballo, got out of his black truck, one with a gold star on the side. He had a teasing grin on his face that told Jax he was about to get seriously hassled by his future brother-in-law.

"So my fiancée tells me she hired you a hot house-keeper."

Just what he expected. Beneath the black cowboy hat, Bren's brown eyes were one-hundred percent fun and games.

"I don't know what you're talking about."

Bren shook his head, stopped beside him, crossed his arms in front of him. "Uh-uh."

Jax tried to sock Bren in the arm, but the man ducked out of the way. "It wouldn't have mattered if she was eighty years old with gray hair. She's perfect for the job."

"Yeah? You let all your employees' kids swim in your pool?"

He'd seen them? Well, of course he had. In Bren's line of work, he would observe things most people wouldn't—like kids swimming in a pool as he drove by—while Kyle probably hadn't noticed a thing. That's what he liked about the man. They were a lot alike, the two of them. His sister couldn't have found a more perfect match for her and her son.

"Her kids are great," Jax said. "I couldn't say no when she asked if they could use the pool."

Bren just gave him a look that said plain as day he didn't believe him.

"Besides, I was thinking Kyle could join them later. He'll be tired after he rides."

Bren considered the words. "So you want me to pick him up this evening?"

He was feeling more and more uncomfortable by the minute. "If that works."

Bren's smile was like a dog that had broken into the food bin. "Well, all right then."

"You don't have to leave right away. I miss the days of riding lessons and beers afterward."

He shook his head. "Kyle told me he can handle it from here on out, and he's right. The kid's a natural."

"He is that."

"Besides, I wouldn't want to intrude on your time with the hot housekeeper."

"Hey, now."

His friend laughed. Jax decided to ignore him. The more he denied it, the more grief he'd get. Bren was known for his dry sense of humor.

"I'll tell Lauren the plan. You go have fun."

Fun. Yeah. "You sure you don't want to stick around?"

"Nah. I'll leave you alone with the happy home-maker."

He ignored the remark and, a few minutes later, watched Bren drive away. But the whole time he supervised his nephew he couldn't deny the way his heart rate rose and fell in correlation to the direction of his thoughts.

When he slipped through the tall doors of the arena it was in time to see Kyle leading Zippy through the gate. Man, the kid had gotten good. Of course, with jumping lessons and damn near daily riding sessions, he'd had every opportunity to improve. The only rule was that he couldn't ride alone. Someone always had to be nearby in case something happened, and so Jax busied himself around the barn, doing things his friends the Reynoldses had taught him to do: check horse water, clean stalls, give the horses on the ranch the once-over. Right now the horses were all on vacation. That would change soon. Once his therapist and ranch manager arrived they would decide the best course of action on how to get the ranch up and running. Exciting times ahead.

"Uncle Jax, look!"

He glanced through the bars of the horse stall he stood in. He'd built them that way for exactly that reason—so people could watch what was going on in the arena while they worked with the horses. Kyle galloped around the perimeter, Zippy's hooves kicking up dust, the sun catching the particles and turning them into clouds so that it almost appeared as if Kyle flew. The image was helped by the fact that he didn't hold onto the reins. His arms were out to the side and he tipped his head back, laughing, and Jax rested the muck rake in the shavings and just smiled. This. This was why he'd done what he'd done. Why he'd sunk a small fortune into the place. He wanted to bring joy to people's lives. A joy he had yet to find for himself. But that was okay. He could absorb the happiness of others. That was enough for him.

Kyle grabbed the reins again, sat back. Zippy stopped. "That was fun."

"Probably time to call it quits," he said. "If you want to have time to swim before the sun goes down."

Kyle nodded and pointed Zippy toward the stalls. His nephew was still all smiles, sliding expertly to the ground.

"Looks like you're ready for the championship."

Kyle stepped up to the horse's head, clucking to urge Zippy forward. "Bren said it's okay if I get nervous. Everyone has to step up their game, but that all I have to do is put into action everything I've practiced and I'll be fine."

"Are you nervous?"

Kyle stopped. "No. Not really. I don't think so. I get

this weird kind of butterfly thing in my tummy when I think about it, but I'm not scared."

"Good for you."

"Come on, Zippy. Time for dinner."

They fed the horse, and it was something Jax planned to keep on doing, even once his ranch manager arrived. There was something about the eager look on a horse's face that always made him smile, and then the calming sound of them munching on food.

"Ready?" he asked when they were finished, glancing back into the empty arena. Soon. Soon all his plans would come to fruition.

"I can't wait to swim."

He realized in that instant why he'd wanted Kyle to join him at the pool so badly. He'd needed a chaperone.

He damn near stumbled.

"You okay, Uncle Jax?"

Jax waved a hand, his heart beating like he'd just run from the barn. He didn't want to be alone with her, although strictly speaking he wouldn't be alone. Her kids would be there, too. And that was part of the problem, as well. For the first time in a very, very long time, he was intimidated, and all by one gorgeous redhead and her two kids.

"Let's go," he told his nephew. Kyle just stared at him strangely, as if he knew something was up, but didn't want to push the matter. He'd always been a smart kid for his age.

"Do you like your new housekeeper?"

He glanced over at his nephew as he started the ATV. At first he thought the kid meant like as in *like*...dating-type like. Then he realized he was just asking in the typical ten-year-old, boys-think-girls-are-yucky type of way.

"She's nice."

And a good cook. And a hard worker. His house looked spotless. The other day he'd walked into his master bathroom and realized it smelled like vanilla and lemon. He didn't know what it was, but he would bet it was something she'd concocted on her own. Some all-natural, homeopathic cleanser.

"Mom says she's pretty."

She is that. The words were on the tip of his tongue, but he didn't want to admit that to his nephew. All he needed was some form of the comment to be regurgitated later on.

"Nobody is as pretty as your mom."

Kyle nodded in agreement. Jax's hands clenched the steering wheel as they rounded the side of the hill and his house came into view. He could hear a little boy shriek and a dog bark. Tramp appeared to be having the time of his life.

"Is that the dog my mom was telling me about?"

He'd had a conversation with his sister about Tramp the other night, one that had kept her laughing for at least a half hour.

"It is. Name is Tramp."

"Cool. You going to keep him?"

"Hell, no."

"Why not?"

"He's a Dennis the Menace."

"Who's that?"

He glanced at his nephew, loving the avid curiosity in his eyes. "Never mind."

"How old is her son?" Kyle asked as they pulled to a stop along the side of the house.

"Your age, I think."

"Cool. Gonna change into my swim trunks."

And he was gone. Kyle waved to the crowd at hand and yelled, "Be right back," as he darted by.

Naomi sat up. Tramp skidded to a stop near the edge of the pool, lifted his head and made a beeline for him.

"Tramp, no."

To his complete and utter shock the dog listened, slowing down, tail wagging, canine face wreathed in a smile as he greeted him.

"Where's Janus?"

"Inside," she said with a smile. "Much to his dismay."

She wore a swimsuit.

Jax absently patted Tramp's head, pretending an interest in the dog. Of course she wore swimming gear. They were at his pool. For some reason he wished she'd worn a nun's habit. He didn't need a reminder that she was a sexy, beautiful woman. Not now. Not after he'd stood so close to her and he'd felt...

He didn't know what the hell he'd felt.

"Was that your nephew?" said a voice from the pool. Tramp followed in his wake as he moved to the edge. T.J.'s eager blue eyes stared up at him, his red hair streaming water into his face, the strands turned dark by the liquid. Jax had no idea where the boy's glasses had gone, but he could clearly see something.

"That's him."

"Where'd he go?"

"To change into his swim trunks."

The kid smiled just before he plunged under water again. Jax stood by the side, watching him transform into a shimmering mirage when he pushed off the edge, and feeling more awkard by the second.

It's your house.

Yes, but he really wanted to go back inside and work. He should do that, too, because no matter how often he told himself, he would never take it easy and slow down. He needed to stay busy. The nightmares at night were too vivid for him to ever slow down. So he worked.

"Come." Naomi patted the wooden chaise next to her. "Sit and relax."

It was just a plain black bathing suit. No fancy pattern. No tiny triangles. No body-enhancing tricks, yet it flattered her pale skin and hugged her curves in a way that convinced him all the more that he should go hide inside.

"I should work." A wet nose bumped his hand. He glanced down. Tramp stared up at him imploringly.

"Even Tramp wants you to stay."

"Tramp just wants attention."

She shook his head. "You work too much."

Her daughter sat next to her, and the little girl frowned. Jax wondered if she disapproved of her mother's boss hanging out with them. He wouldn't blame her.

"Come on," she said, patting the seat again.

Don't do it. Ignore her. Go inside and work.

But her smile was as warm and as welcoming as an innocent babe's, the blue of the pool emphasizing the lightness of her eyes, and he knew if he didn't do as she asked, he'd hurt her feelings. He didn't want to do that. He didn't want her kids to think he was a snob. He wanted to make a good impression.

Damned if he knew why.

Chapter 8

He felt tense. Why was he tense when he sat by his damn pool?

Naomi turned toward him. He flinched as if his chaise had suddenly sprouted thorns.

"You know, you could go inside and change into your bathing suit."

The sun glistened on her pale skin and he wondered if she'd put something on to keep herself from burning. He'd never seen skin so fair. It reminded him of his mother's fine china.

"I'm okay."

Tramp turned to look at him, and Jax could swear the look on the dog's face was one of question.

"It's not a crime to actually enjoy your own pool, you know."

Yeah. That's what he'd been trying to tell himself.

On the other side of Naomi, Samantha leaned forward, catching his eye. She didn't have her mother's fair complexion and he wondered if she took after her father. His gaze fell to Naomi's hand. The gold ring still glistened.

So?

If she still carried a torch for her husband it was none of his business, except he knew that to be a lie. It was time to confess, something he always prided himself on doing—complete honesty. He liked her. She might have deplorable taste in dogs, but she was funny and charming and she sure as heck didn't look like someone who'd had two kids. He glanced at Naomi's daughter again. She must have felt his gaze because she turned, gave him the world's cheesiest smile, then went back to watching her brother.

"Cannonball!"

His nephew flew through the air, landing inches away from where T.J. swam. Tramp woofed in approval.

"Stay," he told the dog.

To his surprise, Tramp did as ordered. Inside the pool Kyle broke the surface, splashed water at T.J., then shot off. Naomi's son needed no second prompting. He was off like a sprinter.

He felt someone's gaze upon him. Samantha. He smiled. She looked away, then stood. "I'm going for a swim."

Okay, so it wasn't just the widow thing that should give him second thoughts; he needed to add two children into the mix. Complicated with a capital *C*, and not because he didn't like kids. He loved his nephew. He could just tell by the look on the daughter's face she wouldn't welcome any male attention where her mom was concerned. That wasn't the only complication. Naomi worked for him. He'd never, not once in all his years of owning a business, glanced at one of his employees. Why now?

Samantha went to the far end of the pool, dangled

her legs in the water. She watched what happened in the pool in between peeking glances at her mom.

"At least take off your cowboy hat," said Naomi.

He'd forgotten he wore the damn thing. The boots on his feet should have been a reminder, but he was clearly distracted. Tramp whined. He glanced at the dog, took off his hat, waved it at the dog. "Go on."

He was off like a shot, barking at the kids in the pool. For the first time he saw Samantha smile, cowering away from Tramp when the dog spotted her sitting there and recognized her for what she was—an easy mark. A tongue bath ensued.

"Stop," she cried over the splashing in the pool, using her hands as a shield.

"Thanks for letting them swim." She said the words softly, quietly, but she punctuated them with a grateful smile. "I've got to confess, this was just what they needed. They're not used to life on a ranch. The isolation was…unexpected."

He glanced at Samantha, who tried to push Tramp away. "They'll adjust."

Naomi nodded. "Sam wants to learn how to ride." She glanced over at him. "Do you know anyone that gives lessons?"

"You should talk to Claire's sister-in-law." He glanced at his hands, wondering why he felt the need to clench them. "She gives jumping lessons."

"That's right. I forgot."

"I'm sure she'd give you a deal, too."

"I hope so, because I'm a little short on cash these days." But she didn't say the words as if she felt sorry for herself. It was just a statement of facts.

"And once she learns the basics, she's free to ride the horses here if she wants."

"Really?"

Her squeal drew the attention of the kids in the pool and he knew that he was doomed. Even Tramp had gone quiet, staring at the humans across the pool.

"Yes, really."

She was off her chair and giving him a hug before he knew what was happening, and as her long hair brushed his chin and her warm body pressed against him, he was thankful for his barricade of clothing.

"Thank you," she said emphatically. "This is just what Sam needs."

"What?" her daughter said.

Naomi turned toward her kids and said, "Mr. Stone just agreed to let you use his horses."

He felt his mouth drop open. Talk about spilling the beans. He hadn't meant right now.

"Now?" her daughter asked, her eyes brightening with interest.

"Can I ride, too?" asked T.J.

"Once you guys learn the basics," she said. "I'm going to ask Claire's sister-in-law to give you some lessons. But once you're given the all clear, you can ride."

If she'd expected whoops of delight, she must have been sorely disappointed. T.J. just said, "Cool," then kicked his way over to the side of the pool. Samantha stared between the two of them.

"Aren't you excited, Sam?"

"Mr. Stone really won't mind?"

"Not at all."

Samantha stared into his eyes, and for the first time in a long, long time, Jax began to grow uncomfortable. It was as if Naomi's daughter suspected every naughty thought he'd had about her mother.

"Sam, don't you want to say thank you?"

"Sure." Another cheesy smile. "Thanks, Mr. Stone."

"Wh—" Naomi's sigh was one of confusion. "I don't understand."

Sam stood up suddenly. "I'm going inside."

Naomi stood, taking a few steps in her direction. "Sam, wait."

But her daughter waved her away. Tramp followed in her wake. She slipped out the gate, and Tramp stopped, sat down and watched her disappear around the side of the house. Jax could tell by the slant of Naomi's shoulders that she was devastated by her reaction.

"It's actually supercool that we get to ride," T.J. said, and it looked like Naomi wanted to hug her kid right then. "I'm excited."

"And I can help you," Kyle said.

"Really?"

"My mom and I used to live in the same place you do. I used to ride all the time and play in the hills. There's a really cool lake that you can fish in and the school's awesome. How old are you?"

"Ten."

"Cool. We're the same age. You'll be in my class."

T.J.'s face lit up. "Neat." He shoved off the side of the pool, clearly aiming for Kyle. Kyle shrieked and shoved off even though there was no hope T.J. could catch him. And that was that.

Naomi sank back onto the chaise. "At least T.J.'s excited."

"Samantha will come around."

She spun to face him, red hair backlit by the sun so that it seemed to catch fire. "I don't know what her problem is. Back in Georgia horse posters covered her walls. She's always wanted to learn to ride, but since we've moved in not once has she mentioned them or wanted to see them or ask if could ride."

He didn't like it when her eyes were dulled by sadness, which only solidified his belief that he was getting in too deep.

"She's mad about the move," he said.

He watched as she stared in the direction her daughter had disappeared. "Yes, she is, and damned if I know what to do about it."

Don't hug your boss. He almost said the words out loud, but she'd probably take it wrong. She might be Sam's mom, but she clearly didn't see the possessiveness in her daughter's eyes. Jax did. What was more, he understood. Hell, he even felt guilty about the direction his thoughts had been taking.

"Where are you going?"

He hadn't even realized he'd stood up. "Work." His gaze caught on his nephew. "Do you mind keeping an eye on him for me?"

"No, of course not."

"Thanks."

"You work too much."

Because it kept his mind off things, things like a warm smile and the way she looked in that bathing suit.

"Got a lot to do before next weekend."

He didn't. Not really. She'd done all the work.

"Do you need any help?"

"No. Stay with your family. It's the weekend. Tell Kyle to come get me when he's done swimming."

He needed to escape, to figure out what was going on, why this sudden…weakness.

"You need to get some rest, too, you know."

But that was something he couldn't do around her. Impossible to relax when he kept noticing the way the sun played with her hair and how her black bathing suit made her skin look like pearls, and how much he wanted to say or do something to bring the smile back to her eyes.

"Work is good for me."

Work is what he did best. Relationships…those were for people who didn't have a multimillion-dollar corporation to manage and a head full of crap that always seemed to get in the way of anything meaningful.

"I don't like it here."

Naomi counted to ten before taking a deep breath and facing her daughter across a glass coffee table. T.J. was off with Kyle, the two of them having sneaked Tramp into Jax's home. Any moment now she expected to hear the sound of glass breaking.

"So you're okay if we only see Nona and Papa once a year?"

Her daughter clearly didn't like that particular line of logic. "I'll miss them, sure, but…" She sucked in her lower lip. "I want to go back to Georgia. It's not too late. The house isn't sold yet."

"Look." Naomi leaned toward her troubled daughter. "I know this was a big change. I know it's scary."

For the first time she spotted tears in her daughter's eyes. "What's wrong with going back to Georgia?"

"Nothing, but we can't go back. It's too late. We're here now."

And in California she didn't see Trevor everywhere she went. She wouldn't have to see him in the house they'd once shared, in that broken sink that he'd claimed to have fixed but still dripped incessantly. In the faces of the friends they'd once shared, their sadness and sympathy having never faded. Around town whenever she spotted a landmark they'd once visited. She'd held on to the memories long enough. Time to make some new ones.

"You hate me."

Oh no. Not the "you hate me" argument. She took another deep breath. "Sam, trust me. This is for the best." She sensed the brewing squall—her daughter was as tempestuous as a Southern thunderstorm—so she cut her off with, "It's a done deal, Sam. Crying won't make me change my mind."

Sam bolted for her room, but not before the tears fell. Naomi rubbed her tired eyes. She had no idea why she'd thought this would be easy. Sam had always been surrounded by a posse of friends. Naomi had known she wouldn't want to leave them. Stuck out in the middle of nowhere it would be tough to make new ones, at least until school started, and then she'd have to worry about boys. T.J. was notoriously standoffish when it came to meeting new people, and yet there he was upstairs with his new best buddy terrorizing her boss with a crazy dog.

Her boss.

A man who hid his kind heart behind a gruff exterior. Who worked his butt off to the point that he'd forgotten how to have fun. Who was in need of a vacation more than anybody she'd known.

T.J. came bursting in a few minutes later. He went straight to the fridge, opening it up in search of the ever-necessary snack, all the while saying, "Kyle's staying the night at his uncle's. We're going to get up early and go fishing. Tramp's going to stay with us, too."

"In Mr. Stone's house?"

"Yup."

"And Jax was okay with that?"

"Not really." Her son emerged with a package of string cheese. "When's dinner?"

"Half hour. I just have to put it in."

"What are we having?"

"Fried chicken."

"Cool. Maybe we can feed Kyle since I doubt his uncle will do it."

"You might be surprised."

But her son was already headed down the hall. "Gonna go play with his Wii."

And that would be that. He'd found a new friend. It amazed her. It also made her want to cry. Maybe this move hadn't been such a bad idea after all.

Just then Sam cried out in frustration from the confines of her bedroom. Probably couldn't get through to one of her old friends, or the internet wasn't working right, or her tweet hadn't gone through.

Some things would never change—west coast or east—she was doomed to be deemed a horrible mother either way.

Chapter 9

Someone smothered him.

Jax fought his way back to consciousness, arms flailing, body jerking, heart pounding. A dream. It was just a dream. He had them all the time. Terrible nightmares, except...

He pushed the weight away.

Thanks to the half light of his alarm clock he could see the culprit. Tramp.

"What the—"

A tail thumped. The dog yawned, his big canine body sprawled up against him, paws in the air.

"You are not allowed in here," he told the dog.

Tramp just rolled onto his belly, drew his legs together and curled up next to him. The dog even sighed in canine satisfaction.

"Unbelievable."

He should push him off. Remind him who was master. Exert his will so that it didn't happen again. Except he would just end up in an empty bed, alone, staring at the ceiling. It happened all the time. Sometimes he couldn't even remember what he dreamed about. He just knew it was bad, a memory from the past that'd come back to haunt him.

He got out of bed.

Tramp didn't move. Well, from what he could see he might have moved an eye, as in he opened one, determined nothing fun was about to happen and went back to sleep.

He'd lost his bed to a dog. What had the world come to?

He pulled on a T-shirt and decided to head downstairs for a cup of coffee. It was 2:00 a.m., the perfect time to conduct business overseas. By the time he finished, Kyle and T.J. would be creeping out of bed to go fishing. As he slipped inside the kitchen his eye caught movement on the back patio. He'd forgotten to arm the motion sensors, he realized, a serious breach of his security protocol that had everything to do with the woman who sat outside.

Crying.

He didn't need the light of the moon to know what was going on, although it illuminated her white-robed form. The shaking shoulders. The bent head. The way she'd wiped at her eyes. They might be silent tears, but she sobbed and it left him utterly stunned. She was the Wonder Woman of good cheer. The Elektra of charm and grace. The Peggy Carter of get-'er-done. It was like learning his house had been built upside down.

Who knew how long he would have gone on staring at her if not for Tramp. The dog tried barreling through one of the French doors. Naomi jumped. Her gaze jerked up. It landed right on him. He saw her wipe her face hurriedly, as if she worried he might see her tears. Too late for that. Then she gave a little wave. Tramp tried breaking through the door again.

"Tramp, down."

He'd say one thing for the dog, when he decided to listen, he did it well. Clearly someone had tried to train him because he sat at the door, peering over at him as if to say, "Hurry up and open it."

Except he knew if he did that he'd go straight to Naomi, probably paws first, probably knocking her over.

"Stay."

He should leave her in peace. Keep his distance. Let her cry her sorrows away.

He opened the door and slipped outside.

"Hey," she said softly, and he could hear how clogged her nose was, further evidence that she'd been bawling her eyes out. Not that there was any doubt.

"Hey," he said back.

"Fancy meeting you here."

There she was. The woman who ate sunshine for breakfast every day. Crying.

"Are you kidding?" he heard himself say. "I'm out here all the time in the middle of the night."

He wasn't. He much preferred standing and staring out the windows of his office when sleep and his hyperactive brain collided.

"Mind if I join you?"

"Sure." But there was a catch in her voice, as if she might start crying again, and if she did that he...

He didn't know what he'd do. He knew what he *wanted* to do. But he couldn't do that. It tore at him, too. It shocked him how much it bothered him that he couldn't comfort her.

"Couldn't sleep?" he asked. It was as inane a question as a person could ask, but he couldn't think of a single other thing to say.

"Sam isn't taking the move well."

This he could deal with. Having a sister gave him an insight into the female psyche. "Give her time. She's at an age where everything is going to be drama."

"You think?"

"I know." He thought back to when Lauren was her age. They had ten years between them, which meant he could perfectly recall her teenage years. "I remember one time Lauren planned this big outing with her friends—dinner, a movie, the whole nine yards—and at the last minute, my mom decided she wanted to go out that night instead. I was home on leave at the time, but I still remember the dustup."

She nodded, wiped at her eyes. "It's just that it's so hard being the bad guy all the time. I wish Trev—"

She looked away, her red hair burnished silver by moonlight, but he didn't need to see to know she'd started to cry again. Without conscious thought his hand moved to her shoulder, and no sooner had he touched her than he thought *what are you doing?* but he couldn't seem to stop.

"I know what it's like," he said softly. "My own parents, they're not around a whole lot." The shirt she wore had been warmed by her skin. "It's not that they're bad parents, because they're not. They're just not all that involved with Kyle. They were raised in a different era. Kids were to be seen, but not heard, and so they're distant. I know Lauren hides it well, but it's been difficult for her. I didn't realize how hard until I went to visit her and I realized she was barely hanging on and I felt like a jerk. Here I was making all kinds of money and what had I done with it?" He shook his head. "I used it to make even more money. It was a game changer for me. I realized I'd done so little for anyone other than myself, just like my parents, and so I resolved to change that. Fate stepped in because Ethan called me about an idea he had for wounded warriors, and Hooves for Heroes was born."

She had stopped crying and with his own silence came the beat of his heart.

"Sometimes," he said, "doing what's right for everyone takes a huge leap of faith, but I promise you, it will work out all right in the end."

She turned to face him and he warned himself not to move. Not to stare at her lips. Not to lean in close to her.

"You're a good man, Jaxton Stone."

No, he wasn't. He was having all kinds of inappropriate thoughts about her. Wondered what she would do if he bent and brushed her lips with his own. But he couldn't. Damn it all, he just couldn't.

It was the hardest thing in the world to let her go.

"And you're a good mom," he heard himself say, forcing himself to relax and to stand. "Have faith. Trust your heart. It'll never lead you astray."

She peered up at him, blue eyes wide and pooled with tears, her hair spilling around her shoulders and he felt himself falling...falling...

"Good night."

He ran.

Have faith.

Naomi tried to remember the words as she said goodbye to her kids the following day. She would have thought Sam would be excited. Their trip to Disney World had been in the works for so long. But her daughter still held on to her grudge. T.J., however... T.J. could barely sleep last night. He was excited about flying on his own. Excited about seeing his grandparents. Excited about the trip. Sam would have nothing to do with her. When Naomi turned her kids over to the airline escort, her face heated in embarrassment when Sam took off without her.

"Bye, Mom." T.J. kissed her, having to slide his glasses back up his nose afterward. "Don't worry. I'll talk to her."

"Thanks, kiddo."

"And I'll come back with some Mickey Mouse ears to cheer you up."

She wanted to cry. Instead she hugged him, hated to release him, wondered if she should tell Jax she'd changed her mind. But, no. Sam needed time. And space. The trip would be good for her, so she reluctantly let T.J. go.

And he was off. She watched them both disappear behind a door. Their grandparents would meet them in Florida. Afterward, they'd all fly back to Georgia together. That hadn't been the original plan, but Sam had begged Naomi to let her go to Georgia with them. One last time to see her friends, she'd said, and Naomi hadn't had the heart to say no. Rose and Walt would finish packing up their house with the kids' help and then fly out to their new home in the desert with the kids in tow. They'd all be living in California then. They could settle into a routine. Well, as routine as it would get.

Because she had a crush on Jax Stone.

Her first crush since Trevor. Oh, there'd been interest from the opposite sex, but she'd turned them down cold. Nobody could ever fill the shoes of Trevor. She'd been convinced of it…until she'd met Jax. Was it any wonder, though? They were so much alike. Both gave so much of themselves. They would do anything for friends and family. They would never turn their back on someone in need. They'd both served their country. One of them had died for it. But the sad truth was she could never let her feelings for him get out of hand. Sam would disown her if she threw dating someone into the whole mix.

Naomi barely recalled the drive back to the ranch. All she could think about was how much of a fool she was. Jax was her boss. Yet her heart began to beat when the ranch came back into view. She wondered if he'd meet her outside, or if she'd see him later, by the pool. If he'd touch her again.

He was nowhere in sight and she had to fight back disappointment. Janus was the only one to greet her, his paws scratching at the door before she opened it. The dog looked past her.

"They're gone." He must have picked up the sadness in her voice because he stepped back and then bumped his head into her hand. "You're here, though, aren't you?" And Tramp. Although, the dog was living with Jax, something she would have never believed possible when she'd first met the man. They'd had no luck finding his owner. No chip. No nothing. Jax hadn't said a word about her failure. He'd just taken the dog in—further proof that her boss was just about the nicest guy she'd ever met.

Should she go outside? To the pool? Was that too obvious? And what if she did? What if he went out there and touched her again and she felt the same thing? What if she wanted to bury herself in his arms, to inhale the scent of him, to lean back and…

No. She wouldn't go down that road. Instead she told herself to stop it. She refused to be "that woman," the one who threw herself at her boss. So she stayed up until she knew her kids had made it to Florida safe and sound, and then she went to bed, though she couldn't keep herself from peeking outside from time to time.

She tossed and turned all night. Janus crawled into bed with her at some point, nearly suffocating her until she won the battle for the pillow, but her dreams were haunted by Jax. When she woke up, she listened for him. All was quiet.

She found out why a half hour later.

She had a message from him, and her smile faded when she read it. He'd left. Work had called him away. He'd asked her to keep an eye on Tramp, which was about as close he'd come to admitting he was keeping the dog as she'd expect. He also told her the Hooves for Heroes open house was in her hands. She'd be in charge of helping to get their new ranch manager settled in, too. She read it and then reread it. The message shouldn't come as a surprise. He'd told her his job took him all over the world at the drop of a hat. That was why he'd needed a live-at-home caretaker, but with everything going on this week, it still surprised her. She would have thought he'd want to be on hand to keep an eye on things. Instead he'd given her instructions on which apartment their new ranch manager would live in, and how to get in touch with the hippotherapist, and then left without so much as a goodbye and it…stung.

Why did it sting? It was no more than she should expect. He was her boss, nothing more.

Which was why she needed to stop this right now. She couldn't get caught up in feelings for him. She doubted she would ever truly let go of Trevor. Not really. Whatever feelings she might develop for Jax, they'd be short-lived at best. That was the way these things went. Bright sparks that always fizzled.

Always.

Chapter 10

The sun was setting when his wheels touched down at the Santa Barbara airport.

"Have a safe drive home, Mr. S," his pilot of ten years, Ben, said. The man had flown for the Navy before becoming a private pilot and Jax didn't know what he'd do without him.

"Thanks, Ben. Have a great weekend."

He'd stayed away an entire five days. Honestly, he hadn't needed to, he'd just felt it would be more prudent given the thoughts that'd gone through his head. He might have cut it a little too close, though. The big party was due to start in a few hours and he had no idea if they were ready or not. When he slipped into his truck, which he'd left parked at the airport, he realized he had less than three hours to get back to the ranch, check to ensure all was ready and get dressed. It'd been a huge leap of faith to leave everything in Naomi's hands, but somehow he knew she wouldn't disappoint.

Sure enough, when he pulled in less than an hour later, she already had signs in place directing people to park at the barn. That was where she was, he would bet, because his house was completely deserted. He debated whether or not to head down that way, but he decided to text her instead.

Home.

That was all he said. He let himself inside, pausing by his front door to listen for the clatter of dog paws on marble. She must have Tramp with her, and it was funny because he almost felt something like disappointment that the big dog wasn't around.

His phone chimed.

Welcome back! All is ready. Can't wait for you to see what we've done. You should come look.

He wanted to do exactly that. What he wanted more than that, however, was to see her again. It took every ounce of his willpower to type:

Tired. See you in a bit.

He *was* tired. A six-hour flight on Monday to New York where he'd visited clients for a day, followed by a twelve-hour flight overseas to settle the feathers of yet another big client. Twenty-four hours on the ground, followed by a flight back to New York. They'd hit a hell of a headwind on the way home. Ben had said the jet stream wreaked havoc on the arrival times of commercial airlines across the nation. It seemed to take forever to get back home and now here he was. Jet lag didn't begin to describe how he felt.

Somehow he managed to squeeze himself into a penguin suit. They were trying to impress, she'd said in one of her emails, and she didn't think cowboy boots and jeans made any kind of statement. He would wear the damn tux, but his cowboy hat would still be on his head. That he refused to give up.

Why are you avoiding her?

He should be down at the arena, making sure everything was okay. Helping out. Checking that nothing had been forgotten. Instead he was hiding out in his home like a damn fugitive and waiting until the last minute to drive down. The party would start in a half hour, their first guests could start arriving at any moment, and he figured he'd cut it as close as he could.

Behaving like a damn chicken, that's what you're doing.

The sun had long since set, and so it was in total darkness that he headed to the arena. She'd bought solar lights, he noticed, to help guide guests down the road. Smart. He was sure it was the first of many finishing touches she'd arranged for the night.

He damn near hit the brakes, though, when he spotted the arena. Just in case someone might have trouble finding the place, she'd rented spotlights. They lit up his property and drew patterns in the sky. As he drove closer he could see that the massive double doors that usually closed off the arena were now open. Inside he spotted the big-top circus tent she'd rented. The pointy part stood dead center. The doors to the barn aisle were open, too, but she'd somehow managed to light the "HFH" carved above the door.

"Can I help you?" said a man he didn't recognize and it instantly set his survival instincts atwitter. It didn't matter that he was at his own ranch, and that logic dictated the man was one of the waitstaff Naomi had hired; he instantly found himself surveying the man for a weapon.

Stop it.

His time overseas had messed with his head. This wasn't the Middle East. He was in Southern California, at a ranch he'd built to help men who suffered from PTSD way worse than he did.

"I'm looking for Naomi."

The man smiled, nodded. "She's right over there."

He pointed toward the big top. On a wooden floor there were dinner tables set up beneath the circus tent, and Naomi stood on the far side of them all, by what looked like a buffet table, talking to a woman wearing the same type of outfit as the man who'd greeted him.

"Thanks."

A horse nickered, and it was the only sign this was, in fact, an arena and a barn. The animals that would serve as center stage to his program each had their own nameplate now, and she'd had some type of rubber floor put down, presumably so their guests could wander down the aisle without fear of dirtying their shoes. Whether it was temporary or permanent, he didn't know, but he would bet it'd all cost him a pretty penny. How much, he didn't know. Frankly, he really didn't care. Traveling to a different continent had been good for him. It'd reminded him of how tough other countries had it. Visiting with his overseas staff, many of whom had been with him for years and had the battle scars to prove it, had helped him to recall his purpose back at home. Of what he wanted to accomplish, even though it hadn't lessened his thoughts about Naomi one little bit.

She turned toward him then, and her whole face lit up when she saw him, and he tripped on the floor. That's what he told himself, but deep inside he knew he lied.

Holy—

She looked like an actress on the red carpet. Or a model about to walk the runway. Or a woman born to play hostess, in her strapless red dress that hugged her upper body and then flared into a long skirt beneath.

"My liege," she said with a twinkle in her eyes.

God, he'd missed her.

How it was possible that he could know someone such a short time and already come to crave her warm smiles and irreverent humor was anybody's guess. The last time he'd seen her she'd had tears in her eyes, so he knew that at times it was all an act. That deep inside she was still haunted by the loss of her husband. That she missed Trevor and would probably go on missing him for the rest of her life. That she felt bad about uprooting her kids, even if it was for the best. One of those kids, Samantha, was all the more reason to put an end to this…this…whatever it was he felt for her. Her daughter clearly didn't want her mom to see other men.

"Nice dress," he heard himself say.

She glanced down, spread her arms as if surveying herself for the first time. "This old thing? I've had it forever." But her eyes told him she was joking. "It's actually Natalie's. She wore it to some big movie premier. Did you know she's friends with Rand Jefferson?"

All he could do was nod because he'd somehow lost the ability to talk. He had never, not in his life, seen a woman look as beautiful as she did with her hair piled high on her head and her flawless face.

"And that's my other big surprise. Guess who's coming tonight?"

He had to clear his throat. "Rand."

"Yes." She bounced up on his toes. "And he's invited all his Hollywood friends and it's going to be crazy, Jax.

I've been dying to tell you, but I wanted to see your face. We're going to have paparazzi here tonight. The media exposure will be out of this world. I'm so excited for Hooves for Heroes I could just spit."

He bet she would, too. Despite looking like the cover of a magazine, he had no doubt that she was the type of woman who could hawk a loogie as well as the boys—she was just that type.

His type.

He'd spent a week away from her and rather than cool the flames, it'd only fanned them.

And all he managed to say was, "Please don't spit." Which made her smile, at least until he asked, "How are the kids?"

"Good." She forced a smile. "T.J.'s having a great time. Sam and I sort of talked it out. I think Rose and Walt had a talk with her." At his look of confusion she said, "That's their grandparents. They've asked if they can keep the kids with them in Georgia for a few more days once they get back from Disney World."

Which meant he'd have her to himself for a few more days.

Stop. You should not be thinking about her like that. Who was he kidding?

He'd been thinking about her all week. Had she not been his employee he would have called her up, checked on her, asked how she was coping with Sam's hostility, but he hadn't wanted to cross the line.

"Come on. Let me show you what we've done." She hooked an arm through his own and it was all he could do not to pull away. She smelled like cotton candy. It baffled him how one second he wanted to put some distance between them and the next he wanted to lean into her.

"We're using half the arena because the Reynoldses are doing a special performance at the other end. I can't wait to see what they've cooked up. I have the barbecue guy out front. That's what you smell. He's got prime rib slow cooking out there. Doesn't it smell divine?"

She smelled divine.

"Amanda is in charge of the waitstaff." She drew him toward the barn aisle. "And I hired a few people to guard the front gate. They'll be checking names to make sure nobody crashes the party, but I made a deal with a few members of the media. They'll be in the background taking pictures, but I gave them strict instructions about approaching our guests. If they want an interview they have to clear it with me first." They paused in the middle of the floor. "Don't the decorations look great?"

Decorations? He hadn't even noticed. He could barely tear his eyes off her animated face.

"I love the popcorn containers. And the gerbera daisies are so bright and cheerful." For the first time the light in her eyes dimmed. "I wish my kids could see it."

"They would love it."

She nodded. "Especially T.J. He's still at an age where everything is cool. Sam likes to think she's too old for stuff like this."

"You've done an amazing job."

She turned to face him fully, her skirt swirling around her legs. "You like it?"

"If you didn't already have the job, I would have hired you on the spot."

She smiled and he realized she had a grin like a movie starlet, the kind that could light up a screen with its brilliance.

"I can't tell you how thrilled I am with how everything turned out, especially on such short notice. I was a little worried nobody would come, but Claire started working the lines. Apparently she made a ton of contacts when she held a benefit for her son."

After helping her son battle cancer, Claire had dedicated her life to helping others. So had her son. The entire Reynolds clan was pretty amazing. He should have known they'd pitch in to help.

"It'll be great no matter who shows up."

Her expression lightened up again. "And look at you." She motioned with her hands to his outfit. "All svelte and swanky in your duds."

He glanced down at his suit. "Thanks. I think."

That expressive face of hers flickered. "You look good."

She turned away, as if she were afraid to look at him any longer. "There's Amanda. Come on. I'll introduce you."

Why did he have a feeling she was only too happy to change the subject? And why was she suddenly rushing away from him?

He hung back a second, the reason all but hitting him in the face.

Because she was attracted to him, too.

A few hours later Naomi found herself standing at the side of the arena, watching as easily a hundred guests sat or stood or milled around Dark Horse Ranch, a feeling of pride causing her chin to lift.

"You done good, Red."

She couldn't contain her cry. "Ethan!"

Her husband's best friend opened his arms and she sank into them. She hadn't seen him since she'd arrived.

According to Claire, the vet clinic where he worked kept him busy 24/7, but she was glad to see him now.

"Wow," she said after drawing back. "You clean up nice."

He glanced down at his tux self-consciously. "Do I?"

"You know you do." She glanced past him, scanning the room. "Where's Claire?"

He pointed over his shoulder with a thumb. "She's talking to one of my clients. Levi Daniels. Breeds Malinois. Lives pretty close by, but they've never met."

Claire's organization for MWDs was one of the few approved nonmilitary rescues in the country. "I bet they have a lot in common."

She followed his gaze to the tall blond who stood talking to Claire. He had the same bearing as Ethan. Broad shoulders. Proud. "Let me guess, Marine?"

Ethan smiled. "Navy, but good guess."

She studied her friend's face, looking for signs that Ethan was thinking of him, too, of Trevor. The ghost in the room.

"You can take the man out of the military…"

"…but not the military out of the man," he finished for her with a smile.

"Do you miss it, though?" she asked.

"What? Patching together shot-up dogs? Watching as their handlers get shot, too? Dealing with…"

He didn't need to finish his sentence. He'd been her husband's best friend. He'd been the one to escort his body back home. And Janus, too. Thank goodness he'd followed the dog back to Claire's ranch and the rescue organization that'd been about to re-home him. Claire's operation. It was how they'd met.

"I better go get Claire before she goes into her 'dog breeders are bad' speech."

She smiled. "I have a feeling that man could hold his own."

"I have a feeling you're right." He bent, kissed her cheek. "It's good to see a smile on your face."

"I could say the same about you."

He smiled, nodded. "She's a remarkable woman."

"And you're a remarkable man."

He turned, but before he'd taken a step said, "Great party, by the way."

"Thanks."

She watched him cross to Claire's side, kiss her bare shoulder. He said something to her and she turned, waved. Naomi waved back.

Ethan was right. It was a good party. Everyone seemed to be having a good time. Jax could have no reason to complain about how the event had turned out. So far it'd exceeded even her own wildest expectations. The Reynolds clan had performed, Natalie wowing the crowd when she'd ridden her horse without a bridle. They'd just finished the most scrumptious dinner she'd ever had, and the best part of it all, people were hanging around for the dancing. The big band she'd hired was warming up on a flatbed trailer they'd pulled into the far end of the arena.

"Well, there's the hostess with the mostess," said a deeply masculine voice with a Texas twang.

Colby Koch.

"Howdy," she answered back.

And...*wow*.

The new ranch manager looked gorgeous in a tux he'd rented from goodness knew where and a black cowboy hat that looked the same as Jax's. A pair of eyes the same color as the big jays that perched in the trees were framed by thick, dark lashes. He might wear a hat all the time, but he was tan, and he must smile a lot because he had crow's feet, and the skin was white in the cracks where the edges crinkled.

"Quite a party."

"I know, right? I can't believe I just directed Rand Jefferson to the little boys' room."

His smile was as wide as the Texas plains he rode in from. The man was more handsome than half the male actors who'd shown up tonight and she felt…nothing. His light blue eyes, square jaw and five-o'clock shadow hadn't stirred a single feminine bone in her body. It'd been that way all night. Men most women fantasized about, and they were right there in front of her, but she had eyes for only one man.

Jax.

He looked so sexy in his black tux and black hat that matched his black hair. She'd watched him smile and laugh with his guests, and take pictures with celebrities, and make small talk with starlets, and all she could think about was how perfectly at ease he seemed, and how wonderful it was that so many people had come together to make this night a success, and how she couldn't be more proud because it was clear Hooves for Heroes was poised to be an amazing success…and all because of Jax.

She had it worse than she thought.

"So have you had a chance to relax?"

"I ate dinner." Barely. She was still pretty keyed up, hoping everything would go as planned. It was all but over except the dancing.

"Then I suppose it's okay to ask you to dance?"

What? "Well, I don't know—"

"Come on." He smiled. "The music's just about to start."

As if waiting for his cue, she heard the countdown tapping of the band master, and a few seconds later the musicians started playing something she didn't instantly recognize, but by the time Colby had led her to the dance floor she had it pinned down: "Chattanooga Choo Choo." They were the only ones at first, but then she saw Natalie and Colt Reynolds head to the floor, and then Claire and Ethan McCall. They weren't much quicker than Rand Jefferson and his longtime girlfriend, who happened to share the same name as her daughter, Samantha.

"Just relax," Colby told her as they took center stage. "I'll guide you."

Guide her to do what? And then he pushed her out and she felt like a rag doll when he immediately pulled her back to him and she realized he was swinging her. Dear goodness, she hadn't done a swing dance since…

She gulped.

Trevor. They used to love it. For a moment she was overcome by sadness, but then she picked herself back up, because tonight should be a night for celebrating. And so she smiled and relaxed and Colby must have realized she knew what she was doing because he smiled, too, and soon he was pulling her out and in and around and under his arms and she was laughing. She hardly even noticed when the music changed; it was too much fun to watch her skirt swirl around her legs. Naomi would bet Natalie had never taken the dress out for a spin like she had.

"You're a good dancer," Colby yelled over the music.

"My husband taught me."

Colby's eyes went wide. "You're married."

Again the brief shot of sadness to her heart. "Not anymore." She swallowed hard. "He died in combat."

Their new ranch foreman showed he had a heart right then by squeezing her hand and shooting her a look of sympathy. "I'm sorry."

"Me, too." Okay. Change of subject needed. "Were you in the military?"

"Two tours."

She wasn't surprised. "What branch?"

"Army."

She nodded. "From Kazakhstan to cowboy. Crazy."

"I've always been a cowboy. My family owns a big ranch."

"What made you move out here?"

He shrugged, swinging her around before saying, "Needed a change."

She smiled. "Don't we all?"

The music ended and suddenly everything went quiet, but only for a moment. The soft notes of "Moonlight Serenade" began to play.

"Slow dance?"

"Sure."

"Actually," said a voice, "I'd like a turn."

Jax. If her face hadn't already been red from exertion it would have flamed brightly right then.

"You mind?" he asked her.

Yes. She minded. She didn't want to dance with him. She'd already had enough sleepless nights, thank you very much. She didn't need her imagination to have ammunition for more.

"Sure," she said.

Sam would have had a fit. But Sam wasn't here.

He nodded to Colby and she wondered if they'd met. Well, of course they had. He'd hired him—

He pulled her to him. Their hips touched and their chests brushed and it was all she could do to keep her breathing regulated. She didn't just have it bad. She had a full-on case of hero worship.

"Just relax," he said, pulling her even closer. "I'm not going to bite."

He said the last words in the shell of her ear and all she could think was how badly she wished he would bite her. She could imagine what it would be like to have his teeth lightly nip her lobes and it made her shiver. If only things were different...

"Cold?"

"No," she choked out.

I'm in lust with you.

What would he do if she said the words? Because that was what this was. She didn't believe for a moment that it was anything more. They'd just met, and he'd been so kind to her and he had such a good spirit. Nobody could build all this—she glanced up and around her—and not possess a big heart. He might try to hide it behind his gruff exterior, but it was there deep inside.

"You did an amazing job," he said, his breath stirring the hairs on her neck.

"Thank you."

"Inviting the chief of staff from the local hospital was a master stroke."

"That was your sister's idea." She wanted to lean back and look into his eyes, but she didn't dare. She was afraid of what he might see. "She thought he might be able to help refer people into your program."

"He already has." He drew back a bit and she took a deep breath before meeting his gaze. There was such a look of pride and gratitude on his face that she gulped once more. "Looks like we'll have our first guest by the end of the month."

"That's wonderful."

His smile turned crooked. She loved that tilted smile.

"*You're* wonderful," he said softly, and then he seemed a bit stricken. "I mean, you've done a wonderful job."

She couldn't look away from him. He held her hand. He drew her close and all she could do was keep on staring into his eyes, and something inside her began to swirl around, although maybe that was her head. She didn't know what this was she was feeling except it made her dizzy. Something she kept hidden within her bubbled to the surface. Her inner happiness. She hadn't had time to do anything but put one foot in front of the other since Trev died, so she'd buried her need for fun, for her kids' sake. But now, staring into Jax's eyes, she felt it gurgle to life again.

She looked away. She had to. Suddenly, she wanted to cry.

The music changed. She hardly noticed. He still held her close even though the tempo had picked up.

"Hey," he said softly. "What's the matter?"

Deep breaths. Deep breaths. Deep breaths.

"Nothing." She sniffed.

She felt him move, knew what he was about to do, and sure enough, a hand tipped up her chin.

"You're crying."

"No, I'm not," she said with a wide smile. "Just tired."

"Why are you crying?"

Quit asking me questions. "I'm not, really. It's just been so long since I danced. I'd forgotten how exhausting it is."

Lies, lies, lies. But she didn't want him to know how deeply he'd affected her.

"Do you want to stop?"

As she thought about Trevor and what he would think of her dancing in another man's arms, she instantly said, "No." Trevor would be happy for her. He wouldn't have wanted her to close herself off to the world. He would have wanted her to go on. To have fun. It was Sam who would prove to be a problem.

"Was your husband the one to teach you to swing like that?"

Could he read her thoughts so easily?

"Yes."

He smiled softly. "Well, I'm glad he did, because I'm going to make sure to dance your toes off you tonight."

"You don't have to do that."

"By the end of the night, you're going to wish you'd worn slippers."

"Jax—"

He pulled her close and she gasped, but then he pushed her out and started to slowly swing her around and she couldn't help it—she laughed. He smiled, and for a moment she was perfectly happy, but that happiness faded when she felt a tap at her shoulder. She stumbled a bit, turned.

America's favorite heartthrob stared down at her. Rand Jefferson. Hawkman. Star of big screens and little. A man voted Sexiest Man Alive last year.

And she wanted to tell him to go away.

"Natalie tells me I have to dance with you." He shot Jax an apologetic smile. "And I always do what Natalie tells me to do."

If someone had told her that she'd be asked to dance by one of America's hottest actors and that she'd actually be *disappointed*, she would have called them crazy.

"No. It's okay." She glanced at her boss.

Your boss.

She took a deep breath. "Jax should probably dance with some of his guests."

He didn't want to give her up. She could see it in his eyes and that made her want to cry for a whole other reason. He liked her. Not like a boss liked an employee. He liked her, liked her.

Dear goodness.

Heaven knew what she would do about that.

Chapter 11

He'd left her alone for the rest of the night. He'd had to. If he'd held her in his arms one more time he didn't think he'd let her go.

"Good night," said Amanda, the waitstaff manager.

"Night," he said, lifting a hand. "Thanks."

"My pleasure."

Was that a flirtatious grin on the woman's face? He had a feeling it was. Maybe a few weeks ago he would have taken her up on the invitation in her eyes. Right now all he wanted to do was find Naomi.

"Great party."

Colby Koch, his new ranch manager/foreman, slipped out of the shadows. "I have a feeling you'll be booked solid in a week."

"Maybe," he said, forcing himself to smile.

He hadn't liked seeing the man twirl Naomi around. Not one little bit.

"When's your fancy horse therapist arriving?"

By that he meant Brielle. "She asked for another week off. Something about a family emergency."

"Well, she better get here quick," he drawled in his Texas accent. "Gonna get crazy around here soon."

That he couldn't deny. And then he caught sight of a red dress coming from the back of the arena and he saw Colby take a step toward Naomi before he cut him off with, "Thanks for your help tonight. Naomi and I couldn't be more pleased."

He'd caught the man by surprise. Jax saw him glance in Naomi's direction, saw the question in his eyes, and he knew his new employee understood what he meant.

Back off.

"If you wouldn't mind closing up down here, I'll take Naomi back home."

He was giving the man the wrong impression. He and Naomi weren't a couple, but he was certain it sounded that way, especially when he called to her, "Ready to go?"

She was closer now, her skirt gathered in one hand, her heels dangling from her other hand, and she wouldn't look him in the eye when she said, "I can walk."

He released a snort. "You are not going to walk."

Why was she shy all of a sudden? Did Colby notice? Did he care if he did? All he cared about was that she looked exhausted and every protective instinct inside him made him want to rush to her aide.

"Come on," he said gently, holding out his hand. She stared at it, then looked him in the eyes, and he saw it then, a yearning that he recognized within himself, and every nerve ending in his body suddenly fired. Their dance. That one dance. It'd changed everything.

She took his hand.

"Good night, Colby," she said softly.

"Night," he echoed.

When they reached his truck he wanted to lift her into it. Instead he opened her door and helped her up, but his hand lingered in her own and the tension increased and he wondered how the hell he'd drive her home without slamming on the brakes and trying to kiss her.

You got it bad, buddy.

He closed her door. He almost leaned against it. Instead he took his hat off and ran his fingers through his hair.

Get a grip.

She was tired. Exhausted. That was why she looked at him so softly. He was reading the situation wrong. He needed to rein things in before he made a huge mistake.

So he walked around the front of his truck, tossed his hat in the back seat when he opened the door, climbed inside and told himself not to look at her.

"Close your eyes. Be there in a sec."

She didn't say anything and that was good. He was grateful the drive was so short. When he pulled up in front of her apartment, he had to force himself to open the door and get out before touching her. She already had her own door open, was already slipping out, and he reached for her, to steady her, he told himself, but she reached for him, too.

"Thank you," she said softly.

"Do you need help?"

She smiled a bit. "No. Really. I'm okay."

She stepped away and his hand fell to his side and he felt such a keening sense of regret it was almost a physical ache. But then she stopped. Turned back to him, her dress once again clutched in one hand.

"Before I forget to tell you, I think it's amazing what

you're doing here. You're going to help so many people. You're a good man, Jaxton Stone."

He froze. He couldn't breathe all of a sudden. She started to walk away and he rushed to her side before he could think better of it, touched her elbow, and she turned back to him and God help him, he knew he was about to do something crazy.

Just crazy.

For one terrible moment, he thought he'd misread the situation, but then the look in her eyes warmed and he found himself leaning down and kissing her and he realized all his fantasies were nothing like the reality. Every nerve ending fired. His head swam. His body heated. She tasted fifty times sweeter than anything his imagination might have cooked up, like a dessert he'd waited to eat, vanilla and chocolate with just a hint of coffee.

He pulled back. He had no idea he'd been about to do it, but somehow he did, gasping out, "We can't."

"I know."

He set her away from him. She didn't move. Why didn't she leave? Because for the love of God, his willpower only went so far.

"I loved my husband," she said softly. "He was my best friend." She tipped her head sideways, the loop of hair that'd fallen out about to completely break free. "But tonight, when you held me, Jax, when you danced with me, I was reminded of what it was like to be a woman. To be young again and carefree and it made me want…" She shook her head. "It made me want…"

He leaned forward and said softly, "What?"

She looked him square in the eye. "You."

Her words were like a sucker punch to the groin. If she knew how tightly he held onto control, she wouldn't say such a thing. She would know that he was about to do something very, very foolish. That he could only hold out for so long.

"I know this might be a mistake. Goodness knows Sam can't ever find out. But I don't care. She's not here and we are and I want… I want."

"Naomi—"

She shushed him in a hand. "I just *want*. In the morning we can talk about tomorrow. We can decide what to do about Sam, and about my future here, but for tonight… Damn it, Jax, I just want you."

He closed his eyes. How long he stood there, he didn't know. Long enough that his knuckles started to ache from clenching his hands.

"I don't think one night will be enough."

"One night is all it can be, at least for now. At least until things settle down with my kids. I can't spring a new job and an affair with my boss on them, too."

He opened his eyes again. She held out a hand. God help him, he took it.

WHAT ARE YOU DOING? What are you doing? What are you doing?

The words marched the same rhythm as her steps.

It's not too late to change your mind.

She stopped in front of her door. *His* door. This was *his* place. She worked for him.

And she didn't care.

Tonight she didn't want to be boss and employee. She didn't want to think about what tomorrow would bring. She didn't want to *think*, period. She just…wanted.

She opened the door. He followed, and there came a moment when she knew she could still change her mind, when she knew she could turn to him and tell him this was a bad idea, and he would understand, he wouldn't pressure her. He would just walk away because he was that type of man. Instead she dropped her shoes and turned to him.

Janus wedged himself between them.

"Janus, no," he ordered.

"It's okay," she said. "Just kiss me."

She didn't know where the words came from, she just had a feeling if she didn't give him exact instructions he would take the chivalrous route and do something like hug her and hold her and she didn't want that. Oh no. She was miles away from her kids. Alone. In an apartment with a man she truly thought of as the sexiest man alive. Yes, sexier than Hawkman, and she was dying—no, absolutely craving his kiss.

"Naomi, I—"

She shook her head, closed the distance between them, but not before kicking her shoes into a corner and saying, "Stop talking, Jax. For the love of God, just kiss me."

And she pulled him toward her, although she didn't remember reaching for his shoulders. She knew she won when she heard him groan. She groaned, too, just before his lips found her own and she tasted the salty essence of him for the second time that night.

She wanted.

There was no other way to describe how he made her feel. He roused every feminine desire within her, even ones she didn't know she had—like the one that made her want to touch him in places that made her blush, because she'd never been the one to be brazen. Trevor had always been the instigator, the one to gently seduce her and touch her and bring her pleasure. But with Jax she wanted things she'd never wanted before.

She bit his lip. He gasped. She took advantage of

his open mouth and slipped her tongue inside. Even this was different. He was bolder than Trevor, his own tongue twinning with hers, sucking and making her groan all over again. She arched into him, and the feel of his body up against her own made her senses reel. She never would have thought she'd be the type to grab a man by the lapels of his jacket, but that was exactly what she did. She pulled away and tugged him toward her bedroom, although at some point her hand slipped from his jacket and down his arm until their fingers entwined.

What are you doing?

It was the voice of reason that asked the question. The one that reminded her that tomorrow would come and there would be consequences to their actions, but that had always been her problem: she thought too much. So when she reached her room she didn't give him time to question; instead she pulled him to her again and kissed him with enough pent-up passion that he had to know she meant business.

He jerked her up against him.

Yes, like that, she tried to tell him with her mouth and her hands and her body. And just in case he missed the point, she slipped a hand between them and...

He gasped.

She pressed harder. Her zipper slipped down and it took her moment to realize he'd pulled it free. She wore no bra, so when the bodice sprang free there was nothing between them and he didn't hesitate to cup her, and she pressed against him because it was what she wanted. When his mouth broke free she mewed in disappointment, but then he bent his head and captured the tip of her breast in his mouth and she forgot her discontent because his tongue swirled around her nipple and she went limp in his arms.

It'd been so long. So very, very long…

He nipped her. She gasped, buried her fingers in his hair, shifted in a way that told him she wanted more. She knew they moved, although it was only distantly, but suddenly she was up against the bed and she didn't mind that he set her down first, or that he pulled his mouth away. She could sense his next move, and sure enough, he tugged the dress down, only to freeze when he spied her underwear. She hadn't been able to find a strapless bra that fit her right, but she'd found the sexiest pair of red underwear on God's green earth, and she'd bought them because, heaven help her, a part of her had wondered, had maybe hoped…

"You're going to be the death of me."

She lifted her hips, shoved the dress the rest of the way down. A part of her thought she should probably pick it up and do something with it because she hated to know how much the darn thing had cost; another part of her admitted she didn't care about anything other than the way Jax stared at her lying there in nothing but her scarlet-red satin. She knew she was ready for him. She could feel just how ready.

His head lowered. She started to pant. His lips found her hips first, and then his fingers brushed the wisp of fabric and she felt them move. She helped him along, wiggling out of the fabric until she lay in front of him, naked, her leg hanging off the bed, exposed to him in a way only one other man had ever seen her.

Don't think about Trevor.

He kissed her there, right there, no preamble, no gentle teasing, just his lips and the very center of her, and she cried out in pleasure as he helped her to climb higher and higher.

And then he pulled away.

Her eyes opened in disappointment. Those eyes of his. They'd gone as dark as a feral cat.

"I'm going to do things to you, Naomi."

Yes, please do.

"I'm going to make you beg me for release."

That was what she wanted.

"Turn over."

It was as if he knew he battled the ghost of Trevor. Her first love would never have demanded she do such a thing. He would have been all sweet words and kisses. Not Jax. Oh no. He urged her over, and she knew he readied himself for her. She heard the rip of the foil pouch, knew he must have carried protection with him, how convenient…

He leaned into her.

She opened for him. She felt him there and she moaned. Her hair lost its battle with bobby pins because it suddenly came tumbling down and she didn't care because he pressed into her, all warmth and hardness. His hands moved around her side to her breasts and he cupped her at the same time he kissed her and drove himself home.

"Jax," she cried.

And this was what she wanted, what she'd craved from him. She didn't care that he was her boss, and that she was a mother of two, and that her daughter would pitch a fit, or that in the morning there might be consequences. All she wanted at the moment was him inside her, and to never stop climbing higher and higher…

He gently turned her. She didn't want him to stop, but he made her slow down and suddenly things changed.

Suddenly she stared into his eyes as he gently claimed her once more and her frenzied need to reach the summit subsided because there was something in his blue eyes, something that made it difficult to breathe.

He kissed her.

He still wore clothes but she didn't care because he kissed her and stroked her so very, very gently, and for some reason it made her eyes well with tears. His tongue slipped between her lips and his kiss was as gentle as the petals of a flower and pleasure began to build again, but this time in a wholly different way than before. This time her hands moved to the nape of his neck. This time she pulled him down tight, as if she could never get enough of the taste of him, and she went on kissing him and kissing him until she couldn't take it anymore and she arched and cried out her release.

He held her.

He wrapped his arms around her while she soared and glided and floated back to her.

And cried.

She cried because it'd been so long. Because she didn't think she'd ever feel the passion of a woman again. Because she'd found the perfect man to bring her back to life.

"Jax," she softly sighed.

He kissed her. She wrapped her legs around him because it was his turn. She wanted to give back. To hear him cry out in pleasure, and he must have been waiting for her because it didn't take long. Naomi felt sexier than she ever had in her life when she heard him cry out. Only then did she let him go. Only then did she pull him onto the bed with her. Only then did she snuggle up next to him and rest her head on his chest.

It was the last thing she remembered.

Chapter 12

He awoke to the sound of someone panting, and it wasn't Naomi.

Janus.

"Go away," he ordered the dog softly.

Janus eyed the woman in the bed, brown eyes conveying his desire to lick her face, but all it took was one softly uttered "no" to get Janus to change his mind. He scampered off to wherever he'd been hiding and Jax pulled Naomi closer. He was surprised Tramp wasn't barking to be let in, although he seemed to like the backyard. For now all was quiet. The feel of her cuddled up next to him and the realization that for the first time in a long, long time he'd slept the whole night were revelations.

Jax glanced outside. Through a window that overlooked the back patio he could just make out the steel gray of an early dawn. Morning had arrived, and not a single nightmare had plagued his sleep.

She stirred. He held still, not daring to breathe. She lay in his arms, her hair bunched up beneath her. In sleep, her lashes fanned against her face like a line of watercolor brushes and he realized they were a perfect mirror of the shape of her eyebrows. Her cheeks were flushed, or was that makeup? He somehow doubted it, because the rosy tinge stained her jawline and hair line, and he admitted that even sound asleep, with the weakest of sunlight illuminating her face, she was still the most beautiful woman he'd ever seen.

And he shouldn't have slept with her.

His heart began to pound in a familiar way. Anxiety. A by-product of his days in the military and being shot at every day. It was why he hardly slept at night, except last night. Last night he'd slept like the dead, but now morning had come and with it cold, hard reality. Only an idiot slept with an employee. It didn't matter that he trusted her, and that he doubted she'd ever be the type to cry foul. He was her boss, and she was his employee, and she had a kid that he was pretty sure didn't like him. All of it could present some very real problems down the road.

One night, she'd said. Only he couldn't imagine never doing this again.

Quietly, gently, he disentangled himself from her arms and slipped on his pants from last night. He tossed the jacket, shirt and tie across his arm and scooped up his shoes. He told himself it was because he needed to work. He hadn't checked email in more than twelve hours. No doubt there'd be all kinds of fires to put out.

That was what he told himself.

When he softly padded down the hall to his home, he hoped like hell he hadn't woken her. He took extra care not to yank the door closed, the lock catching with a soft *snick*.

Tramp whined from the backyard. That was all he needed—a bark to wake her up.

"Shh," he softly hissed as he let Tramp inside, then he whispered, "Heel."

The dog licked his hand before falling into step alongside him. He'd be lying to himself if he didn't admit a sense of relief when he closed his office door.

"Go lie down," he told Tramp in a more normal voice.

The dog did exactly as ordered, and Jax stood there for a second in surprise. Maybe they were finally getting through to him. Or maybe Janus had worn off on him.

"You're not staying here," he told the animal.

Tramp's tail thumped in response.

Work proved to be just as big a distraction as he'd hoped. He had at least a dozen messages to his home office about last night's event. People wanted to know more about the program, how they could sign up, what it cost. He should have anticipated this happening, but he hadn't and now he wondered what they would do if they ended up with more business than they could handle. So he answered emails and phone calls and he might have done so all day but for one thing: bacon.

Tramp smelled it, too; the dog lifted his head. She'd done it again. Like Aladdin rubbing the genie's lamp, she knew exactly how to summon him downstairs. Or he could open a window. It had turned into a beautiful day outside. He could hold out and go on trying to avoid her because that was exactly what he wanted to do.

His stomach growled.

"Damn," he muttered.

He stood. Tramp stood, too.

"Let's go."

The sunlight from outside painted mirror images of the window frames on the steps. The smell of bacon only increased as he stood on the landing, and still he hesitated because for some reason his nerves were stretched taut.

"Good morning," she said when he paused in the door of the kitchen, her smile as wide as triangles on a beach ball. She stood in front of the stove and something sizzled in front of her. The bacon.

"That smells good."

"Of course it does." She flipped the meat over. "There's French toast in the oven. Sit down. I'll serve some up."

"You don't have to do that."

"Yes, I do. Sit."

He watched in silence as she pulled a plate from the oven, and then scooped some bacon out of the pan. His stomach growled again.

"Are you going to eat?"

"I already did." Her smile turned crooked, and he could have sworn she blushed because she looked away for a moment. "Worked up an appetite last night."

And she looked just as beautiful this morning as she had last night, with her hair loose around her shoulders. She wore jeans and a long-sleeved blouse over a white tank top. She'd rolled the sleeves up while she cooked, and compared to her red dress last night, the whole thing was as plain as day, and yet he found her more attractive this morning than he had when he'd first seen her across the dance floor.

"Speaking of last night," she said.

And he realized this was it. They were about to have "the conversation," the one he'd been avoiding all morning and that he'd been hoping to delay by at least a couple of hours. Leave it to her to take the bull by the horns.

"Jax. Last night was..." She worried her bottom lip

and out of nowhere came the urge to kiss her. "Amazing."

He would have said mind-blowing, but he'd take amazing.

"But it can't happen again."

He froze. All morning he'd been telling himself pretty much the same thing. Yet hearing her say the same words…it took the wind out of his sails.

"My kids will be back soon. We can't ever let them know anything about what happened. My daughter would kill me, but even T.J. would probably freak out. What kind of example would I be setting for them if they knew I'd jumped into bed with my boss?"

He felt something roll around in his stomach. The bite of French toast he'd taken. It suddenly wanted to come back up.

"Add to the fact that I just moved all the way out from Georgia for this job, and so if things don't work out, I'll be out of a job, and, well…"

There was no possible way they could call this a good idea. That was what she was trying to say. What was more, he knew she was right. It was why he'd slipped from bed without her knowing. Why he'd been avoiding her. He'd arrived at the same conclusion. But knowing she was right and agreeing with her didn't mean he had to like it.

"So you want to act like nothing happened."

She nodded, and she looked so worried and sorry it jabbed at his heart. "If it will make you feel better, I'll sign something. You know. A nondisclosure agreement or something."

"Don't be ridiculous."

She was biting her lower lip again. He hated when she did that.

"You're mad."

"No," he instantly corrected. Just disappointed. She'd slipped beneath his defenses. He had no idea how she'd done it, but she had, and damned if he knew what to do about it.

"I'm not angry." He forced his tone to soften. "Hell, Naomi, I'm not even surprised. We both knew this was a mistake going into it, didn't we?"

She came around the side of the island. "Not a mistake, Jax." Her eyes were soft and so blue they reminded him of colored eggshells on Easter morning. "Never a mistake."

She would have touched him if he hadn't moved away at the last moment. He knew, though, that if she touched him, he might do something rash, something that he might regret later and that might lead to another "mistake." She knew it, too, because she let her hand fall back to her side. Her smile faded and sadness entered her eyes.

"I never thought I'd meet another man who'd tempt me to do what we did last night." She forced a smile again, this one full of gratitude.

Gratitude.

Like he was a prized stallion and she thanked him for his service.

"You're a remarkable man, Jax."

Yeah? he wanted to say. Apparently not remarkable enough.

Chapter 13

Stupid, stupid, stupid. She never should have let her crush grow into full-on lust like it had. What had she been thinking to climb into bed with her boss?

She managed to get through the rest of the day without seeing him, although that wasn't hard since it was Sunday and she had the cleanup to do after the party. She would have to face him again tomorrow, though, and she wasn't looking forward to it. At the crack of dawn on Monday, she was awoken by a call.

Georgia area code, but not her kids. Thank goodness it wasn't about her kids.

"Naomi Jones?"

"Yes?"

"This is Harrison Giles."

It took her a moment to place the name, but when she did, she shot up in bed. Her Realtor. What time was it in Georgia? She glanced at the clock and quickly did the math. It was 8:00 a.m. He'd called her first thing.

"I have some good news for you."

No. She couldn't believe it. Not this quickly.

"I've sold your house."

It was both the most bittersweet and the most beautiful thing she'd heard in years. Her house. Her beautiful house—the one she'd shared with Trevor and the kids—would no longer be hers, and though she'd been expecting the news sooner or later, she'd figured it'd be later. Way later.

"Are you there?" Harrison asked.

"Yes, of course. That's great."

"And it's for the full asking price, too," Harrison said, excitement in his words. "They absolutely fell in love with it. The buyers have family right down the street, so they can't wait to move in."

She clutched the covers up to her tighter. "That's great."

"They want to close escrow quickly. So I'm going to open up escrow at a title company near you. Where are you at exactly?"

"Via Del Caballo, California."

"Oh, wow. Yeah. I forgot about that. I must have called you early."

Her heart pounded. It was sold. So soon. "I have some stuff in the back that I didn't move out west with me. Can I have my in-laws come by and get it?"

"Of course, although I'm pretty sure the new owners would love to keep the yard the way it is."

It was her bench, the one she and Trevor would sit on whenever he'd come back from overseas. They'd planned their whole lives on that bench and suddenly she wanted it, even though she'd been telling herself for weeks it was old and falling apart and she didn't need it.

"I'll send someone over this week."

"Okay, then," Harrison said, the excitement back in his voice. "I'll send the offer over to you immediately. Do you have a fax? We'll need you to sign it and fax it back. The rest of the paperwork will have to be done through a title company."

She gave Harrison Jax's fax number, hoping he wouldn't mind her using it for personal business. Somehow she doubted he would, but it would mean seeing him again, and sooner than she would like.

"Can you send it right over?"

"Sure."

Maybe Jax wouldn't be up. Maybe she could slip upstairs without him noticing.

She got up from bed, her body still sore in places that made her blush. Best not to think about that, she told herself as she pulled on a dark green sweater and jeans. She needed to put all that behind her.

She'd sold her house.

She should be elated. It meant financial freedom. It meant she could quit her job if she needed to and maybe find another one. But she didn't want to do that. She liked working for Jax. It was a great job, and she'd always intended that money for Sam and T.J. to go to college, not for herself. It was what Trevor would have wanted her to do.

Then why did she feel like crying as she slipped into Jax's home and lightly made her way upstairs?

"You sold it."

She about jumped out of her tennis shoes. Of course he was awake. Why wouldn't he be? The man was a workaholic.

"I sold it." She noticed a sheaf of papers on his desk, papers that she would bet belonged to her. "I hope it was okay to give my Realtor your fax number."

"Of course it is."

She nodded, looking anywhere but at him.

"You've been crying."

She jerked her head up. "No, I haven't."

"You look ready to."

Good heavens. Could he read her so well? "I'm just tired." She forced a smile. "Busy weekend."

Their night together was the elephant in the room and she waited for him to say something about it, but he didn't. Instead he slid the papers across his massive desk. "If you sign it now I'll fax it back."

"Shouldn't I read it first?"

"Of course. Have a seat."

"No thanks, I'll just bring them back—"

"Sit, Naomi. Read. And if you want, I'll read them, too."

She felt her whole body go to mush. "That's okay."

"I insist. Hand me a page when you're through with it."

She sank into his chair even though she wanted to go hide in her apartment. He was right, though. Two sets of eyes were better than one, and so she reached for the papers, although if she were honest, most of the words were a blur. Reading the offer, seeing it all there in black and white, the finality of it all.

"What's this about fixtures in the backyard?"

She looked up. "Just some stuff I thought I didn't want, but I guess now I realize I do and so I'll have to have my in-laws go and get it."

He set the paper down, his gaze intense. "This is hard on you, isn't it?"

Why did the kindness in his eyes bring her to the brink of tears? Was it because she knew he cared for her and all she wanted to do was fall into his arms? That was crazy, because she suddenly missed Trevor more than she would have thought possible, and yet she wanted to be in another man's arms.

"I didn't expect it to sell so quickly," she admitted.

"But it's a good thing, yes?"

"It is." She took a deep breath, mostly to keep the tears at bay. "But it's also sad."

He stared at her a bit longer, but then he nodded. "It's the end of a chapter."

Despite her best efforts, her eyes welled with tears. "The start of something new."

That wouldn't include him, that couldn't include him, and that broke her heart, too. Good gracious, she was such an emotional wreck.

"It looks good to me," he said a few minutes later. "Of course, if you'd like, I can have my attorney look it over."

"No. That's okay. I'll just sign."

And she did, scribbling her name even though the letters blurred when she did. He took the document from her, stood and sent it through the printer/fax machine behind him.

"Thank you," she said.

"Do the kids know?"

Dear heavens, she hadn't even thought about that. What kind of mom was she? "No." She took a deep breath. "I think I'll wait and tell them when they get back."

He nodded. She waited.

For what?

She didn't know. She had a whole list of things to do this morning, mostly housework, so she should get going, but suddenly she didn't want to leave him.

Move.

"Thank you."

She left. He let her. She knew it was for the best. Keep busy. Keep moving. Keep ducking her head. It wasn't like she didn't have a million things on her plate. She suspected Jax would keep busy, too. She'd known the party would be a success, she just hadn't known how much until she opened her email later that morning. Messages. Dozens of them. Some from the contacts she'd made, more than a few forwarded from Jax, all of them dealing with Hooves for Heroes and how to book guests and wanting more information about the program and asking if they could take a tour of the ranch.

She didn't see Jax that whole Monday and a part of her wondered if he'd tried to avoid her. She wouldn't blame him, and, if she were honest, she was happy to have some space. She needed time to deal with the emotions that had come along with selling her house, with missing her kids, with wishing things could be different between her and Jax. Her handsome, virile boss who always treated her so kindly.

Stop.

Her cell phone rang and she about jumped out of her skin.

"Meet me out front in twenty minutes," he said without preamble. "We're headed out of town. Pack a bag."

He disconnected before she could say a word.

Pack a bag?

What did that mean? Where were they going? Was this a *date*?

Any notion that he was trying to whip her away for a romantic getaway vanished when she spotted him standing by his truck, looking the essence of a cowboy in his black hat and blue jeans. There was no welcoming smile. No nod of greeting. He'd gone back to the Jax she'd first met, the stone-faced man of few words.

"Where are we going?" she asked.

"Airport."

Wait. "What?"

He opened the passenger door of his truck, but she didn't move.

He must have seen her need to know on her face because he said, "I got a call today from a doctor back east. He saw a clip about our facility on the news."

"Oh?" She'd known the party had been picked up by the local news media, but she'd had no idea it'd gone national. How exciting. The free publicity had worked. That explained the volume of emails they'd been receiving.

"Seems he's got this guy in his care. Real bad deal. Medication isn't touching his condition. He'd been doing some reading on equine therapy and when he saw the news clip on us he said it was like a message from heaven. Picked up his phone and called me right away."

"That's incredible."

"I told him we weren't exactly open yet, but he doesn't care. Wants the guy here sooner rather than later. He pretty much begged me to take him. I figure he can help Colby around the ranch until our hippotherapist arrives. He agreed. Told me he'd get him flown out here ASAP if I agreed, but I figured we'd go get him."

"We?"

"He's in Atlanta."

She drew back in surprise. That was only an hour or so from where she lived.

"I know. Crazy coincidence. So I figured Colby could take care of the dogs for us. We could fly back east and you could get what you need from your house, pop in and see your kids, then fly back west tonight. Maybe even with your kids if you want."

She wanted to cry. Just bawl. It was the kindest thing he could have ever offered to do, even though she knew

Sam would balk at coming home early. The kindest thing *anyone* had ever done for her, really. If he was trying to knock her socks off, he'd just succeeded.

"We'll be in Atlanta by nightfall."

She hated flying, she really did, but she was so grateful all she could do was gush, "Thank you."

He nodded, swung the truck door open a little wider, his meaning clear. She climbed inside. He jumped in a few seconds later, but he didn't look at her when he started up the truck. Didn't smile. Didn't do anything other than stare straight ahead.

She hated it.

She wanted the old Jax back, the one she'd charmed out of his shell. Who'd danced with her at the party and kissed her senseless Saturday night. That was the man she'd started to fall in love with.

She jerked in her seat.

"You okay?"

She nodded, and the urge to touch him, to grab his hand, to hold onto someone solid and real nearly overwhelmed her. Not the hand of a ghost. Not Trevor's hand. His hand. And it scared the crap out of her.

"I'm fine."

But she wasn't. It wasn't just nerves about the flight they were about to take that made her heart pound like a sledgehammer. She stared out the window at the oak trees that dotted the countryside. She hadn't pushed him away because of her kids or because he was her boss or because it was somehow wrong. She'd pushed him away because she was terrified, absolutely petrified, of loving him. There'd only been one love of her life. Just one. Nobody was lucky enough to find it twice.

Not even with a man as remarkable as Jax.

She hardly remembered the trip through the coastal

mountains. Her hands had started to shake, but that was just nerves, she told herself, not anxiety about the realization that she had feelings for Jax.

"So you do this kind of thing all the time?"

She couldn't stand the silence anymore, hoped that talking would help to distract her.

"What do you mean?"

She motioned toward the front windshield, hoping he didn't see her hand shake. "Fly out at the drop of a hat."

He nodded. "I do it when I have to. I spent a lot of years building DTS into what it is. It's my baby."

There was a tone to his voice, one that made her think he was trying to tell her something. Had he somehow guessed her feelings for him? Was he trying to warn her off? "You're lucky to be so passionate about something," she heard herself say.

He took a moment to consider her words and she told herself to relax. He wasn't trying to tell her something. But she wasn't so distracted that she couldn't admit to the truth. This was what she missed. He might seem gruff on the outside, but he was easy to talk to once he opened up.

"The men who work for me. All of them. They were handpicked by me. Their security and their safety are in my hands. That's not something I'll ever hand over to someone else."

She should have known it was something like that. His sister had told her how protective he was of her and her son.

He steered the truck off the freeway, passing in front of tall palm trees and heading toward a building with an adobe roof. Out behind it she could see jets parked on a tarmac, and beyond that, a big commercial jet starting to taxi down the main runway.

Her mouth went dry.

"Is one of those yours?" she forced out.

He pulled into a parking spot out in front of the building. "Mine is probably in a hangar for preflight."

"Do you pilot it yourself?"

She didn't know what she would do if he said yes. Probably grab a paper bag to breathe into, because for some reason the thought of him piloting a plane made her want to hyperventilate.

Instead he released a tiny huff of amusement. "Hardly. This place is an FBO. Fixed-base operator. They have hubs throughout the world." He must have seen the confusion on her face because he said, "They're sort of like jet hotels. You fly into them, you park your jet there, and if they need any maintenance, they do it for you. And they fuel them up, too."

Despite being on the edge of a nervous breakdown she heard herself say, "Because everyone needs a place to park their jet."

He smiled again. "It's a convenience." He turned his truck off.

"Hell of a convenience." She slipped out of the truck, her hair blowing back in her face. This close to the coast the wind had a kick to it. She'd worn jeans and a maroon-colored sweater, but she should have worn a jacket, too. No time to think things through.

"Mr. Stone," said a woman who stood behind a chrome-and-glass reception desk inside a lobby that looked like something out of a four-star hotel. "Your pilot said to go on through. He's ready for takeoff."

"Thanks, Kris."

The woman nodded, her grin about as sincere as a restaurant hostess's. Naomi wondered what she thought about the man in the cowboy hat and his unkempt com-

panion with the wild red hair. She was probably used
to sleek and polished celebrities.

She followed Jax through a pair of glass doors. They
opened into a hangar that smelled faintly of fuel and
lemon cleaner. An older man came toward them, a handsome man, one with a wide, extremely white smile and
all the bells and whistles of a former naval fighter pilot,
including the close-cropped gray hair.

"Mr. Stone," he said, holding out his hand. "Got you
all fueled up and ready to go. Mark's already on board."

"Thanks, Ben." Her boss shook the pilot's hand before heading toward a narrow set of steps that led up to
the doorway of the jet.

If her pulse had raced back at the house, that was
nothing compared to now, and it wasn't just because
she'd suddenly realized she was falling in love with
her boss.

"I feel like Julia Roberts in *Pretty Woman*."

She wasn't sure Jax heard her, but the pilot did because there was a smile on his face when she glanced
back at him.

"Except I doubt you're headed to the opera," Ben
said.

Which meant the pilot knew his boss well. All work
and no play. Why? Why was Jax so serious all the time?
The only time she'd ever seen him do something fun
was when he watched his nephew ride. That was it. But
then she stopped inside the opening of the jet, because
the posh interior took her aback.

"Wow."

Cream-colored leather seats. Plush off-white carpet.
Chrome accents. There were at least six seats, but they
weren't like a commercial airliner. There were two seats
that sat opposite each other with a mahogany table in

between. Jax plopped down into one of those. Across from them was a couch. Beyond that were another two seats, single ones. She didn't want to sit behind Jax because to be honest, she was so nervous she didn't want to be back there all by herself. She moved because another man, the copilot Mark, she guessed, stared at her from the cockpit.

"Hey." She waved weakly, then turned to take the seat opposite Jax.

"Buckle up," Jax ordered, pulling a laptop out of a compartment in the table. "Even on a private jet you need to wear a seat belt."

"Thanks."

How could he not hear her heart pounding? She glanced out the window, at the cloudy sky. She hated flying when she couldn't see the sun.

He cocked his head at her. "You seem nervous."

Why did he have to be so observant? But she had the perfect excuse for her shaking hands. "I guess this is not the time to confess that I hate flying."

He glanced up at her casually, only to do a double take because he must have seen the terror on her face. Little did he know that the terror had a lot more to do with *him* than with flying.

"Are you okay?"

She nodded weakly.

He stood up. "Do you need something to drink?"

"Beg your pardon?"

"Whiskey? Gin? Vodka? I have it all."

Of course he did. Probably a full bar in the back of the plane. Sure enough, that's where he headed, stopping in front of a sideboard at the tail end.

"Can you bring the whole bottle?"

He grabbed something, what she couldn't see, and poured her some amber-colored liquid.

"Drink," he said, holding a crystal glass out to her.

She drank.

Whatever it was, it burned like liquid fire and it immediately warmed her chilled body. "Ugh," she said with a shutter, slamming the glass down.

The plane lurched.

"I didn't even hear him start the engine."

She had his full focus, and she didn't know if it was the alcohol or the sudden smile on his face that made her go all wonky inside. She had it bad.

"They moved it out of the hangar with a pushback."

The warmth continued to spread. She rarely, if ever, drank, and the effect of eighty proof went straight to her bloodstream.

"Oh."

Beneath his cowboy hat, his eyes watched her intently, his laptop forgotten. He leaned back.

She glanced around. "No stewardesses?"

"I don't need someone to serve me drinks."

"Maybe I should do that for you. I am your housekeeper, after all."

"You're a lot more than that."

There it was again, that intense look that made her want to squirm in her seat. She wondered if he'd ever joined the mile-high club.

Naomi.

Her flush worsened, which made her look down at her hands. Her head snapped up, though, when she heard an engine start. Any hope that flying on a private jet might make air travel feel less stressful faded when she realized they were about to depart and that she was on the verge of her usual panic attack.

"It *is* safer than driving."

"I know." She glanced out the window. "And I know my anxiety is driven by a perceived lack of control. And that, statistically speaking, only one in three million planes crash. I know that. It doesn't matter. Still scares the crap out of me."

He smiled.

No. Don't do that, she wanted to say. *Don't be kind to me. I don't need more reasons to fall in love with you.*

"Relax."

He reached for her hands. She'd placed them on the table and hadn't even known it. Or maybe she had known. Maybe deep down inside she'd wanted this, wanted him to touch her and tell her everything would be okay. Trevor had done the same thing. He'd always laughed at her irrational fear, too.

"If we crash at least it will be a quick death."

That sounded like something Trevor would say, too. "I'll remind you of that as we plummet to earth."

He laughed and she admitted she loved touching him. Maybe it was the drink. Maybe it was the feel of his hands. Maybe it was the way he wouldn't release her gaze, but calm overcame her. The jet engine revved. She realized they'd been cleared for takeoff. She knew they were moving. Slowly at first, then faster and faster, but she didn't know if it was the jet that made her heart race, or something else. Her stomach dropped as if she'd plunged off the top of a roller coaster. She held his hand tighter, and then tighter still, until sunlight suddenly blinded the cabin and she realized they were soaring above the clouds.

Only the jet wasn't the only thing soaring. As she stared into his eyes, so did her heart.

Chapter 14

She'd fallen asleep somewhere over the Midwest, due, in part, to the giant glass of whiskey he'd poured her. Jax had covered her with a blanket and gone back to work, all the while marveling at how keyed up she'd been over flying. For someone so brave and clever he'd found her irrational fear somewhat amusing.

He would have let her keep on sleeping, but they'd begun their descent into Atlanta, according to Ben, and that meant he'd have to wake her soon. His pilot always insisted on seat belts, but for now he watched her sleep and he had to admit, she looked so different. She'd been really upset about selling her house. He knew why, too. She'd have to let go. It was the last of the things she'd shared with her husband. Her last anchor to her memories. That had to be scary.

He'd had a revelation, too, as they'd flown over the Midwest. He'd put away his laptop, turned off his cell phone and arrived at a decision. He wasn't going to let her slip away. To hell with the fact that she worked for him and that she had kids and that she was still hung up on Trevor. He would take a leap of faith and hope it landed him her heart because he saw in her something remarkable. A woman who'd had a tough go in life, but who'd still maintained her strength and sense of humor and dignity.

"Naomi," he said gently, shaking her lightly. "Time to wake up. We're landing."

She shot up so fast she damn near clocked him in the chin. "We're landing?"

Her left cheek was creased where it'd lain against a crack in the leather seat and her hair stuck up on one side. And yet even with her makeup smeared she still looked beautiful.

"In about fifteen minutes."

She glanced out the plane's window. It was late afternoon. The sky was a light, luminescent blue, and it meant the sun would set in a little bit.

"I hate landing," he heard her say.

He sat in his seat and contemplated what to do. She didn't want to get involved with him. Fine. He understood that, and her reasons why, but that didn't mean he had to accept them. He might be opening himself up to trouble, but he just didn't care, and so he sat down next to her, tipped his cowboy hat back and pulled her into his arms. She was stiff at first, but he refused to let her go and he eventually felt her relax.

"If we die, we'll die together," he told her.

"Thanks."

"Do you want another shot?"

She shook her head. "Only if it'll knock me out. You can wake me when we get to the ground safely."

"Come on. Let's get buckled in before Ben comes out to do his pre-landing check of the cabin. He's a bit of a hard-ass when it comes to following regulations."

She leaned away from him. "Actually, that's a good

thing. It means he's conscientious and thereby less prone to crashing."

He stared at her lips, and man he'd like to kiss them, and for a moment he wondered if he should—but it was too much too soon. He'd have to woo her. Slowly. But he was patient, and in his experience good things came to those who waited.

He would wait as long as it took where Naomi was concerned.

She survived the landing.

Jax, bless his heart, held her the whole way down. She should have pushed him away, but she hadn't. She'd succumbed to her fears and the overwhelming need to be held by him. Thank goodness he'd let her go at the end. And that he hadn't tried anything. She wasn't at all sure she'd have resisted.

"So how long will you be here for?" she asked as he drove her toward a rental car agency. He already had a car to drive—a brand-new BMW—because apparently when you had a gazillion dollars, you didn't have to worry about anything as plebian as regular rental cars. You just jumped off your jet, grabbed keys and off you went. Jax had explained there was no need for paperwork when they had a jet as collateral sitting in their hangar. She supposed he had a point.

"Just in and out. I'd like to get this guy back to the ranch as soon as possible. Ben's on standby as I work the details out."

Another perk of being wealthy. Your own personal pilot. It was a good thing she wasn't a gold digger because it was awfully hard not to peek at the good-looking man sitting next to her and not think he was quite a catch.

"Speaking of helping someone out, I can't thank you enough for bringing me out here. I promise I'll make it quick. Shouldn't take more than a few hours to get things arranged."

The GPS shouted instructions and her stomach flipped over because soon she'd be driving home. Her last time driving home. Everything had become a list of lasts as soon as they'd landed. The last time she'd step off a plane and feel the cloying, sticky air of the South, at least until she could afford to visit for a vacation. The last time she'd ever see the inside of a luxurious jet center because she sure as certain would never be on a private jet again because she planned to fly home on her own. Probably the last time she'd ride in a car as luxurious as this one, too, although to be perfectly honest, she much preferred his truck.

"You know, I could drive you to your place."

She turned toward him so fast her rear end slid on the leather seat. "Oh no. I couldn't ask you to do that. Columbus is a million miles from here. Well, not a million, but an hour and a half. That's too far. I'm sure you have more important things to do."

He was quiet for a moment. She stared at his fingers wrapped around a leather steering wheel and tried not to fidget.

"I've got a confession to make."

The eyes beneath his cowboy hat were soft and blue and they made her want to look away. She had a feeling she knew what he was about to say. Didn't want to know if her suspicions were correct because if she was correct, that would make him the kindest, most heroic man she'd ever met—next to Trevor—and she didn't want to delve into that too deeply.

"I didn't have to fly all the way out here to pick up that soldier."

She knew it. Of course she did. If the man he'd come to pick up was still in the Army's care, that meant the Army could have made their own arrangements to get him to California.

"He's at Fort Benning, isn't he?"

"What a coincidence, right?"

Not really. It was one of the biggest Army bases in the nation. The reason why she lived in Columbus. Why she wanted to get away. Too many reminders.

"You do realize you're making it awfully hard not to hug you."

He smiled.

She loved him.

She knew it right then as he stared down at her and admitted with tenderness in his eyes that he'd done this for her. All for her.

"Why do I have the feeling if I insist on renting a car, you'll just drive me anyway?"

"Because you'd be right."

What was with her? Why was she so emotional all of a sudden? This whole damn situation made her want to cry. It was like she was stuck in one of those horrible dreams, one where your feet were like cement bags and you couldn't move. On the one hand she wanted to turn to him and tell him she gave up. That she was willing to give it a try. To be his girl.

Her eyes began to burn.

"Hey," he said gently. "What's wrong?"

He wasn't a hard-ass. He wasn't made of stone. He was about the best man in the world she'd ever met. Who else would fly all the way across the country not just for her, but for some strange man he'd never met but whom he wanted to help.

"I'm suffering from an anxiety attack," she muttered.

He slowed down, and she knew what he was about to do.

"Jax, no."

But he pulled over anyway. They must look so strange to people passing by. The man in the luxury car wearing a cowboy hat and the woman sitting next to him with drool stains on her chin and tears in her eyes. What a hot mess she was.

"Why are you fighting this?"

"Fighting what?" she asked through a nose clogged with tears.

"Us."

Oh, dear Lord. He knew. He knew she was in love with him. Or maybe he'd just reasoned out that she'd begun to fall for him and it scared her to death. And that she wasn't the type of woman who could have sex with a man and not care.

"Jax, I—"

"Please, Naomi. Whatever there's been between us, we've always been honest with each other. You feel it, too, don't you?"

He was right. She wouldn't deny it. She was fighting this…this *thing* between them.

"I do."

Behind him, the Atlanta skyline stretched tall, a host of windows sparkling in the early-evening sunlight. This was her home. Or it used to be. A place she'd wanted to escape. To California. The land of golden opportunity.

"I don't know if I can do it, Jax."

"Do what?"

She gulped. "Say goodbye to my home."

The tears that had been hanging on by a thread suddenly broke free. She inhaled deeply to stanch the flow of even more tears, but it didn't help.

"You can. You will."

She wanted to believe him, she really did, but for the first time she wondered if her tears weren't just because she'd sold her house. If they were because she suddenly wondered if she'd done the right thing. If moving to California had been for the best. If maybe Sam was right. Maybe it'd all been a mistake, one she still had time to rectify.

Chapter 15

"Mom?"

Naomi caught Sam in the midst of climbing down the stairs when she walked into her in-laws' plantation-style home.

"Surprise!" she said, suddenly wanting to cry all over again.

"Mom!" she yelled, and any fears Naomi had that Samantha might be permanently mad at her faded at the look of joy on her daughter's face. It was pure happiness. "You're here."

"I'm here," she echoed as her daughter flew into her arms.

"I knew you'd change your mind. I knew it. I knew it."

"Mom?" she heard T.J. say. His little head peeked around the corner of the kitchen and then he, too, was wrapped up in a hug.

"My word!" said a woman's voice.

"Okay, everybody, back off." Naomi looked up, meeting the gaze of her mother-in-law.

"What in heaven's name are you doing here?" asked Rose.

Naomi winced. She'd never really been close to Rose Jones. The woman and her husband loved the kids, though.

"I thought I'd surprise you." She didn't want to tell the kids that she'd sold the house they'd grown up in. Not yet. "My boss had to come out here for business and he offered to bring me along."

Sam stared up at her, disappointment filling her eyes. Naomi stroked her head, trying to reassure her that it would all be okay, hoping Sam wouldn't go back to hating her again when she heard the news that their house had sold. She looked into Rose's eyes, and it was clear the woman knew something was up. Naomi had never met someone who looked so stern all the time. The only time Rose's face softened was when she was dealing with her grandkids. With her short-cropped gray hair and light blue eyes, Naomi had told Trevor once she resembled her old high school math teacher, a woman who'd never liked her.

"Kids. Why don't you go upstairs to your rooms and give your mother and me some time to chat."

Sam didn't look like she wanted to leave her. Naomi often wondered if she sensed the tension between her and her grandmother.

"Go on," Naomi urged.

And still, her daughter didn't move. Naomi shot her a silent *please* with her eyes. Sam took a step away. T.J. seemed to be waiting for his sister to set the mood because his shoulders slumped as he headed upstairs.

"Let's sit," Rose said, pointing toward the couch in the front room. Trevor had once told her that his mom loved the couch so much, she and Walt had scrimped and saved to get it, and she'd vowed never to get rid of it. Naomi was pretty sure the story was true. That would explain why Rose had never replaced it in the fifteen years she'd known the woman. And why it was harder than a park bench.

"Where's Walt?" she asked, trying to distract her.

"Golfing."

Of course he was. It was part of the reason they were moving to California. Year-round golf.

"What happened?" her mother-in-law asked the moment they'd taken a seat.

"What do you mean?"

Blue eyes just like Trevor's narrowed. "Don't play coy with me, young lady. I didn't watch you cry your eyes out for months on end not to recognize when you've been bawling."

See, and all this time she'd thought she'd done a pretty good job concealing her grief from her mother-in-law. Little did she know.

"I sold the house."

A brow popped up. She would know if her mother-in-law ever had plastic surgery because the day she could stop doing that was the day she'd had her skin stitched up. She was forever giving her the Spock brow.

"And that upset you?"

Not just that. I had an affair with my boss. And I think I'm in love with him.

It shocked her how close she was to saying exactly those words, except she didn't want to give the strait-laced Rose Jones a shock. Not at her age.

"I don't think I want to move the kids."

Rose leaned back. "I thought you wanted to stay close to us."

"I did. But then I—" *jumped into bed with my boss*

"—thought about it and I'm wondering if it's really the right thing to do."

Rose crossed her arms in front of her. Naomi went on high alert. The only other time she'd ever done that was a month after Trevor had died, when Naomi had gotten a little too caught up in the grieving process, or so Rose had told her. Never mind that she'd had every right.

"You had an affair with your boss, didn't you?"

"I—" She couldn't speak for a moment. "What makes you say that?"

"The kids told me you two seemed cozy."

"No."

"Well, Sam told me that. T.J. is just like my son. More interested in fun and excitement than paying attention to what's going on around him."

I did not have an affair.

The lie was right on the tip of her tongue, but she'd never been dishonest a day in her life. She wasn't going to start by lying to her mother-in-law, and so she kept quiet. Nothing wrong with pleading the fifth—in an indirect way.

"Did he make a pass at you?"

The question almost made her laugh. Jax make a pass at her? As if that would ever happen.

"Well?"

"No."

That, at least, was the truth. She'd been the one to touch him first. Or had she been? To be honest, she couldn't remember, but what did it matter?

"So you were the instigator then." And she didn't say it like a question, she said it like a fact, and Naomi decided to take the fifth again. Actually, what she decided to do was change the subject.

"How was your vacation with the kids?"

Rose simply stared.

"Did T.J. freak out about any of the rides?"

And still, she stared. Naomi felt her face begin to heat like a Bunsen burner. Curse her fair complexion. This was not a conversation she wanted to have with her mother-in-law. There were times when she wished she had a friend. A good friend. Someone she could confide in. Trevor had been her best friend. She'd told him everything: about the snobby mother at the kids' school. And the horrible boss she'd had when the kids were younger. Even her own suspicions that his mother didn't like her, which he'd denied, even though Naomi still thought the woman didn't think her good enough. She'd always felt like an interloper, too. Trevor had dismissed her concerns, of course, but some things never changed.

And Rose still stared.

"I think I'll go break the news to the kids."

"Sit."

She sat.

"Naomi, I'm an old woman. I do not have time for games. Something happened while you were in California. It's written all over your face. I'd like to know what."

She recognized another look on Rose's face, this one from the how-long-has-it-been-since-you've-bathed conversations they'd had after Trevor had died. Good times.

"Okay." She glanced up the stairs. The last thing she needed was for the kids to hear. "So maybe something did happen."

She expected condemnation. She expected disgust. She might have even expected contempt. But none of those emotions filled Rose's eyes. Instead what she saw could only be identified as...

Sadness.

"I've been wondering when this would happen."

As if from a distance she heard herself say, "When what would happen?"

"When you'd find someone."

I didn't "find" anyone, she wanted to say. She'd had a crush on her boss. It'd turned into something deeper. She would nip it in the bud before it could become anything more serious.

"He's just a friend."

"But you slept with him."

For an older woman she sure had a frank way of conversing about such a sensitive topic. Clearly, she'd been watching too much of *The View*.

"Just once."

And even to her own ears it sounded ridiculous. As if the frequency with which you slept with someone somehow negated the intimacy of the act. She stared down at her hands. The woman must be so disappointed with her. The glint of her wedding ring caught her eye. She played with it, wondering what Trevor would say.

"I'm surprised it was just once."

Yup. Just as she'd thought. Her mother-in-law had lost complete respect for her.

"If I'd gone as long without sex as you have, I'd have given it a week or two before calling it off."

Naomi's head snapped up. "Excuse me?"

Was that... No. That couldn't be... Kindness. Patience. Understanding. It was all there in Rose's eyes.

"Naomi, you loved my son. I had my doubts at first, I'll confess. You guys were so young. Ask Walt.

I thought for sure the only reason he married you was that you must be pregnant."

It was nice to know she hadn't been far off the mark as far as Rose's feelings for her.

"But when you toughed it out all through basic training, and then you stuck with him through his first deployment, I knew it was the real deal. You loved him. What's more, he loved you."

Were those tears in the woman's eyes? She couldn't be certain. She'd never really seen Rose cry before. Not even on the day they'd buried Trevor. She'd just stood there, mute, her eyes welling with tears, but never actually crying. Today she looked ready to do exactly that.

"We were both very lucky."

"Yes," Rose said softly. "You were." She leaned forward. "But for the love of God, Red, it's time to move on."

She drew back as if the woman had hit her. Rose had never, not once since Naomi had known her, called her by Trevor's pet name.

"He would have wanted that."

"I know," Naomi said over the lump in her throat. "I hear his voice in my head all the time. He always told me if something happened to him that I was to go on living my life. That I wasn't to live like a nun."

"But that's exactly what you've been doing."

She didn't know what surprised her most: that her mother-in-law thought she'd been living like a nun, or that she heard disapproval in her voice when she talked about it.

"The next time Magic Mike comes to town, I'll invite you to come along. We can both cut loose."

But her attempt at humor was lost on Rose.

"I want to tell you something, Naomi. Something

that happened a long time ago. Before Sam was born, but before I tell you, I want you to promise me that you won't be angry with me for keeping it from you for all these years."

That sounded ominous. So was the look on Rose's face. Ominous and troubled.

"I promise," she managed to choke out, even though something deep inside told her she might not want to hear it.

"It was the year Trevor was on that training mission in Germany."

No, no. She did not want to hear this, especially not now, because she perfectly recalled the time and she had a feeling she knew what Rose was about to reveal. She and Trev had been trying to have a baby, but she hadn't been able to conceive. She'd been mad at Trevor for having to take off, even though she knew there hadn't been anything he could do about it. He'd gone away in a huff, and for the first and only time in her marriage, she wondered if things were going to work out.

"He met her at a coffee shop."

"No." She stood. "I do not want to hear this."

"Sit down."

She would have done Tramp proud in that moment because she refused. "I'm serious, Rose. I don't want to know."

"You have to know," her mother-in-law said, standing, too. "For years I've watched you put my son on a pedestal, worship the ground he walked on, when all the while I carried this secret. This terrible secret..."

And it was why she'd always been so cold. It wasn't dislike. It was dismay. She'd been afraid to let something slip. Had chosen silence as a way of valor. Dear Lord. How could she have been so blind?

"He stayed there for an extra week," Naomi heard herself say.

"He was trying to decide."

Stay? Or leave.

She closed her eyes. Funny thing was, she didn't cry, didn't feel hurt, didn't feel anything because she knew. Deep inside she'd always known something had happened in Germany. She'd been afraid to probe too deep to find out what it'd been.

"So if you're waiting for this magic, perfect love to come again, Naomi, you're kidding yourself. No love is perfect. Heck. Do you know how many times I've wanted to bash Walt over the head with a golf club? That man will be buried with his nine iron."

She shouldn't find the comment funny. Now was not the time to laugh. But it was the first time she'd ever heard her mother-in-law make a funny. Even more crazy, Rose smiled, too.

"One of these days I'm going to find him in bed with his clubs, you mark my words."

Naomi smiled.

Rose's expression turned serious again. "My son was no saint, Naomi. He loved you. Of that I have no doubt. He came back to you. As far as I know, he never strayed again, and the next year you had Sam and then T.J. soon after. He was happy. Come to think of it, I don't think I've ever thanked you for that, for making my son so happy. I might have had my doubts at the beginning, but I didn't at the end. Never at the end."

How did one go from smiling to crying in the next instant? She had to wipe at her eyes.

"Thank you," she said.

Rose took a step, but she hesitated a moment before she opened her arms. Naomi took the guesswork out of the gesture. She opened her own arms and for the first time since Trevor's death, hugged Rose.

"You were good for him. You brought out the best in him."

She drew back.

"You'll be good for another man, too. And he'll be lucky to have you."

Chapter 16

His house seemed ridiculously lonely without her. Even Tramp seemed to notice her absence, the animal unusually subdued.

"You miss her, too, don't you?" he asked him the morning after he'd arrived back home. She'd asked for a few days off, to think, and he'd gladly given them to her, but he hated the silence.

"To hell with this."

Tramp lifted his head again. Jax reached for his cell phone:

Took Tramp to the shelter.

He sat back on the bed. He didn't have to wait long.

What?!!

He smiled. So she wasn't completely ignoring him. Good to know.

They're prepping the gas chamber right now.

He glanced at Tramp. The dog seemed to roll his eyes. It made him smile all over again.

Haha. Very funny.

So much for scaring her.

They said they could try and adopt him out, but he's too ugly.

She replied quickly.

Beauty is in the eye of the beholder.

See, that was what he missed. Her witty comebacks. Her ability to see the humor in a situation. He missed her. The house wasn't the same without her. He missed her humming while she cleaned. He missed her dancing in the kitchen. He even missed her waffles. He didn't know what she put in those things, but he would never eat them frozen from a box again.

So he lifted his phone and shot a picture of Tramp lying on the edge of his bed, the dog doing his part by looking soulfully into the lens.

He misses you.

And Jax truly thought he did. There could be no other explanation for his melancholy. He waited for a response.

Janus probably misses you, too.

"Oh, what the heck."

I miss you.

He waited, breath held. Nothing.
"Damn it."
But then his phone beeped and his heart lifted.

I just want to say thank you, Jax. For everything.

Wait. *What?* What the hell did that mean?
He typed the words out, waiting for a response, and when he didn't get one, shot out of bed from nervous energy. Tramp didn't. The dog just lay there while he got dressed. He wondered if there was something wrong with the animal. If maybe he should call Ethan. His friend was a vet. He could maybe give him a quick once-over. Besides, calling Ethan would give him something to do. He arranged for his friend to come over and killed time by checking emails.

His inbox showed he had new messages, and somehow he knew what one of them would be. Sure enough, there it was.

"I'm so sorry."
That was the subject line. His heart started to pound as he read the content.

Dear Jax:
I know this is probably the cowardly way to do this, but I've changed my mind about working at your ranch I know, I know—after everything you've done to help me out, here I am, telling you've I've changed my mind. You must think I'm the stupidest person you've ever met.

No. Not stupid. Just very, very conflicted.

I know this will leave you in the lurch, and I'm so sorry. I guess in the end what it boils down to is I'm afraid to let myself fall again. Afraid of what it might do to me. And not just me, but the kids, too. T.J. adores you. Sam? Well, I think she suspects how I feel about you, and I know she'd come around eventually, but if I mess this up somehow, if it doesn't work out, I don't want to break their hearts again. They've already been through so much.

His gate alarm beeped—a signal that someone had arrived. A quick check of the monitor revealed Ethan driving up to the house.

I'm still planning a move to California, but we'll all live with my in-laws until I find a new job. I'll send Ethan over for my truck. Claire said they can store it until I get back to California.

I hope you know how much you mean to me, Jax. How much I admire you. You're perfect in so many ways. I'm afraid I'm not perfect enough for you.

Tramp's ears pricked forward when he heard the vehicle on the drive. His tail began to wag. He rushed to the office window, excitedly dancing around.

"It's not her, buddy."

The dog didn't believe him. Jax just sat there. He couldn't move, devastated.

The doorbell rang. Tramp barked. He thought about ignoring him, but Ethan would just keep bugging him.

"Hey," Ethan said when Jax finally let him in.

Jax lifted a hand in greeting. "Thanks for coming over on such short notice."

Ethan cocked a head at him. "You look like you just saw your best friend get killed. What's wrong?"

He wanted to deny it. To tell his friend he was just worried about Tramp. That's what he should do.

"Naomi quit," he admitted.

Ethan drew back in surprise. "Wow." He cocked his head. "You mind me asking what happened?"

Yes, he did mind. He didn't want to talk about it. Instead he heard himself say, "Want a beer?"

Ethan called the dog over to him. Tramp reluctantly complied.

"Hey, buddy," he said to the dog. "You look okay. You missing your friends?"

"Is that what the problem is?"

Ethan straightened. "Probably, but I'll have a look at him in a minute."

Jax tried not to vomit as he headed to the kitchen. He hated to do it. It was a reminder of her. He could still see her there, leaning against the counter, a smile on her beautiful face.

She's gone.

For now, he firmly told himself. He wasn't a quitter. He wouldn't let her be one, either.

"He looks good," Ethan said, taking the beer from him. "I doubt there's anything wrong with him."

"I wish I was good."

Ethan took a swig of the beer. "Well?"

Jax took a deep breath before saying, "Your pal Trevor must have been a heck of a man."

"He was."

"She's still hung up on him. Plus, I think she's afraid of what her kids might think of me."

Ethan nodded, rested the beer on his knee. They both looked out at the property Jax had built. At the dream they'd both shared. It was because of Ethan that he'd moved to Via Del Caballo in the first place. Because of him that he'd committed a huge part of his life, and his money, to a project that they both believed in—helping wounded vets. Ethan was a good man. If he told Jax to leave Naomi alone, he would.

"So you two hooked up then?"

Jax didn't bother to deny it.

"I kind of figured you would."

That caught his attention. "You did?"

Ethan's smile was rueful. "Well, not me. Claire predicted it. So did your sister. The two of them were like game-show hosts. Some kind of matchmaking reality flick. You should have heard them plotting what Naomi should wear to the big gala."

Jesus, Mary and Joseph. He should have known.

"Tell them thanks, but it didn't work."

Ethan glanced over at him. "You fall in love with her?"

He'd asked himself the same question a million times. "I did."

"Figured as much."

They both sat there. That was the thing about Ethan. He was quiet. Calm. Reassuring. It was what made him a good veterinarian. They'd met way back at the beginning of their military careers, had always stayed in touch, and Jax thanked God for him every day whenever he got up and looked out his front window, at the scenic valley where he now lived.

Heaven on earth.

Moving to Via Del Caballo had done more to heal the scars of war more than anything else. It'd done the same thing for Ethan. He'd have been content here. But then Naomi had come along and he realized there was more to life than his business and his home and his new ranch. So much more.

"You should go after her."

"I know," Jax said.

Ethan half turned to him, his bottle dripping with condensation. "So what's holding you back?"

Jax stared at the brown glass, observing the way the sun glinted off its surface, worked the edge of the label free while he contemplated his friend's words. "Scared, I guess. She claims she's afraid, too. I almost emailed her back and told her I felt the same way."

"She emailed you that she wasn't coming back?"

Jax nodded.

Ethan frowned. "Brutal."

Jax glanced over at him. "Thanks for your honesty."

"Sorry." Ethan stared down at his bottle, too. "You know that dog of hers, Janus? You remember me telling you about how at first Naomi didn't want him?"

Jax nodded. "Claire was supposed to adopt him out."

"She didn't want him because it hurt too much. That dog was a big reminder of what she'd lost, but here's the thing. Janus loved her. That damn dog took one look at Naomi when she came to the ranch and almost mowed her down. He remembered her. Loved her. Not the same way he loved Trevor. That was a different kind of love. That was a bond between animal and handler, a bond that was forged on the battlefield. Janus and Trevor were inseparable. When he died, a part of Janus died, too. But then he saw Naomi and it kindled a different kind of love. And then later, when he went home to the kids, yet another kind of love—protecting his young. Trevor's young. Never seen anything like it."

Jax knew what he was trying to say. He'd seen it

with his own eyes. That dog loved his tiny humans. It was remarkable.

"There are all kinds of love in this world," Ethan said. "Working with animals, I've seen it in every form. Horses love their owners. Dogs adore their handlers. Hell, even cats can love."

"Surely not cats."

Ethan smiled a little, nodded. "Cats get a bum rap."

"You think."

"Pretty sure."

They both sat there in silence again. Tramp shuffled over without him realizing it, rested his head in his lap, brown eyes gazing soulfully into his own. Jax rubbed his wiry fur, leaned his head in closer.

Go get her, the dog seemed to say.

"That dog knows I'm right, too."

If only that were true. If only the dog could talk. Maybe he needed more reassurances. All he knew was that he'd never been more scared in his life. Not when he'd been in combat. Not when he'd first gone into business. Not when he'd watched his nephew fall off a steer for the first time.

"What if she says no?"

"What if you change her mind?" Ethan asked.

What if, indeed.

Chapter 17

T.J. didn't take the news that Naomi wouldn't be working for Jax anymore very well. Seemed he'd had his heart set on being a cowboy, and none of the excuses she handed him amounted to any good.

"Can't I visit?" he'd asked. "I liked Jax and Kyle."

"I'm afraid not, buddy." And she hated the look of disappointment on his face. It was just what she'd been hoping to avoid.

"Plus, I'm going to look for work closer to Nona and Papa. Won't that be great?"

That had been the other surprise. In the days following their heart-to-heart Rose had really opened up. It made Naomi wish they'd spoken so honestly sooner.

"This is bunk," T.J. had said, storming off.

Sam had just watched her little brother, then fixed her gaze on her mom.

"Whatever." That'd been her response, but Naomi had seen a flash of something behind her eyes. Relief? Regret? What?

She almost didn't want to know.

So she helped Rose and Walt pack their home. Fortunately, she had the house money coming and she could use some of that for living expenses. By the time she found a new place to move to in California, the kids would be ready to start back to school. It would all work out.

"I'm going to miss this old house," Rose admitted as she slapped tape on yet another box.

"Me, too."

Her mother-in-law stared at her intently. Had she sounded sad? Was that why she looked at Naomi like that? Rose had made no bones about the fact that she thought she was crazy for giving up such a great job in California.

"It's not too late to change your mind."

"I can't do that."

He hadn't even called her. That stung. Sure, she'd been the one to quit on him, but she'd thought he'd at least put up a little fight.

"We're going to need more of these." Rose shoved the box she'd just packed off the side.

"They're out in the garage."

"I'll go get them."

"No. It's okay. I'll do it."

Trevor's mom had been working too hard. So Naomi pushed herself to her feet and headed outside.

And there he was.

He stood across the street, leaning on the driver's side of a luxury car, cowboy hat still firmly in place, and her heart leaped. It just leaped in pure joy.

He moved, opened the car door, but not before looking both ways, and she saw him then.

Tramp.

The dog had seen her, too, and it was a good thing no cars were coming because he ran straight for her, a canine woof of joy escaping just before he collided with her midsection.

"Tramp, down," she cried, blinking away tears. "You big goofball."

The dog wouldn't listen, though, just kept trying to get to her face, and she realized he wore a bow. She tried to fend him off as best she could while she watched Jax approach.

"He missed you," Jax said.

"I can see that."

"And since I miss you, too, I thought maybe we'd fly in for a visit."

Tramp finally settled down. Well, he went over to Jax next, dancing around at his feet.

"You flew all the way out here just to bring Tramp for a visit?"

He shrugged.

"I don't know what to say."

"Tell me you've missed me."

She had missed him. Terribly. He'd missed her, too. He hadn't actually told her he loved her, but she'd known it was headed in that direction for him, too. All she had to do was look into his eyes to know how right she'd been.

"Stop looking at me like that," she said softly.

"I also came to give you this." He held out an envelope she hadn't seen before.

"What is it?"

"Look."

It wasn't an invitation. It was a card.

HOOVES FOR HEROES GRAND OPENING.

She smiled. "You're finally opening for business."

"Well, we've actually been open for a couple weeks now. A soft opening. I arranged for that war veteran to come out right away. But next week we're actually cutting the ribbon. Our first guests have arrived and Colby and Brielle have both been hard at work. I'd really like you to come and see it."

"Jax, I don't have time to fly out there. I'm helping my in-laws now, and packing up the last of my own things that I need to drive out to California. There's still so much to do. We have at least another week of work…"

"That's why I'm sending my jet. You'll be back and forth in a day."

"No," she said with a firm shake of her head, trying to hand the card back to him. "I would never ask you to do that."

"I know. That's why I'm offering."

"And I'm declining."

Tramp had settled down around their feet, and he must have caught Janus's scent because he suddenly began to sniff around.

"I'm not giving up on us," he said.

"You should."

"Give me one good reason why I should."

"Because I'm in love with another man."

"You're in love with a ghost." He took a step closer to her. "With a memory."

Her heart had begun to pound in her chest. "Please don't."

"Don't what?" He took another step. "Don't remind you of what it's like to have a flesh-and-blood man? You love me, Naomi. I know you do. Maybe not the same way as you loved Trevor, but it's there."

Yes, she did, although how it'd happened so quickly she had no idea. She loved him. Terribly. Just not enough to give her the courage she'd need to take such a huge step with Jax.

"I'm sorry."

He stood there, staring down at her. "I'm sorry, too."

She bent, held out her hand to the goofy dog who'd captured her heart, too. "Goodbye, Tramp."

The dog wagged his tail and she felt tears begin to build again. She straightened, held out her hand, Trevor's ring glinting on her finger. "Goodbye, Jax."

He wouldn't take it, just turned, Tramp pausing by the edge of her yard to take one last look before bounding away.

It was the last time she would ever see him.

She cried herself to sleep that night. She'd known she'd done the right thing. She was a mom. Moms made sacrifices. Right now she needed to live life for her kids.

"You told him to leave."

She'd been sitting at Rose and Walt's breakfast table, a tiny little wooden thing that would be donated to charity once they were ready to leave Georgia, and to be honest, she'd thought at first that the words had come from her own internal monologue. It took a moment to realize they'd been uttered by Sam.

"Excuse me?"

Her daughter peered at her across a plate of pancakes, her fork lifted halfway to her mouth, syrup oozing off the end. It smelled like maple in the kitchen because of it.

"Jax. I saw you talking to him, but then he left."

T.J.'s head jerked up. "Jax was here?"

His sister nodded. "And Tramp."

"Is Kyle here, too?"

"Sit down, Teej," Sam said. "It was only Jax and Tramp, and they left already."

T.J. seemed utterly devastated and it made Naomi's stomach flip.

"You had a thing with him, didn't you?"

"Sam!"

Where was this coming from? Why was her thirteen-year-old daughter suddenly talking to her like she was the adult and Naomi the kid.

"It was while we were with Nona and Papa, wasn't it?"

"What's a thing?" T.J. asked.

"Nothing," Naomi said, shooting her daughter a look that she hoped Sam knew meant she better be quiet. She should have known better.

"You've been moping around here ever since you've been back. T.J., too, although his crying I understand. He wanted to be a cowboy."

"I wanted to learn how to ride," T.J. amended.

"Same thing," Sam said before her gaze met her own. "You're in love with him, aren't you, Mom?"

"In love with who?" T.J. asked. "Tramp?"

"No, nitwit. Mr. Stone."

For the first time T.J.'s eyes lit up. "Really?"

Sam nodded, leaned back in her chair, crossed her arms in front of her. "Only Mom told him to go away." She cocked the trigger before unleashing the verbal bullet. "Because of us."

"Why?" T.J. asked. That was the thing with kids. Questions got boiled down to the bare bones.

"Because she's using us as an excuse. She doesn't want to admit her feelings to us, that she loves another man."

For the first time Naomi caught a glimpse of what

this was all about. Sam was in pain. Not because her mom had fallen in love with another man, but because her own love for her father still burned brightly. Clearly, she resented her mother's ability to move on when she couldn't seem to do the same thing.

"I'm so sorry, Sam."

"For what?"

"For thinking you were over the loss of your dad."

She drew back, her eyes instantly welling with tears. "Why would you think that?"

Naomi shook her head. "I don't know. Maybe because it's been a long time since I've heard you cry yourself to sleep, too."

Sam flicked her chin up. "I'll never stop loving him, Mom. Not as long as I live."

"Me, neither," she admitted.

"But you love that man."

She took a deep breath. "I do."

"How can that be possible if you love Daddy, too?"

She shrugged. "I don't know, Sam. I just do."

T.J.'s gaze shifted to Sam, waiting for the next volley, and when his sister didn't say anything he asked, "Are you going to marry him?"

"She told him to go away," Sam answered for her.

"Why?"

"Because she thinks she needs to be some kind of supermom, I guess."

"Wait a minute," Naomi said. "I thought you didn't like him."

"He's okay." Sam shrugged, and that was probably the best she'd ever get from her daughter when it came to admitting she approved. "He's not a creep, that's for sure. And I knew it was bound to happen sooner or later."

"You mean Mom wants to be a superhero?"

Sam smirked. "Something like that, Teej."

"So you don't hate me for liking another man?" Naomi asked.

"Why would I do that?" Sam asked. "It was weird at first, seeing you flirt with him."

"I never flirted with him."

"Well, you might not think so, but I saw the way you were looking at him. It weirded me out at first, but then he flew you all the way out here just to get Dad's bench and I had to admit, that was pretty nice. But then you said you'd quit and I thought maybe I was mistaken, but I could tell by watching you I was right. You're in love with him."

She wilted back in her chair, the fight suddenly drained out of her.

"And you want to know something weird, Mom?"

T.J. stared at his sister avidly. He nodded.

"I was actually disappointed," Sam admitted. "I'd seen you light up in a way I hadn't seen before, and suddenly that light was gone, and it made me realize how selfish I'd been."

Suddenly Naomi wanted to cry. She'd been telling herself her daughter was growing up too fast. Only now did she realize how true it was.

"You've been sad for too long. I miss you being happy."

Oh, if only it were that simple. "I'm afraid," she admitted to her kids. "No. Terrified."

"Of what?" asked T.J.

"Doing it again."

"Doing what?" This time it was Sam that asked.

"The whole relationship thing. The ups and downs. The good and the bad. The moments when you're not in love. The times you want to pack up your bags and leave. The times you're so blissfully happy you're afraid it will all disappear. The days when you're so horribly angry it's all you can do not to throw a coffee cup at someone's head. Afraid of all that. Afraid of what it means for you. Afraid of what it means for me."

There was silence around the table and she realized this was the conversation she'd needed to have, with her kids, to explain. Not keep it all bottled up inside. She'd been fooling herself. She wasn't there for them. They were there for *her*. She needed *them*. Not the other way around.

"What does it mean, Mommy?" The fight had gone out of Sam's eyes. She was her little girl again. The one who didn't understand something and needed her mother to explain.

"It means I'm in love, kiddo." She swallowed over the lump in her throat. "And sometimes love isn't pretty. It's not what they sell to you in movies and on TV. It's not perfect. It can be ugly. It can be beautiful. It can be utterly terrifying, too. It's all those things at once and sometimes only one of those things at a time—if that makes sense."

"It's like my Legos," T.J. said matter-of-factly. "I would be really upset if something happened to them. But I love my Legos. You could love my Legos, too, Mommy, if it'll make you feel any better."

She wanted to smile, she really did, but she was trying too hard not to cry. "Thanks, buddy."

Sam just stared. "Did you hate Daddy sometimes?"

Naomi thought back to that time when he left for Germany. "Yes, honey, I did, but only for a while, and then I loved him all over again. More, once you were born."

"And you're afraid of going through that all over again?"

Boiled down to the nuts and bolts. "Yes. And I'm afraid of putting you through it, too."

"So you're not miserable because of us?"

"Oh, honey." She got up from her chair, crossed to her daughter's side. "Of course not."

She thought Sam would ignore her at first. She was a teenager after all and subject to mercurial mood swings, but she felt her daughter slip her arms around her. She cuddled her head in her belly just like she used to do when she was tiny and barely stood past her knees.

"I love you, Sam."

"Don't be afraid, Mom." She felt Sam stir. When her daughter tipped her head back, there were tears in her eyes. "We'll be here for you, T.J. and me. No matter what happens, you'll always have us."

She felt her face crumple because it was true. No matter what, she would always have this. Sam in her arms. T.J., too, because he came around the side of the table and snuggled up next to her, too. Her kids. Her and Trevor's kids. A little piece of him next to her heart. Always.

"Kids. How would you like to go back to the ranch?"

T.J. jumped back. "Oh, boy. Yes!"

But it was Sam she looked to for an answer. For some reason, she needed her daughter's approval.

"I hate how sad you've become."

That was as close to an answer as she would get, but that was okay. Naomi would take it.

"Oh, kiddo. Me, too."

Chapter 18

The day of his grand opening dawned beautiful and bright. Jax couldn't have ordered better weather if he'd had a direct line to God.

"It's almost a pity we're going to be inside," Claire McCall said. She paused beneath the entrance to the stable. Someone had hung a sign that said CONGRATULATIONS over the doorway and she looked up at it and smiled. "I'm surprised the horses aren't freaking out at the balloons."

Jax would bet it was Brielle who had dolled the place up. His new hippotherapist might not live at the ranch full-time, but she made the most of her hours.

"They're therapy horses," Jax said. "Nothing fazes them."

Those horses were tied to a rail inside the arena, and Colby stood nearby. As the ranch foreman, he was in charge of preparing the animals, something Jax was grateful for. Although he'd learned a lot in recent weeks, he was no expert.

He heard someone laugh. Chance Reynolds and his wife, Carolina, stood in front of the grooming stall,

Caro petting the nose of a horse. Beyond them Colt, Natalie and Lauren's future husband, Bren, stood talking to a male guest. Next to them stood another guest, a woman. Kaitlyn had been in a chopper accident. A bad one. She'd lost feeling in her right leg. Learning to ride would help her with balance and slowly build her core strength, all goals of the program.

Mission accomplished.

Jax stared down at his hands. He'd done it. He'd really done it. He'd created a state-of-the-art therapy program from scratch. He'd done the research. He'd built the facility. He'd hired the right help. Well, one of them a little too right.

Naomi.

He hadn't heard from her in the week since he'd flown to Georgia. He didn't know what he'd expected when he'd gone to see her. Maybe a pledge of undying love. Maybe not. He hadn't expected to be told that she was still in love with her husband. He understood, even suspected. It still hurt, though.

"Looks like our first member of the media has arrived," Lauren said.

Was it ridiculous that his heart rate increased when he spied not a news van, but a regular car? That he peered inside to see if it was a rental driven by Naomi? It wasn't, of course, and he felt like a fool for even considering it.

It was a pattern that repeated itself as more and more people arrived. At one point someone drove a truck toward him and he actually stopped breathing. Ridiculous. Ethan had transported her truck to her in-laws' new place in Palmdale, and as far as he knew, she was already living there. See, that was how bad it was. Every time someone arrived, his heart leaped, only to crash back around his feet. He greeted guest after guest. Jax admitted more people had shown up than had been invited. That was good. Even one of the major networks had made an appearance. He watched from a distance as they filmed Brielle working with Mitchell Robertson, a patient at the ranch.

"Uncle Jax, can I help Brielle give therapy to the soldiers? I told her I could help lead the horse around, but she said it was up to you."

In the center of the arena, Brielle walked alongside the soldier, her long blond braid swaying back and forth and she glanced from her patient to the horse, then back again. She had to help him to stay on, her blue eyes focused on her task. The man had lost the use of his legs in a recent conflict and every time Jax started feeling sorry for himself, he remembered Mitchell. Whatever life had dealt him recently, it could be worse.

"I don't see why not, as long as it's okay with Brielle."

Kyle did a jig of excitement. "She said she didn't mind as long as you didn't."

"Fine by me."

"Cool." He glanced toward Brielle, and was that hero worship on the boy's face? Did he have a crush on his pretty new hippotherapist? Jax thought he might.

"Maybe we can help that man walk again."

He forgot all about boyhood crushes then because that was the whole point. His cup should be running over. He'd built his ranch. He had guests/patients in residence. He had a full staff, and he'd inspired his nephew to volunteer his time. What more could he want?

Naomi, he instantly answered. She should have been a part of this. She was all that was missing. Her and Tramp.

He glanced around.

Tramp. The dog had been right at his feet a moment ago. He walked toward the edge of the arena, glancing around. No sign of him.

"Tramp," he called.

No answering bark. He wasn't too concerned. The dog had never wandered far. He was probably out back, in the pond. He'd never seen a dog more addicted to water, but he wasn't in the lake.

"What's wrong?" his sister asked.

"Tramp." Jax scratched his head in thought. "He's not here."

She turned in place, scouring the countryside. "Maybe he's in the back pasture with the horses?"

"He can't get in with them. Colby put that wire up last week."

His sister glanced toward the arena. "I'll go look inside."

"I'll go walk around the arena. Maybe he's off chasing a squirrel or something."

They both met up in the front of the barn a few minutes later. "Not here," his sister said, and by now Brennan had joined in.

"What's the problem?" he asked.

"He can't find Tramp."

"Did you check the house?"

Ever the efficient lawman. Leave it to Brennan to state the obvious. "I'll go do that right now."

"You need me to come with you?" Lauren asked.

"Nah. He's probably at the house like Bren says. Stay here and keep an eye on our guests."

His sister nodded. The couple laced hands as they turned back to the arena.

Jax jumped into his all-terrain vehicle. It was a short

drive up to the house, and as he rounded the side of the hill, he heard the dog before he saw him.

Thank God.

He shut off the ATV and jumped out. It surprised Jax how much the dog had gotten under his skin. Last week he'd even flown Tramp up to San Francisco with him. Everyone in the office loved him. Tramp loved everyone right back, but he still missed Naomi. Every time Jax brought him home, he did the same thing. Scoured the house from end to end, always ending up at the door to the apartment. He hadn't hired anyone since Naomi had left. He doubted he would. Nobody could replace Naomi.

He heard laughter. A boy's laugh, and for a moment he thought he might have missed Kyle coming up to the house, but he'd left the boy in the arena.

"He's funny, Mom."

And he knew.

Tramp started barking again, but this time it grew louder and Jax knew he was about to be discovered, not that he'd sneaked up on them. They'd probably heard him, which meant he was about to come face-to-face with—

Tramp nearly knocked him down. "Hey. Whoa."

The dog bounced. Up, down. Up, down. And then he bounded off for Naomi, as if to say, "See who's here? See?"

I see, he silently told the dog.

"Mr. Stone," T.J. said. "It took us hours to get here. Just hours. We had to drive to my nona and papa's new house and drop Janus off. And then we had to drive here. And my mom wasn't sure if you were still having the party today so she wanted to stop off at the house first even though Sam told her nobody was here, and it turns out she was right, so we were just about to drive down to the stables, and— Is Kyle here?"

And suddenly Jax wanted to laugh. And smile. And ask him to slow down because Jax was pretty sure he hadn't caught everything T.J. was trying to tell him. By "we" he meant his mom and sister. Sam leaned against the familiar blue truck. Naomi's vehicle.

"Hey, Mr. Stone," she said, waving, looking so much like her mom in that instant even though he'd always thought T.J. was the one who mostly resembled her.

"Hey," he said back.

He looked into Naomi's eyes. Naomi's remarkable, stunning blue eyes. The ones that reminded him of secluded lakes and crystal-blue skies and precious gems all at once.

"Surprise," she said.

Boy, she had that right.

T.J. leaned up on his toes. "I'm going to run down to the stables."

"I'm going with you," Sam said, peeling off from the car. The teenager sauntered by, and she had the strangest smile on her face. "Bye." She gave a little wave.

And they were alone. Well, aside from Tramp. The dog had stayed with him, eyeing his two favorite humans as if silently asking what was wrong with them. Why weren't they frolicking through the grass and licking each other's faces and climbing all over each other? Never mind that that was probably the weirdest thing Jax had ever thought of. He really had a feeling that it was true. It made him smile. No, Naomi made him smile.

"You're here," he said, and suddenly his smile faded. She hadn't run up to him. Hadn't hugged him. She hadn't kissed him. For all he knew this was a social call and nothing more.

"I'm here," she echoed.

He didn't want to move. Wouldn't move. It was her turn to move. He'd chased her all the way across the country and back. Twice. Not this time.

"Jax," she said softly. He saw her eyes change colors. They grew darker and he knew from experience that meant she was close to tears. "I just—"

To hell with it. He closed the distance between them. She opened her arms.

And he wondered if it was a dream. If he'd somehow not woken up this morning and this whole day was a figment of his imagination because she couldn't really be in his arms.

But she was.

Her heat seeped into him. Her arms held him tight. Her head tipped back and she pushed up on her toes and he bent down and kissed her.

And all was right in the world. She'd come back to him. She tilted her head sideways and he deepened the kiss and admitted he might never let her go.

A long while later she drew back. He pulled her up against him, rested his chin on her head.

"What changed your mind?"

She was quiet for a moment, and that was okay. He would have been content to hold her for the rest of the day. Hell, for the rest of his life. Until the world came to an end. She was his world.

"Sam," she said quietly. She drew back. "My daughter helped me to realize that I wasn't afraid you'd come between me and my kids, I was afraid of love itself. Afraid to surrender myself to the ups and downs and ins and outs of being in a relationship."

"And now?" he asked gently. "Are you still afraid now?"

She shook her head. "No." But then her eyes grew concerned. "But my kids. T.J. has two speeds—on and off. He's either running around or crashed on the couch. And Sam. She's a handful, Jax. She's a teen. Do you know what it's like living with a teen? And a girl teen?"

"I do," he admitted, remembering what it was like to grow up with Lauren.

"No, you don't. Or you've forgotten. It's like having Maleficent, Snow White and Elsa all rolled into one. Some days you'll want to kill her. Other days she'll make you cry, for a good reason. She'll say the sweetest thing. And then she'll make you laugh. And she'll be your best friend. And then she'll turn into Maleficent again. So I feel I should warn you, because if you're in love with me, we're a package deal. Me, my kids and my dog."

If he loved her.

"I wouldn't care if you came with a two-headed dragon, Naomi. I love you. I love everything that's a part of you, most especially your kids."

Her eyes had turned dark again, and the look on her face...it was one he committed to memory. The look of a woman who'd found the center of her universe, and never wanted to leave.

"I love you, too." She reached up on tiptoe again and he needed no second invitation. He kissed her as he'd dreamed of kissing her the past few weeks. Like a man who'd found the key to perfect happiness. And he had found that, just as long as she was always in his arms.

"Marry me," he asked a long while later. "The sooner the better. I need to make an honest woman of you in front of your kids."

She had tears in her eyes when their gazes met. "I'll marry you on one condition," she said softly.

"What's that?"

"You have to promise me that you'll never, not ever, make me mop your granite floors again."

He threw back his head and laughed, hugged her tight, kissed her again. "That," he said between kisses, "is a deal."

Epilogue

"Captain's log. Stardate 2.0.3102. Kyle and I have entered a strange new world. What appears to be a barn transformed into a church for our parents to get married in."

T.J. glanced at his cousin-to-be, a smile coming to his face when Kyle laughed.

"You really can't even tell it's an arena, can you?" Kyle said.

They were hiding out in the hayloft, a secret place they'd dubbed "the bridge" on one of their many excursions to the barn. Kyle was teaching T.J. how to ride. In exchange, T.J. was teaching Kyle how to fish. It was something T.J.'s dad had taught him before he'd died. And that, too, was something they both had in common. They'd lost a father, but they were both gaining one on the same day.

"You think they'll smear cake in each other's face?" T.J. asked, trying to loosen the dang tie they'd forced him into. They had a perfect view of inside the arena from where they sat, hidden from everyone by a thick beam. In the middle of the arena his mom had arranged to have a temporary floor put down on the dirt. It'd been super fun to run around on it last night before they'd had to set up those darn chairs. Hundreds of them, it seemed. To his right stood an arch with all kinds of flowers and ivy and twinkling lights. It looked too girlie for him, but he had to admit, the Christmas lights around the railing and in the rafters looked pretty cool. Especially since it'd dawned a cloudy day. He and Kyle were hoping for rain.

"I'd be disappointed if they didn't."

It was Christmas Eve, although T.J. had made a face when it'd been announced that his mom would be getting married the day before Christmas. His soon-to-be aunt, Lauren, had explained to him that she'd wanted to share her wedding day with his mom. Lauren had originally picked the day because it seemed as if she and her son were getting a gift in the form of Bren Connelly. Now his mom would be getting Jax Stone and so it seemed to fit. When they'd told him that, he understood, although he'd wondered if that meant he'd get fewer presents for Christmas. He hadn't, because there was a boatload of gifts under the tree. They were celebrating tomorrow in his soon-to-be new home, a place as big as a palace, with a Christmas tree as big as the ones in the forest. Seriously. Huge.

"There sure are a lot of police officers here," T.J. observed, spotting yet another man in uniform.

"That's because Bren's the town sheriff and he knows absolutely *everybody*."

"My mom said Rand Jefferson would be here."

"I know," Kyle said, tossing a flake of alfalfa toward the ground and watching it fall to the barn aisle below.

The horses had all been moved to the pasture, which was kind of a bummer. T.J. really liked petting them.

"I've met him before, though," Kyle added. "He's really nice."

"Oh, look, here come Ethan and Claire." T.J. pointed.

Both boys watched as the couple split up outside the arena. Claire would be in the wedding. So would Ethan. The two kissed, making T.J. grimace, and then Claire headed toward one side of the arena while Ethan headed to the other. Music started to play. Some kind of fancy instrument band that T.J. wasn't really fond of, but later they had a really cool band coming, the same band that'd played at the big party his mom had planned but that he couldn't be at because he'd been in Georgia. He couldn't wait, although it might be hot in his suit and tie. It was supposed to get really cold later today, though, so maybe not.

"Come on snow," Kyle murmured.

"You think it will?" T.J. asked, watching as Chance and Carolina Reynolds also parted company. After that it was one guest after another. T.J. lost count of how many people arrived. One of Ethan's friends, Mariah, and her husband, Chase. Some other guy named Wes and his wife, Jillian, and then what seemed like half the town of Via Del Caballo.

"There's my grandparents," T.J. said, pointing to them as they took seats near the front.

"Mine are here somewhere," Kyle said, scanning the crowd for them. "First time I've seen them in a year."

"Not mine," T.J. said. "We've been living with—"

"Boys," someone called from down below them.

They both peered over the edge.

"There you are," said Brielle. "I've been looking everywhere for you guys. Come on."

"All right." Kyle sighed.

T.J. knew how he felt. He wasn't looking forward to

walking down the aisle ahead of his mom and Kyle's mom, but he supposed it was for a good cause. His sister had to walk, too, although she was his mom's maid of honor. She'd had to dress up, too, and she didn't look half bad with her dark hair up on her head. Brielle looked better, though. Kyle said Brielle was hot. He had a feeling his friend had a crush on the older woman. He couldn't blame him, though. His mom said Brielle looked like a Disney princess, the snow queen one.

"Where have you been?" said his mom, and he stopped in his tracks when he saw her. He had never, not ever, seen his mom look so pretty in his life.

"Wow, Mom. You look great."

His mom seemed to light up. "Thanks."

"You look good, too, Mom," said Kyle.

Lauren glanced down at the dress she wore before saying, "Thanks. I think."

"You both look good," said Sam. She wore a red dress that matched the stupid ties they'd been forced to wear.

They were all gathered at the end of the barn aisle, hidden from everyone's view. They'd walk outside and around to the front, something they'd rehearsed last night, and then each of them would walk to the first row.

"We wanted to see everyone arrive," he explained.

"You guys need to get over to the other side with the men."

Kyle rolled his eyes. T.J. just shook his head. It was stupid that Jax and Bren had to stay away.

"Let's go," said Kyle.

They slipped through a door near the foot of some stairs, his mom waving goodbye, his sister sticking her tongue out at him. He just ignored her, but when he stepped outside, he stopped. Kyle did, too.

Snow.

He couldn't believe it.

"Is that really..." Kyle held out his hand.

A big, fat flake landed in his palm. They looked at each other and said at the same time, "Snow!"

They ran to tell their soon-to-be fathers. All the men—Bren, Jax, Ethan, Chance and Colt—went outside for a moment, but then they were being ushered back inside and he and Kyle had to walk down the aisle, slowly, like they'd practiced. The minister who'd be marrying his mom to Jax and his soon-to-be aunt to Bren already stood there. He smiled at him and T.J. had to admit, it was kind of cool to see all the faces staring back at him, and the arena looked really neat with all the twinkling lights and giant red ribbons tied to the backs of the chairs. The same color ribbons were wrapped around the necks of Janus and Tramp. The two leashes were being held by Brielle, and he spotted the way Kyle waved at her, although he'd probably tell him later he was just greeting the dogs, which would be an out-and-out lie, but whatever. They took their places next to the pastor, then Colt and Chance walked up and stood next to them. Ethan got to stand next to Bren and Jax.

"Here we go," he heard Ethan say.

The music got louder and Janus and Tramp started to wag their tails, the two of them having become best friends, and he realized his sister walked down the aisle. She didn't stick her tongue out at him, though. And then Carolina walked toward him in a dress that matched his sister's, followed by Natalie. Finally Claire came in and he knew this was it, the moment everyone had been waiting for.

The music changed. Everyone stood.

It was finally happening. After months of hearing

his mom talk about it, and after all the problems getting things arranged in such a short amount of time, his mother would finally marry Jax, a man T.J. really, really liked. Of course, Jax would never be his dad. Well, not his *real* dad, anyway, but he made his mom happy. Happier than T.J. had ever seen her, and as he watched her say her vows he wondered if his own dad was watching and what he would think about all this. His dad would be happy for her, he decided. He'd be happy for them all.

"Ladies and gentleman," said the pastor. "I now pronounce Mr. and Mrs. Brennan Connelly and Mr. and Mrs. Jaxton Stone."

His mom turned to his new dad, and he could see that she was crying, and for some reason that made him want to cry, even though he took pains to hide the tears from Kyle. Except Kyle was crying, too, and that made him feel better.

His mom took off down the aisle toward a carriage waiting outside, the covered kind of stagecoach like you saw in the bank commercials. He hadn't even heard the darn thing pull up and it was his favorite part of the wedding. The guy said they could get rides afterward.

"You did good, twerp," his sister said, pushing him lightly while they waited for their mom and Aunt Lauren to get into the carriage with their new husbands. Behind them the wedding guests started to file out.

"You did, too," he said, glancing at the sky. Snow. He still couldn't believe it.

"I'm going to freeze walking back to the house."

The carriage took off. He caught a glimpse of his mom as she waved at them both.

"She looks happy," he said.

"She is," Sam said.

"That makes me happy."

"Me, too," Sam said.

"Here." T.J. handed her his jacket.

"You don't have to do that."

He handed it to her, anyway. He and Kyle would get warm running behind the carriage. That was the plan. And then they'd ask the guy for a ride.

"Tag, you're it," said Kyle, and then he ran after the carriage.

"See ya," T.J called to his sister, chasing after his friend.

Inside the stagecoach, snuggled up next to her new husband, Naomi stared into the eyes of the man she loved.

"Another spectacular event planned by my wife," Jax said tenderly.

"Yeah, but this one was ever better than the last," Naomi said.

On the bench seat opposite, Lauren pulled her gaze away from her own husband and said, "It really was amazing, Naomi. It didn't even look like an arena. You should do this professionally."

She glanced up at her husband.

Her husband.

She loved the sound of that word. And as she placed a hand on his lapel, the diamond he'd bought her sparkled, and she remembered the fuss he'd made when he'd given it to her. He'd asked her to marry him again in front of her kids, but only after he'd asked for their permission. It was one of the things she loved about Jax, the way he included her kids in everything. There were other things to love, too. He spoiled her rotten. Encouraged her to explore her talent as an event planner. He even put up with Sam and her pubescent teen-ager mood swings.

"I love you," she said softly.

He stared down at her and she could see an answering love in his eyes.

"Just remember who said it first."

He kissed her. Across from them, Bren kissed Lauren, right as the stagecoach hit a hole that made them bump noses, which made them all laugh as outside the snow began to fall harder.

"It's perfect," she heard herself say.

Jax grabbed her hand, and she squeezed his back. "You're perfect."

This time when they kissed there were no potholes to disturb it. In the distance the kids laughed. Inside Naomi closed her eyes and kissed the man of her dreams, the man who would carry her through the good and the bad, who would shelter her from the storm and run naked with her through the snow, who would laugh and cry with her, and who would never leave her side.

* * * * *

*"[Kathy Douglass] pulls you right in from
page one, and you won't want to leave."*
—**New York Times** *bestselling author Linda Lael Miller*

*Ten years ago, the love of Raven Reynolds's
life disappeared without a trace. Now Donovan Cordero
is back, standing on her doorstep. Along the way,
Raven had the rancher's child—though he didn't know
she was pregnant!*

*Read on for a sneak preview of
the next great book in the Sweet Briar Sweethearts
miniseries,* The Rancher's Return *by Kathy Douglass.*

"You'll still get plenty of time with him," Raven said as Elias
ran off.

"You're being nicer about this than I'd expected you to be."

"What did you think I'd do? Grab my kid and go sneaking off
in the middle of the night?"

Donovan inhaled a sharp breath.

"Sorry. I didn't mean that the way it sounded."

"I'm just a bit sensitive, I guess."

"And I'm a bit uncomfortable. Have you noticed how many
people are staring at us?"

"They're not staring at us. They're staring at you. You're the
prettiest girl here."

Raven laughed. "There's no need for flattery. I already said you
can spend time with Elias."

"It's not flattery. It's the truth. You're gorgeous."

The laughter vanished from her voice and the sparkle left her eyes. "No flirting. We're not on a date. We're here for Elias."

"But we are getting to know each other. Not for the purpose of falling in love again. I know you're engaged and I respect that."

"Who told you I was engaged?"

"Carson. Congratulations, I hope you'll be happy together. Just so you know, I have no intention of interfering in your life. But if we're going to coparent Elias, we need to find a way to be friends again. And we were friends, weren't we?"

She nodded and the smile reappeared. Apparently he'd said the right thing.

Donovan stepped in front of Raven and took her hands in his. Though she worked on the ranch, her palms were soft. "I'm sorry."

"Sorry for what?"

"For putting you through ten years of hell. Ten years of hoping I'd come home. For not being around while you were pregnant or to help you raise our son. All of it. I'm sorry for all of it. Please forgive me."

Her eyes widened in surprise and she blinked. Was what he'd said so unexpected? He didn't think so. Just what kind of jerk did she think he'd become? He replayed the conversation they'd had that first night. It must have looked like he was playing games when he hadn't fully answered her questions. But Raven was engaged to another man, so his reasons for staying away really didn't matter now. They'd have to start here to build their relationship.

"You're forgiven."

"Clean slate?"

She smiled. "Clean slate. Now let's catch up to Elias and play some games. I plan on winning one of those oversize teddy bears."

Looking for more satisfying love stories
with community and family at their core?

Check out **Harlequin® Special Edition**
and **Love Inspired®** books!

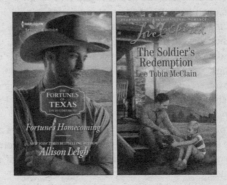

New books available every month!

CONNECT WITH US AT:

Facebook.com/groups/HarlequinConnection

Facebook.com/HarlequinBooks

Twitter.com/HarlequinBooks

Instagram.com/HarlequinBooks

Pinterest.com/HarlequinBooks

ReaderService.com

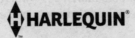

**ROMANCE WHEN
YOU NEED IT**

HFGENRE2018

Love Harlequin romance?

DISCOVER.

Be the first to find out about promotions,
news and exclusive content!

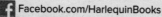

f Facebook.com/HarlequinBooks

Twitter.com/HarlequinBooks

Instagram.com/HarlequinBooks

P Pinterest.com/HarlequinBooks

ReaderService.com

EXPLORE.

Sign up for the Harlequin e-newsletter and
download a free book from any series at
TryHarlequin.com.

CONNECT.

Join our Harlequin community to share
your thoughts and connect with other
romance readers!
Facebook.com/groups/HarlequinConnection

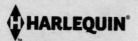

HARLEQUIN®

**ROMANCE WHEN
YOU NEED IT**

HSOCIAL2018